His kiss promises
the most wicked desire…

... ... What are you so afraid of?" Nick nuzzled the corner of Gin's mouth, making her nearly swoon right off the blasted dock.

Gin's knees went even weaker, but Nick caught her all the more snugly against his chest, leading her into temptation. "Aren't you curious about how it would be between us?"

"Curiosity killed the cat," she pointed out, trying to sound aloof and utterly failing.

"At least the cat died happy. Kiss me back," he ordered her again. "You know you want to. I've seen the way you look at me. Like in the cave."

She bit her lip in yearning at the memory of his glistening, hard body and pulled back to look into his eyes. "It doesn't mean anything if I do," she warned, her pulse racing with anticipation.

"No," he assured her with a whisper of amusement, "not a thing."

Then he kissed her again, and her feeble resistance melted away.

By Gaelen Foley

GAELEN FOLEY

The Secrets of a Scoundrel

A V O N
An Imprint of HarperCollins*Publishers*

This is a work of fiction. Names, characters, places, and incidents are products of the author's imagination or are used fictitiously and are not to be construed as real. Any resemblance to actual events, locales, organizations, or persons, living or dead, is entirely coincidental.

AVON BOOKS
An Imprint of HarperCollins*Publishers*
195 Broadway
New York, New York 10007

Copyright © 2014 by Gaelen Foley
ISBN 978-0-06-207605-2
www.avonromance.com

First Avon Books mass market printing: July 2014

Avon Trademark Reg. U.S. Pat. Off. and in Other Countries, Marca Registrada, Hecho en U.S.A.
HarperCollins® is a registered trademark of HarperCollins Publishers.

Printed in the U.S.A.

10 9 8 7 6 5 4 3 2 1

The Secrets of a Scoundrel

Chapter 1

Scotland, 1816

*K*eys clanking, the brawny, kilted guard opened the iron door before her. Armed to the teeth, he stepped aside, beckoning her into the secret dungeon where the Order locked away its most valued prisoners. "This way, milady."

She followed, sparing a brief glance up at the weathered stone arch above the doorway. She half expected to see Dante's famous quote carved there, welcoming visitors to Hell: *Abandon hope all ye who enter here.*

Inferno Club, indeed, she thought.

Then she left the bleak, midday gloom of November behind and crossed the threshold into the darkness that had swallowed up the man she had come to save.

A fallen hero. A lost cause, to some.

She dared to think that she knew better.

The burly guard lifted a torch off the wall and proceeded to escort her down the stone tunnel, descending ancient stairs carved into the limestone. She lifted the hem of her dark-hued gown a little, but her booted footfalls were firm and sure as she followed.

Ever deeper the guard led her into the bowels of the mountain beneath St. Michael's Abbey and the Order's ancient school, where wellborn boys were gradually turned into deadly warriors.

Like the man in the cell below.

Only he could help her now. If there were any other way, she would have gladly considered it.

But the situation was dire. There was no time to dither over less dangerous solutions.

Nevertheless, she shook her head to think that of one of her father's top warriors, caged like a wild beast in this dungeon. "How long has he been down here?"

"Six months, ma'am. Came to us in May. Only a quarter of the way into his sentence, I believe."

She gave a slight shudder.

Of course, two years in a cage was only a slap on the wrist for a man trained to endure enemy torture. But this punishment had been handed down to him by his own superiors—a private disciplinary action taken against him by the graybeards who ran the Order. And justly so, from what she understood.

Still, it was quite a sentence for a man who had recently taken a bullet for the Regent. Unfortunately, Nick, Baron Forrester, had committed the unpardonable sin.

He had tried to quit the Order, and that was not allowed. If the organization was a kind of family, bound by secrecy and blood, he was its black sheep.

"How's his health?" she asked, noting the dank conditions.

"Sound, far as I know. Ach, he's fairly indestructible, this one. In fact, milady . . ." The guard paused on the weathered limestone stairs and turned to her, the light from his torch flickering over the walls. "For your own safety, don't stray too near the bars."

She arched a brow. "I can handle myself, thank you," she said in a prickly tone.

He lifted his bushy eyebrows at her cool, steady gaze. "No offense intended, ma'am. I'm just warnin' ye, he hasn't seen a woman in months. No tellin' what he might do if you get too close. Half-mad, if you ask me."

"I didn't," she clipped out. *Rotten bastard he might be, but he's still worth twelve of you.* With a cold stare, she nodded toward the torchlit tunnel that led ever deeper into the mountain. "Shall we?"

He blinked in startled indignation but complied. Turning around again, he added under his breath with a measure of sarcasm, "Aye, she Virgil's daughter, all right."

She smirked at the back of his thick head as they continued on. In the next moment, they came to the bottom of the stairs and passed a few empty cells along the dungeon corridor. With walls of stone, each cell was only the size of a box stall.

But then she furrowed her brow, hearing the sound of loud, rhythmic panting coming from the last cell in the aisle.

Ahead of her, the guard stopped and banged his truncheon on the rusty bars. "On your feet, you scum!"

"I'm busy, arsehole, as you can see. What do you want?" a low voice growled, rasping with effort.

She sauntered closer, setting one foot warily after the other until the prisoner came into view.

Down on the cold stone floor, a large, shirtless man was doing one-armed push-ups. The torchlight played over his sinewy, naked back.

My, oh, my.

Gin watched, impressed in spite of herself, as he switched arms without missing a beat and continued his regimen with explosive vigor, rudely ignoring the guard.

"For God's sake, put a shirt on, man," the guard grumbled. "There's a lady present."

"A what?"

He froze mid push-up, peering up through the wild tangle of jet-black hair hanging in his face. His stare locked on her. "Well, I'll be damned," he uttered.

He jumped to his feet with fluid grace, tall and sculpted, sweat glistening on his bare chest.

She watched it heaving with unabashed admiration.

A man could be a lovely thing sometimes.

"And who might you be?" he panted, wiping the sweat off his face with a rough pass of a thickly muscled arm.

He flashed the same crooked smile that had made her quiver as a seventeen-year-old.

Not that he'd remember that.

Seeing him half-naked, his skin flushed with the virile glow of exercise, his muscles warmed and hard, it took her half a heartbeat longer to collect her thoughts and remind herself, namely, that she was not a young girl anymore; that he was a disgraced agent who'd gone rogue, not to mention a trained assassin with a higher-than-average kill rate.

Standing there smiling at her, his midnight eyes full of reckless charm, distrust, and angry secrets, he was as dangerous as they came.

She should know; her own father had trained him.

And although she cowered from no man, when the panting Lord Forrester sauntered closer, prevented from touching her only by the bars of his cage, she had to stop herself from taking an instinctive step backwards.

That would not do. Not if she was to take custody of him.

It was vital to show him from the start who was in charge. With the candle burning behind him on a little battered table covered in books and maps and papers, he was a dark silhouette, wide-shouldered, menacing, and powerful.

Hers to claim, with full permission of the graybeards. Hers to use for her own purposes.

If she could control him.

And if not, if the rogue agent gave her any trouble, she had full permission to put a bullet in his handsome head. But as her gaze traveled over his exquisitely honed physique, she had to admit that that would be a very great shame, indeed.

A man's mind started playing tricks on him after a few months of solitary confinement, and so Nick was not yet fully convinced this wasn't a dream.

One could never be too sure.

Moments ago, he had thought he smelled a whiff of some enticing perfume wafting toward him on the dank dungeon air; that he heard a faint rustle of satin skirts and a light, whispering prowl of some softer stride echoing behind the guard's heavy, clomping footfalls.

But he had ignored these tantalizing hints of beauty, tired of his own delusions and hating the shameful loneliness that spawned them.

Then, to his astonishment, it turned out he was right.

A gorgeous, pale-skinned mystery woman had stepped into view, and maybe he *was* dreaming because she looked like a fantasy.

On second thought, he did not have *that* good an imagination. It was the first time in ages he'd seen a female of any kind, and this one was . . . spectacular.

He could not tear his gaze away.

She seemed real enough. The only way to be sure, of course, would be to reach through the bars and touch her, but he didn't dare, for fear of offending her, scaring her away, and being left alone again for God-knew how long.

He strove to focus on the obvious question instead. What was she doing here?

The woman glanced around at his cavelike quarters—grim accommodations, indeed, for a nobleman, however empty his coffers.

To say nothing of his soul.

"Cozy place you've got here," she remarked.

"Isn't it, though?" he countered. "I'd offer you a drink, but the service here is terrible."

She looked askance at Nick from the corner of her blue, blue eyes, offering a slow, wary curve of her lips; her canny little smile got him slightly drunk.

Ross, the ever-charming Scottish guard, did not approve of his cautious flirtation. He whacked the bars again and made the metal thrum like Nick's awareness of her. "Put your shirt on, man! I'm not going to tell you again! You're in the presence of a lady!"

"Oh, I don't mind," the lady drawled in a worldly murmur. She studied Nick's abdomen in unmasked appreciation.

He grinned, glad he'd used his time in prison well to hone his body. There was little else to do. That, and rue his life's choices, make friends with the mouse who lived in the corner, and, of course, read. God bless his friend and Order teammate, Lord Trevor Montgomery, who had saved his sanity by sending him books.

Nick supposed his eyesight would be ruined by the time he got out of here, a sad state of affairs for an expert sniper. One candle could hardly stand up to the all-consuming gloom of this place. But he had needed something, anything, to carry his mind beyond these dungeon walls.

So he had begrudgingly resorted to reading spectacles. Depressing, really. Just another symbol of his squandered youth.

Five times over, he had read the book from Trevor until he had nearly memorized it: the first published account of the journey of Messieurs Lewis and Clark into the American wilderness.

Under the circumstances, Nick had a new appreciation for the total freedom of that untamed place. As soon as he got the devil out of here, that was where he had made up his mind to go.

He had already planned his journey up to the edge of the map. From there, he could hardly wait to push out past the charted territory into the unknown, nothing but a rifle across his back and a haversack of supplies.

To hell with civilization. He was obviously not cut out for it. He had sampled all its charms and walked away bankrupt in more ways than one, jaded to the core.

Bears, Indians, poisonous snakes.

These didn't concern him after the enemies he'd already faced. God's truth, he'd enjoy it. On the far side of the ocean, pristine virgin territory waited to be explored by a man who knew what he was doing . . .

In the meanwhile, the lush mountains and mysterious valleys of the woman standing out of reach on the other side of the bars both lured and taunted his animal instincts.

He looked her up and down, perhaps a little rudely, but he deemed this only fair since she was openly doing the same to him.

Nick didn't mind a'tall. He leaned against the bars, happy to let her look all she pleased, while he did likewise, hoping, nay, praying—probably in vain—that she was a high-end harlot, generously sent to him by his more scoundrelly brother-in-arms, Sebastian, Viscount Beauchamp.

Trevor, newly married to the pastor's daughter, would send him books and food and useful things not to tempt his sinful nature.

Beau, however, the former ladies' man before he, too, had been snared in the vicar's mousetrap, was sure to have a jollier understanding of what Nick needed most after six months in jail.

When his stare drifted down to the creamy silken V of the woman's chest displayed in a tailored white shirt, layered beneath her dark-hued gown, and opened low enough to show off exquisite cleavage, he cursed the iron bars and gripped them rather desperately, offering her a hungry smile. "Pray, would you like to come in and sit for a while, my dear?" he drawled with a wicked smile.

His beautiful, delicious-smelling visitor merely arched a cynical brow at him, amusement her answer to his leer.

Alas, the air of command in the jut of her chin and the even hold of her piercing blue eyes made him doubt this queenly female had ever been for sale.

Do I know her from somewhere? he wondered vaguely. She seemed somehow familiar. He was sure he'd have remembered meeting such a fascinating female. But the thread of recognition danced away.

He was distracted, too busy savoring the way the torchlight danced in gold and ruby spangles on her dark auburn hair. She had long, velvety lashes. Plump, sensuous lips—

"Whenever you're ready to put your eyes back in your head, Lord Forrester, we can get down to business."

He snapped out of his lustful daze and shot back at her, "Likewise, madam."

Ross banged his truncheon on the rusty bars once more. "Mind your manners, you scoundrel!"

Nick glared at him. "You make a charming chaperone, old boy, but I daresay the lady and I are old enough to be left alone."

"You wish," he shot back.

"It's all right, Sergeant. Leave us," she ordered.

"But, ma'am! 'Tisna safe to leave ye alone with this brrrrute!" he said, rolling his Scottish r's grandly.

"Never you mind, I know how to handle a rudesby," she said in amusement. When the guard hesitated, she sharpened her tone. "Thank you, that will be all."

Ross didn't like that, but it seemed he had been ordered to obey her.

Well, well, thought Nick, still amused himself, Her Highness must be somebody, indeed.

Ross grumbled his compliance, bowed, and withdrew, and Nick studied the mystery woman in reluctant awe.

She chose not to flaunt her miracle-working power. After Ross had gone, she merely turned to him with a rueful smile and a hint of compassion in her eyes. "I don't think he likes you."

"Strange, isn't it? Amiable as I am," Nick said. "So, where were we? Ah, yes. You were about to tell me who you are and what you want with me," he challenged her.

Not that he was in any position to be making demands.

Her watchful gaze assessed him as if he were either a horse for sale or some unfortunate animal to be used in a scientific experiment.

Neither possibility boded well.

But maybe, just maybe, she wanted something else. After the way she had been staring at his body, he could not help thinking of ancient Roman gladiators being visited by married noblewomen, in search of either a night of rough pleasure or to have their bellies filled with new life born of strong, warrior seed.

That was about all he had left to give of himself at this point, he mused in bitter humor. But the thought that she wanted to use him in that fashion stung his pride enough to help cool his lust. Ah, well, she wouldn't be the first.

Still, he had so little power in this cage that the least he could do was choose not to let her ogle him.

Suddenly self-conscious, he turned away, crossing his cell to go put on his shirt, as commanded.

"My name is Lady Burke," she informed him. "And I am here with a proposition for you."

His mind instantly went to the gutter. He paused in the middle of pulling his shirt on over his head.

"If you agree to my proposal," she continued with a cool stare, "and swear to give me your complete, un-questioning obedience—"

He laughed.

"I can get you out of here. Today."

Nick abruptly stopped laughing.

Instead, he turned to her with a dubious stare, certain he had either misunderstood her or that this was a very cruel trick. He narrowed his eyes, scrutinizing the woman for any faint sign of deception. He detected none. "You don't say," he growled in wary skepticism, his defenses bristling against certain disappointment.

She nodded.

And his heart began to pound. Well, now. Could she really free him? It seemed impossible after he'd been such a naughty boy.

Unless . . . well, it meant either one of two things. Either this woman was incredibly well connected, or she needed him for something that was more than likely going to get him killed.

Nick weighed that possibility for all of two seconds before making up his mind. Anything was better than being condemned to this pit. He tucked in his shirt and approached the bars warily. "I'm listening."

"Perhaps I had better start at the beginning."

"That is usually best."

"Very well." She leaned her shoulder against the bars of his cell and began drawing off her gloves. "A month ago, I took a missing person's case in Town. An eighteen-year-old girl, Susannah Perkins, had disappeared. The mother sought my help. The stepfather claimed she had run off with a boy, but the mother insisted her daughter would never do that without at least telling her friends—"

"Hold on. Beg your pardon, Lady Burke, but you've lost me. You 'took a case'? How's that, then?"

She lifted her eyebrows in surprise, a sardonic smile skimming her lips. "Ah, right. I forgot. It always confounds the *stronger* sex to find a female with a brain and a purpose of her own. Let me catch you up, then. A few years ago, after my husband's death, I found myself at liberty to follow my own interests as I pleased."

Widow, Nick thought, barely hearing the rest. *Praise God.*

"Now, this may shock you, Lord Forrester," she continued, "but life for an intelligent woman of my station can soon grow exceedingly dull."

"And thus adultery is the ton's favorite sport," he countered with a ready smile. "So I'm told."

She shrugged. "Some ladies do embroidery work to fill up their time; others devote themselves to works of charity. Or gardening, or gossip as their favored pastime. For me—" A guarded gleam came into her eyes. "I became interested in helping people who've been victims of crime or some similar injustice. It entertains me to investigate the facts behind their various misfortunes and, where possible, discover the responsible party, sharing this information with the authorities."

He furrowed his brow and stared at her, intrigued. "So, what, then? You're some sort of a . . . lady detective?"

He had never heard of such a thing, but this designation seemed to please her. "Yes, I suppose I am. Don't look so shocked," she chided, a hint of defiance in the lift of her chin. "I can do as I please with my time and my fortune. Who else will help the lower orders when they are wronged and too frightened to come forward? Or God forbid, a woman who should have troubling questions concerning her husband. I help those—discreetly, of course—who have nowhere else to turn."

Nick decided on the spot that he adored her. He made no further sport of her little Bow-Street-ish endeavors. "So where do I come in?"

"I understand from your work in the field that you developed a number of assets among the criminal underworld in London and abroad."

How the hell does she know that?

He was not foolish enough to ask impertinent questions, though, if there was a real chance that she could get him out of here.

"Correct."

To the criminal underworld, he was Jonathan Black: assassin for hire and Very Bad Man.

"You gained the trust of people who trust no one," she continued. "I need you to use those connections on my behalf."

"Which connections? Can you be more specific?"

"Not at this time."

"I see." He folded his arms across his chest as he mulled it. "So, I take it this missing person's case of yours took an unexpectedly nefarious turn?"

"Yes."

"It must be dire, indeed, or you could have simply taken the information to the lads at Bow Street."

"That would not be adequate." She hesitated. "Lord Forrester, I have uncovered a trafficking ring abducting young girls and selling them overseas. Miss Perkins is not the only young girl who's disappeared in recent weeks. I have managed to learn that the head of the ring goes by the nickname of Rotgut. His true name is unknown. He's English, and he captains a ship called the *Black Jest*. That's all I know about him, except for one additional fact. That he is currently set to sell his captives on the underworld auction known as the Bacchus Bazaar. I understand you're familiar with it."

Nick cursed under his breath.

She lifted an eyebrow in grim agreement.

The Bacchus Bazaar was a secretive, underworld auction held every other year, where the top dealers in all sorts of illicit goods gathered to trade their wares, make deals, settle scores, and form alliances.

"We've got a lot of work to do if you decide to help me," she continued. "Time is short. The auction is set for the first half of December."

"Did you manage to get a game piece yet?"

"Well, I did, but that's the trouble. It's disappeared, along with my assistant, John Carr. He went missing a week ago. Considering the nature of the people we are dealing with, I am not optimistic."

"You think he's been murdered?"

"Or added to the roster of captives to be sold." She paused. "He's a very beautiful young man."

"I see," he murmured, indeed, probably more than she cared for him to see. Namely, that the worldly widow did not merely "entertain herself" investigating crimes, but also by enjoying the services of some young, pretty-faced cavalier serviente. Who had blundered in some way and mucked up all her progress.

If she was telling him everything.

Which she obviously wasn't.

Fair enough.

Nick did not know why he should be so irked to hear about her toy boy, but it helped him step back from the snare of her beauty to think a bit more clearly about all this. And remember his own interests.

"Without a game piece, I am stymied," she said, heaving a sigh of frustration as she paced the other way. "I'm shut out from the next round and can't move forward. I know the rendezvous point is in Paris, but if I don't present the game piece when I get there, they won't tell me the location of the Bacchus Bazaar."

"Er, they may also kill you," he pointed out dryly. "You can't go in there acting like an insider and not present your proof."

"That's why I need you. I need to get my hands on a second game piece, and you've participated in the auction before, from what I understand. Time is of the essence. These girls have no hope if we don't act. So will you help me?"

In light of his own unpleasant circumstances, Nick

eyed her warily, fighting the inborn urge to rush to the aid of a damsel in distress. Instead, he simply drawled, "What's in it for me?"

She smiled in cynical amusement. "I thought you'd never ask." Then she pushed away from the bars and paced slowly back and forth before his cell.

Nick watched her with riveted attention.

"You can get out of that cage today, as I said, Lord Forrester. And if you're a very good boy, you won't ever have to come back."

"Really?" He held his breath, shocked.

"Once our mission is completed, the Order has agreed to give you back your freedom—on certain conditions, of course. Put you on parole, as it were."

"How in the world did you do that?"

"Well, as it turns out, I'm not the only one who'd like to see you freed. I understand the graybeards have been under constant pressure for months from your fellow agents. Lord Beauchamp and Lord Trevor Montgomery in particular have been campaigning without ceasing behind the scenes, trying to gain you an early release."

He was stunned all over again to hear this. They hadn't told him. They mustn't have wanted to get his hopes up.

"And you did take that bullet for the Regent," she added.

"Damn," he mumbled, still shocked. Mired in shame over his failures, abandoning his blood vow, Nick had assumed that his brother warriors agreed that he had only got what he deserved, landing in this cell. But they wanted him out?

After what he had done?

He was touched—and slightly chastened—to hear it. But maybe he should have trusted a little more in their loyalty to him, even after his own to them had faltered.

Obviously, his going rogue last year had never been meant to hurt them, nor, of course, to betray his bloody country. He just couldn't take it anymore.

Turning mercenary had simply been a way to make some money so he could then retire to a beautiful island somewhere. West Indies, maybe. No more killing, no more treachery. No more playing dark chess games in foreign courts and living the sort of life where he was constantly looking over his shoulder.

All he had really wanted was to be left alone.

But nothing was ever simple.

Instead, like a dupe, a fool, a mark, he had unwittingly been pulled into an underhanded scheme to frame the Order for the assassination of the Prime Minister.

Of course, it had come to naught. Lord Liverpool was alive and well at home even now, probably eating a beef pie and dreaming up new ways to oppress the ordinary Englishman, Nick mused with his usual cynicism.

Beauchamp had thankfully pieced the conspirators' plot together even before Nick had any idea of how he was being used. His trusty mate had managed to pull him out of the mess he had unknowingly got himself into. To the relief of them all, the sinister plot had fizzled.

But at the last moment, when the conspirators knew their plan was null, one of them had whipped out a pistol in range of the Regent. Nick had seen the gun and acted automatically. Thus the bullet in the belly and the national acclaim.

The glory for his "noble deed" only shamed him the more, for the public had no inkling of the rest of the story.

That bullet had actually saved him from the full fury of his superiors, however. Otherwise, the graybeards might well have put him in front of an Order firing squad.

Agents were held to the highest of standards, and the Order punished its own perhaps even more severely than it punished its enemies.

Obviously, Nick would not have murdered the jackass Prime Minister for anyone—if he had known beforehand who his target was to have been. The type of clients who hired assassins to kill people for them, after all, were not terribly forthcoming, as a rule. Information was doled out bit by bit. He had been sent to London to await further instructions.

Thanks to Beau's hunting him down and warning him how he was being set up, the dark venture had never come to fruition. Nevertheless, at the very least, Nick knew he was guilty of dereliction of duty.

And poor judgment.

And probably laziness, too, among a bevy of other sins, faults, and failings.

Indeed, the worst part about being locked in this cage was that there was no way to escape himself—a man for whom he had lost all respect.

Lady Burke was still explaining. "My request for your assistance in this matter was simply the last straw from the graybeards' standpoint."

Nick frowned, wondering how she even knew the agents' irreverent nickname for the Elders of the Order.

"Obviously, they see that this is for a good cause, rescuing these unfortunate girls," she continued. "So they've agreed to hand you over to my custody. You are being given a chance to redeem yourself, my lord. I suggest you use it well."

He lowered his gaze, a little overwhelmed by this unexpected chance at redemption. Then he shook his head. "I still don't understand. Why would they listen to you?" He looked at her again sharply. "How do you know about contacts I developed in the field? Who *are* you?" he demanded in a low tone.

She gazed at him for a moment with an odd mix of pity and mistrust and, once again, left him in the dark. "If you agree to take this mission, Lord Forrester—and I can't imagine that you'd refuse, given your options—then you must understand first and foremost that you will be taking your orders from a woman. Namely, me. I trust that won't be a problem?"

He shook his head warily. *Wouldn't be the first time,* he thought in chagrin. The queen of the mercenary army he had got mixed up in was a woman, after all.

Of course, *that* hadn't worked out very well.

"So what is your decision?" she demanded in a taut voice. "Mind you," she interrupted before he could answer, "I won't put up with any nonsense. I must be frank, Lord Forrester—may I call you Nick? I've done my research on you, and I already know all your tricks."

Oh, I doubt that.

"So don't even think about trying to deceive me," she continued. "In all, we shall get on handsomely, I think, as long as you're a very good boy for me and do exactly as I say."

"Or what?" he challenged in a low tone. Because such instructions went against the grain of every atom in him.

"Or I'll shoot you in the head," she replied without a trace of humor.

Nick was fascinated in spite of himself but didn't trust her by a mile. "Who *are* you, exactly?"

"I've already told you. My name is Virginia Stokes, Baroness Burke. Gin to my friends."

"Baron Burke . . . your husband," he murmured, searching his memory. "I've heard the name, but I don't believe I ever met the man."

She pursed her lips, as though holding back a comment.

Judging by her expression, it was something along the lines of, *You weren't missing much.*

Seeing that he had read that assessment on her face, the mysterious Lady Burke looked away.

"Wasn't he a nabob?" Nick knew that the Order had a few men based in India. "Was he an agent? One of ours?"

"God, no."

"Are you?" he persisted in a whisper, leaning his forehead against the bars.

There was an edge to her smile as she glanced wryly

at him. "You know the Order does not allow women to serve in that capacity, my lord."

"Then who the hell *are* you?" he exclaimed, pulling away and banging the bars in frustration. "Answer me! I can see there's plenty you're not telling me—"

"You will be given information as it's needed, Lord Forrester."

He glared at her, seething as he strove to figure her out. For all he knew, this could be another trap.

He had many enemies out there to this day. Or the Order could be testing his loyalty. He might be an idiot if he took the bait. "I'm sorry. I just don't understand what's going on."

"No, I don't imagine that you do. You're just going to have to trust me, I suppose."

"And why would you trust me?" he countered. "You see where I am. I don't deny that I belong here for everything I've done."

"What you've done?" she echoed in surprise, her blue eyes flashing with a sudden angry gleam. "You've served this organization and the Crown since you were younger than John Carr. And this is the thanks they give you? A bloody cage?"

Nick was taken aback to realize for the first time that she was not angry at him, but *for* him.

He wasn't quite sure what to say. "I deserve it."

"For wanting to quit? For getting tired of it all?" she countered passionately, to his surprise. "For having your heart broken too many times, facing down an evil that other people don't even know exists? Oh, Nick." Gazing at him, she shook her head almost tenderly, and he went half-mad with the need to figure out where he knew her from.

Then she gave it away softly. "Nick, Nick, Nicholas."

The phrase jerked his head up and put all his defenses instantly on high alert.

Only one person used to say that to him, in tones of fatherly affection . . .

The only father figure he had ever known. The first and possibly the last person who had ever believed in him.

His handler.

Oh, how he'd let the old man down.

He gripped the bars intensely, staring at her. "Who are you?" he demanded in a savage whisper. "Either tell me now, or take yourself out of here. Quit playing games."

She was unmoved. "Do you want to know why I'm giving you this chance? Yes, I do need the game piece. But the reason I'm willing to trust you is because my father did. Explicitly."

"Your father?" He swallowed hard, his brain unwilling to accept this revelation.

She finally relented, lowering her mask of cool control just a bit. "My mother's the Countess of Ashton, and though I am acknowledged as the offspring of her husband, the Earl, the truth is, thirty years ago, Mama took a braw Scotsman for a lover—an Order agent, who sired me. My natural father was your handler, Nick. Virgil Banks."

His jaw dropped.

Virgil's daughter? So that's how she knew so much . . .

"Now, for the last time, will you work with me or not?" she demanded in a hard tone—that suddenly made perfect sense.

Good God! Speechless, Nick could only stare. Before his untimely death, Virgil Banks had been a legend of the Order. The taciturn Scot been like a father to all "his boys," the highborn lads he had handpicked to be trained and turned into agents. The canny spymaster had taught them everything they knew. But . . .

Virgil had a daughter?

"He never told us!" he blurted out. "We were like

sons to him. I mean, I thought he kept the secrets to the mission side of things. But—he never said a word!"

Her lips twisted ruefully. "Would you? Think about it. If you had a daughter, would you introduce her to someone like you?"

"Hell, no," he said without a second's hesitation.

"Well?" She chuckled.

He let out a short laugh, as well, just barely managing to shake off his astonishment. "Well, I'd do anything for the old man." *Including keeping his daughter from getting herself killed.* "Of course you've got my help."

Clever as she was, he doubted the lady investigator had any real idea of the sort of people she was dealing with. Only the worst of the worst attended the Bacchus Bazaar.

But if he had this one chance left to do something good, maybe even save his soul, he'd keep her safe. Keep her out of her own investigation as much as possible . . .

Meanwhile, she held his gaze with a sweet, girlish blush filling her cheeks, relief easing into her blue eyes. "Oh, thank you! I was so hoping you'd say that. It's a lot to take on by oneself."

"I know," he answered softly.

"I'll go get the guard," she said. "Let's get you of there, shall we?"

He nodded. When she turned away, Nick stared after her, still entirely astonished.

Well, so much for bedding her, he thought wryly after a moment. He had enough problems without also being haunted from beyond the grave by her father's angry ghost.

What a shame.

Chapter
2

She returned with Ross, who gave Nick a warning glower and told him to pack his things: He'd be leaving.

Nick complied uneasily, still filled with a sense of unreality. Part of him feared this was all a cruel hoax soon to be reversed, but he took out the single box he had arrived with and placed in it the few belongings he'd been allowed to keep, along with the various small comforts sent to him by his friends. He took the map of America down off the wall, folded it somberly, and put it in the box in which all of his possessions now fit.

Then Ross unlocked his cell, not to grant him his usual one hour a week outside but to remand him into the custody of the lovely Lady Burke.

With his wrists and his ankles shackled, Nick was first escorted upstairs for a final meeting with the graybeards. There was paperwork to fill out, a short but intense interrogation, dire warnings issued.

This, he was advised, was his one chance to prove to them he could still be trusted. One chance to clear the slate. *Good God,* he thought while their lecture droned on, *what did this woman want from him, really?*

It had to be a lot worse than anyone was admitting for them to let him go. Ah, well. If it was for Virgil, he was in.

In any case, the last thing the graybeards did before he left was to return his signet ring to him. Feeling rather dazed, he stared at it for a second as if he had never seen his family's coat of arms before: a black wolf on a scarlet ground.

Despite the awkwardness of the shackles on this wrists, he managed to slip it onto his pinky finger, and thus became the baron again.

Heir to an ancient, but quite bankrupt family.

Not exactly cursed bloodlines, but damned unlucky—and plagued by a self-destructive streak.

Lady Burke looked at him. "Is there anything else you need before we go?"

Nick shook his head, mute and overwhelmed. The only thing he wanted was to be gone from here.

Before the bastards changed their minds.

"This way, then. Come with me." Concern flickered in her eyes at his lost expression; she gestured toward a waiting coach-and-four in the square.

He stepped outside, blinking in the light.

He was not so far gone not to feel the searing sting to his pride when he had to cross to her carriage in front of all the young students, with his chains clanking like a cautionary tale. *Now then, pupils, pay attention. Here's an example of what not to do in life. Always follow orders, do not think for yourself, or you might end up like him.*

He kept his head high and stepped up into his new owner's coach, then sat down with his shoulders squared and a stoic stare fixed straight ahead at nothing.

Lady Burke said her good-byes to the graybeards with a murmur that she would be in touch. Nick saw Ross (how he'd miss him—!) give her the key to his manacles, but when she joined him in the carriage, she did not release him from them. Not that he could blame her.

He wouldn't have trusted him, either. Even now, low, dishonorable thoughts of escaping at the first opportunity were going through his mind. Of course, he ignored them. This was Virgil's daughter. He could no more betray or abandon her than he could give in to the pull of lust that he felt already heating the space between them.

Any other woman in the world, he'd have been happy to cheapen with his long-pent-up needs, but this was Virgil's little girl. No, he stoutly informed his starved libido. He would treat her as chastely as if she were a nun. At least, he'd do his damnedest to try.

After all, if he made a move on her, and she didn't like it, she could send him back to prison. For the first time possibly in his life, Nick resolved to be an angel.

The mysterious baroness rapped on the coach, commanding her driver to make haste; in the next moment, the carriage rolled into motion.

They were off.

Good riddance, Nick thought.

$\mathcal{W}$atching him intently, Gin wondered how he was doing. Expert assassin or not, on a very human level, the man beside her seemed overwhelmed to taste freedom once again—such as it was, considering he was still in chains.

The stench of the prison still clung to him. He needed washing, fresh clothes, a few weeks' worth of good meals, and Heaven only knew what else.

Considering all he had been through, she realized that, realistically, he might need a day or two before he was ready to start their mission.

Well, she wasn't made of stone. She was a mother,

after all, with a certain nurturing instinct. Besides, she needed him strong for the challenges ahead.

Physically, he was obviously more than fit, but mentally, emotionally, it was hard to say.

Yes, she could spare a day or two to let him recover and get his bearings, Gin mused as she discreetly watched him gazing out the carriage window.

He was absorbed in staring at the bleak November countryside, and though Gin could only see his face in profile, his expression looked stricken, his dark eyes wide, his sculpted lips parted slightly.

She bent her head a little, masking the fact that she was studying him with increasing concern. Perhaps she should simply leave him alone, but how could she ignore his pain? The man seemed quietly distraught.

"Are you . . . all right?" she inquired with cautious tact.

He kept staring out the window. "Everything's more beautiful than I remembered," he answered in a slightly strangled voice.

"Ah." Gin was embarrassed for having intruded on his anguish. She looked away, reminding herself that this was the first time in months that the man had been set free from the confines of the prison.

When he sat there a moment longer, still brooding, she attempted to lighten the mood. "You have interesting taste if you find this day is beautiful. Wait till the sun comes out at least. Today is all gloom! The fields are so brown, the sky is gray—"

"The sky. Exactly," he echoed. Then he glanced over at her with a rueful half smile that nearly stole her breath.

Gin gazed at him with a pang of understanding but was reluctant to admit even to herself how his words, indeed, his vulnerability in this moment thawed some of the frost she was so careful to keep around her heart.

A protective layer of indifference.

"Well," she managed at last in a wry tone, "they do say beauty is in the eye of the beholder."

He smiled at her, then gazed out the window again, his starved stare greedily consuming all there was to see.

The carriage rolled on.

*A*fter a time, her prisoner must have looked his fill for the time being.

He stretched out his long legs as best he could in the cramped carriage; with his manacled hands resting on his lap, he put his head back and finally closed his eyes.

Till now, he had been acutely vigilant, but the rhythmic rocking of the carriage must have finally lulled him into a state of relaxation. Or perhaps he was just saving his strength to give her a fight later.

She knew better than to trust him, of course. But on the other hand, she couldn't stop staring at him with an odd and gratifying sense of ownership, possession . . .

You're all mine, for now, she thought in amusement.

She couldn't help but furtively study him, this novelty. Her father's problem agent. The unpredictable one.

He wore no cravat, of course, and she soon became fascinated by the elegant line of his neck and his Adam's apple. Her gaze roamed casually over the sleek waves of his dirty black hair, in need of washing.

The inky fringe of his lashes.

His sculpted lips.

The scar not quite hidden by the dark stubble on his jaw. Why, he even looked like a proper cutthroat, and so he was, she thought, but she could not deny that he was a beautiful man.

Older, wiser, no doubt scarred by the world, but just as appealing now as he had been the first time she had seen him, only in a different way. She had been seventeen . . .

As she watched him doze, her thoughts drifted back to the day many years ago when she had tailed her father to a fencing studio in London to get her first look at "Virgil's boys."

After hearing her father, her dearest friend and confidante, heap praises on the new crop of agents he was training (though he would never say it to them); hearing the warmth and pride in his voice when he spoke of them; the respect he had for each of these brave young warriors who became like sons to him while she was merely a daughter, she had grown jealous, resentful.

Who were these strangers who took so much of her father's time away from her? She even feared that he might love them more than he loved her, his illegitimate daughter.

Virgil had obviously not known how much she had needed his attention at that point in her life. Hoping that at least she might be included in that aspect of her father's secretive existence, she had asked to be introduced to these supposed flowers of chivalry.

He had forbidden it. He wanted her nowhere around them, for a long list of reasons. Well, as disappointed as she had been, a spymaster was not the sort of father that even so rebellious a daughter as she disobeyed lightly.

Nevertheless, she had inherited from him a certain talent at sneaking; in her jealousy, she had decided to go and see "Virgil's boys" for herself. Spy on the spies, as it were, just once—so she could see them and prove to herself that they weren't so great as all that.

That she, too, could've become just as skilled as they if only her father would give her a chance.

But Virgil refused that, too, beyond some basic training in self-defense and reading people.

Females were not allowed to join the Order. She had hoped to be the first, but he would not hear of that, either.

At last, after furtively tailing her father to a London

fencing studio where the lads were having a casual training session one afternoon, she had finally glimpsed the group of them, all in their early twenties, one more beautiful than the next.

Fighting like demons against each other in practice, then laughing and roughhousing good-naturedly like brothers between rounds.

Though their vibrant male beauty had left her breathless, their close-knit warmth had struck her like a stab in her girlish heart.

For this, she had realized, was her father's real family, and she was just as woefully excluded from it as she was from the family she lived with.

The Earl of Ashton's palatial home had been a very chilly place for the redhead who wasn't quite His Lordship's daughter.

Gin lowered her head, tamping down the pain from the memory of that lesson; it still smarted. In any case, her most vivid memory of that day had been of Nick, the young Lord Forrester, leaning by himself against a column, sharpening his blade.

She had picked him out when one of the others had called his name. He had looked over, and her stare had homed in on him: she knew that name.

Now she could put a face to the one who drove her father to distraction. "Nefarious Nick," as his brother warriors called him, was her father's greatest headache.

To be sure, the young, intriguing, black-haired knight was deadly. But Order teams were trained to work as a seamless unit, and Nick had always been a bit of a lone wolf.

Apparently, the Order's prison was where his stubborn, independent streak had got him.

How she could relate to that.

For, indeed, her own stubborn, independent streak had landed *her* in a prison of sorts herself for a number of years: marriage.

But she wouldn't be making that mistake ever again.

Putting the past out of her mind, she closed her eyes and leaned back beside him as the carriage rumbled on.

*A*fter three hours of travel, it was necessary to stop and change horses. They pulled into the cobbled yard of a busy, galleried coaching inn called The Owl.

It had a pub on the ground floor, guest chambers above, and a livery stable in the back.

Nick lifted his head from the squabs, eagerly watching out the window at the hustle and bustle of ordinary life going on. Travelers spilled out of newly arriving stagecoaches; others filed into departing coaches while the tin horns blew.

Gin glanced at her prisoner when they both caught the scent of food coming from the pub. She heard his stomach grumble loudly in response and gave a sympathetic wince.

She wished it was possible to release him so he might come in with them—it would probably do him good—but she did not dare. Not here, in a busy transportation hub.

If he took it into his mind to escape, there were too many opportunities for him to grab a horse and go. She would never see him again. And then there would be hell to pay from the graybeards.

"Would you like to get out and stretch?" she offered.

He shook his head. Cynicism flickered in his dark eyes when he realized she had no intention of taking the shackles off him. But his pride outweighed practicality.

"No, thanks. I'll wait," he said, stone-faced.

"Suit yourself." She gave her two grooms strict orders to guard him. With a nod, one brought his hand to his pistol, then they both went to stand on either side of the carriage doors.

Gin strode into The Owl to make the arrangements for the horses and order food.

Inside, she stayed near the window to make sure her valuable prisoner did not try to overcome his pair of guards and get away. Meanwhile, the coachman unhitched the horses from the last stage and traded them for fresh ones.

Before long, the food was ready. She carried it outside, distributing the small hampers of provisions to her men before climbing back into the carriage.

"Beef stew or chicken pie?" she asked her prisoner when she returned to her seat.

He looked startled by the question and blurted out, "I have a choice?"

Gin paused, feeling another unexpected pang of compassion. "Actually, why don't you take them both," she mumbled. "I don't have much of an appetite today."

As the coach rolled into motion once more, Nick asked to start with the beef stew. She reached into the hamper the innkeeper had prepared and carefully gave him the bowl of stew and a spoon. His chains clanked as he took the precious substance in his hands.

"This goes with it." She handed him a light, fluffy dinner roll. He took it reverently; she watched, bemused, as he lifted it to his nose and inhaled the buttery smell of it as though it were some rare perfume.

He squeezed it between his fingers gently, savoring the texture.

Gin smiled and wished she had bought more. *Poor man.* Slowly, he looked over at her, wordless thanks in his dark, soulful eyes. She held his gaze; he didn't need to say it aloud. Then she looked away to let the starved lone wolf eat in peace.

Unfortunately, it soon became clear that it was difficult for him attempting to eat soup in a moving carriage while wearing heavy iron manacles.

Gin did not dare offend his pride by offering to help him, but when calamity struck and a particularly large pothole sent the dinner roll flying out of his hand, he let out a vile curse.

She raised a brow.

He mumbled, "Sorry."

She brought up her hand and showed him that she had caught the dinner roll in her hand before it fell. She gave it back to him, then decided to move closer, crossing the carriage to sit beside instead of across from him. "Why don't you let me . . ."

He watched her every move as she took the bowl of stew from him, along with the spoon.

"You could unchain me," he pointed out in a low tone.

She just looked at him. Then she filled up the spoon and fed him a mouthful of the stew. He accepted it, staring into her eyes all the while. She proceeded to feed him.

But the intimacy of this act soon had her squirming and casting about for some way to dispel the climbing tension between them.

"So," she started in an idle tone, "what about this bullet you took for the Regent?"

He snorted. "Oh, yes. I am one heroic son of a bitch."

She looked at him in surprise. "Such language in front of lady."

"Is that what you are?" he challenged her with a taunting gleam in his eyes. "Traipsing into a dungeon to buy a traitor's freedom isn't exactly delicate behavior."

"You're not a traitor."

"Well, they didn't put me in that cell for being a saint, love. And you weren't even chaperoned."

"Unless we count this." She lifted the hem of her gown just high enough to pull her pistol out of its garter holster. She gave the black barrel of it a kiss.

Nick grinned. "I think I'm in love."

She flicked a playful scowl at him, her lashes bristling. "Don't annoy me, or I can always find another cell to put you in." He gawked at her stockinged leg as she put her gun back away. "There's always room in the kennel where I keep my hounds, and if they won't share, I'm sure I find an extra chicken crate."

"Lady, I have been called many things, but never chicken."

"Obviously not. You slapped the entire Order across the face, then stepped in front of a bullet to save the life of a man I wager you don't even respect. Why?" she prompted in a confidential tone, glancing into his eyes. "Why did you take that bullet for the Regent?"

"What makes you think I did it for him? I'm a selfish bastard. Didn't you read that in my file? I did it to save my own neck, of course. Put me back in the Order's good graces."

She considered his answer for a moment, then shook her head. "No. Here's a better use for that mouth of yours than telling lies." She fed him another mouthful of beef stew, leaning closer.

As she did so, she could feel his raging sensual interest—and her own response, the quickening in her blood.

He swallowed the mouthful of stew, then licked his lips. "Delicious," he remarked with a stare that made her wonder if he was talking about the food. She looked away but could feel him studying her. "Your turn to answer a question for me, I think."

"You're in no position," she chided, though she was intrigued by his interest in her.

"How did your husband die?" he asked bluntly, scrutinizing her as he waited for her response.

The question startled her. "In the war."

"Combat?"

She shook her head. "Fever hit the camp."

He must have noticed something darker in her demeanor than mere wifely grief. His fiery stare intensified.

"What is it?" he murmured.

Gin abruptly remembered that Order agents were trained to read people, and right now, he was reading her.

She didn't like it.

Her father used to do that, search her out as if he wished to comprehend her every mood.

Difficult to hide anything from these men.

"Nothing." She fed him another spoonful of food to silence his questions. It was not as if she could tell him that her husband's death was her fault, indirectly. How could she ever tell anyone that she was responsible?

At least, she *felt* responsible.

But that was between herself, her dead husband, and their Maker. She'd have to answer for it someday, in the next world, if she ever saw Burke again.

Until then, she hid her guilt away.

Nick saw her refusal to talk about it and shrugged the question off. "As you wish."

When he had finished the beef stew, she gave him the chicken pie. This was not quite as messy a dish; he could manage it on his own. So she returned to her own seat and leaned against the squabs, gazing out the window.

After another hour passed, she reached in boredom for her newspaper. "You were reading something in your cell. Would you like your book?"

He shrugged. "Why not."

Because of his chains, she fetched it for him. The groom had stowed the box of Nick's things in the compartment under the opposite seat. She lifted the lid, exposing the storage area. She immediately spotted the book he had been reading. It was right on top of the box.

She picked it up and read the cover. *A Journal of the Voyages and Travels of a Corps of Discovery, by Sergeant Patrick Gass, 1807.* When she saw what it was, she handed it to him with a rueful half smile. The caged warrior had obviously spent those months locked up in his cell dreaming of the ultimate in liberty.

"You find my choice of reading material amusing, Lady Burke?"

"Not at all. I just don't know where President Jefferson found men mad enough to want to go out into that wilderness."

"I'd go," he said.

She laughed. "Of course you would. Not I, thank you very much."

"Ah, come. Does it not intrigue you just a little? Wondering what might be out there . . . ?"

"Not in the least," she assured him with an arch smile. "I am a creature of civilization. The Americans are welcome to their wilderness. I am looking forward to Paris, actually, once we get our game piece."

He snorted. "Philistine," he teased.

She smiled back at him. "Barbarian," she answered.

Then they both settled into their seats side by side and read together in relative contentment.

*E*very now and then, Nick sneaked a glance at her from over the edge of his Lewis and Clark book. "So, um, where are we going?" he asked hastily when she caught him gazing at her once again.

"To Deepwell, my estate in the North Riding. Won't be long now."

"Ah, Yorkshire. I have always appreciated the North," he remarked. "Good people. Who mind their own affairs."

"And where are you from?" she asked, turning to him.

"But my lady, surely you already know. You seem to know everything about me." He arched a brow, waiting for her to tell him how she knew so many details.

Surely, Virgil had not told her all their life stories over tea.

But the baroness just looked at him, unwilling to share her sources. Then she lifted her newspaper again and turned the page.

Nick snorted under his breath and turned to stare out the window at the landscape again. He soon became absorbed in it, his very soul starved for the autumn beauty that unfurled before him.

Sun rays angled through a moody sky and lit up the sweeping green valley below, dotted with woolly white sheep.

The woods around the edges of the valley were clad in all the colors of autumn: the ash trees golden, the oaks maroon, chestnut trees a glorious orange; and on the distant brow of the next emerald hill, the sad medieval ruins of an abbey with its scattering of ancient gravestones lying all around like broken teeth.

The carriage rumbled on, winding through a quaint stone hamlet. They passed through the angled shadow of a weathered stone marker at the cross, then out the other end of the little village, taking a country road.

It followed the ridge he had seen from the last highway, out into the countryside. From there, they climbed a hill. The tired horses slowed a bit.

"Here we are," Lady Burke murmured when, at last, the carriage turned in through a pair of towering wrought-iron gates and proceeded up the wooded drive to the stately manor house ahead.

The grounds of her estate struck him as especially beautiful.

Everywhere he turned his gaze, the landscape seemed carefully orchestrated to delight the eye and inspire the soul. Either Capability Brown had created a masterpiece here, or Nick had merely been imprisoned too long.

Then he frowned, wrinkling his nose. "Bloody hell, that smells worse than I do. I think you've got a dead deer out there somewhere in the park."

"No, that's the odor from the hot springs on the property. It's in a limestone cave, over there." She quickly pointed out the mossy and mysterious opening of a cave in the wooded hillside as they drove past. "I'm told the water contains sulfur, iron, magnesium. Bathing in it has been known to cure all sorts of ills. Everything from gout to infertility."

"Really?" he murmured in surprise as the cave mouth disappeared behind the trees. "Rather like the waters at Bath, then?"

She nodded. "There are several such springs throughout the area. I'm just lucky enough to have one on my property."

"Except for the smell."

"You get used to it. Smells like home to me." She chuckled at his skeptical glance. "My husband's ancestors discovered it in the late 1500s. You are welcome to take the waters if you like, before we set out on our mission."

"Not if I come out smelling like that."

"I daresay it would be an improvement to how you smell right now, my lord," she said dryly.

He scowled at her.

She laughed. "You should try it. It's good for you! Besides, it feels wonderful."

"I see." He eyed her in guarded amusement. "So you got me out of the dungeon to bring me to a health spa. Not bad. Not bad a'tall."

They drove on toward the house.

Nick was glad to note that, thankfully, her husband's ancestors had had the good sense to set the mansion far enough away from the "healthful" odors of the sulfur spring.

When the coachman brought the weary horses to a halt in front of the house, Lady Burke turned to Nick with an earnest, searching gaze.

"I'd like to take the shackles off you if you give me your word that you won't run." Her neatly manicured fingertip came down to rest on the chain between his wrists. "I know it hurts your pride, and I have no desire to subject you to anything worse than you've already been through. So can I count on you to honor our agreement and not try to escape?"

He looked into her eyes. It had been a long time since anyone had put any value in his word of honor. "Of course," he mumbled. "You have my word, of course, my lady."

Where else would I go?

He had no family, other than a mother who had always had better things to do them worry about him.

He still had the loyalty of his friends, his former teammates, but he did not want them to see him in this condition. "I'm not going anywhere," he assured her in a low tone, holding her stare. "You helped me; I help you."

The softening around her tender lips did strange things to his insides. She slipped the key to his chains out of her décolleté where she had hidden it close to her heart. She held his gaze and thrust it into the hole. Nick swallowed hard, wanting her to the point of pain as she turned the key and made the iron lock pop.

As the manacles released, he nearly groaned.

She removed the little key from the manacles and handed it to him. He leaned down and unlocked the cuffs around his ankles.

The iron shackles dropped to the carriage floor, an unutterable weight taken from him, like a very anchor that had been holding him underwater, placed there by all those who were just waiting for him to drown.

Straightening up, he gave her back the key. "Thank you," he said in a low, earnest tone.

Again the hint of a silken smile tugged at her lips. "After all you've done, you deserve better than to have my staff see you in chains."

Nick searched her face for any sign of irony. He found none. Yet for his part, he barely knew what she was talking about—"everything he had done."

All he could remember these days was the bad imputed to his account. The guilt. The disappointment he was to those who had invested so much in him. Prison had a way of making a man forget the good about himself if he had ever really known it in the first place.

Then the carriage door opened.

Lady Burke alighted, her hand resting on that of her groom. Nick rubbed his chafed wrists as he stepped down after her, leaving his shackles behind as he stepped out into the sunlight.

"This way." The baroness turned to him with a steadying gaze, as if she knew how disoriented he felt as he stood there in the drive, a free man, more or less, for the first time in months.

Damn. It was so moving to taste freedom again that he, Nick Forrester, trained assassin, hardest of the hard, had a lump in his throat.

A sunbeam caressed his cheeks as he turned his face to the open sky above him.

"Come." Lady Burke touched his elbow gently after a moment. "Welcome to Deepwood, my lord. If you'll follow me?"

He opened his eyes and found her watching him. Her curious stare brought him back to earth, then he trailed after her as she went ahead of him into her grand, porticoed mansion.

Nick was almost beginning to feel like a real human being again as she introduced him to the butler, Mason;

the housekeeper, Mrs. Hill; and the first footman, Edward, who would be looking after him.

Young, squeaky-clean Edward looked slightly terrified to have been assigned this duty, but he needn't have worried. Nick had no plans of causing trouble.

Indeed, it seemed Virgil's daughter had done the impossible—had inspired the old Scot's problem agent to be a good boy.

And that in itself, thought Nick, was probably cause for alarm. Then he trailed after her, damned near ready to do whatever she said.

Chapter

3

*G*in watched him climb the stairs with a weary, prowling stride, like the pitiful big cats kept on public display at the Tower of London's menagerie. Embittered and broken as the animals became from too many years in a stone cell, they were still capable of mauling a well-meaning keeper on occasion.

She knew she would have to be on her toes with him, and yet he was beautiful, dangerous as he was, with an innate nobility. "Lord Forrester?" she called, as he followed Edward to the landing of the staircase.

He turned. "Yes, my lady?"

"Do you have a favorite dessert, by chance?"

He did not seem to comprehend the question.

"Dinner is served at seven, and since you are our guest, we would like to make you happy."

"Anything," he forced out with a catch in his voice, as though he had become so unaccustomed to kindness that he almost preferred cruelty. At least cruelty was predictable. "Anything," he repeated in a stronger tone, clearing his throat slightly.

"Very well."

Edward continued up the steps. Nick started to follow, then hesitated. "I have always been rather partial in autumn to a baked apple pudding in pastry."

"Ah, apple pie?" she answered with a startled smile.

He nodded. "As it is also known. But it's not important—"

"I'll see what I can do."

He smiled back cautiously, then they went on their way and soon disappeared as Edward showed him up to his room. As Gin stood there, pondering the presence of this hard, dangerous man in her home—and hoping she wasn't making a big mistake by bringing him here—she got the feeling he did not quite know what to make of her gentleness with him. It was not difficult to see that his mode of life had often been unfair to him and robbed him of all ability to trust.

Blazes, the only reason he had the connections she so desperately needed was because the Order had wanted him to walk the line between spy for the Crown and criminal. Who could be surprised that moving in that world would eventually affect him?

Well, she thought, he ought not to place too much trust in her, either. Her expression darkened. After all, she had only told him the bare minimum about her quest.

With that, she summoned Mrs. Hill. "Have Cook prepare an apple pie for our guest. Also to ensure that large quantities of food are available over the next couple of days. I fear the baron has been much deprived of late."

"Yes, my lady."

"Mason." She next turned to the butler. "Send down to the village for Dr. Baldwell to come and examine my guest."

"Right away, my lady." Mason hesitated with a look of concern. "Is Lord Forrester ill, ma'am? If there's anything we can do to make him more comfortable—"

"No, it's all right. He's spent too much time in unhealthful surroundings of late. I just want the physician to look him over and assure me about the state of his health before I send him into danger."

Her staff knew the nature of her investigations, and though they worried for her safety and rather disapproved, they were unshakably loyal.

"Very good, ma'am." Mason took leave of her and went to send one of the younger servants off to the village to fetch Dr. Baldwell.

*N*ick shed his filthy prison clothes and wrapped a towel around his waist, then went into the bathing room, where the tub was almost full. His architecturally inclined friend Trevor would've been so impressed with the hot running water at Lady Burke's estate, he thought.

The water that came out of the pipes was ordinary well water, not the mysterious healing flows from the hot springs outside. But no matter.

Nick shut the door, removed the towel, and stepped into the hot water, feeling like a veritable king as he lowered himself into it.

He bathed with gusto, submerging himself under the suds, washing his hair, soaping himself all over, and getting the stink and the coldness of the dungeon off him, hopefully never to return.

It was already starting to feel like it all had been nothing but a bad dream.

Meanwhile, in the next room, Edward dutifully aired out the three sets of clothes that had been stored in Nick's box of belongings during his incarceration.

The tidy young footman pressed his shirts, coats, cravats, and trousers, then shined his boots for him in the next room. This done, he left to go and burn Nick's prison clothes, as ordered.

In the bathing tub, meanwhile, Nick took a razor in one hand and a mirror in the other and gave himself a careful shave. It seemed a great luxury.

During his sentence, he had only been permitted to use his razor once a week, and he had to give it back as soon as he was finished; knowing his skill with a blade, the guards took many precautions about such things.

He was not a vain man, but he had no intention of letting himself start to look like some half-wild hermit from a Wordsworth poem. He'd got accustomed to shaving in near darkness, so the sunshine streaming in through the window astonished him with its beauty—and made his task much easier.

In due time, he emerged from the bathing room, feeling like a new man. With a towel wrapped around his waist once more, he walked, barefoot, across the luxurious bedchamber to the chest of drawers with a mirror.

There were a couple of bottles of masculine cologne on the dresser. Nick smelled each of them and chose one with a faint scent of frankincense and citrus. But before slapping it on himself, he paused and looked over at Edward, who presently returned. "Say, did Baron Burke used to wear this scent?" he inquired.

He did not wish to smell like her dead husband.

"No, sir," the lad answered in surprise. "Those are just for guests."

"I see." Nick arched a brow at him. "And does Her Ladyship get a lot of male guests here at Deepwood?"

Edward blanched. "That's not what I meant, sir. Sometimes the young master brings his friends home from school. The young gentlemen often use this guest room."

"The 'young master'?" Nick echoed in confusion.

"The current Lord Burke, sir. Phillip."

Phillip? he wondered, intrigued.

"Sir, might I ask which of these clothes you prefer to wear tonight to dinner?"

Still wary about all this, Nick prowled over and inspected his three choices. He winced at the sight of his full-dress military uniform; it was the last thing he had worn before they'd put him in his cell.

He had been escorted by the Order's kilted guards straight from the Regent's ceremony at Westminster Abbey, honoring them for their service with showy medals and all pomp and circumstance, immediately north to the Order's Scottish headquarters and down to the gloomy dungeon to pay for his misdeeds.

At least the graybeards had spared his pride, refraining from having him shackled in front of the populace there at Westminster Abbey.

Thankfully, they had chosen to handle his punishment as an internal matter, hidden from public view. But that was the Order way.

"Sir?" Edward prompted.

Nick shrugged off bad memories, determined to put the past behind him now that Lady Burke had given him a second chance. "The black merino wool."

"Very good, my lord."

While Edward went to finish getting his clothes ready for him, Nick wandered over to the box of his belongings that had been returned him. Of course, the graybeards had kept his weapons, the bastards, but what could he do?

In the bottom of the box, he found his necklace—the one they all wore—the white Maltese cross on a silver chain, the hard-won symbol of the Order of St. Michael the Archangel. He had worn it for years like a talisman to ward off the danger that lurked in every shadow during their years of fighting the rich and highborn members of the Promethean conspiracy throughout Europe.

In time, the necklace had come to feel more like wearing a tag of ownership that one would put on a dog.

Now it just looked like a symbol of Nick's disappointment in himself. He left it in the box, turned away, and started getting dressed: short drawers. He tied the drawstring. Black socks. He hooked them onto the knee straps, then pulled his white shirt on over his head. The clean white linen felt blissful against his skin. He smoothed the open V of the neck down his chest, feeling almost like a human being again.

After pulling on his black trousers, Nick stopped cold. "What the hell?" he uttered, shocked at the change in how his clothes fit.

They hung off him. He drew the waistband of his black trousers away from his waist, astonished to find several inches of excess fabric.

Good God, he had kept up with his regimen of daily exercises as best he could in prison to avoid wasting away to nothing. But the restricted rations must have cost him a good stone of weight that he hadn't needed to lose.

Jolly good thing he had a pair of suspenders among his belongings, he thought indignantly. Then he leaned closer toward the mirror, finally noticing the gauntness under his cheekbones, the sharp angles of his jaw, the hollows around his eyes.

No wonder Edward seemed afraid of him. He looked as lean and hungry as a wolf. And yet he remembered that Lady Burke had not seemed intimidated. But then, she was Virgil's daughter.

"Waistcoat."

The footman bravely held it up and stepped forward; Nick slipped his arms in the holes.

Edward next fetched his freshly ironed cravat, reaching out his arm to hand it gingerly to him from the greatest distance possible.

"I'll do it myself. I'm not going to kill you, Edward."

"Of course not," the lad said abruptly with a nervous gulp followed by short laugh of relief. "Thank you, sir."

Nick eyed him warily. "What did they tell you about

me?" he asked as he stood in front of the mirror tying his cravat.

"Oh, nothing, sir."

"Something, surely?" Waiting, he glanced at the tongue-tied footman in the mirror.

Edward plainly cast about for some polite escape from this question. "Oh, just some whispers in the servants' quarters, sir. Nothing important."

"Humor me, please. I won't hold it against anyone, I promise."

"Well, sir, one of the maids overheard Her Ladyship telling Mr. Mason that you had been trained by Master Virgil." Edward shrugged. "Seeing the sorts of things that Master Virgil also taught Her Ladyship, we just put two and two together. That you work for the Order," he whispered, wide-eyed.

Not that I was in prison? He was touched she had shielded his reputation. "So Virgil came here to visit?"

"Oh, yes, sir. Quite a lot. Her Ladyship and her father were very close."

Nick stared at him in fascination, absorbing this. *Why, you old fox, with your secrets.* It seemed their taciturn handler was growing even more mysterious in death than he had been in life.

Just then, there came a knock on the door. "Lord Forrester?"

Edward glanced toward it. "That'll be Mr. Mason, sir."

"Come in," Nick called just as he finished tucking in the tied ends of his cravat.

The butler stepped into the guest chamber and clasped his white-gloved hands behind him, nodding politely. "Lord Forrester, allow me to present Dr. Baldwell, our local physician."

A little gray-haired man with stooped shoulders and a black leather bag stepped into the room behind him.

Nick stared at the newcomer, instantly suspicious.

"Her Ladyship has asked that Dr. Baldwell give you a

brief examination to make sure you are in the best possible health," Mason informed him.

Nick looked at him in shock. "Has she indeed?" he retorted, bristling at this new request. "Whatever for?"

Lady Burke herself appeared in the doorway, apparently anticipating his resistance. "Considering your recent living conditions, I want to make sure you're well enough for duty."

"I'm well enough for duty!" He scoffed. "I don't need some quack poking and prodding at me to confirm my health. No offense, Doctor."

"You will cooperate," she informed him. "I cannot risk your passing along anything catching to my staff. Check him," she ordered the physician, then shot him a no-nonsense look. "Cooperate, Nicholas. You gave me your word."

He narrowed his eyes at her. So he had.

With that curt order, Her Ladyship left him scowling and gritting his teeth. But was it worth it to fight?

One had to choose one's battles, after all.

"I didn't give my word to agree to be inspected like a bloody farm animal," he muttered more to himself than to them. He glared at Edward, who quickly scurried out behind the butler.

Dr. Baldwell then proceeded to ask him all the usual impertinent questions that were part of taking down a patient's history. The old, unflappable physician was no more affected by Nick's resentful glares than he would have been at the tantrums of a child with the chicken pox.

He measured him by various methods, height and weight; inspected his tongue; bounced the light off a little mirror into his eyes; peered into his ears with a little funnel thing; checked his head for lice; banged on his knees with a dainty hammer; checked his pulse; listened to his heart; and palpated his abdomen, checking the healing around his solar plexus where he'd taken the bullet for the thankless bloated Prince of Whales.

"Tell me about this bullet wound," the doctor said, inspecting it.

"It hurt," he drawled.

"Did it pierce the bowel or other internal organs?"

"No," he said with a sigh. "The distance saved me. It hit the muscle and went flat. Hurt like hell, though."

"I imagine so." He paused. "You're very lucky."

"You wouldn't think so if you ever saw me in a card game. I'm bloody cursed."

The doctor snorted. "Drop your trousers."

"But we only just met."

The irked physician shot him a baleful glance. Then he made him piss in a cup and examined the color of his "water" by the sunlight.

"Are we quite through here?" Nick demanded, sufficiently humiliated for one day.

"Don't button up just yet."

Good God! Nick let out a wordless exclamation as the old country doctor finished his inspection by checking to make sure he didn't have the French disease.

"Good news, no mercury for you."

"And why exactly does she want to know the condition of my cock?" Nick asked cynically while the old man, through with him, went to wash his hands.

Dr. Baldwell gave him another disapproving scowl. "Her Ladyship is only trying to help you."

"Good riddance," Nick muttered when the old man left a moment later, leaving him alone to fasten his clothes again and make himself presentable once more.

But the question he had asked aloud still gnawed at him. What exactly would his duties to this baroness entail?

The question left him bristling with renewed mistrust.

Was he going to be expected to service her on top of everything else? He was not sure how to feel about that. Obviously, he was attracted to her, but that wasn't really the point. He had thought his time of being used as some rich woman's plaything was over. He'd been down that road before, and it hadn't ended well.

The more he brooded on her unknown motives, the angrier and the more suspicious he became.

So why, then, was Lady Burke being so kind to him? Taking such good care of him? What did she really want? He growled under his breath as he put his clothes back on.

After all, when something looked too good to be true, it usually was.

Well, it was plain to see she was a woman of the world, with her young lover. She had better not be assuming Nick would take over where her missing toy boy had left off just because she said so. A man had his pride.

If she thought her arrangement with the graybeards gave her leave to use him for a bloody male whore, she was misinformed.

If he could resist her.

Torn between lust and resentment, all he knew was that he did not like her control over him one bit. *Don't be so quick to trust her just because she's Virgil's daughter.*

She was keeping as many secrets as her father.

Spooked to wonder whether this chance at earning back his freedom would cost him the last few remnants of his pride, Nick decided that until he figured out what this woman really wanted from him, he had better stay on his guard.

Dinner was sure to be interesting.

*T*hat evening, Gin took a sip of wine as she sat at her dressing table in the candlelit alcove of her opulent bedchamber, legs crossed. Clad in a silk peignoir before dressing in her dinner gown, she reviewed Dr. Baldwell's notes from his examination of Lord Forrester.

She was surprised at the degree of her own relief to find that his health was sound, from head to toe and at all points in between. Not that it should have mattered, beyond the practicalities of his basic readiness for the mission ahead.

But as she trailed her fingertip over the physician's diagram, she shook her head with a pang at all the places on Nick's body where the doctor had recorded the presence of scars. Burns, slashes, healed-over breaks, shrapnel, and, of course, a couple of bullet holes, one more recent than the rest.

She couldn't help feeling that every one of them was her father's fault, and since he was dead, that she was somehow responsible for all the damage done to this agent. Years ago, Virgil, in his early role of Seeker, had gone around to various aristocratic families and handpicked the lads he wanted for his unit before they were even Phillip's age. It must have been heartbreaking, knowing the kind of danger he was recruiting these mere children into, but all of them had been eager to go.

Nick, especially, according to her father.

She let out a sigh and put the notes down on her dressing table, saddened. As her thought drifted, she remembered how she had raged so many times at her sire for stubbornly forbidding her to try to become the Order's first female agent.

But Dr. Baldwell's little drawing of all the scars on Nick was proof positive that her father had been right.

If the enemy could inflict this kind of pain on one of the Order's hardiest warriors, what might they have done to a female spy associated with the organization if she were ever captured?

With such a hostage, they could have wrung deadly concessions out of the graybeards and every honor-bound male agent in the field.

Ah, well. She had long since realized that her father had only stopped her out of love. As much as she had hated it at the time, living vicariously through the tales he told about "his boys" and their perilous adventures, she had come to understand a parent's need to protect his or her child once she had become a mother, herself.

In the mirror on her dressing table, the look in her eyes turned steely. The Order was never getting their hands on Phillip. They'd never leave these kinds of scars on her darling son.

Just then, a soft knock sounded on the door.

"Come." She glanced into the reflection behind her as her lady's maid stepped in.

"You sent for me, my lady?"

"Yes, I have to dress for dinner." She rose with a languid motion. "The emerald satin tonight, I think."

"Very good, ma'am." The maid hurried to fetch the gown from the large, adjoining dressing room.

Soon, Gin was dressed in the luxurious green gown and seated once again before the mirror while the maid braided small sections of her hair to add interest to the topknot that would be held in place with pearl-studded combs.

In the reflection, Gin noticed the smile tugging at the maid's mouth and realized it had been there since the woman had come in. "You seem rather merry this evening, Bowland. What's afoot?"

"Oh, it's nothing, ma'am," she assured her with a quick smile as she worked.

"Come. This wouldn't have something to do with our guest, would it?"

"Well, the girls belowstairs couldn't help but notice His Lordship's awfully handsome, ma'am."

"That he is. He's also very dangerous. Not a man to be trifled with. Let them know I won't countenance any nonsense."

"Yes, my lady. I will tell them." Bowland dropped her gaze with a chastened look.

Gin knew the stern precision with which she ran her household was not much fun for her staff, but she did not intend to let the maids go throwing themselves at Lord Forrester.

She did not need her silly-headed servant girls tempting a very worldly man who had been starved of sex for the past six months.

Somehow, she could not shake her own, acute awareness of that fact. Nevertheless, the rogue agent was as much her hireling now as the maids were, and like them, he would jolly well live up to her standards while he was under her roof.

She just hoped she could hold up to them herself. She sent herself a stern, warning glance in the mirror. *One false move, and he'll take control of everything.*

That's not going to happen, she assured herself. She might have taken the manacles off him, but she still intended to keep her trained wolf on a very short leash.

Then she turned with a rustle of satin and proceeded down to dinner.

$\mathcal{N}$ick remained on his guard at supper that evening. Still suspicious of her motives, he refused to let the wine lull him into lowering his defenses, nor her beauty to turn his head. It was impossible, though, not to feel the impact of her allure.

She was ravishing, and God, it had been so long since he had known the pleasures of a woman's bed. The emerald hue of her gown turned her blue eyes sea green and made them sparkle like a warm, tropic sea.

Her intricate coiffure was a work of enchantment to behold, and her skin . . . her rosy cheeks, her alabaster throat . . .

The creamy expanse of her chest bared by the low, pointed neck of her gown, tortured him with a cruel show of cleavage.

But considering that she held all the power, at least for the moment, his cool demeanor toward her was the only act of defiance he could afford, under the circumstances. It wasn't easy. They were both wary and polite, not talking much at table.

The spread of food was lavish. After the privations of the past year, Nick fought himself not to devour everything in sight. Hell, for all he knew, the sumptuous feast before him might only be intended to fatten him up for the slaughter, he thought wryly.

They sat at the two distant ends of the long, formal dining table. Between them, the staff laid out a rapturous spread of dishes, symmetrically arranged—elegant blends of textures and tastes, contrasting and complementing, with new bottles of wine to sample with every course.

All the while, from its place of honor above the white fireplace, the large, gilded portrait of a weak-chinned man in uniform stared down at them in prim disapproval.

The husband.

Nick eyed the pasty-faced figure warily as he chewed. *How the hell does a chap like that get a woman like her?*

Lady Burke noticed him looking at it and supplied the answer to his unasked question. "The late Lord Burke."

"Tell me about him," he invited her, keen to gather information about his mysterious hostess. "Nabob?"

"His family has had various lucrative enterprises under way in India for decades. He was sent over there after his graduation from Oxford to familiarize himself with the holdings he'd inherit. He spent a decade there, then returned to England to settle down and find a bride."

Nick stared at her. "Well, he was obviously successful in that quest."

"Oh, yes," she said with a bland smile and took a drink of wine.

This reaction intrigued Nick in the extreme; and now he couldn't leave it alone. "I am sorry for your loss. It must have been very difficult for you."

Not really, said her cool gaze. "Thank you," said her lovely lips.

You despised him? Nick thought. *He bored you to death?*

"How did you two first meet?" he asked in a cordial tone.

"Well . . ." Lady Burke glanced at the dining-room door, making sure that none of her servants were in earshot. "It's a funny story, actually."

"Do tell."

"He originally started out courting another girl in my debutante class, but I stole him."

"Oh, really?" Nick was both astonished and amused. "You stole him from a friend?"

"Oh, no, not from a friend. An enemy," she answered with an arch smile. "That was why I did it. Of course, I was very young. Seventeen. I had no idea my mischief would end up in marriage."

"What happened?"

"The girl Burke was courting at the time was the bane of our lives—all the other debs, I mean. I won't mention any names, but she was a horrid little beauty. Arrogant, spoiled in the extreme. Had to be the center of attention at all times."

"I know the type."

"She wheedled her way into favor with the Patronesses of Almack's, then began her reign of terror. As our first Season wore on, this young lady took to the habit of bullying my dear friend, Elizabeth. Torturing her in Society with mockery and intimidation. So I decided to put the queen bee in her place."

"By stealing her beau?"

"Precisely. It was shockingly easy. But I never anticipated that I would then be forced to marry him—for appearances' sake."

Nick winced. "Poor thing."

"It wasn't so bad. His family did own diamond mines."

"Well, there's a consolation."

She shook her head, shrugged, and let out a sigh. "I suppose it was no worse than any Society match."

Nick pondered this for a moment, staring into his

wineglass. "Did he ever find out the real reason you first began pursuing him?"

"Oh, yes. That was pleasant." When he glanced at her, he could see she had not anticipated this question.

The smile faded from her face. A shadow passed behind her eyes. "It became difficult after a time to hide my true feelings."

Disgust, Nick realized. He paused. "Was that what sent him off to war?"

"Yes, and he never returned." She gave him a look that informed him this was all she intended to say on the topic.

He did not press for more.

They lapsed into silence as they continued eating. But every now and then, he looked at her, more intrigued than ever. She barely knew him, so why tell a virtual stranger such an intimate story? Why share what must have been the most devastating mistake of her young life?

Maybe she was trying to show him that he wasn't the only one who had ever made a misstep, considering where she had found him. It was generous of her if that was her motive.

Nick lowered his gaze, but even when they brought out the exact dessert he had requested, he eyed her with furtive uncertainty.

He still had no idea what to make of her: the sensual baroness, the carefree widow, the lady detective?

Countless questions about her swam through his mind as they finished the meal and repaired to the drawing room, where she offered him a cheroot and, to his surprise, took one for herself.

"You smoke?" he exclaimed.

"On occasion. You disapprove?" she drawled.

"Just surprised. Not the done thing for ladies, I thought. Or have things changed so much since they locked me up?" he asked in amusement as he held the match for her, then lit his own.

"No, you're right. I'm an odd duck. Always have been." She smiled as she puffed on the cheroot to get the tip fully lit. He did the same. "Terrible habit, isn't it? I picked it up from my father."

"So did I," he replied.

"Let's step outside, shall we? I don't want the smell to get in the house." She slipped her gloved hand through the crook of his elbow and led him through the French doors out onto the terrace.

"Thank you for the dinner. Especially the apple pie. Extremely thoughtful of you."

"It's my pleasure."

"Cold?" he asked as his breath misted in the night's crisp chill.

"Not yet. It feels good. Bracing."

He nodded. The November sky was black. She let go of his arm and stepped away from him. Nick tilted his head back and gazed up at the stars.

It was the first time he'd been outside at night in so very long, stuck in his cell. The white half-moon wrapped in ebony silk was even more beautiful than he remembered.

Lady Burke must have noticed his taut silence, for she spoke soothingly of idle things, drawing him back from his momentary anguish with the nearest, easy topic. "Oh, yes, I've become a great fan of the leaf from the Carolinas," she said in a musing tone, inspecting her cheroot. "I know I ought to quit, but somehow I always order more . . . though I tell myself I only keep them on hand for my gentlemen friends."

Her words jarred him with a reminder of the various bottles of cologne on the dressing table in the guest chamber he had been assigned. "And do you have many of those here, my lady? Gentlemen visitors at Deepwood?"

She turned to him in guarded surprise, her slender eyebrows lifted. "A few. From time to time. You disapprove again?"

"No, of course not. It's your life. You're a grown woman." He paused for a moment. "I just wondered if you have them all inspected for the French disease first."

"Ah, I knew you were still peeved about the doctor!" she exclaimed.

"I think I have a right to be," he said. "The state of my health is none of your business."

"I had to make sure you're fit for service."

"And what service might that be, exactly? I'd just like to know what all is going to be expected of me."

She had the decency to blush. Indeed, he could feel the blaze pouring off her cheeks in the cool night air. It told him all he needed to know. "You have to trust me, Nick. I do have your best interests at heart."

"Right."

"What?" she demanded. "What's the matter?"

"I agreed to help you, Virginia—" He used her Christian name with insolence, since she had felt free to use his. "But that doesn't mean you own me. I'll kill whoever you want, but I'm not your plaything. Unlike your little toy boy," he added under his breath.

Her jaw dropped. "Excuse me?"

"Well, he is your lover, isn't he? This chap who's gone missing."

"Not that it's any of your business—but, no!"

"Ah." He absorbed this, unsure if he believed her. But the vehemence of her denial left him feeling like a bit of an ass. "Then it seems I owe you an apology," he said in cool, sardonic reproach.

"Yes, you do," she declared, staring at him in astonishment. "I suggest you go to bed now, Lord Forrester. The strain of all our travel seems to have robbed you of your manners."

He cleared his throat, slightly chastened. "Indeed. Then I bid you a fond good night, my lady." Avoiding eye contact, he turned to crush out his cheroot in a garden urn filled with sand for that purpose.

"Lord Forrester!"

Heading back to the French doors, Nick turned warily.

"You're a pretty fellow, but my only interest in you is for the case."

"Good," he answered smoothly. Then he gave her a polite bow and withdrew, his ego smarting.

At least her tart answer had put his mind at ease about her having ulterior motives.

He just hoped that, having laid out his boundaries, he did not regret telling her in so many words that he had no desire to bed her. Because that was a bold-faced lie.

*G*ood Lord.

Gin stared after him in fiery indignation, her cheeks still flaming brightly. Blast the man, he was too perceptive by half.

Clearly, she would have to work harder to hide her wild attraction to him.

Shaking her head at his barbarity and her own foolishness, she folded her arms across her chest and took another pull off her cheroot, trying to calm down.

How rude could someone be? And as for her . . .

Idiot! And here she had thought they could be friends.

She should have known not to trust his quiet, guarded demeanor tonight. All the while, he had been sitting there seething over the medical exam, she realized. Eyeing her with suspicion, and—ever the spy—collecting information on her, which she had freely shared.

Damn, she wished she had not told him the true story of her marriage. Why not just tilt back her head and offer him her jugular?

She did not even know *why* she had done it. But, no, if she was honest, on second thought, of course she did.

She had seen the way he had looked at her husband's portrait, as though baffled by the match, and she had felt embarrassed. She had always been embarrassed of the weak, lazy, self-indulgent coward she had married.

Even though she had brought it on herself, the whole match had been such a bitter disappointment—especially when, as a girl, she had always expected to end up with some bold, dashing Order hero.

Well, she mused, if tonight with Nick was any example of what that would have been like, then clearly, she was better off.

If only he weren't so beautiful. If only his midnight eyes did not beckon her with his loneliness and need . . .

Damn it. She shook her head and stared off into the bleakly bare garden, silvered with moonlight. She was going to have to do better than this, be more careful about keeping things businesslike between them.

The wine at dinner and the darkness of this seductive autumn night was obviously too dangerous, too tempting, when she already had a secret weakness for this man—as though she were still an infatuated seventeen-year-old.

It would not do.

She cringed to wonder how great a fool she might have made of herself. But no matter. If he had detected her desire for him, it didn't mean that she had ever intended to act on it. Besides, she would remedy her error merely by treating him all the more coolly on the morrow.

In any case, it was official: Her father's problem agent was her headache now.

Chapter
5

The next morning, Gin went down to breakfast with her plan for the day firmly set in her mind.

After making their final preparations this morning for the dangerous mission ahead, they would set out for London this afternoon.

By tomorrow night, they should be ready to proceed to the Topaz Room in Southwark, where they would confront Hugh Lowell, the owner of the notorious gambling hell.

But when Gin stepped into the dining room and inquired of her staff whether Lord Forrester had appeared yet this morning, Mason informed her that His Lordship had been up since dawn and had gone out to the hot springs.

Gin went motionless, hearing this.

Though she had told Nick he was welcome to bathe in the hot springs—that, indeed, it would be good for him after all his injuries—she had never meant for him to go unchaperoned.

Her immediate response was a tightening of fear in

her chest, then her heart began to pound. God, the cave was so close to the front gates and the perimeter of her property.

What if he had lied to her staff, merely using a visit to the hot springs as a pretense to cover his escape?

She was instantly furious at herself for trusting him. An agent willing to abandon the Order itself would surely not hesitate to desert her on her investigation. It was clear he hardly took it seriously, after all, since she was naught but a lowly female. His indignation about the medical exam and their quarrel last night would have only fueled his desire to escape.

Waving off an offer of breakfast, she clipped out a command that her horse be saddled at once and brought round. Why, oh, why hadn't she specified to him and her staff that he was not to leave the house unsupervised?

Why hadn't she set a guard on him at all times, the way the graybeards had advised and, in truth, had assumed she would do?

Because I wanted to trust him, she thought as she marched out through the entrance hall and snatched her cloak off the wooden coat-tree in the corner.

She wanted him to take this chance to stand up and be the man her father had known Nick had the potential to become. He was so beautiful and fearless, yet so bloody difficult . . .

She wanted to believe the best of him. That there was still a man worth saving behind the cynicism, bravado, and despair. A man of honor.

A true knight of the Order.

We'll see. Pulling on her coat, she stalked outside into the gray November drear.

Her tall, powerful dapple gray swiveled his fine head, pricked up his ears, and snuffled a horsey greeting when he saw her. "Morning, Trebuchet." She gave him a brisk pat, nodded tersely at the groom holding the bridle, then sprang up onto the sidesaddle, gripping the pommel with one hand. The groom handed her a riding crop.

She nodded to him to back away, then she was off, cantering briskly across the acreage of her estate for the hot-springs cave, and praying she had not made a huge mistake.

But one thing was clear. If Nick needed to be treated like a convict, as she had been warned, then that was precisely what she'd do.

If he was not already long gone.

The drizzly morning's chill seeped into her bones and made steam rise from her horse's spotted hide. The bare, sparse branches raked the leaden skies overhead; from beneath her horse's flying hooves, chunks of emerald turf flew up as she cantered across the green expanse of lawn.

But when she guided Trebuchet into the woods, following the well-worn path to the cave, the thick blanket of wet fallen leaves crushed underfoot filled the damp air with the smell of autumn.

Surely, Nick was not that dishonorable, she thought, her stomach still churning with dread as the muddy path rose toward the cave's mouth. He might be many things, but surely he would not abandon her when she had explained how he was the only one who could help her get the required game piece to the vile Bacchus Bazaar.

Innocent girls' lives were at stake.

As the cave's mossy entrance came into sight, she decided that if he was not in there—if he was gone— then she had truly misjudged him. And for that matter, so had her sire. Trying not to jump to conclusions, she would not have to wait much longer to find out.

Arriving at the cave, she dismounted, steadied her gelding, then tied his reins around a nearby tree.

Still clutching the riding crop, she lifted the hem of her walking dress to slog through deep mud up to the ankles of her boots, clambering up to the slippery stone entrance of the cave.

The bubbling pool of medicinal waters lay at the end of the murky tunnel. Inside, the cave was dark and warm, filled with hollow, dripping sounds. The mineral smell was strong, but Gin quickly got used to that.

Trailing a gloved hand along the smooth limestone wall of the tunnel to guide her on her way, she ventured into the darkness while her eyes adjusted.

Halfway down the tunnel, she saw a glow of light ahead. The staff left oil lamps and fresh towels here, knowing the hot springs were often used. But Gin remained cautious.

Just because the lamp was lit did not mean her guest was still here. It could be another ruse, meant to buy him time. Her heart pounded as she neared the end of the tunnel, stopping just in time to avoid stepping with her mud-coated boots on a pile of clothes near her feet.

She looked down at them and felt a rush of hope, then immediately glanced ahead toward the pool.

Her knees went weak with relief.

He was there, lounging in the water—his black hair slick with moisture, his arms spread wide, elbows resting along the stone edge of the pool.

With his head tipped back, his eyes were closed, the harsh angles of his face softened with sensual pleasure.

Gin swallowed hard at the sight of his glistening body. She stepped around the pile of his clothes, drifting nearer, her heart pounding. His lifted his lashes and gazed at her with a lazy smile, the fire in his coal black eyes banked to a golden glow. "Am I ever glad I listened to you," he greeted her in a purr.

Gin smiled, hoping that the riot of her emotions upon finding him here did not show too plainly on her face. She was so relieved he had not run off on her that she did not know what to say.

Secretly chastened that she had doubted him, she

tried her best to seem natural—and not to stare too much. With a discreet gulp, she lowered her gaze to toy with her riding crop.

Nick eyed the object curiously. "Just what are you planning on doing with that, dare I ask?"

"Oh, um, nothing. I just . . . forgot to leave it in the saddle holder. I rode up here," she added.

"Ah." He nodded slowly, staring at her. Reading her once again, she feared. "Are you going to join me?"

Her eyes widened; her head snapped up to meet his gaze.

"The water's blissful," he added, his midnight eyes full of dangerous invitation.

This from a man who had informed her in no uncertain terms last night that there would be no naughtiness between them.

She wondered at how many women had wanted to strangle him over the years.

"No, I—that is, we need to get our day started. Ahem." She cleared her throat and looked around at the rocky protrusions of the cave walls. Anywhere but at him. "I hate to ruin your fun, but we've got work to do. We leave for Town this afternoon."

He heaved a great sigh. "As you wish, my lady." Nick sank down into the water, disappearing, and then he stood up, visible to the waist. He brushed the water off his face, then squeezed it out of his slick hair, shrugging his broad shoulders, and flexing his neck from side to side.

He let out a sigh of satisfaction: Gin could not take her eyes off him. The muscled elegance of his sculpted body filled her with raw yearning.

He turned around and climbed, naked, out of the pool. Her pulse pounded, her mouth watering, as her stare slid down the strong, sweeping lines of his lower back to his taut buttocks and his lightly furred thighs.

He grabbed a towel, dried himself a bit, then wrapped

it around his waist, turning back to her. "I know I had some clothes on when I got here. Now where the devil did I . . . ?"

"Here," she meant to tell him, but her voice had disappeared.

"Ah, there you are." He approached his clothes, his body warm and glowing, a relaxed expression on his face that made him seem almost like another man entirely.

He eyed her in amusement, as though well aware of her staring. His glance flicked to the riding crop in her hands. "Not sure I trust you with that thing."

"Don't make me use it," she shot back in a breathy tone, to her dismay. At least she had recovered her bravado in time to avoid making a complete cake of herself.

He laughed softly and bent to pick up his clean linen drawers near her feet. He looked at her, then cast aside his towel, and stepped into them.

Throbbing with his nearness, Gin bit her lower lip and dropped her gaze while he proceeded to dress, but she could feel him studying her. "Are you all right, my lady?"

"Yes. Why?" She swallowed hard.

"You look, I don't know. Nervous." She jumped slightly when he touched her face, wiping away a fleck of mud that her horse must have kicked up. "Something wrong?"

I thought you betrayed me, her heart whispered. But outwardly, she managed a taut smile and shook her head. "Just eager to get on about our business."

He nodded. "I'll be ready in a moment."

"I'll wait outside." If she stayed in here much longer, alone in the dark intimacy of the cave with him, she had a feeling they were both going to end up naked in that pool, and that was not allowed to happen.

Somehow, she dragged herself back out to the threshold of the cave, savoring the bracing chill of the morning now. But as she waited for him, staring out at the gray drizzle of the day, she reminded herself once again that he was a spy—trained to manipulate, deceive, charm his targets into doing things that were not in their best interest.

Which was all the more reason not to let him know the truth. That she had been incapable of loving her dead husband because he could never compare in her eyes to the breathtaking men who worked with her father.

Men like Nick.

And she knew perfectly well why Virgil had never wanted her to meet any of them. He had known what would happen. That she, passionate, rebellious, would fall desperately in love with one or the other of them, but that, given his warriors' deadly obligations, it could only end for her in agonizing heartbreak.

It might yet, she thought, as Nick sauntered out to join her near the cave's mouth.

As her gaze flicked over him, she could not help smiling a little. No cravat, no waistcoat, but at least he had his trousers and boots on; he was still tucking in his loose white shirt and pulling his black jacket on as he approached.

"Nice piece of horseflesh," he remarked, nodding at Trebuchet, who was eating the leaves of some nearby bush.

"Come," she ordered. "He's strong enough to carry us both."

Nick followed her down over the slippery rocks outside the cave's entrance to her horse. They took the bulky side saddle off him so they might ride together; Nick carried it back up into the cave for one of the servants to collect later.

Soon, Trebuchet was moving along at an easy, swinging walk with both of them on his back. Nick rode behind her, his hands resting lightly on her waist.

Gin was acutely aware of his hands and the unyielding hardness of his body behind her, his breath warming her neck as she held the reins.

They passed through the drizzling woods in silence.

"You thought I'd gone, hadn't you?" he asked at length, his voice low and intimate at her ear. "Don't lie," he chided softly before she could deny it. "I saw the relief on your face when you stepped into the cave."

Gin considered how to respond. "You've defied my expectations," she admitted.

"You've certainly upended mine," he replied.

She wasn't sure what he meant by that, but maybe it was better not to know. Whatever assumptions the cynical ex-spy had made about her were likely to be a tad insulting: She refused to rise to the bait.

"I'm not going to abandon you," he said. "I agreed to help you, and I will. I do have one speck of honor still."

"Good," she forced out. "I'm counting on you. And so are those kidnapped girls."

"Right. Well, what's next?"

"Weapons practice. Let's make sure you haven't lost your touch."

"Me?" He laughed idly. "I was born with a sword in my hand, don't you know?"

She glanced over her shoulder at the irresistible rogue. "I'll be the judge of that."

$\mathcal{S}$ he fed him well and let him play with guns. Nick was not the type to fall in love, but these two points put Lady Burke as close to being his ideal woman as he had ever met.

There was also the lesser fact that the more time he spent with her, the more curious he became about what she would be like in bed. Tender and sweet? Needy and demanding? Shy or insatiable? Would her façade of cool control melt away into frenzied submission, or would she try to master him, fight him for dominance?

Envisioning the many possibilities heated his blood so much that he avoided meeting her gaze for fear she'd read the drift of his dirty thoughts in his eyes.

He was *not* getting himself sent back to prison by offending her. Only a dolt would fail to realize he had already pushed his luck. Therefore, Nick gave no sign of his desire: He was a very angel, on his best behavior. For once.

They spent an hour in target practice with an assortment of guns, shooting toward the steep hill behind her house to ensure that any stray bullets pierced nothing more than turf.

Not that there *were* any stray bullets. Nick *hadn't* lost his touch, as it turned out, and as for Lady Burke, why, the beautiful baroness was an impressive shot.

She favored her little silver pistol. He was more of a rifleman, himself.

At length, the gray gloom cleared, and the skies parted to admit some slanting, golden sunshine. It immediately began to dry the soggy grass and lit the bleak autumn world around them with its mossy, melancholy beauty.

A footman marched out of the house as if on cue and quickly dried off the garden furniture nearby: a wrought-iron table-and-chairs set on a circle of flagstones under a giant, bare-branched oak.

The two of them continued shooting toward the hill, but once the furniture was dry, more servants brought out refreshments, which they placed on the table: hot mulled cider, a few slices of excellent firm cheese, and soft pumpkin bread, still warm from the oven and slathered with fresh butter.

Feeling like quite the king of all that he surveyed, Nick finished brushing up on his skills with the firearms and took his place across from the baroness at the little table to enjoy their late-morning snack.

The lady knew how to live, he'd give her that.

Afterwards, it was on to bladed weapons. Nick picked up a sword. He savored its well-balanced weight in his grasp, the pleasure of its slicing through the air as he whipped through a few speedy figure eights.

He lowered the weapon as a grizzled older man approached; Lady Burke introduced him as a local fencing master she had summoned to put Nick through his paces.

Nick shook hands with him, then switched to one of the blunted practice blades. As Lady Burke sat back and watched him brushing up his moves against the fencing master, Nick felt a little self-conscious under her scrutiny, as if he were some nervous adolescent trying to impress a girl.

With some additional effort, he blocked her out of his mind and focused on the fight. The fencing master was good; Nick was better. Moves drilled into him since boyhood had long since turned into reflexes. It all came back to him quickly. When they paused for a break, he took a swallow of the now-cold cider, his muscles burning, his chest heaving—yet this was the best he had felt in a long time.

He glanced over and saw and met Lady Burke's gaze in wordless gratitude. She smiled knowingly. Then she called in the next expert to engage him, in fisticuffs this time.

After a rigorous hour with the blades, another forty-five minutes with the pugilist was all he had left in him, especially after the brutal trainer landed several blows around Nick's solar plexus, where his Regent-saving gunshot wound had only just settled into a healed-over scar.

When the old injury grew sore, he took care to block

his midsection better, but still, he didn't see any point in pressing his luck unnecessarily. He appreciated the practice, but he wasn't stupid. He finally called a halt.

At least now he was aware of the weakness so that he could guard against it when the fight was for real.

Lady Burke rose from the garden chair on which she had been sitting the whole time, watching patiently. She thanked, then dismissed the boxing trainer. Equally winded, the giant bald man bowed to her and to Nick, and took his leave.

Still panting and streaming with sweat, Nick collapsed into the wrought-iron chair beside her.

"Having fun?" she asked, eyeing him in amusement.

"Is that why we're doing this? For fun? And here I was starting to wonder if you were trying to kill me."

"Don't be a baby. It's good for you."

He laughed in exhaustion, dabbing his face with a hand towel. "God, you *are* your father's daughter." He helped himself to another swig of the leftover cold cider.

She was watching him intently. "What was it like working with him?"

Nick looked at her in surprise. "Well . . . he was tough."

"I know he was very hard on all of you."

He shook his head and took another drink as his heartbeat finally slowed back to normal. "We were grateful for it. Felt like torture at the time, but later on, it saved our lives. Actually, a little bird told me that your father gave you some training, too."

She smiled ruefully. "He wouldn't let me join the Order like I wanted—"

"*What?* You wanted to join?"

"So what if I did?" she challenged him.

"God," was all he said.

She snorted. "Humph. Well, he wouldn't budge on that, but at least he agreed to teach me a few basic skills."

"Oh, really? Let's see 'em."

She sent him a dubious glance. "I don't have to prove myself to you," she drawled.

"Besides, if we're headed into danger together, I want to know what you can do. Come. Show me."

"Very well." Taking his offered hand, she allowed him to pull her up fondly out of her chair.

Her touch, though brief, put his weary senses on high alert. She let go of his hand and went languidly to pick up one of the blunted practice swords, as well as a wooden knife for her left hand.

Nick followed, but he only took a sword. He had to give her *some* advantage, after all, just to make it reasonably fair. As they both got into position on the lawn, standing a few feet across from each other, Nick raised the wooden practice sword before his face in a formal salute.

She did the same. "Prepare to die, thou scurvy knave," she taunted with a pleasant smile. "En garde," she added. Then she attacked.

Nick defended himself in delight. She was quick and agile, and what was more, and he could see her sharp mind working as she skillfully parried his blows, feinting to the right and coming at him from the left.

"Not bad for a girl."

"Fight back! You're not even trying."

"You're a lady!"

"Oh, am I?" With that, she swiped her dainty foot behind his heel and tripped him.

Nick fell back with a merry yelp and landed on his elbows on the ground. He looked up at her for a second in shock, then immediately rebounded, vaulting acrobatically to his feet.

She arched a brow in aloof amusement. "A pretty move."

"You haven't seen anything yet."

"Show me," she taunted in a whisper, circling his blade with her own.

Nick let out a lusty laugh.

She lunged as if to run him through; he captured her extended arm, stepping back beside her; she brought her dagger neatly across her body to demonstrate how she still could've stabbed him in the eye.

"Well, well," he murmured, laughing softly.

Then he tripped her in return, brushing her feet out from under her so that she went tumbling down in a whoosh of skirts and petticoats. She landed on her back, her chest heaving, both hands still clutching her sword and dagger.

Nick dropped to his knees astride her, plunging his practice blade into the soft turf by her head.

She tried holding him at bay as best she could, laying the wooden blade flat against his chest, but he ignored it, disarming her, and pinning her wrists to the ground.

"Damn you!" she said through breathless laughter, struggling against his hold to no avail, thrashing beneath him.

"Now, now. You'll only make it worse for yourself if you fight me. This doesn't have to hurt. Unless you want it to."

She glared at him, but there was more than one type of frustration in her deep blue eyes.

Nick stared down into them, wanting with everything in him to make love to her. "Never play-fight against a trained assassin, my dear. And now for the coup de grace."

"Ruthless," she accused him, arching her neck as she tried in vain to sit up.

"Very. Lie back for me." Leaning closer, closer, he bent his head until his lips hovered at her throat; he was panting more from lust than from exertion.

"Nicholas," she warned, trying to sound stern and failing miserably, for her voice came out as a sensual whimper, full of unspoken, unacknowledged need.

He wanted with everything in him to fulfill it.

"There, there," he whispered with a wicked smile as his lips grazed her throat. "Would you like me to deal you a little death, my lady? *Un petit mort?*"

Otherwise known as an orgasm.

She huffed and shook her head, her cheeks turning even redder. She refused to meet his gaze. "You are a demon."

"But I'm your demon now. So what do you say? I have rethought my position on this thing. Now that I know you're not demanding it of me, I think I'd be happy to pleasure you."

"Thanks, but I'm rather busy at the moment," she answered dryly.

Amusement danced in his eyes, but he couldn't stop staring at her creamy chest. "Perhaps some other time, then?"

"You wish."

"Guilty as charged." Not wishing to scare her, he released her wrists and ventured a light caress on her cheekbone with his fingertips.

She looked up at him uncertainly at last.

"You are a remarkable woman, Virginia Burke," he murmured. "Thank you for getting me out of that cage. I was dying in there. My soul was dying."

"I know," she whispered, reaching up to cup his cheek in return for a fleeting moment.

He throbbed at the softness of her touch. God, it had been so long, and she was not like any woman he had encountered before. He positively craved her.

But at just that moment, Nick heard something in the distance. He did not move from his position atop her but lifted his head and turned to stare keenly down the drive.

"What is it?" she asked, still seeming quite content to lie beneath him.

"Expecting someone?" he mumbled, narrowing his eyes as he stared toward the drive. "You've got visitors."

"What?"

He quirked a brow at her. "Don't tell me you've hired yet another expert to come and beat me up."

She shook her head. "I'm not expecting anyone. Off with you before we're seen." She slapped at his thigh still straddling her hip.

Nick got up, immediately bending down to offer her a hand. She clasped his palm; he pulled her to her feet.

She brushed a leaf out of her hair and dusted the dirt off her dress as she went striding toward the carriage, which was presently pulling up in front of the house.

Nick gazed after her, privately marveling at the woman. Her walk was a thing of beauty to behold.

He blew out a quiet exhalation, trying to will his hunger for her into submission.

Then the carriage door banged open, and a young lad of about fifteen, with a shock of dark red hair, jumped out.

Nick arched a brow as the baroness stopped in her tracks. "Phillip!" she cried. "What on earth are you doing here? You're supposed to be in school!"

"Sorry, Mum, I got suspended."

"*What?*"

"Mother—don't explode—I can explain. It was all just a misunderstanding . . ."

Nick stared, wide-eyed. *Mother?*

"Who's that?" the boy suddenly demanded, glancing past Lady Burke at Nick. "Oh, perfect. Another one?" he cried.

"*How dare you?*" his mother thundered, but Nick laughed aloud at the lad's highly impertinent question.

Hearing him laugh, she sent him a wrathful glower over her shoulder: Nick quickly stifled his humor.

"Get inside," she ordered her son. "I want answers, now, young man. Go!"

The boy glared at Nick as he slouched toward the front door, a mere puppy, but all bristling protectiveness toward his mama.

Nick stared after him, marveling with a pang of remembrance as the truth hit home.

The kid was Virgil's grandson.

Chapter
6

$\mathcal{T}$he library was the room in their home long since designated for lectures and scoldings. As Gin marched her wayward son thence, her temples throbbed with agitation.

What's he done now? she wondered, though, to be sure, Phillip's getting into trouble was nothing new. He had always been a handful, too smart for his own good and as stubborn as a donkey.

Taken off guard by his arrival, she had no idea what to do with him, considering that she and Nick were about to leave for London.

Most of all, she was furious at herself for nearly letting her child find her rolling around on the ground with a strange man. Some example! She felt like a terrible mother, and that only made everything worse. What was she thinking, allowing Nick to take such liberties, anyway?

She was in severe danger of losing all control of the situation—and before Phillip's intrusion—just for a moment there, she had barely cared. Damn it, was she so willing to let her pet prisoner take the upper hand? Why?

Just because he happened to be everything she had ever dreamed of in a man? *Fool*. She shook her head at herself. God, where might their playful, heavy-breathing sport have led if her son's carriage had not arrived when it did?

With a shudder, she vowed to pull back from this dangerous attraction between herself and a man she had just sprung from jail. Thankfully, her son's unexpected arrival had brought her back rudely to her senses.

Closing the library door behind her, she took a deep breath and turned to fix her boy with a quelling stare. "Well?"

"Well, what, Mother?" he retorted, flinging himself down onto one of the thick leather couches. He crossed his long legs out before him and folded his arms over his chest, glaring at her in disapproval.

"What do you have to say for yourself?"

"I might ask the same of you. Who is th-that *person?*" He jabbed a finger toward the window. "Another new 'gentleman friend'? Already? What happened to the last one? The yellow-haired idiot? What's-his-name, Carr."

"You'd better watch your mouth," she warned, lowering herself to sit on the padded arm of the couch.

"I'm only trying to protect you, Mother."

"Why did they send you home from school? What did you do? Come. Tell me at once."

Phillip scowled and handed her a crisp piece of parchment that turned out to be an indignant letter from the headmaster. When she came to the end of it, she lowered her head with a groan.

Phillip shot to his feet. "You should be proud of me by all rights, not angry!"

"Proud? Fighting? Causing a ruckus? You did serious injury to another boy."

"The class bully—and besides, he's two years older than me. Ha!"

"Whoever he was, it says here you sprained his shoulder and beat him nigh senseless."

"God made him senseless, and he's lucky I didn't break it," he declared.

"Phillip, this is serious. It also says here you threatened a division master."

"You mean Professor Marquis de Sade?"

She let out a stifled yelp at his words. "I don't want my fifteen-year-old knowing about the Marquis de Sade!"

"I'm not a prude, Mother," he informed her in a worldly tone, folding his arms across his chest.

"Oh, sorry!" she retorted, before gesturing to the letter. "So, what happened with this tutor?"

"He's a pervert, for one thing."

She shut her eyes and groaned under her breath. She knew the most expensive private boys' schools had a certain reputation for creating a brutal environment, the better to prepare the lads of the upper class for their harsh futures in politics, war, and empire.

Unfortunately, there were sometimes men in control of the children who abused their privilege and enjoyed their places of authority a little too much.

Apparently, Professor Marquis de Sade had not counted on her son, known to his friends and his Mum as "the Red Terror." And not just for the color of his hair.

"The maths don is an even bigger bully than the senior I thrashed," he informed her. "I swear it entertains him, beating boys on their bare arses—"

"Phillip! God."

"Well, it's true. And he's long since singled out the weakest little nancy in our class, Alastair Ponsonby, for his abuses. I got tired of hearing the pitiful creature crying each night after lights-out. So I asked him what the hell was wrong, Mother. And he told me.

"This senior, Dwight Cotler, was ruthlessly torment-ing him. Cotler had thrown little Alastair's math as-signment in a mud puddle, and there wasn't time for him do it over again, so that merely put him afoul of Professor Marquis de Sade, and likely due for another bare-arse beating in front of the class.

"So," Phillip said with a shrug of feckless bravado, "I decided to stand up for him. Protect him. From them both. That's what Grandpa Virgil would've wanted me to do. Defend the weak. Isn't it?"

"Oh, Phillip."

"When I saw Cotler starting in on Alastair as usual the next day at breakfast, let's just say I got involved."

Gin bit her lip, wondering how it was possible to love someone so much and, at the same time, want to throt-tle him.

"This letter says your 'involvement' included sprain-ing Dwight Cotler's arm and knocking him over the head with a food tray so hard that he was unconscious for a quarter hour."

"Just long enough for me to get to maths lesson," Phillip said, nodding. "Nobody dared tell on me until Cotler himself regained consciousness. That made things easier."

"So, what happened with the teacher, then?"

"When he collected our assignments first thing and found that Alistair had nothing to turn in, he had the expected reaction. All I did, Mother—I swear it on my honor—was stand up and vouch for Alistair, why he didn't have his assignment. That it wasn't his fault. I told him what happened, but he didn't even care!" Phillip exclaimed, shaking his head in wide-eyed inno-cence at the world's unfairness. "That brute said there were no excuses. That if a boy couldn't learn to make his way in school, he wouldn't be able to make his way in life. Then he summoned Alistair to the front for his beating.

"I blocked the way, and said, 'Why don't you pick on someone your own size?' He started taunting me, asking if I wanted to take Alistair's beating in his place. I told him, try it. And when he picked up that blasted paddle, I grabbed it out of his hand and broke it over my knee."

Gin stared at him.

Phillip shrugged, and conceded, "I might have raised the broken piece of the paddle at him. I don't really remember—I was so furious. But I wouldn't have hit him, Mother. You must know that. I'm not stupid."

"Oh, Phillip."

"I don't care if they expel me, anyway!" he said vehemently. "In fact, I'd be glad. What's the point of my going there, anyway? We both know where I should be going to school—up in Scotland."

By which he meant the Order school at the Abbey above the dungeon where Nick had been locked up.

"Don't you dare start that again," she warned, staring at him for a moment in suspicion. He dropped back down onto the couch and crossed his ankles in leisurely fashion once more, a very rakehell in the making. "Is that what this is about?" she demanded. "Are you deliberately trying to get expelled? Because if that's what you're planning, you can forget about it, Phillip."

"Mother!"

"You are not joining the Order. End of discussion."

"Why not?" he cried, sitting up straight with a quicksilver motion. "I can do it! We both know that's where I belong! It's my right! It's my heritage!"

"It's never going to happen."

"You think I don't have what it takes? But I do! I just need training—"

"No." She blocked out his protests and headed for the door. "I'll write back to the headmaster and try to smooth things over. But you will be going back there once you've completed your suspension."

"Ugh!" He dropped his head back and glared at the ceiling.

"In the meanwhile, you will be confined to the house, and you're not to have any visitors. You'll carry on with your studies here at home while I'm gone—"

"Gone? Where?"

"I'm leaving for Town in a few hours."

"London?" He sat up eagerly. "Can I come with you?"

"No. I just told you. You're staying here—out of trouble." With a pointed glance, she pivoted and headed for the library door. "I'll summon your old tutor from the village to come and look after you—"

"I'm not an infant, Mother!"

"No?" She paused, glancing at him. "Then prove it by staying on your best behavior while I'm gone. I don't want to hear any bad reports from Mr. Blake."

Phillip glowered at her. "You're not going to be in control of my life forever, Mother."

"Well, I am for now, so you might as well forget about it."

"Why?" he cried. "Why can't I have a dream?"

She stopped and paused, gazing at him. "The Order took my father from me. They're not getting their hands on my son. You, my darling, are going to live a nice, long, happy life—"

"Boring! Dull as dishwater, Mother! Am I supposed to entertain myself when I grow up with a stream of lovers like you do?"

Gin gasped at his impudence. "How dare you?"

"Who's this one? I demand to know who've you brought into our house *this* time."

"You're a child. It's none of your affair!"

"Affairs. You'd be the expert on that," he muttered.

"You watch your mouth, young man!" She hesitated, routed by his accusation, especially since there was a grain of truth to it. She did not want her son thinking ill of her, nor did she wish to be a bad example.

She glanced warily toward the window. "That man is not my lover. He was—" Her words broke off.

"What?"

Against her better judgment, she gave way. "He was a friend of your grandfather's."

Phillip gaped at her in stunned silence. "Are you serious? That's an Order agent out there?"

He flew to the window to stare.

"Just leave him alone, Phillip. He's helping me with a case."

"Why? Is it an especially hard one? Oh, this is amazing!" Then he frowned. "But what happened to your idiot assistant?"

"Well, that's the problem, sweeting. He's disappeared."

"Ran out on you? Eh, Mother, I told you that one was no good."

The boy was more right than he knew.

Then she answered, "Lord Forrester is going to help me find him and get to the bottom of this."

"Wait, Forrester?" he echoed, wide-eyed. "As in *the* Lord Forrester? The chap who took a bullet for the Regent?"

She nodded. "That's him. You leave him alone," she warned. "I mean it. Keep your distance. I don't want you bothering him."

And I don't want him filling your head with grand tales of adventure about his missions.

She already had her hands full trying to rein in her headstrong son on that particular subject.

"But, Mother! Please! He knew Grandfather—and now he's a guest in my house! Oh, I don't believe this. Brilliant!"

"Oh, Phillip," she murmured yet again in dismay.

"If you won't let me join up, myself, at least let me talk to him. I can talk to him if I want to!" he added with a pugnacious frown that reminded her ever so much of Virgil.

"No, you can't."

"Why not?"

"Because I said so, and I'm your mother."

"Tyrant lady! That's no reason! I have rights!"

"He is a dangerous man!"

"Nonsense, Mother, he's a bloody hero!"

Gin blinked, less worried by her son's language than by the hero worship that suddenly shone from his youthful face.

"All of them are! It said so in the papers. That's why the Regent gave them the medals at Westminster Abbey. I wonder if I could see one of his medals!" the boy suddenly added with a gasp of awe.

"Phillip, stay away from him. The man's a trained assassin."

"Really?" He whirled to face the window again, and whispered, "That's fantastic."

She shook her head, seeing that her attempt to scare Phillip away from Nick had only had the opposite effect. Maybe she *should* let him meet Nick, she thought. Then he might see the toll that sort of life took on a person. It might curb his enthusiasm. But, no. Why risk it?

"Lord Forrester and I will be leaving for London shortly to try to get some answers on a case. I'm going to send for Mr. Blake to come and mind you. I don't need you getting into any further trouble. Now, behave," she warned before pivoting and leaving him alone.

Sulking a little, Phillip grumbled under his breath as his mother marched out of the library.

Tyrannical woman.

It was always awkward and disgusting to find her with one of her lovers, though he supposed that was only the way of the world.

Every boy in his class thought she was the most beautiful lady they had ever seen. Which only made him roll his eyes and feign gagging. *Try living with her,* he was fond of retorting. *She's bossier than the Queen.*

Thank God, it sounded like she had improved her tastes if she had finally found herself one of Grandpa Virgil's warrior-heroes. Burning with curiosity, Phillip stared through the glass.

Out on the lawn, minding his own business, the big, muscular, black-clad man was practicing with throwing knives.

"Crikey," Phillip whispered to himself as one blade after another whipped through the air to crowd into the target's center ring. He stared in awe, shaking his head.

A real Order agent, right there on his very own lawn!

Suddenly, Phillip set his jaw in stubborn determination that he had inherited from his grandsire the spymaster—though, to be sure, it had not skipped a generation.

No matter what Mother said, he had a *right* to talk to Lord Forrester, man-to-man. His own father was nothing but an unsmiling portrait and a name bequeathed to him, along with properties and fortune.

Phillip gathered from the things his mother *didn't* say that his father had been a bit of a dud.

Of course, few men could have lived up to the standard set by Grandpa Virgil.

Not that their connection came without cost. After all, many of Phillip's relatives on his father's side didn't accept him on account of her being the Scotsman's by-blow.

Some of his cousins had even taunted him once by calling his mother a half-blood, and that, to be sure, had won his ire.

Nobody insulted his mother.

But although he'd never admit it, their rejection hurt. Indeed, it had convinced him over time that his *real* family lay with the Order, if only he would be allowed to join them.

And now, at last, here was this visitor, a living, breathing connection to that whole, mysterious world.

Phillip simply had to talk to him.

Lord Forrester was one of the most famous Order agents, handpicked and trained by Virgil himself. This seasoned agent would be able to judge better than anyone the great question that obsessed Phillip's heart: whether he had what it took to be accepted into the Order's school. He was pretty sure they would've taken him simply because of his bloodlines: *He* knew he had the blood of heroes in his veins.

But all Mother cared about was keeping him safe, as if he were an egg.

She only did it because she loved him, he supposed, but she was such a mother hen. She just didn't understand.

Sometimes in this life a man had to do what a man had to do. *Like now.* His mind made up, he opened the library window, then climbed out in a most spylike fashion, jumping down silently onto the lawn.

From there, he marched off to go and interview their mysterious guest for himself. Like Grandpa Virgil always used to say: *Easier to ask forgiveness than permission.*

$\mathcal{N}$ick was still practicing when he looked over and saw Lady Burke's son striding toward him. He stopped what he was doing and turned, furrowing his brow, as the youngster hailed him.

"Hullo there! Lord Forrester, isn't it? I'm Lord Burke. Thought I'd come and introduce myself. I'm Phillip!"

Instantly wondering if the boy had seen him on the

ground with his mother, Nick cleared his throat and bowed, feeling awkward. "Pleased to meet you, Lord Burke."

The kid joined him, staring eagerly at Nick as if he expected him to perform a circus trick. Juggling, perhaps.

Nick frowned, a little unnerved by his beaming scrutiny. He turned away and made himself busy wiping some mud off one of his blades.

"So, Mother says you knew Grandpa Virgil!" he blurted out at last.

Nick paused, looking askance at him with caution. "Yes."

"Brilliant. He trained you?"

"Yes. You know about the Order?" he asked warily.

"Oh, I know lots! Let me see if I have this right. You're . . . the expert sniper on Lord Beauchamp's team."

"Was," he mumbled ruefully, arching a brow. "All the teams have been disbanded since we were exposed. You know Beauchamp?"

Phillip gave a sheepish shrug. "Know of him, that's all. But I did get to meet Lord Falconridge once! Capital chap!"

"Yes," Nick agreed.

"He didn't know who I was. I mean, that my grandfather was Virgil. It's been a family secret, y'see."

"So I gather." Nick hid his amusement. But to call the existence of Virgil's daughter and her son a "secret" was putting it mildly. More like a damned shock. "Pretty impressive how he kept all his own trained spies from finding out about you and your mother."

"He didn't want me getting chosen. But I wish I had been!" he added eagerly.

"Ah, no, you don't," Nick muttered.

" 'Course I do! It's brilliant! You fellows are like . . .

heroes or, or the gods of bloody Olympus! Well, the ladies seem to think so," the boy jested.

Nick sent him a dark look, extremely irked by such outlandish praise, but Phillip was beaming with his fantasies of adventure, derring-do, and the admiration of pretty girls. "Where's your mother?" he asked uncomfortably.

"Writing a letter to the headmaster. I got kicked out of school," he added rather proudly.

"What for?"

Phillip's chin came up a notch. "Thrashed a bully. Senior. He deserved it."

He proceeded to tell him the story. Nick listened as he threw, finally nodding to admit he was impressed with the stand the kid had made against the cruel older bully and oppressive authority.

That simple nod seemed to make Phillip grow two inches taller right before his eyes. "So, what's all this, then?" Phillip nodded at his throwing knives.

"Just practicing a bit."

"Can I try?"

"Not sure your mother would approve—"

"I'm practically sixteen!" he protested.

Nick shrugged, remembering all the times Virgil had shown patience to him when he was that age. "All right. Here. No, not like that. Hold it here, by the base of the handle . . ."

Phillip threw a few times without much success, but his enthusiasm was undimmed as he ran and collected the knives when they landed.

"Wait. Look at me. Watch," Nick ordered. "Smooth and steady. Bring it over your shoulder, steady with the left, and *release*."

Thwack!

The knife shuddered into the distant bull's-eye.

"You're way too good at this."

"Years of practice." He smiled. "I was worse than you when I first started. Keep working at it. You'll get better."

So he did, and thankfully managed not to slice his own hand off.

"I suppose I ought to ask you your intentions toward my mum," the pup remarked at length, casting Nick a wary look askance before staring downrange again at the target, then throwing the blade just like Nick had shown him.

"I don't have any," he replied, startled. "I'm here to do a job, then I'm going to America."

"Really? Why?" He stopped and turned to him, his auburn eyebrows arched high in surprise. "Do you have a mission there?"

"Hardly. I want to see the wilderness. Maybe stake out a claim west of the Allegheny Mountains."

"But that's Indian territory! Aren't you worried you'll get scalped?"

"No," he answered in amusement.

Phillip pondered this. "But will you come back? You have a title. Don't you already own some land in England?"

Nick shrugged. "I don't care about my title. You ask a lot of questions."

"I think I have the right," he shot back with startling impertinence, "considering you want to take my mother to London."

"It's not like that," he said with a frown. "She's the one taking me. Don't worry, I have no designs on her. She's far too good for me. I'm only helping her with a case."

"*Helping* my mother?" Phillip echoed with a dubious stare. "The woman who never needs any help from anyone, especially from a man?"

Nick laughed. "Apparently, she's in over her head on this one."

Phillip instantly sobered. "Should I be worried?"

"I'll take care of her," Nick assured him.

The boy was silent for a moment. "Does this have to do with John Carr? She told me he went missing."

"Yes, her assistant." Nick looked askance at Phillip when he snorted in disgust.

"That weasel! Sickeningly in love with her. Maybe he finally gave up on her and went and hanged himself." The boy shook his head. "I never trusted him."

Nick weighed Phillip's words uncertainly. "Well, your mother seems very concerned. We're going to see if we can find out if he's all right or if something's happened to him."

"Maybe I could come along and help—"

"No, I don't think that would be wise," he cut him off. It was too dangerous.

Just then, Nick heard Lady Burke call her son's name.

"Phillip!" she barked at him across the lawn. "Get back inside! Now!"

"Ah, blast it," the boy muttered under his breath.

She was striding angrily over the lawn, headed their way. "I told you to go to your room!"

"Nice meeting you," Phillip mumbled.

"Likewise," Nick answered.

"You know, sir, if you did . . . like my mum, I think I'd give my blessing."

"Thanks," Nick replied, bemused.

Then Phillip slunk away toward his mother, who was clearly on the warpath. "How dare you disobey me? First, you are suspended, then you deliberately ignore what I said!"

Nick did not wish to hear the scolding, so, to spare the lad's pride, he walked off down the range and went to collect his half dozen throwing knives out of the target where he'd sunk them, and out of the ground— Phillip's work.

Good kid, he thought in amusement, though, at the moment, Phillip's mother did not seem to think so.

He took care to stay out of earshot. He could not make out specific words, just the blur of an angry woman scolding her headstrong son.

In truth, Nick was deeply touched by his meeting with the cheery redheaded lad. *Virgil's grandson. Fancy that.* He shook his head in wonder at this revelation.

He couldn't wait to tell Beau and Trevor and the rest. This kid might not have a father, but Phillip was soon to find himself surrounded by a dozen doting, stand-in uncles who'd be glad to take an interest in his welfare. Whether his mum approved or not.

A furtive scan of the territory revealed Phillip trudging into the house. Lady Burke had stayed behind, apparently waiting to speak to Nick. Standing near the wrought-iron furniture, she folded her arms across her chest. He noticed her bristling posture, but what startled him as he approached was her cold stare. "A word with you, please."

Did I do something wrong? he thought as he went to her, his compliments on her boy temporarily forgotten. "What's the matter?"

Her mouth was pursed, her gaze flinty. "Don't take this the wrong way," she clipped out, pausing only briefly, "but stay away from my son."

Nick went motionless, taken off guard by the ice-cold rejection packed into her words.

The hurt made his mind go blank for a second. Then he dropped his gaze and understood why she had said it.

He couldn't really blame her, considering she had just got him out of prison. He was not quite the knight in shining armor Phillip seemed to think and not at all what a good parent would probably consider a positive influence on her child. How many men had he killed, after all?

Still, he had not been braced for this particular ice

pick in the heart. He looked away, filled with a breath-taking surge of shame. He turned away with a nod and managed a taut, "Of course."

She stood there a moment longer for some reason, staring at him, but with his heart knotted up and stuck in his throat, Nick refused to look at her.

He couldn't.

Any hope he had felt about the connection between this woman and himself dissolved like the morning mist—even though he understood. The lioness was merely protecting her young. It didn't matter whose head she bit off in the process. Still, he'd had gunshot wounds that hurt less than this succinct condemnation.

So that was how she saw him. Not even worthy to *speak* to her son.

All right, then. Foolish thoughts away.

He made himself busy wiping the mud off his fine blades that her kid had thrown into the ground.

"We leave for Town in an hour," she informed him.

"Fine."

She hesitated a moment longer, perhaps realizing how she'd hurt him. But it did not signify. She was a pain in the arse, anyway. The wilderness waited.

He'd get her blasted game piece to the Bacchus Bazaar, then he'd be on his way, just like they had agreed.

He shut her out that simply.

He was very good at that. Nobody got close enough to make him feel that kind of pain. Not anymore. It had been folly to let her start to get under his skin, but he hadn't been able to help himself. She was Virgil's daughter. That was all. That had given her an extraordinary advantage, bypassing many layers of his usual distrust.

Perhaps noticing that she had just ceased to exist, at least for him, the baroness pivoted abruptly and marched back into her sprawling house, and Nick went back to practicing, hurling his knives with a newfound vengeance.

God knew, they were not as sharp as her tongue.

What a fool he was, thinking anyone would ever want to get close to him, care for him. Not even his own mother had done that.

This woman, like all the others, had a purpose for him. That was all. She was using him, and he, as usual, had agreed to let himself be used.

He cursed under his breath as he suddenly nicked his thumb with a careless angle of his blade, thanks to his angry distraction.

A small line of crimson appeared at once, but the pain, though small, served to focus his mind and him back to himself . . . the dismal facts of who he was.

An assassin and spy who had let the darkness in which he moved get inside him and slowly destroy all sense of meaning, until nothing mattered anymore. Not his once-shining crusade, not even his blood-proved love for his brother warriors. Indeed, now and then over the years, he had hated them all for tying him to that mysterious shadow-life that no one was ever allowed to leave.

They needed him, and so he had been there, year after year after year, while the shadow slowly hollowed out his soul.

If only he could have kept believing that all their sacrifices were not ultimately in vain.

He had tried, pathetically—illogically—to prove to himself that there was indeed an order to the universe by his own particular usage of mathematics, continuously defying the odds, testing God by taking on deeds that should have killed him, and tempting fate at games of chance when he was at his leisure.

All he ever wanted was a sign that any of it mattered.

Clenching his jaw, Nick put his knives back neatly into their case. As he closed it, he wondered if he might truly find the purpose of his life someday in the wilds of America.

In his heart of hearts, he had to admit it seemed unlikely.

But at this point, it was the only place left on earth where he hadn't looked for whatever the hell it was he was trying to find. If it wasn't there, it was nowhere.

And if so, then there was truly nothing left for him.

When they set out for London at two o'clock that afternoon, it did not take long for Gin to notice that the wind had most definitely shifted between her and Nick.

Rather, a cold front had swept down from the arctic.

And in this bitter chill, oh, joy, the two of them were stuck together, confined inside her traveling chaise, for a journey of twenty-four interminable hours.

It was the longest, uneasiest carriage ride of her life.

As the golden day faded into autumn's early night, Nick remained as silent as the distant planets in the black sky, brooding out on the edges of cold space like Jupiter or Saturn. The bright crescent moon in all its haunting beauty was cheerful by comparison as it watched them traveling on through the night.

She tried to sleep. The cushioned squabs were comfortable. The company was not.

After another hour, Gin wasn't sure what to think.

She felt guilty and apprehensive, aware that she had truly hurt this man, though she hadn't really meant to. Damn it, she should have known he'd take it wrong—

her warning about Phillip—sensitive soul that he was behind the warrior's stony exterior.

Once more, Nick seemed like a different person. Gone was the hard-edged, cynical bravado of the prisoner she had transported from Scotland. Gone also was the more playful, seductive side of him that she had experienced on the lawn.

With one sentence, she had turned the fragile intimacy that had been born between into a desolate canyon.

And why should she be surprised? She knew full well she could be a bit of a hard-nosed bitch. Still, she hadn't expected this. His demeanor toward her was so distant that she was afraid he was done with her as a person. And she was shocked by how much this possibility alarmed her.

Then it made her angry at herself.

Hadn't she vowed never to let a man get the best of her? She despised the urge to explain herself to him. She refused to wheedle or cajole. Ever.

If he wanted to sulk, then let him, she thought. She had bigger things to worry about than a man and his moods.

As the carriage rumbled on toward Town, she wondered if he was disgusted enough to abandon her along the way and try to escape. Despite this possibility, she had dared not put the manacles back on him for the journey.

In this state, it wouldn't take much to push him over the edge, and she was well aware that, if he really wanted to, he could easily overpower her and her driver and grooms and get away. He could do it in seconds.

Yet, he stayed, even though he seemed to hate her at the moment.

She wanted to believe he was angry at a great deal more than only at her. At fate, at life, at everything.

All the same, she wished she would've weighed her angry words a bit more carefully before she had spoken them. Or at least had modified her tone.

Blinded by the fiery wrath of a mother's protective instinct, she had lashed out and hurt a man who was already in too much pain.

Unfortunately, she knew just as certainly that she could not apologize. Not if she wanted to keep any control over the situation.

He was a warrior; he'd read any offering of the olive branch as groveling or weakness. Then he might even try to exploit such a show of vulnerability, just like he was trained to do.

She did not dare give him the chance to take the upper hand. She'd been warned not to trust him overmuch.

Indeed, it was important to keep it in the forefront of her mind exactly who and what he was, not to be taken in by the ex-spy's occasional glints of charm. He was skilled in manipulation, trained to lie. A hardened prisoner who had been remanded into her custody to carry out a particular task.

Apologize? Be a stupid, soppy female?

No.

Why hand him the keys to the castle? The Order was counting on her to keep him under control.

So she held her silence hour after hour, while the carriage glided along behind the team of trotting horses.

Seven hours and three changes of horses into the journey, boredom set in.

She looked at her fob watch and sighed with vexation to find it was only 9:00 P.M. She considered attempting conversation by telling him about her son's act of valor, since in truth, she was secretly bursting with pride in Phillip for sticking up for a weaker boy, even against the school authorities.

Virgil would have been so proud.

She had a feeling Nick would have appreciated the tale, too; but considering that it was over her son that she had cut him with her words, on second thought, maybe it was better to keep her maternal pride to herself.

Stifling a sigh, she went on ignoring him back and busied herself in reviewing her case files on the missing girls. She squinted at her papers, then turned up the light on the tiny oil lamp whose glass sconce was built into the side of the carriage interior.

Even so, its dim illumination was enough to give her eye strain. The shaking of the carriage did not help, with the result that she shut the file a few minutes after starting and turned to Nick.

Of course, he'd be happy that she was the first to break, but restless boredom was driving her out of her mind. "So."

She gazed at him for a moment where he sat across the carriage from her. He stared back at her, his eyes wintry black.

She refused to be unnerved, but the small space of the chaise suddenly seemed much too close and intimate in the lamp's flickering glow.

"So what?" he rather growled at her, barely audibly.

"Tell me about the owner of the Topaz Room," she ordered in a businesslike voice.

He sat up slightly straighter, his change in posture signaling a wary willingness to engage, at least on the relatively safe topic of their shared mission. "There are only two gambling hells in England through which interested parties can obtain the game pieces that serve as tickets to the Bacchus Bazaar. The Caravel in Brighton, and the Topaz Room in Southwark."

"Yes." She nodded. "I got the first game piece at The Caravel. That's why I can't go back there. It took me weeks to establish myself with the owner and win his trust enough even to broach the subject of a game piece. I understand, however, that you are on friendly-enough terms with Hugh Lowell, the owner of the Topaz Room."

"Lost more money there than I care to remember," he said dryly.

"What can you tell me about Lowell?"

"He knows his business. And he reminds me of a giant, bloodsucking tick. What else would you like to know?"

She grimaced with distaste.

"Describe the layout of his establishment."

"Three floors. Gambling hell on the first. Bordello upstairs. He keeps a stable of about a dozen girls. Calls them his Jewels, given the title of the place. Diamond, Ruby, Sapphire, and so on."

Gin nodded.

"Downstairs," Nick continued, "there's a Jerusalem Chamber that handles the debts his guests incur, as well as the kitchens and service areas, and a labyrinth of tunnels under the building where his office is hidden. Highly secure. He keeps an army of henchman on hand for security, of course."

"I see."

"My preferred approach is by the river. The casino has its own private dock with ferryboats to shuttle passengers back to the respectable side of the Thames after they've had their fun. Place opens at six and closes at dawn. I'd like to go during open hours. Such meetings are always simpler with a crowd of people on hand to witness any unpleasantness."

"How much, er, unpleasantness do you expect?"

He shrugged. "At least a little."

"I can easily get you some help. I have a fellow, Haynes, retired Bow Street Runner who sometimes—"

"No."

She stared at him. "He's very capable."

"Indeed?" he murmured with a bit of a leer.

"That's not what I meant!" she shot back hotly, realizing the unspoken accusation in his answer. "You think I'm a real trollop, don't you?"

"Takes one to know one," he drawled.

Struggling for patience, she refused to be offended

since it was clear the jackanapes was trying to make her angry. "Mr. Haynes is in his sixties, Lord Forrester. You, on the other hand, act like you're about thirteen."

He snickered.

She ignored it, jaw clenched. "So, I ask you again. How much trouble do you anticipate in procuring this game piece for me?"

"Nothing I can't handle. Don't worry, you'll have it in your hand by this time tomorrow night. And then I guess that means our business together will have been concluded."

"Yes," she murmured warily.

That *was* their agreement. Still, vexing as he was, it was strange how quickly she had got used to having him around. "Where will you go when we're finished? Have you got a place to stay?"

"Beauchamp's house for a day or two, most likely. His wife was always kind to me. Well, at least she tolerates me."

"The other Order wives don't?"

"They don't know me. And for my part, I don't like strangers."

"I see." Gin mused on what she knew about their tight-knit little group. "Beauchamp seems a lot of fun," she said at length.

Nick snorted wryly. "Most women think so."

"Many ladies were quite crushed when he married Lord Denbury's niece. We've never been introduced, but I've seen her now and then in the ton. She strikes me as a clever, lively, young woman. I'd like to meet them both sometime. I was never allowed to when my father was alive." She looked at him expectantly.

But if she was hoping for Nick to take the hint and offer to do the introductions, she was dreaming.

He shrugged, slouching in his seat, his hands lightly clasped across his chiseled stomach. "Do as you like. They're often enough in Society."

Patience, patience, she told herself.

"Is there anyone you'd like to see in London?" she tried again a moment later while the moonlight slanted in through the carriage window and played across his sculpted face. "I'd be happy to take you about in my carriage. Any family you'd care to visit?"

He laughed. It was not a pleasant sound.

"Come, there must be someone," she persisted, unsettled by the undertone of bitter mockery in his low laugh.

Finally, Nick relented. "I don't know," he mumbled with a shrug, glancing out the window at the dark, silvered countryside. "A few friends, maybe. They're rather sickening, though," he remarked, staring wistfully into the distance. "Newlyweds. Babies on the way."

"What's wrong with that?"

"Sounds boring as hell to me, but if that's what a man wants out of life, then bully for him."

"What do *you* want out of life?" she pursued, out of curiosity.

He flashed a dark smile. "*Out* of life."

"Nicholas, don't say such things," she chided in mild exasperation. "You don't mean that. You could've killed yourself by now at any time if you really wanted to."

"Eh, hope springs eternal." He eyed her dubiously. "I ask you the same question: What do *you* want out of life?"

Gin considered the question for a moment, then shrugged. "I don't really care. As long as I can make my own decisions, I'm content."

"You *do* like being in control, don't you?" he murmured, studying her from the shadows.

"It's better than being someone else's pawn."

"I wouldn't know," he answered dryly. "Do me a favor. Try not to overcontrol your son, or he'll hate you by the time he's twenty."

"*What?* Phillip would never hate me! I'm his mother! He's a good boy." She scoffed. "What sort of blackguard hates his own mother?"

He just looked at her.

"Oh, dear." She sat back as understanding dawned. "Why do you hate your mother?"

"I never said I did."

"You didn't have to."

He shook his head. "I don't hate her. I don't understand her, that's all."

I don't understand her, either, Gin thought. What sort of mother could hand her young son over to the Order?

In this case, to Virgil, in his role as Seeker.

A sense of gravity washed over her as she wondered if a part of Nick hated his beloved handler, too—the man who had recruited him for the Order when he was just a boy. The one perhaps most to blame for Nick's early loss of his innocence. Virgil was gone now, so whatever buried anger Nick might still feel toward her father, maybe all he could do now was take it out on her in some small way.

And that made one thing very clear: It seemed there wasn't going to be any lasting sort of bond between them, after all. It was a sobering realization, and rather made her heart hurt.

She let out a sigh, and for a long moment, they rode in silence, lulled by the clip-clopping beat of the horses' hooves and the rolling sound of the wheels beneath them on the smooth, macadamized road.

At length, she looked at Nick inquiringly. "So you have no interest in continuing this quest with me once I've got the game piece?"

"Not really, no." He sized her up with a keen stare. "Were you planning on forcing me to? Will you be changing the rules of our agreement midway through?"

"No, of course not."

"Good."

"But . . . you have many skills that ought not to go to waste. It's a good cause. If you changed your mind, I'd make it worth your while."

"Pardon?" he echoed, lifting his eyebrows with a wicked smile of innuendo.

She gave him an arch look. "I mean I'd pay you."

"Oh," he said with a show of mild disappointment, the rogue. "No thanks."

She stared at him. "Hmm."

"Hmm, what?"

She shrugged. "It's just that I would've thought a man who spent as many years as you have fighting evil would've cared a little more about these poor abducted girls."

"Well, life is sad."

"Nick!"

"What? It happens all the time, this sort of thing. Cry about it every time, you'll spend your life in tears."

"So you really don't care about them?"

"We've all got our problems. Don't worry, I'm sure he's got them on a ship somewhere headed for the Bacchus Bazaar, once they learn the location. They're safe enough for now, I should think. As long as they don't give him any trouble, they're in no immediate danger, I assure you."

"What makes you so sure?"

"Nobody wants to buy a girl who's starved thin and bruised purple. They're his merchandise, this Rotgut fellow. He's got a vested interest in treating them well. Plump and rosy, they'll fetch a better price," he added, "especially since most of the buyers are probably Turks."

She stared at him in disbelief. Even though she realized he was only speaking in terms of how the slaver viewed his kidnapped girls, Nick's callous indifference was more than she could stand. "Good God."

"Why are you looking at me like that?"

"Because I am starting to wonder if your time as a spy robbed you of all humanity and left you incapable of any human feeling!"

"Of course it did," he answered coolly, staring at her. "What else did you expect?"

"Oh, my God." She shook her head in shock, then signaled her driver to halt.

When he did, she got out of the vehicle and slammed the door behind her, muttering "fiend" and climbing up to ride on the carriage roof.

Maybe he had only said those things to get rid of her, but she didn't care. Better the starry chill of the late-autumn night than the bitter coldness of his heart.

This man was clearly beyond her power to save.

*G*ood riddance.

"More room for me," Nick said cynically, just loud enough for her to hear up on her perch among the luggage. "Heh."

Well, he trusted he had succeeded in pushing her away for good this time.

Mission accomplished.

When she had gone, he folded his arms across his chest, stretched his legs out, crossed his ankles, and rested his feet on the bench across from him, which she had vacated.

He shut his eyes stubbornly and attempted to go to sleep. But his churning thoughts still roiled.

Daft woman. Really, what did she take him for, a monster?

He was not continuing this quest *with* her because he fully intended to handle the foul business alone.

It was much too dangerous for a woman. Being Virgil's daughter did not change the fact that she was still a civilian.

The wilderness would just have to wait.

Somewhere along the way, or maybe from the very moment she had got him out of his dungeon cell, this quest to penetrate the vile, biannual Bacchus Bazaar and free those girls had become *his* mission, not hers.

As was proper.

Hell, Virgil would haunt him from beyond the bloody grave if he allowed his handler's daughter anywhere near that twisted gathering.

No, she'd be staying home for this one.

She might not care enough about her own safety, but her son needed her alive and well. He'd take care of this himself.

It was as good as done.

*T*he next day, they arrived at Gin's smart London town house. Bleary-eyed from travel, she suggested they take a few hours to rest so they would be fresh for the late night ahead. They'd both have to be at their sharpest. By late afternoon, they were making their final preparations before finally setting off for the Topaz Room that night.

At last the hour had come: Midnight.

Gin was secretly rather amazed that she had got this far—that her plan was working. She had persuaded the graybeards to let her borrow Nick, and here they were, approaching the Topaz Room even now.

She should have a game piece in her hand before the dawn. And she had better. For the stakes were much higher than Nick had any idea.

She had no desire to tell him the rest of the story, especially since he was planning on leaving after this task was done. Maybe he'd have changed his mind if he knew about her father's journal, but unpredictable as he was, it was impossible to guess how he might react.

The thought of John Carr's treachery and the potential catastrophe quietly waiting in the wings to unfold made her shudder.

She thrust her secrets out of her mind for fear Nick might read them somehow in her eyes with his spy skills. Instead, she focused on the task at hand.

They were presently gliding across the Thames in a slow-moving ferry. A brisk night wind raked across the river, while the moon shone down on them like a malevolent eye. Nick sat in front of her, quiet and remote, tension thrumming through his big body.

She could see his readiness for battle in the broad lines of his shoulders as he leaned into the boat's motion.

Ahead, twin lanterns marked out the riverside dock belonging to the Topaz Room, just as he had described.

The ferryman drew them on inexorably toward it, and the closer they got, the more Gin shivered with nerves and uncertainty.

The gambling hell was a brown brick building, quite plain from the outside. The lights glowing in the curtained windows reflected on the river's streaming current.

"Is this the place?" asked Haynes, seated beside her.

Gin nodded. She had called in the retired Bow Street Runner despite Nick's insistence that he didn't need any help.

In his early sixties, the gruff, burly Liam Haynes was an experienced thief-taker and private investigator whom she sometimes hired to follow leads that she could not take on herself, for one reason or another.

She appreciated his experience in dealing with the criminal world. Haynes was armed to protect her if she needed it, as well, a gun concealed in the roomy pocket of his long, wool greatcoat.

Gin, likewise, had tucked a little silver pistol into her reticule, but neither of them were as heavily armed as Nick.

At last, the ferryman maneuvered his boat up to the

private, wooden dock reserved exclusively for visitors to the casino. Other boats were moored along the creaking wooden dock for the same purpose, their bored, shivering pilots waiting to take passengers back to the north shore of the Thames when they wished to go.

Their ferryman managed to find a slip and tossed a loop of rope over a weathered upright post along the lanternlit dock. Then he nodded to them that it was safe to disembark.

Nick turned to Gin, his eyes blacker than the night; they glinted with savagery in the lanterns' glow. "This won't take long. Wait here."

She gritted her teeth.

He started to climb out of the boat, then stopped, glancing over his shoulder. "What are you doing?" he asked as he noticed her right behind him.

"What do you think? I'm coming with you."

"No. Absolutely not."

"Oh yes, I am."

"No," he repeated crisply. "That's not going to work. Lowell knows me. He doesn't know you."

"So? You'll be my escort for the evening," she replied in a blithe tone, taking his arm.

He glowered. "I don't want you going in there. It's not a place fit for a lady. Wait here in the boat. Haynes, keep her out of—"

"Excuse me! All right, you want to have this out?" she challenged Nick. "We both know what's really going on here. You don't want me to come because you're still angry about what I said yesterday about Phillip. But, fine. Rather than let you jeopardize the mission with your mood, let me explain to you what I meant."

"I know exactly what you meant," he clipped out coldly. "So why don't you sit back down with Mr. Haynes and let me go and do the job you got me out of prison for?"

"Oh, you'd like that, wouldn't you?" she retorted

while the startled wherrymen looked on. "I should just sit down, be quiet, and do as I'm told. After all, I am only a woman. Sorry, did you think you were in charge?"

Nick rolled his eyes skyward, beseeching heaven for patience.

Gin was not trying to be difficult. But she really had no choice. It was for Nick's own safety and the sake of the mission that she *had* go on in there with him.

Only, she could not tell him why.

Obviously, she could not send the man into the Topaz Room alone, when the fact was, she had only told him half of what was really going on.

Before guilt over her deception could set in, she hiked up her skirts a bit and stepped past him out of the boat, climbing up onto the dock.

"Don't worry, Lord Forrester. You won't have to put up with me much longer. Just keep up your end of the bargain, and you can be on your way. In the meanwhile, I am not in the habit of sitting around like some docile little miss waiting for my big strong man to manage my affairs. We're doing this together. This is *my* mission, lest you forget," she added, turning back. "You're just along to smooth the way and do the introductions. Now let's go. Wait for us," she ordered the ferryman, then she nodded farewell to Haynes and pivoted, her skirts swirling around her legs.

"Virginia!"

Behind her, she heard a low curse, a creaking of wood, and a sloshing of water as Nick sprang out of the ferryboat and followed her.

The long, floating dock snaked and wobbled under their angry strides, but neither of them faltered as they marched toward solid ground.

Her heart pounded, but Gin did not look back.

A show of strength seemed imperative right now; she sensed that if she faltered in this key moment, he'd surely wrest control from her, and that she refused to allow.

"My lady!" he called sarcastically.

She refused to look back. "Come along, my dear!" Taking the same, stern tone she used on Phillip, she kept her stare fixed on the back door of the gambling hell. "I won't get in your way. I just want to make sure the questions I need answered get asked properly."

"You think I don't know how to do my job?" he demanded as he approached from behind her.

"Don't be tedious, of course I do. I just want to size up Mr. Lowell with my own two eyes."

"Well, the size of him is sure to make a lasting impression," he muttered. "Virginia, wait." He grasped her arm above the elbow, turning her to face him. The lanterns' dim illumination slid over his sleek black hair in shades of indigo and auburn; it limned his chiseled profile with a glimmer of gold as he glared at her. "You don't know what you're doing."

"Don't I?" she replied archly.

"What vanity makes you imagine that an underworld kingpin is going to sit there and simply answer your questions—what, out of the goodness of his heart?"

She cocked her head to the side in defiance, but no ready answer came.

"Hugh Lowell rules like a fat, ruthless, little despot over his domain in there," Nick informed her in a low tone, nodding toward the plain brick building. "There is no chivalry in him for you to exploit with your feminine wiles. So if you assume that you'll just bat your lashes and charm him the way you did with the Order graybeards, you are deluded. Firstly, women are not his vice.

"Secondly, if they were, the upper floor above the gaming hell happens to be a bordello. He is surrounded day and night by beautiful girls, who are younger and a great more *accommodating* than you—"

She gasped aloud at the insult. "I beg your pardon!" Yanking her arm out of his grasp, she looked him up and down with the utmost indignation. "You black-guard. I'm not *old*!"

"Oh, darling," he said sweetly with a sly, chiding smile, "don't take my words the wrong way."

She narrowed her eyes at him. "You are the devil."

He gave her a wink. "Pity you made a bargain with me, eh? Now go back to the boat," he ordered softly.

"No." She pivoted and tried to continue down the dock, but to her exasperation, he managed to step ahead of her and stood, looming, in her path, blocking her. "Listen to me—"

"No, you listen to me, Nicholas! As I said, we are doing this together, whether you like it or not! You agreed to cooperate."

"Yes, but—"

"No, you gave your word that you'd obey my orders. Your word. Remember? That was our deal. Now, you either take me in there with you, or I'm sending you back to prison. Is that clear?"

He shut his mouth and stared grimly at her. "So that's the way of it then. You resort to threats. Not that I'm surprised. You are a female, after all."

"Oh, you noticed?" She snorted in haughty disdain. "Pity I'm just too *old* for you."

"I was jesting!" he exclaimed. He stared at her for a heartbeat in bewilderment or something like it.

"What?" she demanded.

"You know bloody well I find you ravishing! But hell, if you're going to send me back to prison anyway—"

He wrapped his hand around her nape and pulled her to him roughly; he claimed her mouth, his other arm snaking round her waist.

Slamming her against his tall, rock-hard body, Nick parted her lips with an insistent stroke of his tongue. He let out a throaty moan of sensual desperation as he tasted her, cupping her cheek.

Gin was reeling but did her best to ward off the dizziness, holding absolutely still. Damn him, he had just turned the tables on her; flummoxed her with unexpected pleasure and the sudden flaming of carefully repressed desire.

As her heart pounded, she did not know what to do. To her fury, he was much too good at this. So much so that she did not have the heart to stop him; for pride's sake, however, she rejected her body's untamed response to him with all her will.

He paused in kissing her and smiled knowingly against her lips though frustration roughened his whisper. "Kiss me back, you little hoyden, or I'll throw you in this river."

"You wouldn't dare."

"Come on, you know you want to. One kiss. What are you so afraid of?" He nuzzled the corner of her mouth, making her nearly swoon right off the blasted dock. Her knees went even weaker, but he caught her all the more snugly against his chest, leading her into temptation. "Aren't you curious about how it would be between us?"

"Curiosity killed the cat," she pointed out, trying to sound aloof and utterly failing.

"At least the cat died happy. Kiss me back," he ordered her again. "You know you want to. I've seen the way you look at me. Like in the cave."

She bit her lip in yearning at the memory of his glistening, hard body and pulled back to look into his eyes. "It doesn't mean anything if I do," she warned, her pulse racing with anticipation.

"No," he assured her with a whisper of amusement, "not a thing."

Then he kissed her again, and her feeble resistance melted away.

Nick tilted his head in the other direction, kissing her more deeply, as his clever fingers curled into her hair. Every inch of her flesh instantly burning for him, she clung to his muscled shoulders and met his kiss measure for measure.

His tongue plunged into her mouth. Everywhere he touched her, pleasure followed. As she ran her hands along his biceps and down his chest, she thought of his gorgeous, naked body in the hot springs, and despaired at the knowledge of how much she wanted him.

This was so unwise.

Yes, he was irresistible, but she was walking right into a trap. The ex-spy was using whatever means necessary to get his way, and she knew it—but the worst part was, she didn't even care.

She shivered violently, but not from the cold November night. The stiff breeze off the river was forgotten in the searing heat that engulfed the two of them. They ignored the ferrymen around them, as well, fairly consuming each other in the darkness, the dock unsteady under their feet.

"God." It ended all too soon as Nick pulled back, leaving her dazed and routed, and craving nothing except him.

He looked at her in amazement, panting.

Then he quickly reached out to steady her when she weaved slightly on her feet.

"That was incredible," he breathed.

"Yes." She swallowed hard, too dazed even to care that some of the boatmen were rudely applauding their display. "Not bad."

Nick turned and gave their audience a sardonic bow.

In spite of herself, Gin laughed, blushing slightly.

He turned back to her, surely the most beautiful man she had ever laid eyes on, dazzling her all over again just like he had when she was seventeen and had fallen in love with him from afar.

He held her stare, his night black eyes shimmering like stars. His lips, still wet with her kisses, shone in the lanterns' glow; then they curved into a roguish half smile that made her shudder with naughty thoughts of pushing the scoundrel down onto her bed and keeping him there for a month.

"Whew," he murmured, running his hand through his hair to fix it after she had rumpled it. Then he gave her a wink. "*Now* you can send me back to prison."

"Where you belong," she jested in a trembling voice.

His lips twisted; he tilted his head and studied her for a moment.

"Well, come on if you're coming," he said abruptly, stepping past her. "Let's go get you a game piece, shall we?" With that, he strode off down the dock and headed for the back door of the gambling hell.

Gin was left standing there for a second, still lost in a softheaded haze of desire. Then she blinked herself back to the waking world after that dream of a kiss and hurried after him.

*O*utside the back door of the Topaz Room, Nick waited for her restlessly, hands in his greatcoat pockets as he paced back and forth. He was doing his best to seem completely back to business as she approached, as if that fiery kiss of moments ago had never happened.

"I can't promise you this will go smoothly," he warned her in a low tone as she joined him. "I still think you should go back and wait in the boat—"

"Forget it."

"But since you're hell-bent on it," he said with a wry smile, "I *suggest* you follow my lead. Don't do anything to rouse Lowell's suspicions. Keep your mouth shut and your eyes open; conform to his expectations. Remember, he's used to women who do as they're told."

"Ah, yes, you mentioned that. *Young,* beautiful, obedient women," she drawled. "What wonderful creatures they must be!"

"If one likes that sort of thing. Some of us prefer a challenge."

She looked askance at him; he winked at her, then

lifted his fist, rapping a few times soundly on the back door of the dubious establishment.

A sliver of light promptly appeared.

As the door cracked open, the noise of the gambling hell tumbled out, disturbing the stillness of nighttime on the river.

Two towering, brawny door guards stood inside the doorway, looming over them as the wedge of light widened.

"Name?" one grunted.

"Lord Forrester. I need to see Mr. Lowell. It's urgent. I'm in the book," he added.

"Just a minute," one rumbled, reaching for the guest-book that recorded the names of the house's previously approved visitors. "Let me find it."

Virginia leaned toward Nick's ear while they conferred. "No alias?" she whispered.

He shook his head. "Not here." He was somewhat irked that Lowell's two giant door guards had not recognized him. Of course, it had been a long time, and they were clearly not the brightest stars in the firmament. But whatever dullness lurked behind their thick skulls, Nick hoped Lowell did not sic them on him. It would not be fun to fight them.

The two brawny guards were close to seven feet tall, about three hundred pounds apiece, and full of themselves, like two sides of beef with an attitude.

While they sought to verify his bona fides with the house, Nick waited, keenly aware of the intoxicating woman beside him. The sensuality pouring off her was electric, like lightning in a dark, silken sky. She had shocked him with her hungry response to his kiss.

Damn. Now he'd probably be obsessed with how it would be to bed her until he had satisfied his curiosity.

Meanwhile, his late handler was probably turning over in his grave. This, apparently, was exactly what the old Scot hadn't wanted: his daughter entangled with an Order agent. Especially not the bad apple of the lot.

"Found it." The giant's eyebrow arched. "But there's a problem. You got a black mark next to your name."

Shite, Nick thought.

"Sorry, sir, but you're going to have to go talk to the moneylenders downstairs first," the door guard said. "Once this matter's settled, then you can come back up and play at the tables all you like."

Virginia looked at Nick in shock. "You owe them money?"

He strove for patience and ignored her. "I am not here to play," he repeated. "I need to speak to Mr. Lowell, as I've already said. Now go give him my name."

"The Jerusalem Chamber is downstairs, Lord Forrester."

"We can settle that business some other time," he ground out impatiently. "Believe me, Mr. Lowell will want to see me—"

"No, he won't. He don't give audiences to people who owe him money. House policy."

"I don't believe this," Virginia muttered under her breath. "So that's why you didn't want me to come in!" She turned back to the giants. "How much does he owe?"

"Don't you dare," Nick warned her. "I really think you should go back to the boat now—"

"Say it again, and *you're* going back to prison," she hissed at him in a confidential tone.

He turned just briefly enough to shoot her a glare while the doorman answered her query.

"We don't keep specifics in the book, ma'am. The bankers in the Jerusalem Chamber have the details. Why? You want to pay his debt for 'im?" he jested with a broad grin.

"She's not paying anything. Stay out of it, Virginia. Now, gentlemen, I don't want to make you look bad in front of your employer and a houseful of clients, but

I'm in a bit of a hurry. So either you take me down to
Lowell's office now, or I'm going to remind you who I
am and what it is I do for a living."

The larger one folded his arms across his chest and
fixed Nick with a sullen stare. "Oh, I'm scared now!"

"Me, too," the other chimed in.

Perhaps it was feeling him tense, gathering for a
strike, that suddenly jarred Virginia into cooperating.

She suddenly took his arm and gave the guards a
charming smile, though her grip on Nick's biceps felt
more like she was discreetly holding him back rather
than the picture she made of a lady flirting with her
escort. "Now, now, Nick, darling, don't hurt the nice
fellows. They're only doing their jobs."

"Wait a second," the slightly smaller giant mumbled,
squinting as if to search his memory. "Nick Forrester?"
His eyes suddenly widened. "*That* Lord Forrester?"

"Humph," said Nick.

"Yes!" she exclaimed sweetly. "You know, the famous
Order agent—and government assassin?"

The two stared at Nick, turning pale.

He gave them an icy smile. "As I said, I'm not here to
play. Now let me in the damned door before I lose my
temper."

The two exchanged an uncomfortable look.

"Well, er, I guess that's different, then."

Nick exhaled slightly. By their worried expression,
Nick gathered that they were aware of their boss's occasional barters with the Home Office: underworld secrets in exchange for the government's leaving Lowell's
operations alone.

"Very well," the larger doorman rumbled, watching
Nick's every move. "We'll take you down to see him.
He's in his office. This way." He eyed Nick warily, then
clomped off ahead of them, his meaty hand resting on
the pistol at his hip.

The second guard remained on duty at the door.

Nick gestured wryly for Her Ladyship to go in first.

She shot him a private glare and shook her head at him in silent, cynical reproach.

He scowled back at her. What business was it of hers if he owed the Tick money?

"Humph." Lifting her chin, she picked up the hem of her skirts a bit and marched ahead of him in the loud, lively gambling hell.

Although from the outside, it was a plain, brick, ordinary building, on the inside, the Topaz Room transported one to a decadent fantasy realm of vice and self-indulgence. A fitting place to forget all about reality and completely lose oneself in feverish play.

The Topaz Room was decorated in the Roman arabesque style with strong, gaudy colors: dark gold walls, deep purple curtains with huge red and gold tassels to offset the greenery of the exotic palm trees everywhere and, of course, the green baize of the tables, the white flash of the dice, and the whirling red and black of the roulette wheel spinning round and round.

All along the edges of the main room were small, sumptuous alcoves with striped satin tent-roofs in the Turkish style and low, cushioned divans and benches.

Lowell's "Jewels," about a dozen prostitutes, ran around the premises dressed as belly dancers fit for a sultan's harem, their eyes lined with kohl and little bells jingling around their ankles and naked waists.

Nearby was the faro table, over there, Macau; to his left, a topless woman dealt at vingt-et-un, and in the far corner, the not-quite-legal EO wheel spun dizzyingly.

A burst of cheering and laughter went up over at the hazard table, where the dice had just been kind to someone.

As Nick crossed the main room behind Virginia and the guard, all around him was noisy and colorful. The place was a seething hive of activity. The whores trolled for men, while the men, lost souls, flung themselves into their reigning passion.

Being there made Nick very uneasy. Not so long ago, he had been one of the damned, sunk in this particular circle of hell. That she should have found out his weakness from the doormen infuriated him.

Hadn't his pride already suffered enough recently when she had first seen him in his prison cell and, more recently, pronounced him unworthy to speak to her son?

Not that he planned on making excuses.

But the shame he felt right now, thanks to her learning of his former vice, was just the sort of dark frame of mind that had made him easy prey for his old gambling mania. He wanted to tell himself that he was only human. That everyone had flaws. He had tried and failed to beat his many times; he had also attempted in vain to keep it secret from his fellow Order agents.

He could not really say why he did it. Why he had set himself up for ruin more times than he could count, as if he secretly wished his own destruction.

He believed that his time in prison had broken the curse for good, and he intended to stay free. He'd never admit it, but this was part of the reason he wanted to lose himself in the wilderness, that pure, pristine, virgin forest, untouched by all these forms of soul-corrupting madness.

But, once upon a time, the cards and the dice had been a kind of religion to him, the last thing he had clung to after he had lost faith in the Order, the cause.

Again and again, he had gone back to the tables, like a dog to its vomit, waiting for the cards or the dice to show him a sign, the meaning of it all. That he had not wasted his life. That his sacrifice since boyhood had not been entirely in vain.

In some not-quite-conscious way, he had expected or at least hoped that evidence would be given him in the form of luck, that what he was doing mattered in the grand scheme of things.

Blind faith claimed that good would be rewarded. So he had convinced himself superstitiously that being dealt a lucky hand was a very stamp of approval by invisible forces greater than himself. Forces that spoke through the elegant language of statistical patterns and the unbreakable laws of mathematics. And that these mystical forces, by letting him win, would reassure him that he—lying spy and trained assassin—was nevertheless a good man.

He begged for that assurance.

But the cards almost always spoke otherwise, cruelly. So for him, every loss rang with doom, until, unnerved, he had finally quit and cursed himself for being so irrational. *Ah, well.* Maybe the fact that he was still alive at all was the very proof he had been seeking, because by all rights, he should have died at least a dozen different times by now.

"Through here," the guard grunted, beckoning them through a door that opened off the adjoining room where food and drinks were served. He ushered them through, then pulled it shut behind them.

From there, he escorted them down a dim service stairway to the lowest floor. The kitchens and other service areas were sunk partly underground and gave way to the murky labyrinth of tunnels and storage areas beneath the building.

Nick was aware that these secret passages had helped Lowell conceal his black-market trade during the war. No wonder the Tick was as rich as a duke, he thought.

Far from the rowdy noise of the gambling hell, it was quiet as the grave the closer they got to his office.

Virginia glanced over her shoulder, sending Nick a dubious look. He gave her a subtle, bolstering nod in answer. She might be rethinking the wisdom of coming along, but there was no turning back now.

At last, they approached the end of the dark tunnel, where another giant henchman was stationed in front of the locked door to Lowell's office.

The bodyguard pushed away from the wall, studying them with interest as they approached. "What's this?"

"They want to see him."

"Mr. Lowell is not accepting visitors."

"He'll see me. Tell him it's Nick Forrester."

The oxlike man shook his head. "You'll have to make an appointment. Come back some other time."

"He's from the Order," the door guard confided to his colleague. "If we turn him away, the boss might not like it. At least let him know he's here."

The other one eyed them skeptically for a moment, then gave a dismissive shrug. "I'll ask. But I wouldn't get my hopes up," he advised, his tone edged ever so faintly with sarcasm. "He's in a mood tonight. The chicken's too dry."

The guard gave a deferential rap on the door before stepping into Lowell's office to inquire.

Nick and Virginia exchanged a dubious look as they waited. He had no doubt that Lowell would see him. Lowering his lips toward her ear, he whispered, "Wait out here for me."

"No chance!" she whispered back. "I'm coming with you."

"The hell you are." He glanced back at the door guard to make sure he wasn't eavesdropping. "It's bad enough you even came into the gambling hell."

"I already told you I want to speak with him personally. You agreed. Care to go back to prison?"

"You're not going to send me back," he whispered, a knowing smile tugging at his lips. "Not after what just happened outside. I'm not stupid, darling."

She stared straight ahead at the closed door. "I told you it meant nothing."

The guard returned while Nick was still struggling against the urge to kiss the hoyden senseless.

The other giant looked surprised by the answer he brought back. "Mr. Lowell will give you five minutes," he announced. Then he nodded to his mate. "Search 'em." He looked at Nick. "Turn, hands on the wall."

Nick rolled his eyes with impatience but complied. While the larger of the two guards patted him down, removing from his person all the weapons that he found, the other fellow examined Virginia.

Nick watched his every move, glowering.

After pulling the little pistol out of her reticule, he ordered her to take off her hat and show that there was nothing hidden in it.

"Watch it!" Nick suddenly exclaimed as the muscled hulk groped his crotch with a little too much interest, then leered at him when Nick turned to scowl.

But he was more concerned about the other fellow, who had just ordered Virgil's daughter to hike up her skirts so he might check for an ankle holster or one strapped around her thigh.

"Do you want to die?" he asked the man, stepping toward him.

"I have to check her!"

"You put your hands on her, I'll break them for you, have you got that?"

Nick stared at him. He did not want to have to kill anyone tonight, but this man was dangerously close to stepping over the line.

Still, even he was a bit surprised at the savagery of his own reaction.

But this was Virgil's daughter.

The guard lifted his hands instinctively, backing away. "No disrespect—sir."

She, meanwhile, had arched a brow at him.

Bloody hell. She was gazing at him with a wicked sparkle in her eyes.

He refused to look at her.

For his part, Nick was torn. He did not want her coming into the office with him, getting any closer to this nasty corner of the underworld than she already was.

On the other hand, after seeing the guard groping her, he was not about to leave her out here in the hallway with these two.

In any case, having been disarmed, they were now permitted in. The larger guard opened the door for them, leering at Nick again as he passed. After running his hands all over his body, he seemed to have taken a liking to him. "Five minutes," he reminded them.

Nick brushed off his annoyance, took Virginia's hand firmly, and led her into the dim, shadowy office of the underworld king.

The fetid smell that hit them just over the threshold was foul beyond description.

Dimly lit, the room itself was choking, airless, close; overwarm and full of clutter; with only one small, high window that had been painted shut. Straight ahead, amid the gloom, sat the hulking, bloated Tick at his desk.

All five hundred pounds of him.

The owner of the establishment was, himself, the main source of the smell. Stale sweat. Greasy body odor: the stench of a man too large around to wash himself properly and too disgusted by his own grotesque form to bother changing clothes as often as he should.

The front of his shirt and waistcoat were splashed with dried stains and drippings from several recent meals.

Everywhere, surrounding him in arm's reach, were different plates of food, some with courses half-devoured, others waiting for him to grab a handful of this or that and gobble it down, which he did as they walked forward slowly.

Good God. Nick knew that Lowell did not believe in wasting food, but there was no telling how long some of those dishes had been sitting there.

Long enough to attract the roaches scuttling over the half-gnawed hambone and crawling up the cake.

This strange sight, the embodiment of gluttony, was quite shocking, even to Nick, who had known what to expect.

He felt Virginia falter by his side and could not help but gloat a little at her revulsion. Well, he had warned her to stay outside in the boat. Then he frowned. *She had better not faint.*

For his part, it took everything in him not to pull out his handkerchief and cover his nose and mouth rather than breathe the dank, stinking air.

Even Lowell would take that as an insult.

Nick resigned himself to breathing as little as possible. But, really, he mused, instead of calling him the Tick, he ought to have nicknamed Lowell after the creature he most resembled physically: one of those huge, tusked wild hogs that roamed the scrub plains of Spain and grew to the most enormous sizes, hundreds and hundreds of pounds of porcine belligerence, like the wild boar of Greek myth, which had gored Adonis.

He had only dubbed him the Tick because as a businessman, Hugh Lowell had no qualms whatever about bleeding luckless gamblers dry.

"Well, well." He went on eating continuously, only pausing to swig a drink or pick something out of his teeth. "Look what the cat dragged in."

"Nice to see you again, too," Nick drawled.

Crumbs spewed out of his mouth as Lowell scoffed at him. "You've got a lot of nerve showin' your face around here, Forrester. You owe me a load o' loot."

"Don't worry, old friend, I haven't forgotten."

"Hmm. Where've you been?" he grunted.

"Here and there."

"Figured I'd've seen you before now. Saved the Regent's life, eh?"

Nick shrugged.

"Nice bit o' muslin."

"Isn't she, though?"

"How do you do," Gin managed.

"Sit if you want to."

"No thanks."

Lowell paused. "Something to eat?"

"God, no," she whispered, placing her hand on her stomach, clearly fighting off a wave of nausea.

Nick suppressed a laugh.

"Well," Lowell said, chewing, "hate to be a killjoy, Forrester, but you can't play in my house anymore. Not until your debts is paid—with interest. Nothing personal. Just business. You know I always liked you, meself, but it's the principle. If word got out that Hugh Lowell has gone soft, I'd be out of business. Rules is rules. I'm sure you understand."

"Of course. But I'm not here to gamble."

Lowell stopped chewing, going suddenly on his guard. "Then what do you want?" he asked through a mouthful of scalloped potatoes and God-knew-what else.

"I need a game piece for the Bacchus Bazaar," Nick answered coolly.

Lowell's eyes widened for a second, then he laughed, picked up a napkin, and wiped off his mouth. "Well, now," he said at length, taking a brief break from his nonstop meal, "that's goin' to be expensive. Now you're really upping the stakes, aren't you? Good lad. Unfortunately, you can't afford it. Unless you've brought me some sort o' useful information?"

"None of that today," Nick said serenely.

Lowell snorted and slogged down a mouthful of ale. "I could always let my bruisers beat it out of you."

"You don't want to do that," Nick replied.

"You got to admit, it would be some entertainment, though! Fine pugilists like yourself, against as many of my hired apes as you care to take on. I pay those lads good money," Lowell declared. "Would be a boon to me to find out if they're worth it."

"Sorry, I don't have time for that tonight. I'm only here to get a game piece."

Lowell shrugged. "Well, pay me for it, and we'll see."

Nick reached into his waistcoat pocket. Virginia glanced at him in surprise. No, he had no money. But he did have two items of value left.

He supposed the most intelligent thing to have done would have been to ask her to stop at Rundell and Bridge's before coming here. Everyone knew the famed jewelers' was the aristocracy's favorite place in London to raise quick money by pawning the family jewels or other objects of value. But for his pride's sake, Nick had not made that request.

He had thought he could get away with it by making her stay outside. Keep her from finding out.

No such luck.

Obviously, Lowell was not going to give him something as valuable as a game piece to the Bacchus Bazaar when he already owed the gull-groper a couple hundred quid.

Ah, well. Lady Burke's opinion of him probably couldn't get much worse, anyway.

Besides, Lowell would be quite tickled with the extremely rare item that Nick intended to use to cover his debts. Its rarity and its meaning made it valuable enough to pay for the game piece, too; and that, in turn, would allow Nick to help Virgil's daughter and save those kidnapped girls, as well. Hell, it was for a good cause, and might just bring him his redemption.

Reaching into his breast pocket, Nick pulled out the most valuable possession he had left and placed it slowly on the table.

"This should cover it."

*G*in gasped, appalled at what he set down on the table. "Nicholas, no! You can't let him have that! Nick, it's your medal for the Order!"

"Is that what that is?" Lowell murmured, sounding impressed.

"It doesn't matter," Nick told her through gritted teeth.

But as Mr. Lowell reached for the ornate white Maltese cross, Gin snatched it off the table. "Give me that! You can't have it," she snapped at the gambling-hell owner. "We'll pay with something else."

"Virginia—"

"No," she answered. "I refuse to let you part with this. It might not mean very much to you right now, but one day, it will." She clutched it safely in her hand—the medal the Regent had personally placed around his neck in Westminster Abbey. "This is something you will pass down to your children! I'm not going to let you throw it away on a gambling debt."

"Well, someone's got to pay it," Mr. Lowell pointed out, while Nick's midnight eyes were full of storm as he glared at her.

"It's all I have," he forced out, obviously shamed.

She shook her head in exasperation and turned to the gambling-hell owner. "Mr. Lowell, would you be so good as to transfer Lord Forrester's debt to me?"

Tucking her reticule under her arm, she took off the earrings she had worn tonight merely because they had matched her gown. "Please, take these. They are Indian rubies with diamond chips, in eighteen-karat gold.

They are surely worth more than enough to cover both items, his debt and the game piece."

"Virginia, please don't do this."

"It does not signify. I have a vault full of such useless trinkets at home. I was married to a nabob, remember? Besides, I need your help anyway for the next leg of my quest," she told him, then she offered the earrings to the rotund man.

Lowell took them skeptically and examined them for a moment. He gave one a small nibble with his teeth to test if it was paste, then he lifted his eyebrows. "Genuine article. Very nice. Very nice, indeed." He glanced from Nick to her again with a bemused look. "I'd rather have the medal, of course, but I'm not made of stone. I can understand why he'd want to keep it."

"I really don't care about the stupid thing," Nick said through gritted teeth.

"Well, I do," Gin declared.

That medal was a symbol of all he had done for his country and his friends, the solid proof of his nobility. She was not going to let him throw it away, even if he could not see the value of it—or himself—right now.

Someday, he might.

"Why are you doing this? I am not a charity case," he snarled at her in a quiet tone, glaring into her eyes.

She could see that he was burning up with shame. But somehow, in that moment, he had never been more dear to her.

How she wished she could just give his face a gentle caress to say she understood. It was just his pride talking. But she knew that if she showed any sign of tenderness, he'd take it as pity, and he'd never forgive her. So she kept her expression aloof. "Don't worry, I intend to make you work for it. I'll keep it as collateral until you've paid me back in full."

"And how exactly am I to do that?" he bit out with a cynical stare.

Lowell's husky laughter interrupted, full of innuendo. "Don't you already have that sort of arrangement with Madame Angelique, Nick, old boy?" he asked dryly. "Wouldn't want to cross her, lady."

"Who's Angelique?" Gin inquired.

Nick scowled at him for mentioning that name. "Never mind it. We came to get a game piece. Will that cover it or not?" he demanded.

"Oh, yes, yes," said Lowell, watching them in fascination.

"That reminds me," Gin spoke up, letting go the mystery of this Angelique woman. Whatever the name meant, she was not entirely sure she wanted to know. She turned again to Mr. Lowell. "Have you ever heard of a man called Rotgut?"

"Might have. Why? What's he done?"

"I have reason to believe he is abducting young girls off the streets and means to auction them like cattle at the Bacchus Bazaar."

Lowell's frown deepened. "Abducting them, you say? Well, I'm no saint, but I don't approve of that sort of thing. All my Jewels come work for me of their own free will. You going after him?" he asked Nick. "Because I don't want any trouble. As one of only two dispensaries in England, it won't be hard for certain people to track it back to me, if you go descending on the Bazaar and start wreaking destruction, as per usual. Those aren't the sort of people I'm keen to cross."

"What, you seem well prepared for any sort of conflict," Nick muttered, nodding toward the door, beyond which Lowell's giant guards waited.

"Nevertheless," the large man replied as he picked up a chicken bone and fingered it nervously, "it ain't good for business." He took a large bite and sank his teeth in.

"Lowell, you may be many things, but a coward isn't one of them," Nick said. "She's paid the debt, now give her the damn game piece."

"With all due respect, I don't know this woman!" he protested, spewing bits of chicken. "If you *really need* to have it for these so-called kidnapped girls, I can give it to you, but not to her. Sorry, ma'am, no offense. This one may be a penniless bastard, but we go back a long time. You, I've never seen before in my life." Then he looked Nick right in the eyes. "So are you in this with her or not?"

Nick clenched his jaw.

Gin folded her arms across her chest and turned to him, even more eager than Lowell was to hear his answer.

If Nick refused to continue on with her, she was out of luck.

She had the money for the undertaking—and her own personal reasons for being willing to spend it; Nick had no money, but he had years of experience in the field— and was approved for the game piece.

But he had wanted to wash his hands of this and be on his way after tonight to start his new life as anything but a spy.

He finally rolled his eyes. "Of course I'll see it through! Just give me the damn thing."

Gin exhaled slightly, eyeing him askance. He still refused to look at her.

"All right, then," said Lowell. Tearing off a final bite of the chicken, he wiped his hands on a napkin, then undertook the taxing process of rising from his steel-reinforced chair with the help of a cane.

As he lurched his enormous bulk slowly upright, Gin winced in sympathy, watching the huge man shamble over to the vault on the far wall.

Mr. Lowell glanced over at them suspiciously before he started dialing in the combination.

While they waited, Gin wondered what to say to Nick after this. His posture was stiff, his face tense; he refused to meet her gaze.

She followed his stare back to the vault, where Lowell was opening a small mahogany box.

From out of it, he lifted an ivory chip carved in the shape of the diamond and engraved with back-to-back B's for the Bacchus Bazaar.

This done, he shut the box and put it back in the vault. Leaning on his cane, he pushed the iron door closed and locked it up tightly once more.

After that came the painstaking process of his turning around again and hobbling back across the room. At last, he sank back into his chair with a sigh of relief.

"Here you are." Slightly winded, he offered Nick the chip.

Nick reached across the desk and took it.

Gin glanced at Mr. Lowell for confirmation. "This will get us in?"

He nodded, heaving for breath and dabbing his sweating brow with his napkin. "Present the chip at the Imperial Suite of the L'Hôtel Grande Alexandre in Paris anytime within the next fortnight. That will get you formally signed in for the auction. At that point, you'll also have to show them what you'll be offering for sale."

"Everyone's got to bring something to sell," Nick informed her, though she already knew the procedure, thanks to her father's journal. "That way, everyone present is incriminated, thus ensuring that all participants will keep their mouths shut."

"Once everyone has registered," Mr. Lowell said, "then and only then, the time and place of the auction will be announced. They'll send you a note. You won't have much time to get there, wherever it is. They change the location every time."

"Any inkling of where it's going to be this year?" Nick asked.

Lowell shook his head. "Last one was in Prague, that's all I know."

Nick nodded. "We won't take any more of your time, then." He headed for the door, but Gin lingered by the desk a moment longer.

She leaned toward the gambling-hell owner. "Are we all square, then, Mr. Lowell? I have your word that you'll erase Lord Forrester's debt from your books?"

He nodded, eyeing her warily. "I'll send down to my Jerusalem Chamber at once."

She smiled at him. "Thank you."

"You are one lucky bastard in your lady friends, Forrester," Lowell remarked, as she followed Nick toward the door. "First Angelique, now this one. Maybe you're not as horribly unlucky as I thought."

Nick sent him a wry glance from the door as he held it open for her. Then he pulled it shut behind them.

Out in the hallway, the guards returned their weapons to them.

Gin could tell by the way Nick moved that he was angry. As soon as he had his brace of pistols and his knives back in their places, he stalked off ahead of her, neither waiting for her nor bothering with a show of gallantry this time.

She got the feeling he was furious about her paying his gambling debt, but what else could she do? Let him hand over his medal of honor to that cretin?

Her father would roll over in his grave.

Through the labyrinth, past the kitchens, back into the stairwell, and up the steps they climbed. Gin lifted the hem of her skirts running up the stairs, trying to keep up with him. He took them two at a time.

Overtaking the guard, Nick let himself out through the door at the top of the stairwell, going back into the gambling hell. The guard frowned after him but waited to hold the door for Gin—not out of politeness, to be sure, but to make sure she left the backstairs region where unescorted visitors were not allowed.

Ahead, she saw Nick striding through the gambling

hell. He looked neither to the right nor the left, as if he did not dare trust himself with so many temptations on every hand. Her heart ached for him even though she wanted to throttle him for his stubborn pride.

Very well, so he was angry, she thought. But at least they now had the necessary game piece.

Moments later, they were back outside, striding down the dock toward their slip, where Haynes waited in the boat. The bracing chill of the night wind was most welcome, blowing the stink of Lowell's office off her, though the smell still clung inside her nose.

Certainly, she had never met anyone quite like Mr. Lowell before; she couldn't help feeling sorry for him even though he was a ruthless crime boss. Then she put him out of her mind. "Nicholas."

"What?" he flung back, stopping to turn around and face her. "What is it now? What do you want from me this time? God, you're as demanding as your father."

She stopped, startled by his vehemence. "And here I was, thinking you'd be grateful!" she exclaimed.

"I don't need your charity," he snarled at her.

He was gripping her game piece tightly in his fist; she still clutched his medal of honor in her hand.

"How could you think to part with this? How could it mean so little to you?"

"I pay my debts. I don't need your help or anybody else's!"

"Well, I need yours!" she exclaimed.

He scowled at her. "Why are you doing all this for me? What are you getting out of it? Just be honest."

"Like you are?" she retorted.

"Why did you really get me out of that cell? Why pay my debt? Why are you interfering in my life?"

She faltered, scarcely knowing what to say. He was in no frame of mind to hear the rest of the truth about what was really at stake.

"Nick, my father loved you like a son. You're a part of

his legacy. I'm not going to let you taint Virgil's memory by throwing away the greatest symbol of everything he taught you." She held up his medal.

He just looked at it, then at her.

Gin lost patience. "Look, all I care about is my investigation! If I help you, it's merely incidental," she lied hotly. "Your life's a mess, your soul's half-lost, your reputation is in shambles. I'm not going to let you darken my father's memory by leaving one of 'Virgil's boys' in this position before the world. Is that what you want to hear?"

He lowered his gaze, obviously stung, but not shrinking from the truth of it. "So now I owe you," he conceded quietly after a moment.

"I know you'll pay me back when you're able. Surely it's better to trust me than to trust that man!" she added, searching his closed expression. "You should have told me you were in debt to Lowell before we went in. With all that's at stake, you should not have let me walk in there not knowing that he had that sort of leverage over you."

He turned away, staring at the river. "You were supposed to stay outside."

"Well, it's done now. Let's both be grateful I happened to wear those ugly red earrings. I never really cared for them."

He looked askance at her, as though well aware she was only saying that to make him feel better.

"The point is," she continued, "now you have to help me. I know it hasn't been easy, figuring out how to work together, but I really need your help. I'm not the expert that you are. Now, if you want your medal back, then stick with me and help me save those girls instead of cutting out on the mission and going your own way, as you planned."

He stared at her. "You really think I would have left?"

"But that's what you said in the carriage!" she cried.

"You said you didn't care about those girls. It's just the way of the world, happens everyday. Am I wrong?"

"I didn't mean it!" he fairly roared.

She blinked. "Well! Maybe you should start saying what you actually mean for a change. How am I supposed to know what goes on in that head of yours? You tried to leave the Order; why should I not expect that you'd desert me, too?"

He winced and turned away with a small, pained laugh.

It was hard telling someone the truth, and Gin half regretted saying it as she watched him smile bitterly in the darkness, shaking his head and struggling to absorb the painfully honest jab.

"Of course I'm going to help you," he finally forced out. "It's what I intended all along."

"What?"

"I didn't want to tell you because I meant to go without you. Anyone with eyes can see you are in so far over your head. You really have no business being involved with any of this. This is warrior's work, and you're just a scared little girl trying to prove herself to her dead father. Do you think that I don't see it?"

She blanched as he skewered her with honesty just as neatly as she had done to him.

Her jaw had dropped, but she managed to close her mouth, not that she could mount any sort of believable denial.

Folding her arms across her chest, she could only shrug, in desperate need of another topic. She steered the conversation elsewhere. "So who is Angelique?"

He flinched, then shook his head with a low, harsh laugh. "Oh, you two would get on so well. I daresay she could teach even you a few things."

Gin bristled even more. "Really? And who is she?"

"Why, you might say she's the female version of Hugh Lowell, my dear. Only she's beautiful. And instead of gluttony, her sin of choice is lust." He paused. "Now that I'm in debt to you, I suppose you'll want to be paid back in the same manner Angelique preferred to accept repayment. So, fine. Let's go. It's all the same to me," he whispered. "Take me to your bed and I'll do whatever you want. After all, you bought me fair and square, didn't you—"

Crack!

She slapped him hard across the face, then stared at him in fury as he slowly brought his hand up to his jaw.

"That's for thinking I'd ever have to pay for it," she informed him.

Then she walked away.

The boat ride home was exceedingly cold. The Thames was as black as the River Styx as the ferryman conveyed them back to the north shore. The lanterns on the boat were but feeble pinpricks of light in the soupy darkness. The water flowed like liquid onyx while the wind whipped, complicating the ferryman's task.

Gin fumed throughout the crossing, keeping to herself. If there were any other way, if there were anybody else who could have helped her, she'd have gladly thrown her partner overboard.

What had her father ever seen in him to choose him for the Order, when a sensible person like herself had not been allowed?

Nick Forrester, loathsome man, was maddening beyond words. He'd been deliberately hurtful. But how could she have expected a trained assassin to be other than at least a little cruel?

She'd be surprised if they didn't kill each other before this mission was over.

He, too, was silent when they arrived on the northern

shore and got into the carriage to return to her town house.

Maybe he regretted throwing it in her face that he had acted as a male whore to this Angelique woman, whoever she was. Or perhaps he was glad to have told her. As if to ensure that he had just killed any interest in him she might have.

The streets of London were all but deserted at this hour. Nick and she seemed to be the only two people awake, but despite being confined inside a coach together, still, they had nothing to say to each other.

The journey home seemed to take forever.

Finally, they arrived outside her town house. The moment the carriage rolled to a halt, she jumped out, not waiting for her coachman to get the door.

Her parting words to Nick were a terse command: "Be ready to leave for Dover by dawn tomorrow. We'll sail from there to Calais."

"Yes, Your Majesty," he drawled barely audibly from inside the darkness of the carriage.

She marched off, not looking back as Nick wearily climbed out of the carriage behind her. He slammed the door behind him.

Gin went into the house, but with the way this night was going, she should have known the fun was not over yet.

Indeed, the lamps were lit throughout the first floor—to welcome home an unexpected guest.

*P*hillip knew he'd be in some trouble for this, but he had escaped his minders at Deepwood and followed his mother and the fascinating Lord Forrester all the way to London in order to prove a point.

That he could do it. That he was resourceful, clever, and brave.

But his point was lost on his mother when she stepped

into the parlor, took one look at him standing there, and gasped. "Phillip!"

"Hullo, Mum!" he greeted her with a forced grin, striving for a light tone in the hopes of avoiding her wrath. "Awfully late to be coming home, even for Town hours, what?"

She flew toward him. "What are you doing here? Where is Mr. Blake? Has something happened?" she cried.

"No, no, everything's fine."

"But—how did you get here?" she exclaimed, looking him over as if to make sure he was not injured. "You should be in bed back at the estate!"

"I'm not a child, Mother!

"Yes!" she countered. "Yes, you are!"

"I'm almost sixteen—"

"Oh, good Lord." She looked like she might go into an apoplectic fit. "You came here on your own?"

"To help you with whatever case you and Lord Forrester are working on!"

He kept talking, telling her how helpful he could be, but he could see that she wasn't listening. She looked glazed over for a second, then his heart sank as she recovered enough from her shock to launch into a rant.

All the yelling attracted another curious party. Phillip looked past his furious mother and suddenly brightened as his new hero stepped into the doorway of the parlor.

"Lord Forrester! There you are!" He walked away from his mother, striding in relief toward the Order agent, which only enraged her the more. "I've come to help," he announced. "Would you please tell my mother to let me be a part of whatever's going on?"

*N*ick went motionless, unsure how to react.

He was glad to see the kid—all the more so because

he knew how much Phillip's arrival would infuriate his mother. It was better than Nick's having to bear all her ire by himself. Still, he was much too smart to get into the middle of this. Especially when Her Ladyship looked over her shoulder and gave him the very Evil Eye in warning: *Don't you dare interfere.*

"Wish I could help," he told the boy in a breezy tone, "but she doesn't listen to me, either. Believe me, my word carries exactly zero weight with the lady in question."

"But that can't be true!" Phillip protested, glancing uncertainly from Nick to his mother and back again.

Softening a bit, he shook his head in regret. "You might as well have stayed at Deepwood, my young friend. I'm afraid the case is nearly solved already, thanks to your mother's cleverness. This one was awfully boring, anyway. Maybe she'll let you help some other time."

Phillip looked crestfallen.

Nick glanced at the boy's mother. "I'm going out for a walk," he told her. Then he looked at Phillip. "Good evening." With a nod to them both, he stepped back outside, leaving them to sort out their domestic squabble for themselves.

As soon as Nick had gone, Phillip looked at Gin suspiciously. "Why the icy looks? Are you two in a fight?"

"Phillip, honestly, you're going to drive your mother mad," she muttered, turning away. His perceptiveness, despite his tender age, never failed to startle her.

"But I thought you liked him!" he said. "And I'm certain he likes you."

"No, he doesn't!" she retorted against her better judgment, turning radish-red. "The man despises me. And he thinks I'm old."

Phillip laughed. "Well, you are! But that's all right, so is he. You're both ancient. I'm mean, you're both over thirty!"

She eyed him ruefully, fighting the urge to tousle his hair. "Don't be adorable when I'm cross at you. It's most annoying."

He grinned at her, then took a bite of an apple. "So you want to hear what route I took from Deepwood? I got here awfully fast—"

"No. I want you to write a letter of apology at once to Mr. Blake for disappearing. Let's hope you haven't killed the poor old fellow from the shock."

"Oh, Mother."

"Don't you understand I'm trying to protect you?" She cupped his smooth, rounded face for a moment between her hands. "I know what you're trying to do, my darling. But I forbid it."

"Why?" he demanded.

"So you don't turn out like Lord Forrester, for one thing!"

"What do you mean? The man's a hero!"

"No. He's a most unhappy soul, who's seen too much and been too many times to Hell and back, all because of the Order. It changes a person, Phillip. Just look at him. Look closely next time. It's made him hard and cold inside. I don't want that to happen to you. I want you to live a happy life and be a part of things and be able to get close to other people. He can't do any of that."

"Don't be daft, Mum, of course he can."

"No, my love. They trained it out of him. He's a hollow shell, and all he's got left is anger."

Phillip shrugged. "Didn't seem like it to me."

"You have to trust me, sweeting. I'm your mother, and I know what's best for you."

He snorted in reply.

"I know right now it frustrates you to hear that, but

someday you'll thank me. Now this matter is not up for discussion. You want to be a hero, and I know that someday you will be. But you'll have to find some other way to make your mark on the world. You're not joining the Order, and that's final. Hate me for it if you must, but I love you too much to turn you over to them for their war machine."

"I'll bet Lord Forrester's mother never babied him!"

She shook her head. "How any of their mothers parted with them, I cannot fathom."

That her own father had been the Seeker to whom those lads had been surrendered by their own families, well, she thought in sorrow, that was Virgil's own private, family curse.

Indeed, their handler had never quite been able to forgive himself for dragging those boys into that dark and dangerous life.

She wondered if Nick or any of them knew the secret guilt Virgil had suffered over that, though he had only been doing his duty, just like the rest of them.

He had made heroes of them, but surely, when they were starry-eyed lads like Phillip dreaming of adventure and great deeds, nobody had seen fit to warn them that heroes were only forged out of sacrifice and pain.

"What's that in your hand, Mother?"

Her son's question drew her from her pained thoughts. She opened her palm slowly and showed him Nick's medal of honor from the Regent.

The boy made a sound of awe and took it from her, staring at it.

"Why don't you hold on to that for me?" she murmured softly. "Keep it somewhere safe until it's time to give it back."

"Can I really?"

She nodded, then kissed him on the forehead and told him in a whisper that he'd better go to bed.

$\mathcal{M}$eanwhile, Nick spent an hour wandering the streets, hands in pockets, hiding in the darkness that had become so comfortable over the years.

He did not have any particular destination in mind, but seeing Phillip with his mother had once more got him thinking of the past.

It was a painful subject.

Like Phillip, he had been raised by a mother alone.

His father had been a bit of a madman, wild and temperamental. Given to highs of exultation countered by the meanest, darkest lows. He had destroyed himself through his loose living when Nick was only three and left the family teetering on the edge of bankruptcy.

But when Nick was eleven, Virgil Banks, the mighty, red-haired Scot, had come to visit, interested in possibly recruiting him for a mysterious chivalric order that was tied to his family bloodlines.

He had been given little tests of his intelligence, played the giant Scot at chess. Tests of his physical soundness, too: his health, his eyesight. Seemingly innocuous demonstrations of his agility, when other boys his age were tripping over their own fast-growing feet.

And then, for the first time in his life, he had been chosen for something special.

Told he had particular value and that he could belong. With the right training, Virgil had told him, why, one day, he could accomplish great things for his country and himself. Be a hero.

Nick had heard the stranger out, both excited and frightened by the secretive door that had been opened to him.

Most of all, he had seen it as a chance to help his mother. She cried all the time and complained ceaselessly about their hard life. Nick knew that if he went, the Order would reward her handsomely, and she might be happy.

He knew that she was lonely after his father died. They had no money, so she wandered around their ramshackle manor feeling sorry for herself, too proud to visit friends who might have cheered her up simply because she did not have adequate gowns equal to her status; nor could she afford the types of leisure pursuits they enjoyed. Nick had known that if he went with the Seeker and let them turn him into a great knight, their family would have a chance at being rich again. Then his mother could return to London and enjoy herself.

Assuring her at the ripe old age of twelve that he would take care of her, take care of everything, he had marched off to be molded into a killer. Too innocent at the time even to realize he was sacrificing his innocence.

He could have lived with it . . . After all, the Order had given him much: his friends, his skills. He'd had the chance to see the world and be a part of certain deeds that, though secret, had helped protect his country. But only three short years into his training, he had received the shock of a lifetime when his mother, restored to Society, had announced she was getting married.

She had found a new husband, and, in no time at all, they had children together, and suddenly she had a whole new family.

Nick had never quite fit in. He felt awkward around the strangers; indeed, he felt as though he had been played for a fool. The cause he had sacrificed himself for had ceased to exist, indeed, had even turned against him, for he had no real place in her new husband's household.

He was an afterthought, an embarrassing reminder of her penniless days and what she had done to escape them: sold her son.

As for her second husband, he seemed to view Nick as a threat, a constant reminder that she had once belonged to another man, his father.

In short, Nick had quickly found he wasn't welcome.

So he had quit going home and turned his back on the need for such connections. Of course, he'd felt abandoned and betrayed, but it did not signify. He had merely sworn to himself that no one would ever hurt him like that again.

He still had very little contact with his so-called family. Both parties preferred it that way. His mother had been proud to hear he'd stepped in front of a bullet for the Regent, but he had made sure that nobody informed her he'd been tossed into the Order's private prison.

Let her keep her illusions about her son, the Order knight. She had her second brood of children to comfort her. Besides, she was daft, anyway.

When he looked up from where his feet had taken him, he was standing in front of her house. The house of her second family, where everyone belonged. Everyone except for him.

He moved closer, up to the edge of the wrought-iron fence that girded the front area. Wistfully, he gazed at the window on the ground floor, but the curtains were closed, and he was shut out in the night.

What was it like to have a family?

Suddenly, to add insult to injury, their dog ran out to the fence and started barking at him.

A quiet, weary laugh escaped Nick. He ordered the dog to be quiet, then wandered on his way—alone—as he supposedly preferred it.

The next day, the morning mists swirled around their post chaise as they set out early on the long but familiar drive to Dover. From there, they'd cross the Channel.

In the interests of convenience and, more importantly, discretion, Virginia had hired the chaise rather than using her own carriage. Though her traveling chariot was far more luxurious, it was also more noticeable on the road.

As for her son, she had left Phillip in the custody of his maternal grandmother until his beleaguered tutor could arrive from Deepwood to fetch him.

As they whisked along, finally clearing the southern outskirts of London, Nick wondered if all youngsters were so much trouble. Of course, at Phillip's age, he wouldn't have thought twice about doing the same thing, no matter whom he inconvenienced. Boys would be boys.

As for the lad's mother, well . . .

Nick peered furtively over his morning paper at the baroness, sitting across from him. Things were still strained between them after all the harsh and cutting words they had exchanged after their visit to the Topaz Room.

He refused to think about the kiss. The woman was impossible, and that was that. She should not even be venturing out on this journey, should have stayed at home with her son and left the bad business to him. By now, of course, Nick realized the futility of trying to tell her that. *Stubborn creature.*

Not only was she blithely meddling with the criminal underworld of Europe—a highly dangerous segment of society that he was sure she did not fully comprehend— but, no. More than that, the lady was in charge.

He was now literally in her debt. Therefore, it was hers to give the orders, his merely to smile and shut up and obey.

At least for now. Hopefully, she would not get them killed in the meantime.

He was just happy she had not clapped him in the manacles again . . . though in certain situations, he supposed that might be fun. Maddening as she could be, at least she was nice to look at.

Sitting across from him, she was dressed in fairly ordinary clothes for their journey in an effort to blend in. But, striking beauty that she was, with that dark red hair and lush body, and the air of confidence with which she carried herself, there was only so much she could do to make herself inconspicuous.

They would probably love her in Paris, he mused, savoring the sight of her. She looked smart and understated in a smooth wool barouche coat: blue-black, three-quarter length, buckled at the waist. The high brim of a dark velvet bonnet framed her ivory face.

He gazed at that face for a moment, the sweet curve of her lashes as she watched, catlike, out the window. The rosy tinge of her cheek . . .

But when his wistful study reached the satin fullness

of her lips, he had to look away, suppressing a small groan. The softness of those lips, the lure of their opening to receive his kiss, was too intoxicating. Already beginning to throb at the memory, he returned his attention to the safer topic of her hat.

Curious things, ladies' hats. Hers was jauntily trimmed with a peacock feather, whose colors suited her beautifully. She had untied the ribbons; his leisurely gaze trailed down the hanging length of one, to where it rested on her bosom.

Back into dangerous territory again.

God, how he had wondered about her breasts ever since that first day in his cell, when she had come to tempt him into accepting her devil's bargain by showing him the cleavage she had no intention of ever letting him touch.

A small sigh almost escaped him before he swallowed it. Letting his gaze linger at her chest, where the barrel snaps of her coat were unbuttoned, he noted her dark green walking dress beneath it.

The lady had style, he thought in secret, fond amusement. As his scrutiny moved on, he was strangely touched by the demure way she had tucked her hands into a big fur muff for warmth. He wasn't sure why, but it seemed so girlish and charming a gesture, an unconscious admission of vulnerability.

Of course, knowing her, she probably had a pistol concealed inside the damned thing, he thought. She was, after all, Virgil's daughter.

"Can I help you?" she clipped out suddenly.

"Hmm?" Nick replied, returning from his daydream. His perusal had got all the way down to her feet, encased in black leather half boots, when he looked up—caught—and met her dubious gaze.

"You're staring at me," she informed him.

"Just wondering if you're warm enough, my lady," he rather purred.

"Yes. Thank you." She searched his face with a stare that made it clear she didn't trust him for a minute.

Smart girl.

"You?" she asked begrudgingly.

"I'm fine," he replied with an even, pleasant stare.

Still regarding him suspiciously, she returned her attention to the landscape. A short while later, they stopped to change post-horses. The hours passed as they pressed on deeper into Kent, finally taking an hour's stop at Canterbury late that afternoon.

He was bored enough from travel to remember that the Black Prince was buried in the great cathedral. If there were time, he'd have gone to pay his respects to the long-dead royal most responsible for the founding of the Order, but Her Ladyship said no.

Back into the chaise they went, and so the day passed.

They did not arrive at Dover until evening.

The wind picked up as they neared the sea; somewhere in the night, half-frozen gulls screamed out plaintively every now and then. The lights of the little harbor town at the foot of the lofty hill beamed gold as best they could against the black November night, whose darkness was so deep it seemed to swallow up the world.

The postillion brought them to a snug quayside inn, where they took lodgings for the night, since the packet ship would not set sail until the morning.

While Lady Burke went to ask the landlord where they could buy tickets for the ship, Nick helped the porter bring their luggage up to their room. He saw to it personally, considering they were carrying an emerald worth a fortune.

The late nabob's gift of the jewel to his wife would be her contribution to the Bacchus Bazaar.

When the porter left the room, Nick closed the door to their room and locked it. Then he unlocked and opened Virginia's traveling trunk, pushing aside a stack of elegant gowns and distracting lacy underthings to take out the little strongbox.

Safe inside its velvet cradle, the emerald sat among the other bits of jewelry she had brought along to wear.

He had raised an eyebrow this morning when he had seen all her luggage. She hadn't liked that.

It's Paris! she had reminded him when he had scoffed and asked her why she was bringing half her wardrobe.

Women.

No wonder the Order didn't let them serve as agents. Who could possibly chase villains across the Continent when a person had to worry about bringing along a whole trunk full of shoes? A male spy could just grab his gun and go.

At least she had dispensed with maids and footmen for the mission.

With a slight smirk, Nick lifted the emerald out of the strongbox and transferred it to the surer protection of his breast pocket. He was not about to leave it in the room. He locked the strongbox again and put it back in her trunk, locked that, as well, then went downstairs to meet her for supper in the taproom.

She had already bought the tickets for the packet ship. Apparently, the inn was deputized to sell them there and then. She had been lucky enough to get the last remaining private cabin. But they would have to bring their luggage over to the dock as soon as they were done eating.

The line's policy was that all passengers' bags had to be loaded at least three hours in advance of their sailing. The tides determined when it was time to go; plus, there was mail on board that had to be delivered on time; all of which meant that no packet ship would be delayed for late-arriving passengers.

Nick offered to bring their trunks over to the dock

immediately, but she said no, they would do it together. There was enough time for a quick meal first since they both were starving.

They ate a supper of pub fare in the inn's cozy tap-room among various other travelers waiting for the ship. Travelers who noticed them likely assumed that they were husband and wife. It was odd contemplating that, Nick mused as he chewed his fish and chips. He couldn't even imagine himself married.

When they were done eating, they went back up to the room, where he showed her he had the emerald in safe-keeping. Then Virginia divided what she would need for sleeping tonight and dressing tomorrow from the rest of her belongings and tucked them into a smaller satchel.

He sat in the armchair by the fireplace in a state of contentment and watched her flitting about while he finished his tankard of good brown ale.

When she was finally ready, they rang for the porter, then Nick helped the lad bring the traveling trunks back downstairs. Upon reaching the ground floor, he set their luggage on a handcart and pulled it for them as they all three went outside and walked across the cobbled street to the dock.

It felt good to stretch his legs after spending all day in the carriage. The bracing cold revived him from the listlessness of the long day's tedium.

There was no one else out on the dock at this hour except the shipping company's employees.

They showed their tickets to the agent on duty. He checked their passports, then added their names to the manifest and called for some sailors to carry their luggage down to the cargo hold. Virginia gave the young porter a couple of farthings and sent him on his way. The lad jogged back to the inn, pulling his handcart behind him.

Lastly, the shipping agent advised them that they'd

sail at dawn. Having made a note of where they were staying, he said he'd let them know if there were any changes to the schedule.

At last, with everything squared away, the two of them headed back up the long, wooden dock. Instead of going straight back to the inn and the intimacy of their shared room, they decided to take a walk on the beach.

It was very cold, but the ceaseless rolling of the white-tipped waves mesmerized him. As the deep layer of large pebbles crunched and shifted under their feet, Nick gave her his arm to steady her.

They did not venture very far, frigid as the night was, especially when they saw some dodgy-looking characters gathered around a bonfire farther down the strand. Instead, they stood in silence side by side, looking at the sea.

"You're freezing. You should get back inside," Nick murmured at length when he felt her shiver.

"I suppose we've got an early start, as well," she conceded with a nod.

When they returned to the inn, they parted ways for now; Nick took a seat in the taproom while she went upstairs. He nursed another tankard of ale so she could have some time to herself to get ready for bed.

She was probably pretty well sick of him by now and could use some time alone. She wouldn't want to have to try to undress for bed with a strange man watching her, especially one so recently freed from a prison cell.

In truth, Nick feared the sight of her peeling off those clothes would be more temptation than he could bear. Better safe than sorry. She was, after all, Virgil's daughter, not to mention pure trouble, head to toe. He sat idly looking at the fire and watching the few stragglers who, like him, had not yet turned in for the night. Finally, he told the barkeep to add the bill to his room tab and went upstairs to the room.

Strangely, his pulse raced a bit as he unlocked the door

with his key. It was much like uncovering the emerald in the strongbox, unlocking this door behind which another sort of jewel lay, snugly tucked into her bed.

Nick chased away any sign of his attraction to her again as he went in, a cool professional once more. She sat propped up against the headboard, surrounded by pillows. He swallowed hard and dropped his gaze.

"Bed comfortable?" he drawled as he locked the door behind him and crossed to set the key on the chest of drawers.

"Not bad," she answered, pointing toward the fireplace. "You can have the chair."

He sent her a rueful smile, tickled by the sight of her in a virginal white night rail with lace-cuffed sleeves. It was buttoned up to her throat.

He wondered if that was what she wore to bed with her "gentlemen friends," of which, apparently, he was not one.

She might as well have put on a chastity belt, he thought sardonically, but, oh, yes, he got the message.

Well, she needn't have worried. He could be a gentlemen on occasion.

But only because she was Virgil's daughter.

He shook out the folded blanket she had left there for him with a pillow and threw it over the armchair, then he took off his coat. He unbuttoned his waistcoat, took off his cravat, and felt her staring as his shirt fell open once these were removed.

He sat wearily and pulled off his boots. Her blue eyes danced as she watched his every move.

"Do I amuse you?"

"For some reason, yes. Very much."

"Happy to be your entertainment, madam."

She smirked, but the sparkle in her eyes was still playful enough to tempt him. "Just so you know," she added, "I'll be sleeping with a pistol under my pillow."

"So will I. So don't get any ideas," he replied. "Good night, my lady."

"Good night, my lord." She blew out the candle and left him in the dark, smiling in spite of himself.

*G*in found it hard to fall asleep with Nick in the room. Her awareness of him was intense.

As she lay awake, filtering all the unfamiliar sounds and smells of this place, she reflected on the fact that she probably should have taken two separate chambers for them at the inn, but she still found it necessary to keep an eye on him. Make sure he didn't steal her emerald and abandon her now that he'd got her the game piece. Make sure the rogue behaved.

Unfortunately, she hadn't expected to find his charismatic presence so distracting. In the darkness, staring at the ceiling, she couldn't stop thinking about all the things written about him in her father's book of secrets—the item that was, in fact, the real reason for this journey—a fact she had not yet seen fit to share with Nick.

She dreaded his reaction. With a knot in the pit of her stomach, she wondered where the journal was right now. *Damn John Carr.*

What had happened was in fact so horrible that she could hardly bear to contemplate it. If all that information should get out or fall into the wrong hands . . .

God, she'd *never* fall asleep if she started thinking about it.

She told herself she wouldn't let that happen, especially now that she had the help of an expert. She just needed to be careful about when she revealed the rest of the story to Nick. Wait until she was sure he was ready to hear it without going through the roof.

When she let out a shaky exhalation, he must have heard her.

"You all right over there?" he drawled in the darkness.

His impertinent tone put a wry smile on her face. "I suppose I just . . . have a lot on my mind."

"Want to talk about it? Ramble all you like. I promise I won't snore if I should fall asleep."

Her lips twisted. "You're very kind. But, no. Go to sleep, Nicholas."

"I would, but this damned chair is nearly as bad as my prison cot." She could hear him shifting around in it impatiently, punching the pillow. "I don't suppose you'd let me—"

"No," she interrupted, fighting a smile. "Perhaps you'll find the floor a little softer."

He harrumphed, and muttered, "Cruel."

She shut her eyes again, smiling, and rather thanking God that he was here.

Much pleasanter than panicking over the journal's location was reflecting on its fascinating contents.

Especially about him.

Virgil had kept careful notes on his boys and their many operations.

That was how she knew these men so well, now that her father had died. Virgil had bequeathed his secret journal to her as her life-insurance policy, should any of his old enemies ever come after her.

She had wide knowledge of the Order and people who could help her if she should ever need it. Knowledge that was all but forbidden to outsiders.

Virgil had known it was a flagrant violation of policy to share this information with her, practically a compendium of his whole clandestine career; but he was a lonely old warrior who had wanted to be truly known by at least one person in this world, and for that, he had chosen her, his own daughter.

More importantly, he had seen too many of those he loved maimed or killed over the years because of his work.

He could not bear for anything to happen to her or his grandson. So he, Virgil Banks, of all people, the legendary spymaster, had broken the Order's *other* immutable law, of secrecy—much as Nick had broken the primary rule, by trying to break free.

Maybe her father and his problem agent were more alike than either man had realized, she mused.

Determined to get some rest before another long day's travel ahead, she thought about her sire's notes pertaining to Nick's temperament, his background, his habits, strengths, and weaknesses, and of course, the record of his many selfless and insanely brave deeds.

That was why she was not concerned about letting him sleep in the same room with her. Nick might not know he was a hero, but she did.

He was a dangerous man, of course, but never to a lady.

Unless, of course, that lady was foolish enough to fall in love with him—a man who could not be tamed.

Gin turned restlessly onto her side and wondered what it would be like, lying in his arms, his hard body curved against hers, spoon fashion, like sated lovers in the aftermath of passion.

She bit her lip to hold back another sigh, lest he start to wonder what the devil was wrong with her.

She knew she was going to have to tell him the whole truth eventually, but not until they had left England, far from the Order's prying eyes.

She did not know how he would react. She did not want him storming out on her for lying to him, turning her over to the graybeards to curry favor with them after his fall from grace; nor could she afford his trying to involve his fellow agents in this mission.

Even though it actually did concern the others—Beauchamp, Montgomery, Warrington, Westwood, Falconridge, Rotherstone, all of them—their involvement would bring too much attention.

Nick, tucked away in prison, had been forgotten by the world.

Besides, he better than anyone would surely understand and forgive her father's breaking of the rules.

No, Gin thought, as long as Nick chose to cooperate, she was confident they could get the journal back and punish John Carr for the theft before any real harm was done, and also rescue those girls. They didn't need his former teammates. The two of them would handle this alone.

*T*he next morning, Nick asked the first mate how the weather looked for the crossing as they came aboard the packet ship.

"Fair skies, at least for now, sir," he replied, "but you never can tell with the Channel."

He was right.

Halfway through the voyage, the winds slacked off, the sea went calm, and they were left to crawl along through the waves at a snail's pace.

What should have been a sail of about five hours was now going on seven, and the fun wasn't nearly over yet. As soon as they reached France, they'd have another, even longer carriage ride down to Paris.

That was sure to be slow going because the roads in France were terrible on account of the wars. Apparently, Napoleon had had better uses for the nation's wealth than fixing roads and bridges. What proper emperor would waste his gold on such mundane repairs when there were still so many delicious countries out there waiting to be invaded?

Ah, well. Bonaparte was now safely under guard around the clock at his island prison of St. Helena— indeed, even while Nick had been locked up in the Order's secret dungeon.

Fancy that, he mused as he sat alone in the tiny stateroom. Never would've thought he'd have something in common with the Monster. God knew he'd killed enough of Napoleon's courtiers, agents of the Promethean conspiracy.

While the afternoon waned, Nick passed the time reviewing the files Virginia had given him related to the case. All the while, he turned the diamond-shaped game piece over and over between his finger and thumb as he worked, glancing over maps of Paris, considering the ground and the various threats they might run across there.

They'd have to keep their wits about them. Of course, the war was over, but France could still be somewhat hostile territory for English folk, less so in the cities.

It had also been for time immemorial a favorite stronghold of the Order's archenemies, the Promethean conspirators. Before the Order had finally defeated the twisted, occult-loving bastards, the conspiracy had been especially strong there, aye, ever since the decades leading up to the bloody French Revolution.

And no wonder, that. Behind the scenes, the rich and highborn Promethean lords had always been the special, hidden patrons of the Jacobins for their own, quite different motives, stirring up the radicals, fomenting any sort of hatred they could turn to their advantage. Whatever they could use. They believed in nothing but their own power and control; to them, the globe was but a chessboard.

All the more reason to hate them, Nick thought. But they were defeated now. Nick and his brother warriors had ended their attempt to take hold of Napoleon's empire from the inside.

If they had succeeded, they would have worked a much darker tyranny over the Continent than the Little Emperor could have ever dreamed of. Bonaparte had built the structure, but the conspirators had thought to take it over bit by bit for their own uses, slowly gaining control, ministry by ministry, region by region, always pretending to obey, help, cooperate.

God, they were vile. He certainly didn't regret killing any of them who had crossed his path.

As he leaned back slowly in his chair, his mind churning on all the information in the files, he suddenly wondered about his traveling companion. Reviewing her notes on these abducted young women suddenly sharpened his instinctive need to make sure she was safe.

Of course, he had scanned the other passengers and determined that nothing on the ship appeared a threat, but she'd been gone a while now. Better go and check on her, he thought.

As he put the papers away, he did not know if she was avoiding him or if she was worried they'd do something they'd regret if they stayed too long together in that tiny cabin.

It was very possible.

Whatever her reasons—and Nick preferred to think it was simple boredom when the ship was becalmed—she had traipsed off to the ship's common room to socialize with the other well-to-do passengers.

Nick hadn't been in the mood to join her when she had invited him to come along, but now seemed a good time to make sure she was all right—and behaving.

Satisfied that their papers were secure, he locked the cabin door, then proceeded through the narrow wooden passageway toward the common room.

Even before he arrived, he heard her laughter. His stomach tightened as he saw her sitting at a table with a small group of people, mostly men.

They were playing cards, gambling.

An idle amusement merely to pass the time, no doubt. But still, with both of them acutely aware that this was his Achilles' heel, he clenched his jaw as he went to her. The handsome blond man sitting across from her stopped laughing and tensed as Nick approached the table, resting his hands on her delicate shoulders.

She tilted her head back and looked up at him warmly. "You're not allowed to join us."

"Your husband, madam?" the stranger asked in a forcedly pleasant tone.

But the timing of their answer went awkwardly awry, for at the same moment Nick bent to kiss her neck, confirming this was so, she replied, "No, he's my brother."

Thus they shocked everyone at the table, for it was not the sort of kiss a brother should ever put on his sister's neck.

Nick let out a wicked laugh—what else could he do?

Virginia turned strawberry red while everyone at the table stared in horror at the incestuous couple.

"Come back to our cabin, sis," he purred loud enough for them to hear. He hooked his finger through her necklace and gave it a light tug, warning her that he was annoyed. "I'm lonely for your company. Besides." He looked at her cards. "You've a terrible hand. Be a good girl and fold."

He had never seen her embarrassed before. It was ever so amusing.

She jumped up from her chair and could not even look at him as she flounced straight out of the common room without a backward glance.

Nick bowed to the cardplayers. "Gentlemen."

Then he chased her as she fled below. Laughing, he caught up with her in the passageway several feet outside their cabin. He reached out from behind her and captured her arm. "Oh, come, you know it was funny."

"You are the devil!" she uttered, whirling to face him, her cheeks aflame.

"Then what does that make you? Tell me, are you going to flirt with the whole crew or just the passengers?" he demanded hotly.

"What's the matter, jealous?"

"Maybe. Isn't that what you want?"

She leaned back against the bulkhead and glared at him, her eyes shooting cobalt sparks. "You don't know what I want," she informed him.

"I think I do," he whispered.

"How can anyone be so arrogant?" she ground out, her chest heaving.

"It's easy." He lowered his head and skimmed her nose with his own. "I want you, Virginia."

"I don't care if you do!"

"What are we going to do about this?"

"We at least ought to get our story straight!" she evaded.

"I agree. Listen." He touched her chin, caressing her face as he lifted her gaze up to his. "I have to tell you something."

"What?" she mumbled, holding his gaze, as though she couldn't look away any more than he could.

"I said some awful things to you the other night outside the Topaz Room. You didn't deserve that. I am sorry."

Her eyebrow shot up.

"I felt foolish for getting myself into that situation, owing Lowell money, I mean. I didn't want you to know. I didn't want you to see me as a total disgrace."

"I don't," she murmured.

"Well, I am, aren't I?"

"Nick, you're not the only one who's ever made mistakes. Believe me."

He lowered his gaze. "I just wanted to tell you that I didn't mean those things I said. I was just embarrassed, but the truth is, you saved my bacon, and I owe you."

"Well, just see this mission through with me, and we'll call it square." She eyed him warily. "I thought you were the fellow who never apologizes."

"First time for everything," he said with a small shrug. "Besides, you deserve it. I was wrong."

She stared into his eyes for a long moment.

"What is it?" he murmured.

"Nick," she whispered. "Kiss me."

The request surprised him, to say the least. He figured she would have continued to try hiding her desire for him.

He tilted his head, regarding her with wry caution. "Is this one going to mean anything?"

"Yes," she breathed, nodding as she held his gaze.

How could he resist when she put herself in his hands like this?

A well of gentleness that he didn't even know he possessed opened within him and began to flow through every inch of his being as he cupped his hand around her nape.

He approached her lips softly, slowly, his heart pounding. There was something sacred in that moment as he leaned down—something that required the truth.

"Virginia?" He paused, close enough to feel her breath puff against his mouth.

"Yes?"

He flinched slightly at the question he had to ask. "Why do you want me to kiss you when you don't even think me worthy to speak to your son?"

"*What?*" She pulled back from waiting breathlessly for his kiss to look into his eyes, furrowing her brow.

He saw some realization enter into her gaze, and she winced and cupped his cheek lightly in her hand. "Oh, Nick, that's not the reason I told you to stay away from him. I don't want him idolizing *any* Order agent. Oh, God, I'm so sorry. I thought you understood that! He's so headstrong, always testing me. So eager to follow in Virgil's footsteps and be a hero."

"I noticed."

"Well, that's how he sees you. When I told you to stay away from him, it was because I don't want you encouraging him. I won't let the Order sink their claws into my boy. They took my father from me. They cannot have my son. Look what they've done to you. How did your mother ever bear to send you off like that? How do any of them? That's what I don't understand." Her words broke off abruptly. "I'm sorry. That was rude."

She searched his face, but Nick just smiled rather sadly. He wished he knew the answer to that himself, but it was a question that, as a rule, he did not let himself ask.

Virginia let it go and laid her hand gently on his chest. "I feel dreadful that you thought that's what I meant. That you're unworthy in any way. That is not how I see you at all, Nick. I just didn't want you saying anything to Phillip that would make the child even more determined to pursue that kind of life."

"Never," he replied in a quiet voice. "I wouldn't wish that sort of life on my worst enemy."

Too hard. Too bloody. Much too isolated from the rest of human life. But it was all in what you got used to.

"If I had known that's what you thought . . . No wonder you were angry." Instead of a kiss, he got a hug as she moved forward and wrapped her arms around his waist.

It was a curious feeling, far from the passion that at least he knew how to navigate. This show of artless, womanly affection rather stymied him.

She laid her head on his chest, holding him like maybe she really *was* his devoted sister or his loyal wife. Nick frowned warily above her, not knowing how to react.

He supposed the done thing was to give her a cautious hug back. So he did.

It seemed to satisfy her. She let out a contented sigh in his arms. He went further, warily smoothing her hair.

"You silly, silly man," she chided with a fond shake of her head against his chest a moment later. "How could you think that I would ever see you as unworthy?"

He shrugged. *Because I am.*

"Beautiful fool," she whispered as if she could read his mind.

Suddenly, the ship's bell clanged, and the cry went out on the decks above them, announcing they had reached the harbor of Calais.

Nick looked at her ruefully as she raised her head.

Stepping back from his embrace, she gave him a tender smile, and the possibility of another kiss was set aside for now.

Interrupted, to be sure, but not at all forgotten.

Then she took his hand. "Come on, you." She pulled him back to their stateroom to collect their things. Nick followed her, in something of a trance. He felt so strange.

So this is what it's like to be an actual person, he thought.

Instead of the bloody angel of death.

The packet ship dropped anchor, and soon they were lowered in a rowboat down into the dip and sway of the waves to be brought ashore.

The rocking, dizzying span from shipboard to land as the sailors plied the oars was good preparation, Gin thought, for entering the whimsical upside-down world that was France, at least to her English brain.

Life was different there. Things that in England were crisp, clean, straight, and narrow, in France became curved, swirling, flowery, and fanciful.

The people were different, too. Where Englishmen made it a point of pride to conceal their true feelings, the French expressed every passing shade of emotion on their faces: a flick of an eyebrow, a curl of the lip, or the world-famous Gallic shrug.

Englishmen liked to agree as much as honorably possible for etiquette's sake; Frenchmen loved to argue about everything under the sun for intellectual stimulation—or mere entertainment. The two tribes had completely different senses of humor, too, and even insulted people differently. The English could cut some poor soul dead with frosty politeness, whereas the French had perfected the art of ridicule centuries ago.

No wonder the war had taken twenty years, she mused wryly. If only their nations could have remained friends, as so many French and English aristocrats were in Society, where they copied each other's fashions and frequently swapped wives. Gin, like most of the world, was simply glad the dreadful war was over.

At last, her stomach turning from the pitching of the waves, she accepted Nick's offered hand and stepped out of the unstable rowboat onto the beach. The first order of business for all arriving passengers was the short, obligatory visit to the Customs House. After filing along through the line, an official checked their papers and asked a few questions about the nature of their visit.

In Calais, they took a room for the night, but their trek was far from over. From there, they had a grueling, two-day carriage ride before they reached the capital.

Given the pitted roads, the worn springs of their hired barouche, and all the jarring, Gin arrived admiring the splendors of Paris feeling like every bone in her body was broken.

But at least she discovered one thing their countries had in common: Carriage drivers in the City of Light were equally as mad as those in London.

She was glad Nick was handling the ribbons, expertly navigating the busy maze of broad, new, imperial avenues and the dark, cramped medieval streets. Merely riding along as passenger gave her half a mind to reach for the smelling salts. Finally, they reached their journey's end just as all the churches in the city began to toll the hour.

The light had faded. In Catholic country, it was time for evening vespers.

Then Nick brought the carriage to a weary halt at last

outside a quaint little inn painted ocher with blue shutters and tiny balconies overlooking the cobbled street. A gold-lettered sign above the door pronounced it LA MAISON DE MAXIME. And like a budding poet sipping coffee at a café, it sat utterly ignoring the opulent monstrosity of the L'Hôtel Grande Alexandre in view across the street.

The little inn's rival was a pillared palace that Gin immediately suspected had once been the home of some guillotined aristocrat before being converted to expensive lodgings for travelers. It had huge, arched windows through which giant chandeliers shone, a pair of gilded lions crouching outside the door.

That was the place where Hugh Lowell had instructed them to go in order to finalize their participation in the Bacchus Bazaar, she mused.

Nick turned to her discreetly. "I'll get us a balcony room at the front of the house here." He nodded at cozy little Maxime's. "This should give a decent view of the people coming and going from the Alexandre. Get a sense of the competition."

She nodded, then let him help her down from the carriage with a small groan of pain.

He frowned in concern.

"I'm fine," she mumbled, as they went into the lobby. "Just a bit sore."

"Your back?"

"All over. Must be because I'm so dashed old," she taunted, leaning on him as she rather hobbled into the lobby.

"God, some people can't take a joke! You're not old."

"Well, I feel about ninety years old at the moment," she grumbled.

"Don't worry, Gran. You can lie down as soon as we get our room."

"One room?" she countered under her breath as they stepped inside. She gave him a droll stare. "Dare we?"

"With such people in the neighborhood, we'd better stick together."

"And get our story straight this time," she added pointedly.

He sent her a sardonic look.

Crossing to the desk in the lobby, they presented themselves as husband and wife.

It was becoming easier every day to carry off the charade though they had only kissed once. Traveling around the clock and living together in such close quarters had bred a familiarity between them that already felt surprisingly natural.

In any case, it was blissful to know they would have a home base of operations for a few nights and would not have to be in motion with the breaking of the dawn.

The maitre d'hôtel was a funny little whirlwind of a Frenchman with a moustache and an apron, who made them immediately welcome.

He neither stopped moving nor talking as he dashed about, running his establishment with obvious pride. "You have shown excellent taste, my friends, by choosing our humble *maison* over that gaudy *horreur* down ze street."

Gin fought a smile. She had not thought "humble" was a word used by any self-respecting Parisian. "Are you Monsieur Maxime?" she inquired, assuming this to be the owner's surname.

"Me? Non, non, madame. I am Claude. Claude de Vence. Maxime is my wife. She is in charge of the kitchens. Her sister runs the boulangerie next door. All our bread is baked fresh there. Me, I manage ze hotel— along with my useless son. Georges! Come, we have new guests!" he shouted abruptly over his shoulder. "Will you wish for supper? Our food is—" He kissed his fingertips. "Exquisite!"

"Certainly, we will. We're very hungry," Nick said, a trace of warm amusement in his voice.

Monsieur de Vence was thrilled to hear it. "Excellent! Let me show you to your room."

"Ah, could we have one at the front of the house, please?"

He frowned. "It's quieter in ze back."

"That's all right. We enjoy watching life go by."

"I see." Monsieur le Vence narrowed his eyes and nodded in approval of these rather French sentiments on the part of an always-hurrying Englishman. "I know we have one open on the second floor. But whether it is finished being cleaned yet, I do not know. Georges!"

A stream of French language tumbled from his lips as he called impatiently to his son.

It was not the sort of fashionable French Gin's governess had ever taught her, but something a bit more earthy and piquant; but though she was rather lost on the exact translation, his meaning was clear enough. To be sure, she recognized the harried look of a fellow parent to a teenaged son. Lord knew she had seen that vexed expression often enough in the mirror.

Running on seventeen-year-old time, the wiry lad eventually rushed into the lobby from the direction of the kitchens. "*Oui, Papa?*" He stared at Nick and Gin for a second with a wide-eyed blink.

"Go and check to make sure Room Nine is ready. Build ze fire while you are there."

Georges bobbed his head, then whirled around, all gangly limbs, and scampered up the steps. Monsieur de Vence smiled at them and tapped his fingers on the desk; while Gin admired a charming watercolor painting of the Seine in the lobby, Nick finished signing them in, then made arrangements with the innkeeper to return the barouche and horses to the Paris station of the same livery company from which they'd hired them.

At last, the boy returned. "*C'est preparée toujours, Papa.*"

The father nodded at their luggage. "Carry up their bags."

Before long, they were all traipsing up the stairs behind their skinny young porter. Poor Georges could not possibly see where he was going, staggering under a tower of baggage that weighed more than himself. But, somehow, he pressed on.

The innkeeper carried another trunk behind them, while Nick hefted the black case that contained their weapons, as well as the strongbox where her jewelry and the emerald for the Bacchus Bazaar were squirreled away.

Zigzagging precariously ahead of them, the sweating Georges showed them to their room. The boy fairly collapsed under his load in the middle of floor.

She rushed to catch the topmost box that slid off the stack in his arms. Then he set everything down, and she rewarded him with a franc for his heroics.

He looked at it, then at her, and bobbed with a bow of thanks.

The room was small and cheerful, unpretentious, a quaint box of creamy plaster walls and ceiling, garden-floral fabrics, and timeworn furniture carved with swirly, round, rococo touches. The fire was already blazing in the modest hearth, warming the space.

Gin felt instantly at home. She let out a great sigh and slowly took off her coat, while Nick stepped into the doorway to confirm that they would have the house supper for two, along with two bottles of wine, one red, one white, of whatever vintage Monsieur de Vence thought best for them.

"It won't be long," their new friend assured them.

Nick nodded in thanks and finally closed the door. At once, he began searching the room for a hiding place in which to conceal the strongbox. He soon found a place to secret it away in a dark upper shelf at the back of the armoire.

Gin felt too battered to be of any help whatever. She simply unlocked the traveling trunk that contained her various nightgowns then dragged herself off behind the painted screen in the corner. While she wearily changed clothes, Nick took out the telescope and evaluated the view of the Alexandre from their balcony.

He was just shutting the narrow little doors that gave access to the balcony when she stepped out from behind the screen, still tying the cloth belt of her dressing gown around her waist.

He smiled ruefully as he pulled the curtains shut over the balcony doors for warmth. "How are you feeling?"

"Like the whole field of racehorses ran over me at the derby."

He smiled fondly. "I'm sure you'll feel better after a good night's sleep. Lie down here, on your stomach."

"Why?" she asked suspiciously.

"Just do as you're told for once." He grabbed one of the pillows and placed it at the foot of the bed.

Warily, she lay on her stomach, facing the fire, her hands clasped under her chin.

"Now then." Standing at the edge of the bed, he leaned down and began running his palms lightly down her back. "Tell me where it hurts."

"Ow. There. Everywhere." She flinched beneath his gentle touch.

"I'll go easy on you, then." And he did. Gradually, she relaxed under his strong, warm, clever hands massaging her, gliding smoothly, gently, over her aching body.

Bit by bit, as they waited for the food to be delivered, he stroked away the soreness, squeezing her shoulders, kneading his fingers deep into her knotted muscles, and spreading relaxation through her, replacing pain with soothing pleasure.

A sigh escaped her. "Mm, that's good."

"So tight," he remarked in a throaty purr as he dealt

with her aches and pains more aggressively now that he had taken the edge off. "There?"

"Yes." It felt wonderful as he dug his knuckles into the knots in the small of her back and pressed his thumb into spots that she hadn't even realized were hurting.

"Where did you learn how to do this?" she mumbled blissfully, resting her cheek on her folded arms.

"Just shut up and enjoy it," he ordered with a smile in his voice. After a moment, he paused, inspired with some new way to pleasure her. "Why don't we try . . . this. Don't move." He went and got her bag of toiletries, choosing a lavender-scented cream.

When he returned, he slipped her satin robe off her shoulders, freeing her arms one by one. He folded her dressing gown back across her hips, draping it over her bottom. "You're going to like this," he promised in a low and husky murmur.

Then he slicked his hands with some of the moisturizing cream and used it to deepen his massage.

Gin was in sheer heaven as his skillful hands caressed her, erasing grueling hours of travel. With a deft motion, he lowered the silk straps on her peignoir, baring her shoulders, and soon, his fingertips marched up the back of her neck with steady, gentle persuasion.

You are dangerous, she thought, as a sigh of bliss escaped her. There was only one way left that he could have pleasured her more . . .

After all, Paris was for lovers, and at this hour of night, there was nothing else to do.

*N*ick was entranced by her beautiful skin.

It was intoxicating to feel the way the tough, proud, no-nonsense lady melted under his touch, her body turning supple, yielding under his caresses. If he could have found a reasonable excuse to justify hitching her silk peignoir up over her long, lithe legs and rubbing cream all over them, too, he would have done it. He wanted to touch every inch of her. But he didn't dare. All of a sudden, he was deathly afraid of making any sort of mistake with her.

This remarkable woman took his breath away. Instead, he was all but mute with yearning, and finally, he flinched when a knock at the door brought her massage to an end.

An expected interruption.

Still, he bit his lip and closed his eyes, struggling to tamp down his hunger for her.

"You are an angel of mercy," she purred, as he covered her up gently with her dressing gown again. Somehow he found the self-possession to go and answer the door.

It was, of course, Monsieur de Vence, delivering their feast on a wheeled cart. He left them to enjoy the house bill of fare, and it did not take long for them both to realize that his wife, the cook, was a born genius.

November meant truffle season in France, therefore the meal was launched in fine style with a silky white truffle soup with asparagus.

Bellies warmed by the soup, they eagerly hurried on to the fish course of *sandre au beurre blanc,* or roasted pike perch with butter. The fish had a succulent, flaky texture and strong, good, pure, simple flavors.

Next came the main course, hearty *boeuf bourguignon,* fragrant with the red Burgundy wine in which the meat had simmered until it was falling apart. There was a lighter offering to choose from: smoked pigeon breast bristling with rosemary springs and smeared with cooked apricots; as well as a side dish of tender roasted carrots sprinkled with parsley.

They were merry with wine by the time they paused for the cheese course, merely a pleasant stop along the way to dessert, as far as Nick was concerned.

"Du fromage, s'il vouz plait," Lady Burke teased him with a tipsy toast, lifting her glass.

"The blue, the brie with apple compôte, or the goat cheese, madame?"

"Oui!" she answered, beckoning him toward her plate.

Her motions seemed unsteady. Her eyes shone a bit too bright. He did not remark upon her state of elevation but served her once again.

At last, they rewarded themselves with the sweets course—vanilla macaroons made into charming little sandwiches filled with sweet pistachio cream.

Nick picked up his wineglass, then reclined on his elbow on the bed, watching her lick the cream from between two macaroons.

"I think I've gained five pounds just now," she remarked in a wryly philosophical tone. "Which makes me wonder."

"About what?" he asked indulgently.

"Why Hugh Lowell doesn't move to France?"

Nick started laughing.

"I mean it! He is obviously a great gourmand, and the food here . . . well, it's France."

"I don't think they'd have him," Nick drawled.

"Of course they would! He's not so bad."

Nick shrugged. "He was more cooperative than I expected, I admit."

"That's because I charmed him," she replied.

"No, you frightened him, I think. God knows you frighten me."

She sent him a long-suffering look. "How did you ever end up in debt to the likes of Hugh Lowell, anyway? Smart fellow like you. It seems . . . out of character."

"Isn't it obvious?" he countered warily. "Bad luck at the tables."

She shook her head. "You perplex me. Why play there in the first place?"

He shrugged. "At first, it was just a matter of establishing my cover in that world. Gain his trust. I had to be convincing. And then, later on, oh, I don't know. I guess I didn't want anyone bothering me whenever I wanted to play."

"You mean like Beauchamp and Montgomery, trying to stop you?"

He sent her a mild, warning look. She was toeing her way onto sensitive ground.

"Why didn't you just borrow money from one of them instead of using Lowell's moneylenders? All your friends are wealthy men."

He shook his head. "I don't do that. I don't take advantage of my friends."

"Hmm. So, what's your poison, then? Hazard? Faro? Whist?"

"Whist?" He looked askance at her. "Whist is for old ladies."

"Well, then? What's your game?"

"I don't gamble anymore," he replied, bristling a little.

She gazed at him.

"But . . . in my day," he admitted a moment later—rather ruefully—as if a part of him needed to talk, "I would've bet on anything. I especially liked the prize-fights. Horse races. Any stupid thing, really."

"Why?"

"Why?" he echoed. "I don't think I ever had a reason."

"Of course you did. You're Nick Forrester. You don't do anything without a reason, not you. So what did you like about it?"

"This is a stupid conversation," he informed her.

"Really? I find it fascinating. I find *you* fascinating." She bit into the macaroon.

He scoffed and looked away, startled, not the least because he could feel his face flush with boyish embarrassment at her interest in him.

She swallowed the dainty mouthful and washed it down with a sip of Riesling. "Well, you are," she said. "I want to understand you, Nicholas."

"Why?"

"No reason. I want to know what makes you tick. For instance, what made you want to join the Order? What made you want to quit?"

"Oh, Lord," he drawled, falling onto his back on the bed with a weary sigh.

"Tell me," she persisted.

"Tell you what, precisely?" he asked, not at all sure he was ready for an interrogation.

"The real reason why you gambled."

He was silent for a moment. "I guess it boils down to being oddly superstitious," he confessed. "I mean, I should have died many times over in the field. But I always walked away in one piece, and it just seems to me that there's got to be a reason—beyond being good at what I do, I mean. Either I've got nine lives like a cat, or there's some reason I've been spared. Something maybe I'm supposed to do or be or see or figure out . . . I don't know. I sound ridiculous, like some raving mad old gypsy woman."

"It doesn't sound ridiculous at all," she replied, smiling. "So you wanted to try to find a pattern? A sense of meaning."

"Yes," he said, sitting up in surprise to stare at her. "Exactly so." Her immediate grasp of his bizarre motivation startled him but made it seem all right to say a little more. "I guess . . . I just wanted a sign. Some sort of sign that what I was doing mattered. That it was right."

"Did you ever get one?"

"No," he said with a wry, sad laugh. "I lost my bloody shirt. Obviously." He sighed.

She stood up slowly, bringing her wine with her. "Did it ever occur to you that maybe the gaming tables was the wrong place to look?"

He watched her in wary fascination as she came to him and sat down on his lap. "What are you doing?" he murmured.

A naughty half smile curved her lips as she glanced down at his mouth, and whispered, "I'll give you a sign, Nicky boy." She tilted her head and kissed him gently.

He shivered with pleasure, but held himself back, his pulse already drumming. "You're drunk, my lady," he said in fond, chiding amusement.

"So?"

"I'm not going to take advantage of you," he said with heroic resolve.

"Please?" she breathed, skimming her lips against his ear.

God. "No more wine for you."

"But we're in Paris."

"That's no excuse," he teased softly. When he lifted her glass out of her hand and set it aside, she draped her arms over his shoulders and leaned nearer.

"I want to tell you a secret," she whispered.

"Hmmm?"

"One day, when I was but a girl of seventeen, I followed my father to one of his meetings with you."

"What?" He pulled back a few inches to chuckle at her.

"That's right. I spied on you all. My father and his protégés."

"Why did you do that?"

"Curiosity. Jealousy. I didn't like being shut out of all the excitement! So I had to find out who or what was stealing so much of my papa's attention from me. And there you all were, at the fencing studio. Hiding in plain sight, just like he taught you to do."

Nick shook his head in astonishment.

"I remember you," she murmured. "You were standing apart from the others, leaning against a column, looking annoyed."

He smiled ruefully. "For some reason, they considered me difficult to work with on occasion. I have no idea why."

"You started arguing with Warrington. Nobody argues with Warrington! The Beast."

Nick rolled his eyes at the mention of the Order's most vainglorious hero. "Dukes always think they walk on water. Somebody's got to take them down a peg."

She smiled as she clasped her hands behind his neck and gazed into his eyes. "Well, here's the secret. You, Lord Forrester, became my favorite from that very day."

"Did I, indeed?" he echoed, pleased.

"Strange, isn't it?" she teased in a flirtatious whisper, while his heart pounded faster at this revelation. "Usually, the ladies all go mad for beautiful Beauchamp. And Lord Trevor Montgomery is so much nicer than you. So much more of a gentleman. Lord Falconridge as well. Then there's Lord Rotherstone, who's obviously cleverer than you—"

"No, just more devious," he insisted with a smile.

"Warrington's the mightiest—"

"Ha."

"And then there's Drake, Lord Westwood. I don't know *what* to make of him."

"Nobody does, believe me. Touched in the head, that one."

"Yes, he is an enigma. But so are you, in your own way. Personally, I like a mystery."

"And you know all this from one reconnaissance mission as a little, seventeen-year-old miss?"

"No, of course not. My father told me all sorts of things about you. All of you."

"Did he really? He must have trusted you immensely."

"Of course he did. We were the best of mates. He took care not to mention names, but I could usually figure out which one of you he was talking about." She shrugged. "I don't think he even realized that I was really listening. He just needed to get things off his chest. And who else could he talk to, really?"

"I wonder why he never introduced you to us all."

"Isn't it obvious? He didn't want me falling in love. But he was too late." She stroked his hair.

Nick was a tad bewildered. Surely this was just the wine talking. "Well, ahem, I'm sure a young girl like that is, um, prone to infatuations."

"Yes, but I am thirty-four, and I fear I'm still not cured."

Once more, he was blushing like a callow youth, staring at the floor, trying with all his might to hold himself back. Never had a woman talked to him this way. Not in all his life. He did not usually allow them close enough even to try. Normally, he'd have been done with her and on his way by now. But with her, well, even now, he could not look away from her dreamy, cobalt gaze.

"Is that why you came and got me out of prison?" he asked softly. *You can't seriously be saying you're in love with me.*

She bit her lip and stroked his hair. "I hated the injustice of what they'd done to you. Locking you up in that hellhole after you'd given your whole life to the Order. Ever since you were a child."

"I was never a child."

She gazed at him thoughtfully. "You never did answer the question I asked you on the ship. How your mother ever agreed to it, how she parted with you."

"What do you mean? I did it for her sake," he answered. "To make her proud of me. And comfortable. And happy."

"Did it? Make her happy?"

"No. She's a miserable person. But I didn't realize that till recently."

"Oh." She paused. "Did it make you happy, at least? Being in the Order?"

"Sometimes."

"But eventually that changed?" she prompted softly when he did not elaborate.

"Yes."

She toyed with the collar of his shirt. "So you went into the Order for your mother's sake. What made you want to get out?"

He stared at her for a second. "They shot Trevor right in front of me. The enemy did. Shot him in the back, and down he went. My God." He shut his eyes and shook his head, wincing at the memory. "*That*," he uttered, "was my sign."

"What do you mean?"

"Trevor, of all people. The good one. It should have been me. He's too good a man. They never should have put him in the field."

"My father never would've sent an unqualified agent out on a dangerous mission—"

"That's not what I mean. Don't misunderstand. He's a damned fine agent. But he's so bloody honorable. You can't be, out there. Your father knew it, too. That's why he put him with me. To stop me from going too far. Because he always knew that, one day, I would."

"Too far how?"

He shook his head and pushed her away, moving her gently off his lap.

She stood up and frowned in thought, studying him.

Thankfully, she spared him the demand for a definition. She did not want to know how willing he had been to kill for the cause.

She picked up her wineglass and retreated to her former seat nearby. "At least you managed to save Trevor's life."

"Just barely," he muttered. "You obviously don't know the rest of the story; otherwise, you'd have been cured of your infatuation and wouldn't keep looking at me like deep down you still think I'm some sort of hero in spite of everything."

She arched a brow at him, keeping her distance at last. "Then perhaps you'd better enlighten me."

"Yes. I should." That would lay to rest her misguided admiration of him.

Still, it took him a long moment to come out with his confession.

"While Trevor was convalescing from the gunshot wound, I made up my mind, you see, to quit the Order. I didn't give a damn anymore after seeing my best friend nearly slaughtered right in front of me.

"Unfortunately," he continued, "Trevor is not the sort who'd ever lie to our superiors. That meant that as soon as he reported back to the graybeards and told them I was a deserter, they would send out agents either to drag me back to face the consequences or shoot me dead if they couldn't take me alive.

"On the other hand, they couldn't send snipers out to kill me if they knew I had one of our own in custody somewhere."

Her eyebrows shot upward. "Oh, dear. So, you . . . used your best friend as a hostage?"

Nick nodded. "Hell, I saved his life. I figured it would not be too much trouble if I allowed him to save mine."

"And how did he react to being held prisoner?" she asked in a dubious tone.

"Eh, he didn't even realize it most of the time. He was wounded, out of commission for several weeks. He just thought I was looking after him—and I was." Nick heaved a sigh, staring at the floor for a second. "It was only a couple of months. I just needed to get some funds together so I could start a new life elsewhere, under a new identity. Far, far away."

"Oh, Nick."

"When Trevor finally started getting stronger and asking why we weren't headed back for England, that's when the trouble started. Because at that point, I actually had to lock him up. Several times we came to blows when he tried to escape. The man can fight," he said.

"So that's why the graybeards put you in that cell."

"Oh, no, darling, it gets much worse."

"Go on."

"As I said, I needed funds. And I do have a rather particular set of skills. That woman, Madame Angelique . . ."

"Ah, the female version of Hugh Lowell, I believe you said?"

"Yes. Let's just say I went to work for her. I needed money. She was getting death threats. I took care of them for her."

"Oh," she said with a small gulp.

"When you take a job as a hired assassin, they don't usually tell you up front who you're supposed to kill. At first, they only tell you where and when, and then, in due time, once you get there, the target is revealed."

She was silent.

"Angelique set it up for me. I didn't know who the target was, honestly. I had no idea. As soon as I found out, of course, I refused. Even though backing out of something like that usually means you're dead."

"Who was the target?"

He held his breath, dreading her reaction. "The Prime Minister, Lord Liverpool."

She covered her mouth with her hand and paled.

"Somebody set me up to frame the entire Order. The charge was to have been that the Order had nurtured a conspiracy plotting to overthrow the government."

"My God," she whispered.

"They used me—or nearly so—to try to incriminate the whole organization. Fortunately, Beauchamp was working the same problem from another angle, and so we ended by teaming up to stop the *real* conspiracy. We managed to expose them and take them down. If it hadn't been for our friendship, and how much we trust each other even in a situation like that, we'd all have been destroyed."

"Is that when you ended up taking a bullet for the Regent?"

"Yes. God's truth, I wished at the time that it had killed me. Facing my friends after what I'd done was harder than dying. At least I didn't have to face your father. Virgil was already dead by the time all this took place."

She nodded, taking it all in. "So instead of gaining your freedom and the new life you longed for, you ended up in that cell."

"I deserved it. Believe me, I'm not complaining. They could have hanged me. Might have done, too, but Beau and even Trevor himself spoke on my behalf. As did the Regent."

"Trevor forgave you, then?"

"I told you he was too good-hearted," Nick said wryly, then he shrugged, relaxing a little as he saw she had not fled the room in disgust of him. "Besides, it actually bore good results in his life."

"How's that?"

"If I had not, er, detained him, he'd have rushed back to London to be reunited with his former fiancée. That woman was all wrong for him. Instead, he missed his chance with her—she had given him up for dead and married a new beau. As a result, Trevor found a new girl, ended up married to the right one for him, a pastor's daughter. I haven't met her yet, but apparently this Grace woman is just as virtuous and sensible as he."

She cast him a wan smile.

"So, you see, at least some good came of what I did," he said wryly. "Still, it's hard to live with. Knowing how I failed."

"Nick. You're not the only person in the world who's ever done anything wrong, you know. We've all done terrible things."

"Not you?"

"Yes, even me," she whispered.

"Like what?"

She was silent as she licked her lips, betraying a hint of apprehension. "Well, if it's to be a night of trading secrets . . ."

Nick waited, his brow furrowed as he studied her. She lowered her head for a second. Taking a deep breath, she lifted her gaze, looked him frankly in the eyes, and said: "I killed my husband."

$\mathcal{N}$ick held stock-still. "Come again?"

"It's true. I am responsible for his death."

"I thought you said he died in the Peninsular War. A fever hit the army camp."

"On the face of it, that's true. But he never even should have been there. He wasn't a soldier. I drove him to it, you see. I couldn't stop comparing him to you . . . and the others. All my father's dashing, handsome, fearless secret agents. I came to hate the sight of him. Isn't that horrible? Remember, I was forced to marry him to avoid a scandal, after I had gone out of my way to steal him from the debutante bullying my friend."

He nodded, remembering what she had told him.

She shook her head and looked away. "I disparaged him, even insulted his manhood, until one day he came home and threw it in my face that he had bought a commission in the cavalry. He was going to war, he said, and *then* I would respect him. And now my son will never know his father."

She lowered her head again with a pained look, avoiding his gaze. "That, too, my dear Lord Forrester, is very hard to live with."

He leaned closer, filled with the urge to comfort her. "Seems we've both been through it."

"Yes, we have."

When she glanced up warily and met his gaze, Nick cupped her cheek in his palm and bent forward, pressing a soft kiss to her lips. His heart pounded as he ended the kiss, though he did not release her face from his gentle hold. "I saw your husband's portrait back at Deepwood," he murmured, unable to help himself. "Forgive me, but the man in that picture wasn't good enough for you. It sounds to me like you were trapped in a prison of your own, just as I was."

"Yes," she breathed, nodding, her eyes closed as she nestled her cheek against his hand.

He kissed her brow. "You fought against your cage. Because you have a warrior's blood in your veins."

"It doesn't excuse the way I treated that poor man in my immaturity. I was petty and cruel—"

"He wasn't strong enough to handle you," he corrected her in a husky whisper. "I'd never let you get away with that if you were mine."

She gazed into his eyes. "If I were yours, there'd be no need." She leaned forward and suddenly kissed him.

Nick held very still as she pressed her lips to his, tasting him in searching speculation. Once more, he fought with all he had to hold himself back. The temptation nearly overpowered him.

He could have no doubt of her intent as she cupped his jaw and brushed her satin lips longingly against his, teasing him. "Do you know what I want for dessert, hmm?"

His pulse pounded as an idle smile passed over his lips. Her touch felt so good it was nearly painful. "The macaroons weren't enough for you?"

"Not nearly."

"We shouldn't do this," he murmured breathlessly as she toyed with his hair.

"We both want it."

"Yes. But some of us don't deserve it."

She kissed his cheek. "Don't deserve to be happy?"

He stopped her, grasping her arm firmly to force her back a small distance, making her meet his serious gaze. "I'm not some perfect knight, Virginia. You know that now. If you're still caught up in girlish daydreams about me, once the truth sinks in, you're going to hate me. You might even hate yourself if we do this. I'm a bad man."

"I'm not afraid," she answered, staring into his eyes. "I know what you are. I also know what you've sacrificed. You've given everything," she whispered. "Until you had nothing left to give. Oh, Nick. I know it's dangerous to love you, but the only way I'll hate myself is if I don't take the chance."

Her words intoxicated and slightly terrified him. *Love me?* He told himself she only meant that one, most dangerous word in the physical sense, surely.

Whether or not this was true, resisting her was futile. The gentle stroking of her fingertips down his cheek crumbled his resolve.

Overwhelming attraction pulled him to her like a planet swallowed up in her field of gravity. Enslaved. Passion gusted through him, a fire taking hold. Irrevocably drawn, he tilted his head as his lips approached hers. "So you like a gamble, too, then, do you?"

"You're worth the risk," she breathed.

He doubted it. Indeed, he was slightly bewildered. He still wasn't sure what all of this was . . . what her sleeping with him meant. Had he gone from being her prisoner to one of her "gentleman friends," or was she merely playing out a fantasy, sampling him just for the adventure of it?

He could not say. Everything in him feared what this could lead to, but when she licked her lips in anticipation of his kiss, he lost the fight. Sensuality glowed in her cobalt eyes, beckoning him, and he was helplessly seduced.

He cupped his hand around her nape and kissed her, slow and hard, his whole body throbbing with need.

It had been so very long.

*C*aught up in his kiss, Gin thrilled to the touch of his hands sliding around her waist, savoring her curves. She was already emboldened by wine, but his soft groan of pleasure inflamed her senses. She moved more firmly onto his lap, astraddle him; resting her elbows on his broad shoulders, she tangled her fingers in his silky, raven hair. Then she pulled his head back a little so she could kiss his neck and throat, and began untying his cravat.

Her fingers trembled with excitement. This was a dream come true. Nick Forrester in her bed. Paris. Together on a mission fraught with danger and excitement, and all night long to give their passions free rein.

He sat relatively still, his eyes closed, letting her do as she liked with him, hers for the taking. When she had done away with his cravat, she kissed her way back up over the stern angle of his jaw, roughened by his day's beard. His chest was heaving with want as she cupped his cheek gently and claimed his mouth once more, wantonly parting his lips with her tongue. She delved into the wine-flavored cove of his mouth to taste him more deeply while her busy fingers parted the V of his shirt.

She stroked his tongue eagerly with her own as her roaming fingertips discovered the sweet, beguiling notch between his rugged collarbones, a tiny spot of vulnerability.

Then her touch ventured downward while she went

on kissing him. She dipped her fingers slyly inside the recesses of his loose white shirt to touch his beautiful body, marveling at the warm, sculpted chest that had inspired her lust since that day in the hot-springs cave.

Nick, meanwhile, ran his big, capable hands smoothly up and down her back, caressing her. His palms slid without opposition over the slippery surface of her satin dressing gown. Then his hands moved to her hair, playing with it as he kissed her.

She could feel his fascination in his touch. With all the time he had spent in that cell—and before that, on the run from the Order, fearing for his life—who knew how long it had been since he had savored the texture of a woman's hair. She wondered ever so briefly about his former lovers. Had there ever been any especially important women to him in his life? Had any of them ever reached his guarded heart?

Could she?

She let the wistful question go when his hand trailed down from her tresses to her breast. He stopped kissing her, as though he had just forgotten how.

She smiled sensually against his mouth when she heard his whispered groan. "Is this really happening, or am I asleep?"

"Shall I pinch you, my lord?" With her hand still tucked inside his shirt, she pinched his nipple lightly in response.

He let out a throaty laugh. "You are such a naughty little baggage," he said in a dreamy purr.

With an arch smile, she gave his lower lip a little love bite in response. "Always happy to help."

He dragged his eyes open, heavy-lidded with desire, and gazed at her. His pupils were as black as the night sea, but their usual fiery expression—soulful, tortured, brooding—had changed to a glow of pleasure.

She was delighted by the change. "What is it, darling?" she prompted in a whisper.

He just shook his head, fixing her with a wary look of wonder.

"Relax," she breathed, and as she pressed a gentler sort of kiss to his lips, he reached for the cloth belt of her robe.

He untied it, parting the edges of her dressing gown like he was unwrapping a present. She supposed he was. But this night was also a gift to herself, the long-awaited culmination of a dream. She hoped she didn't regret it.

But how could she, when she felt how tenderly he stroked her chest? How delicately he moved the strap of her negligee aside and explored her shoulder, as if he had never touched a woman before.

She remembered how rough and rude he had been on the docks that night outside the Topaz Room. *Wicked boy,* she thought. He had certainly been trying to teach her a lesson that night, put her in her place. He was so different now. It seemed tonight he'd let his guard down for her. It was an opportunity she did not intend to waste—and a small, private triumph in itself that she knew she'd always treasure in her memory.

Having bared her breast, he cupped it in his hand with the most heavenly touch; he stopped kissing her again, as though all his marveling attention was focused on the curve and the weight and texture of the soft flesh in his hand. Increasingly restless with desire, Gin tilted her head back with a small groan, feeling that her body had been made for this moment. For him. She licked her lips and groaned aloud when he squeezed her swollen nipple softly. "You are beautiful," he uttered, as if the words were wrenched from his very soul.

She somehow managed to lift her eyelids to gaze at him and immediately thought, *So are you.* But she already knew he didn't want to hear it. Nothing could be permitted to break the spell that had gathered around them and encircled the bed in this deepening enchantment.

With a shrug, she let her dressing gown slip off her

shoulders. The satin whispered to the floor. The night air was cool against her bared arms, but her skin blazed with desire.

She helped Nick pull off his black jacket. Got rid of the untied cravat hanging around his neck. Feverishly unbuttoned the black waistcoat he still wore, and shoved it off his shoulders with a growing desperation pounding in her blood.

Their lips barely grazed in a panting kiss as he threw his shed garments aside. Gin pulled his shirt free of his trouser waist, then he paused to lift the shirt off over his head.

A happy little sigh of admiration escaped her at his sculpted male beauty. He smiled and lowered his head ruefully—which only delighted her more. How could such a dangerous man be so adorable? she wondered. She shook her head, mystified, as she gazed at him, then he started kissing her again.

Inspired by his sculpted muscles and velveteen skin, Gin became a woman on a mission. While his heated kiss trailed down her neck, and his fingers plied the hem of her floor-length peignoir, slowly hitching it up over her thighs, she unfastened his black trousers and freed him. She sighed with anticipation as she trailed her fingers up the hot, silken sides of his shaft in a teasing caress. He shuddered when she wrapped her hand around it and vigorously squeezed, then took up a no-nonsense rhythm, stroking, pleasuring him.

Time had lost all meaning, but it seemed barely minutes had passed when he shifted her forward onto his lap, his hands shaking as he gripped her around the waist.

Gin's heart thundered with her yearning for him.

Bracing the balls of her bare feet on the floor, she rose from his lap, kissing him hungrily as she guided him to the dew-slicked threshold of her passage. Then she took him in, inch by hard, velvet inch, lowering herself, and gasping with pleasure at his penetration.

They fit together perfectly—though he was wonderfully large. Her body opened to accommodate him.

"Mmm." She closed her eyes and dug her fingers into his steely shoulders as she settled fully onto his lap, savoring him so deep inside her.

He kissed her shoulder and breathed some utterance, incoherent in his thrall. His motions were gentle as he held her on his lap, but with their bodies joined, she could feel every inch of him throbbing. He was a thunderstorm of hard, needy lust, trying with all his might not to break.

"Quit holding back." She barely mouthed the words at his ear, they were so soft. Yet they made him groan.

"I don't want to hurt you," he rasped.

"You won't," she promised, petting his head for a moment, pressing a dazed kiss to his brow, rooting for him to let go.

She loved a storm. Always had, since her youth. She used to sneak outside when one hit and throw her arms up to the sky, spinning in the rain as it drenched her face, her hair. Admittedly, she had never flung herself into one so powerful before.

Maybe it was madness to bait him, but she wanted to give herself to him. She had no regrets. Anyway, it was too late now. He was deep inside her, there on the edge of the bed. She sat astride him, and it felt more right than anything she had ever known.

Nick had his eyes closed and a rapturous look on his face as he pulled her closer, fixing her more firmly on his member. He could not even speak.

She could see he was absorbed in sheer sensation as he took hold of her hips and began to rock her. She let him move her as he willed, happy to comply; she joined his churning motion as he took his pleasure of her. He gripped her buttocks harder; she set her knees on the bed. After a time, she slowly pushed him down on his back.

Her hair fell forward, hiding them together in a veil of secrecy as she lowered her head to kiss him again and again. She stroked his bare chest as she rode him, but within moments, he'd had more than he could bear. He thrust her roughly onto her back and mounted her, his hard body sweating and heaving, crushing her deliciously under his weight.

She wrapped her legs around him in total surrender as he took her, until, all of a sudden, he gasped out, "I'm sorry, I can't hold back." The words tore from him, ragged with passion and shame. "I need you—"

"It's all right," she breathed with more tenderness than he was capable of noticing at the moment. "Come to me," she whispered, arching her back to brush her breasts against his muscled chest.

Nick obeyed, unable to do otherwise. She thrashed with pleasure, goading him with her body, as massive jolts of sweet torment racked him. He clutched her hair and her shoulder so hard as he came that it hurt a bit. She didn't mind at all, enraptured by his anguished cries of ecstasy.

He pulled out at the last second and spilled his seed into the folds of her peignoir. She supposed that was wise, but her body flinched at the denial. A fleeting thought of having his child only inflamed her the more, especially now that he had left her still craving release.

It was a state of affairs he remedied well as soon as he recovered some semblance of his wits. She lay there watching him, still on fire herself, but so gratified by the glow of pleasure that had come over him.

"Well, that took the edge off," he panted at length.

"It was good?"

"Earth-shattering, I believe, is the word."

She grinned. "I'm jealous."

"Patience, darling." He stripped her naked, getting rid of her ruined silk peignoir with a mumbled "Sorry."

She waved off his apology with a chuckle and a shake of her head. It did not signify. She had dozens more back at home, and he could ruin them all in this manner if he liked. When she took it off, he ordered her under the covers with a smoldering stare.

Then he got up and finished the job of undressing. She leaned against the headboard and folded her arms behind her head and watched him in possessive appreciation.

He kicked off his shoes, then stripped the rest of the way down. When he had shed his black trousers and short drawers, her sultry stare traveled down his sculpted body in leisurely fashion, lingering on his phallus. Still engorged but no longer erect for the moment, it hung thickly from its surrounding tangle of black hair.

"Get a good look?" Nick drawled as he returned to the bed.

"You're a beautiful man," she said with a shrug.

He scoffed as he slid under the covers with her. "Don't be absurd."

"It's true!"

"Right, well, yes, it's always been my life's ambition to join the dandies."

"Cheeky!" When he turned his back, reaching out to check the nearby candle, burning low, she gave his bare arse a playful slap.

He looked over his shoulder at her in astonishment.

She bit her lip, her eyes dancing.

"Careful," he warned. "I might like that. Or maybe you do." He suddenly rolled her over. "Does milady need a spanking?"

"Don't you dare," she whispered, though she could not hide how she thrilled to his warm, taunting caress as he rested his hand on the curve of her backside.

She shrieked when he suddenly clapped her bottom with a hearty, stinging slap.

"What a bad girl you are," he said.

"You are outrageous!"

"And what are you going to do about it?" he demanded.

She forgot to answer when he reached between her legs and began stroking her from behind. Still wet and oh so needy, she let out a desperate little gasp as he slipped a finger into her quivering passage.

"I'll tell you what you're going to do, Virginia," he continued, instructing her with his lips at her ear and his pleasantly scratchy chest against her back. "Whatever I say."

"Never happen," she denied in breathless tones.

"Watch," he replied, an edge of amusement in his whisper. Kissing her shoulder, he brought his fingertip slicked with her teeming nectar to the rigid and acutely sensitized center of her mound. He touched her as lightly as a butterfly. She groaned aloud and arched against his hand, until he laid her on her back and kissed her all over her body.

She was utterly enthralled as his mouth descended down her throat over her chest, where he surely heard the thunder of her wild heartbeat. He spent a good deal of time sucking her nipples, but soon he moved on.

It was torture, waiting, as his lips skimmed down her belly, until at last he pleasured her with his mouth. She ran her fingers through his hair, writhing with his kisses, moans of bliss spilling from her lips. Her arching body begging for release, he made her scream with fraught delight in seconds, but by now, Nick was ready to go again.

The cries of ecstasy had barely faded from her lips when he moved up to cover her with his body, and took her again. He kissed her with brazen aggression, dominating her just as he had promised. There was nothing she could do about it. Nothing she willed to do but anything he wished.

She could taste herself on his lips as he threaded his fingers through hers, pinning her to the bed. "Is this what you wanted, my lady?" he growled in deep, primal knowing.

"Oh, God, yes," she gasped, swept up in her ravishment. She raked her nails down his back, as though marking him, in turn, for her own.

And so it went throughout the night.

He made love to her for hours as the white autumn moon sailed across the black November sky and cast its ancient glow of magic over Paris.

$\mathcal{N}$ick awoke the next morning with Virgil's daughter sleeping in his arms, her head resting on his chest. Awareness returned gradually until he opened his eyes to find the flat gray light of morning filtering in through the closed doors of the balcony.

He felt curiously calm. Everything was peaceful. That was the first thing he noticed.

His constant companions, lo these many years—anger and loneliness—were noticeably absent. Gone. An anchor's weight from which his heart had been unexpectedly cut free.

He marveled at the light sensation as he listened to her breathing, slow and deep and restful, felt the play of each exhalation tickle his chest where he cradled her sweet head.

For a moment, he stared at her, taking in the exquisite rightness of her being there—just where she was, wrapped in his embrace. As if she were always meant to be there.

Damn, he thought mildly, unsettled by his own tenderness as he bent to inhale the flowery warm smell of her hair. *What have I got myself into here?* He had never been the lovelorn type. In fact, he usually mocked such men, but yet the kiss he pressed to her head was about as besotted as that of a newlywed husband.

Well.

All this was, of course, *not* what they were here for. And Virgil would certainly not have approved, considering how careful he had been to keep his daughter away from Nick and his fellow agents. No wonder the gruff old spymaster had always been such a mystery.

All those years he had directed his teams hither and thither digging up secrets across Europe, he had been slyly covering up his own.

Ah, well. His handler, her father, might not have approved, but it was too late now after they'd had their way with each other in every imaginable position all night long. A rascally smile passed across his face when he felt her stir.

She awoke tousled and thoroughly ravished, rolled onto her back with a sigh of contentment, taking a catlike stretch beside him. Then she gave him a sleepy little smile.

"Good morning, lovely."

She touched his face in weary affection. He kissed the dainty fingertip she brushed across his lips.

Then she pushed up from the bed and rose, naked.

"Ow," she remarked as she walked gingerly toward the screen in the corner behind which the washstand with its built-in chamber pot awaited. "God, Forrester, I can hardly walk, thank you very much."

"You're welcome," he replied, punching the pillow into the shape he wanted.

"Don't listen, I have to tinkle."

He chuckled in sleepy amusement. "You think you have any secrets from me now?"

She shot him an indignant pout from behind the screen before she disappeared again. "You *are* a bad man."

"Warned you," he replied, folding his arms under his head on the pillow and feeling quite the sultan of the earth.

He closed his eyes again, simply relaxing until she returned. Then he savored the sight of her sauntering across the room, every lithe, glorious inch of her nude body.

"Goddess," he murmured heartily.

Her nipples stood erect in the morning's chill. The vision instantly heated his blood. He was happy to warm her up. "Where do you think you're going?" he growled playfully when she passed by the bed heading for her main trunk of clothes. He leaned out from the bed and threw his arms around her hips, pulling her to him.

She let out a girlish squeal as he tumbled her back into bed with him.

"I haven't given you a proper good morning, my lady," he said with wolfish innuendo.

"Oh, Lord, I've created a monster," she replied.

"A very *friendly* monster," he whispered.

"Apparently so." She glanced down with a breathless laugh at his raging member nudging insistently at her thigh.

Nick grinned like a pirate.

He swept her nearer, curling her body into his, spoon fashion, but his intents were not exactly for a cuddle.

"Nick!" she protested halfheartedly.

"Come on," he whispered at her ear, stroking up and down her silken side until she stopped fussing uncertainly.

"Honestly. Shouldn't we get a start on our day?"

"Soon, my lady," he breathed. "I want to love you again." His choice of words melted her resistance and startled even him.

It had not been a calculated statement, nor even a euphemism. Somehow that particular verb flowed off his tongue with alarming ease with her.

With any other woman, he was sure he'd have said something far more earthy.

His heartbeat boomed in the morning stillness like the cadets' morning practice at the artillery range as she yielded to him. Given her body's permission, he slipped his needy prick into the velvet welcome of her core as they both lay on their sides. Before long, this position no longer satisfied.

He pressed her forward onto her stomach and took her from behind. Soon she was on her hands and knees before him, and Nick had hold of her hips, kneeling behind her.

"So good," he whispered in mindless bliss.

It turned out to be nowhere near as quick an exercise as he had promised. Not after they had enjoyed their sport so many times last night. If she was using him— and he didn't think she was, not anymore—he had already made up his mind that he didn't even care.

He brought her to a wrenching climax that he believed the whole Île de la Cité heard quite clearly, including the nearby convent.

When he tried roguishly to cover her mouth with his hand to muffle the sound, the vixen bit his finger. He laughed, which threw him off his rhythm. He lost it for a moment, but she endured until he found it again.

Intoxicated with her, he wrapped his arms around her hips as he drove into her, savoring every stroke, until that perfect moment of release.

Pleasure exploded across his consciousness. Lightning ran down his every nerve ending. He clung to her, gasping, burying his face against her silky-smooth back. She stopped him from pulling out this time. Instinct had taken hold of her. She drove her hips back, keeping him inside her. Nick didn't fight it, but sank back to a kneeling position, sitting on his heels; she lifted herself upright, also on her knees, but facing forward, her thighs spread, her splendid body draped across his lap.

He wrapped his arms around her slim waist as her elegant undulations milked his cock of every last drop of his seed. When they both were spent, she laid her head back on his shoulder, panting after the storm.

He remained ensheathed in her, feeling as close to her in that moment as he had ever been to any human being. As though their two spirits had somehow, over the course of the night, become knitted together. He caught himself on the verge of saying, *I love you.*

What the hell? Surely that was madness. He tried to shake it off. But deep down, he knew as he held her that he wouldn't think twice about giving his life for this woman if the moment ever came.

"Mmm." She lifted herself a bit higher on her knees, breaking the seal of their joining, but only to welcome him into her arms when she lay back down on the bed.

Neither of them spoke of the fact that he might have just got her pregnant.

As he laid his head on her chest with a sigh, he doubted he was in any shape for the next thirty seconds or so for catching villains.

He didn't care. Not for the next minute or two. There would always be evil in the world, but sometimes there was love, or at least beauty.

He had faced death so many times that he had learned to treasure those fleeting brushes with the inherent glory hidden behind all things.

She stroked his hair and his shoulder and kissed the top of his head. "Hungry?" she murmured.

"Starved," he purred.

"Me, too."

They had both worked up an appetite last night, to be sure.

"I'll order some food. What do you want for breakfast?" she asked, kissing his forehead tenderly.

"Surprise me," he answered, lazy as a lion.

He moved aside to let her up, then yawned and

stretched and rubbed his eyes and started thinking about getting up for the day.

But as he watched her walk across the chamber, wonderfully comfortable, it seemed, being naked as Eve, he suddenly could not fathom attempting the American wilderness without female companionship.

Then he frowned. Obviously, the sophisticated baroness would never agree to go along with him on the journey. Dark, uncharted forest filled with hostile tribes, poisonous snakes, man-eating bears, deadly rivers that, after a point, became the only roads? Not a modiste's shop nor a ballroom in sight?

No, the woman wasn't a lunatic.

And for the life of him, Nick suddenly couldn't fathom why he had ever wanted to go in the first place.

It was so much better wherever she was.

God, you are an idiot, he told himself, but he didn't care. *Stick to your principles, man.*

Of course, he didn't actually have any of those, now, did he?

And besides, who could say? The luscious Lady Burke might harbor a streak of the pioneer spirit.

She was half-Scottish, after all. She might surprise him. God knew, she had already done that repeatedly last night—and, indeed, from the first moment he had laid eyes on her through the bars of his dungeon cell.

Presently, as he watched her getting dressed with a possessive glow in his eyes, another stray question ran unbidden through his mind. Who exactly were these "gentlemen friends" who had shared a bed with her?

He bristled, shocked by his own reaction.

Not so much by his mild anger at her, that she'd behave that way, putting so little value on the treasure that she was. But utter, blind rage toward the men.

The thought of any lovers' ever treating his goddess in a cavalier fashion made him want to kill all "gentlemen friends" guilty of this crime.

Now, now, he told himself, blinking his way back to reason. She was an adult, free to do as she pleased, and too smart to let herself be taken advantage of.

Then again, she had to know what she was getting into, becoming the lover of a trained assassin.

Nick noted his own fiery reaction and realized this could possibly explain another reason why Virgil had never told his boys about his beautiful daughter.

With all of them vowing to protect her, it could have resulted in a very high body count, indeed.

She might even have become the one woman who could have made them turn against each other. Maybe Virgil had known the sort of effect she could have on them.

Hell, maybe it was his boys rather than his femme fatale of a daughter that the old man had been protecting—their cohesiveness as a unit—knowing how she could easily have made them rivals.

Whatever the answer, Nick did his best to shake off his distraction and tore his gaze away from her. Oh, but this woman brought out the most primal side of him. An animalistic side of him, worthy of the wilderness. Fully ready to kill any rival male who stepped too near his mate.

His mate?

Good God. That was all quite enough. He took a deep breath and forced himself out of the honey trap of that bed, willing himself to remember he was primarily a soldier.

Not some lovesick jackass of a poet.

Stalking off behind the screen, he opened the washstand to perform his morning ablutions while Virginia rang for a servant to bring them the house breakfast.

Sanity returned for the most part after he had splashed his face.

Still, he was covered in her scent, marked by her love bites and the light scratches she had raked down his body in some fit of passion or another over the night's velvet hours. *Whew*, he thought, shaking his head at his reflection in the mirror.

Then he poured more water from the pitcher into the basin and proceeded to wash. But he paused, smiling wryly when he discovered the mouth-shaped bruise at the base of his neck. Well, she *had* promised she'd give him a sign.

And there it was, he thought wryly.

Rather like an owner's mark.

A while later, Nick went out on his own to have a look around inside L'Hôtel Grande Alexandre. He wanted to scout out the territory before them, get a feel for the lay of the land before it was time to present their game piece.

He would mark the locations of the exits, check to see what sort of security the hotel had in place, and keep an eye out for any suspicious people among the hotel guests. He believed he could visually pick them out of the crowd—the sort of shadowy characters who might be also there to enroll in the Bacchus Bazaar.

Gin remained behind to monitor the people coming and going from the hotel through her telescope. Staying discreetly veiled behind the curtains, she had a good view from the glass doors of the balcony, and they had agreed that if she saw anything out of place, she would open the balcony doors and signal to him.

They both were on the lookout for anyone fitting the description of the mysterious Rotgut. Surely, that low criminal would stand out like a fly in a bowl of lemon sorbet in the lobby of the glittering hotel.

Peering through her little brass telescope, she followed Nick's progress from her perch by the balcony doors. A sated glow of luxuriant pleasure and just a hint of possessiveness filled her as she watched him stride in his bold, confident way down the cobbled street.

She smiled to herself to note the almost jaunty spring in his step after the way she had taken care of him last night. Oh, yes, she quite believed she was getting to him. It thrilled her heart to think she had the power to make that hard, dangerous man happy.

Perhaps it was just as well they had parted ways for now, both of them a little overwhelmed by the intensity of the bond that had blossomed between them.

After the whirlwind of last night, she suspected he needed a little time alone to get his bearings.

So did she, which was why she did not insist on going with him.

Honestly, she was stunned and disturbed by the impulse he had revealed lurking in her heart: the secret, shameful craving to be dominated by a powerful man. She, who supposedly loved being in control at all times!

She wondered if he had somehow sensed that contradictory need in her all along, for he had satisfied it in spades last night. Maybe he had simply seen through her, she mused. He knew a lot about the world and people.

And, apparently, women.

And just to prove how deftly he had turned the tables on her, she found herself wondering, like some wistful, seventeen-year-old mooncalf, what she meant to him. How and where and even *if* she fit into his plans?

What did last night really mean to him?

Probably just an affair, she thought, and oh, *God,* it was not a good sign that she already felt her heart clench at the possibility—the probability—that whatever this was, it couldn't last.

Surely such dizzying happiness could only lead to pain. But she could not stop herself. It was too late. She had already made up her mind to take the gamble.

He was everything she had ever wanted, and yes,

he had his problems, but they didn't scare her. She did not require perfection. Eyes open to the risks, she could not pass up the chance to know what it meant to fall recklessly, passionately in love with the man of her dreams.

If it was not to be, well, then, the coming agony was worth it for the chance to have had this time with him.

Even so, it was a little scary. What had become of her hardened attitude, seemingly overnight? He had cracked her worldly shell and found the vulnerable woman's heart beneath it.

Ah, but it turned out the assassin had a softer side, too, she mused fondly as she scanned the street with her telescope, seeing nothing of any consequence.

She had discovered his vulnerable side for herself, indeed, had quite fallen in love with it last night during her "interview" of him.

Somehow, she had coaxed him into letting her in. Answering her questions. Lowering his guard. What she did now with this rare trust from the Order's lone wolf could make all the difference in the world where his life might go from here.

She took it as a grave responsibility. Never in a million years would he ever say he needed to be loved, but it was so plain to her that he did.

He was starving for it, after all he'd been through, and she could do naught but pour out all her tenderness on him in response. She knew it was exactly what he needed. Already the change in him was nigh miraculous, after just one night. Which was why, for however long this lasted, she felt sure she could make a difference for him. Maybe even change the whole course of his life.

He had certainly changed hers.

Yes, she decided, whatever pain might come when they parted ways, seeing Nick Forrester walk away healed would be reward enough in itself.

Through her telescope, she saw him pause on the

curb across from the hotel, waiting as a delivery wagon of some sort went clattering past.

Then he crossed the street, hands in pockets, the wind billowing through his long, dark greatcoat. Head down, he had his collar turned up against the gray drizzle. He walked toward the hotel with the air of a man who knew exactly what he was doing.

A sigh escaped her. But the truth was, taking him for a lover was not the only gamble she had made.

In the midst of all this, she was keenly aware that she had not been fully honest with him yet.

She had not lied, but she had not told the truth, either. Knowing him, the longer she put off coming clean, the worse it was going to be.

But, God, she did not want to break this little magic bubble of happiness in which they two had unexpectedly found themselves yet.

It was too precious.

What if it actually *could* somehow last between them? she wondered. What if he fell in love with her, too?

But he was Nick. He never fell in love with anyone, according to her father's scribblings on each of his agents' temperaments. Nick Forrester, the hard case, the skeptic. Moody, broody, difficult.

But not to me, she thought with a happy little sigh.

She had known she could manage him.

Lowering her telescope to take a sip of coffee and another bite of her very French breakfast of *pain-au-chocolat*, she found herself wondering how her relationship with Nick might impact Phillip's life. Or, for that matter, what her son would say if he wound up with a baby brother or sister as a result of last night. Or even what Society would say if she bore Baron Forrester a love child?

Well, they'd say she was as much of a hussy as her mother, the Countess of Ashton, she supposed.

But to hell with the ton. She had a title, lands, her own fortune. She need answer to no one. Her days of living at the mercy of other people's opinions were long behind her.

In truth, heaven help her, the prospect of having Nick's baby made her quiver with nervous, giddy joy down to her very toes. She loved being a mother, and he was, to be sure, excellent breeding stock.

Of course, if a baby came . . . there was always marriage.

I am obviously losing my mind. She adjusted the focus on her telescope and strove to shake herself back to sanity. Hadn't she vowed never to marry again after that dreadful experience?

But maybe, just maybe, she could make an exception. For the baby's sake, merely. Should a baby arrive.

In any case, daydreaming about what sort of father Nick would be was easier than dealing with the question of how to tell him the rest of the story.

Why they were really here.

You should have told him by now, her conscience accused her.

She did her best to shrug it off. *No, I shouldn't. I wasn't even sure if I could trust him. Look where I found the man!*

Besides, she had warned him from the start that he would only be given information as he needed it.

He hadn't needed it yet.

Admittedly, he was going to need it soon.

Oh, but what if this belated revelation drove him away from her now, that he had only just begun eating out of her hand like a wild horse?

Unpredictable as he was, it was impossible to anticipate what he was going to say when she gave him the full revelation.

It was not that she feared his flying into a rage. She

doubted a cool-nerved agent with that many years of experience would blow up at her.

It was simply that when she admitted her blunder that had led to all this, he would probably assume she had made the mistake because she was a woman daring to take on tasks that were usually the purview of men.

And so help her, if he dared say to her that a woman had no place meddling in such things, she did not think she would ever forgive him.

She knew full well that everyone thought that way, men and women alike, but somehow from Nick, she knew she'd take it personally.

Deep down, she wanted his respect almost as much as she had wanted Virgil's. Real respect, not pretty chivalry, so he'd see her as an equal.

But having to tell him what had happened, admit that she had trusted John Carr more than she ought, was going to play right into that old, wearisome misapprehension that she did not know what she was doing because she was a woman daring to play a man's game. Therefore, any small mistake she ever made was magnified.

Especially mistakes that weren't so small.

She swallowed hard to think of the near disaster she had created. Bloody hell, how was she to know John Carr would betray her in a fit of pique at her rejection?

That little lying vermin of a thief.

But she could not keep putting it off forever.

It was just that she cringed to think of Nick's looking at her the way her father sometimes had when she tried to involve herself in intrigues. That patronizing, I-told-you-so, why-don't-you-stay-home-knitting-dear sort of look.

It was enough to make a spirited woman despair.

Well, she'd tell him soon. She just hoped that when she did, he would not overreact even though the implications of John's theft were horrifying, indeed.

If she did not get her father's journal back before the

auction, in starkest terms, then John Carr would sell the Order's secrets to the highest bidder.

Loyal assets could be hunted down and killed in retaliation long after the fact. Traps could be laid all over the place for the now-retired agents.

All their blood would be on her hands, simply because she had underestimated her hired assistant, all the while indulging him, taking him for a harmless, pretty fool.

Ah, well. She assured herself she'd soon get the journal safely back into her possession. But she was going to need Nick's help, and for that, she was going to have to tell him the full truth.

Which meant breaking this silence of hers and getting over her own stubborn pride.

Yes, she dreaded the thought of losing his respect, but she had no right to keep the secret any longer than necessary when so much was at stake.

As soon as he got back from casing the hotel, she decided, she would sit him down and tell him how her father had provided for her protection after his death.

And how she had thoroughly botched it.

Chapter
15

$\mathcal{P}$ast the gaudy lions and through the frosted-glass doors, Nick stepped into the huge, bustling entrance hall—now the hotel lobby—of the Grande Alexandre.

Sauntering in discreetly, he moved unnoticed among the elegant travelers coming and going. A party of rich, loudmouthed, fashionable matrons waited for their carriage to take them out on their Parisian shopping spree. They talked incessantly among themselves, snapping an order now and then at their attending maids, while their spoiled children ran about at a wild game of sliding on their feet across the sprawling marble floors, slicked by the damp and mud from everyone's shoes. The wee hellions' uproarious laughter echoed under the colonnade.

Nick frowned at seeing all these children on hand when such unsavory folk as the attendees of the Bacchus Bazaar were also in the building.

But where? He kept his eyes open for anyone who fit the bill.

He counted up the exits and the large footmen placed here and there who looked capable of security duty.

Then he turned his attention to the concierge's stand, quite the hub of activity in the center of the entrance hall, several yards from the foot of the grand staircase.

The uniformed concierge, obviously annoyed by the noisy children, strove to answer guests' questions in several languages and to meet the ceaseless demands of the morning crowd of tourists gathered around his desk.

Nick scanned the area, but nothing seemed out of place as the concierge labored on, pointing guests this way and that, giving directions, arranging for carriages, and suggesting plays and concerts, lectures, galleries, and exhibitions that the holidaymakers might enjoy.

Bloody hell, that chap had the patience of a saint. Nick bought a newspaper from the old man selling stacks of them in the corner, then strolled over to the sprawling, once-aristocratic music room, which had been converted to a café for hotel guests and the public. The very wide doorway looking into the entrance hall gave him a good view of everything.

He had a cup of coffee, watching everyone and everything for a while. Though his senses were on high alert, taking in as many details as he could absorb, he had to take care to keep Virginia out of his mind.

He missed her already. How absurd.

Nevertheless, he smiled as he sipped his coffee. It was a happy thought, knowing she was waiting for him back in their room across the way. But he pushed her out of his mind. Thinking of her would only distract him.

A few possibly suspicious-looking people walked through the lobby as he sat there, but Nick homed in on one rugged fellow who trudged into the café and ordered breakfast. He could tell he was English the moment he spoke. Sounded like a Geordie, and then he had to go and order bangers and eggs for breakfast to confirm it.

He was not well dressed, a large man with weathered

skin like a sailor and a scar on his face, all of which made him very out of place in the elegant Grande Alexandre.

Might this be the mysterious Rotgut, captain of the *Black Jest*? Nick watched him like a hawk as he scarfed down his breakfast in a few huge gulps.

When the waiter brought his bill, Nick saw the man ask for a pencil, then scribbled his name and room number, adding it to his hotel tab.

The moment the brawny suspect got up, wiping his mouth roughly on his napkin before tossing it onto his empty plate, Nick engrossed himself in his paper. The man trudged past his table, but as soon as he left the restaurant, Nick rose and moved over stealthily to the waiter's stand to sneak a look at that bill.

It was right on top of the stack, easy to find.

He spotted the name, E. DOLAN, though he doubted it was his real one. *There,* though, on the second line, there was his room number: fourteen.

The waiter returned from delivering food to another table. "Can I help you, monsieur?"

Nick turned impatiently. "More coffee, please. I've been trying to get your attention for some time," he said curtly, distracting the lad from his snooping with a show of annoyance.

"Oh, I am so sorry, sir! I did not see you—"

"Never mind," he grumbled. "What do I owe you?"

He paid and stalked out, eager to pay a call on Room Fourteen. If E. Dolan was in there, he'd confront him. If he wasn't, Nick would search his room and dig up any clues about where Rotgut was hiding his "merchandise," the girls. They had to be freed before the auction.

On the far end of the lobby, he spotted the opening to the main hallway that gave access to the guest rooms upstairs. A mansion of this size probably had seventy chambers for guests. A plaque on the wall beside it spelled out which blocks of rooms were situated where.

Nick headed for it, but marching past the concierge's stand, he overheard a snippet of conversation that stopped him in his tracks.

"Please send a servant up to tell him John Carr is here to see him."

John Carr?

"Oui, monsieur," the concierge replied, and sent a nearby servant running to bring another guest a message.

Nick turned, homing in on the young man in a tan greatcoat waiting restlessly at the concierge desk.

Well, what have we here?

A ridiculously good-looking young peacock, he had taken off his gloves and clutched them in his hand, tapping them nervously against his pantalooned thigh as he waited with his elbow on the edge of the concierge's little desk.

Nick shook his head to clear it, staring at the princely young fellow in his early twenties.

This didn't seem right, or even possible, according to what Virginia had told him. *I thought he got abducted.*

"John Carr" was a reasonably common name, but still, this would have to have been one hell of a coincidence.

It had to be the same man, Virginia's so-called apprentice. More like her toy boy, Nick thought as he approached warily to investigate.

Room Fourteen wasn't going anywhere for the moment.

An irksome beat of jealousy added extra vigor to his pulse. Her "beautiful boy" looked like he'd stepped out of a bloody Raphael painting. Tousled golden curls, fine-boned profile, blue eyes.

Eyes full of fear, Nick noted as he studied him covertly.

Carr's anxious gaze darted all around the lobby; thus, he quickly saw Nick sizing him up.

The pretty fellow must have been used to people staring at him, for he merely gave a taut nod and mumbled a gentlemanly greeting.

At once, Nick decided on a whim to seize the element of surprise. "John Carr?" he asked, going toward him with a cordial smile.

"Yes? Yes!" The lad drew in his breath, then lowered his voice. "Mr. Truveau? I just had them send a servant up for you. I didn't realize you were standing right behind me." With a nervous smile, he put out his hand.

Nick did not accept the offered handshake, for his blood had run cold at the name.

Truveau?

That name belonged to one of the great French families of the Prometheans.

What the hell?

He knew that the old man Truveau, the patriarch, was newly dead. Nick and his colleagues had dealt with many vicious younger members of the conspirators' clan in their day, but one must have survived.

Carr withdrew his rejected hand awkwardly. "Um, I've brought it with me," he murmured, touching the opposite breast of his coat to indicate some hidden shape beneath.

Nick nodded as if he had any idea what the lad was talking about. "Good."

"Of course, it's all in code," Carr said nervously. "I can't begin to decipher it."

"That shouldn't be a problem," he assured him, as if he knew exactly what he was talking about.

Relief filled Carr's face. "I'm glad to hear it."

Nick glanced discreetly around the lobby, wondering how long he had before the real Truveau appeared.

He had apparently stumbled upon a very interesting meeting.

The concierge arched an eyebrow, looking on in curiosity, now that the tourists had finally left him alone. Had the hotel attendant already realized that Nick was not the real Truveau?

"So, um, would you like to see it? I assume you've brought my money?"

"Yes, of course. Give it to me." Nick flicked his fingers impatiently and put out his hand, keen to know what all this was about.

Carr looked at him in surprise. "Here, sir? Shouldn't we go somewhere more private? You're not the only interested party, as I mentioned. Thus the price. I think a couple of them are following me." Carr glanced around again, pale with nerves, and suddenly saw something that made him blanch. "They're coming!" he forced out all of a sudden. "What do we do?"

Nick glanced over his shoulder, following Carr's stare. Three mean-looking men in crisp black clothes were marching toward them.

"Quickly, give it to me." Whatever the item in question was, it was obviously important.

"Not until you've paid me!"

"I'm not Truveau, you young fool," he whispered as the three henchmen bore down on them. "Now, would you like me to stop them from killing you or not?"

Carr looked at him in shock. "Who are you?"

"A friend of Lady Burke's," Nick replied.

At that, the lad cursed, spun around, and sprinted, fleeing past Nick right out the door.

A baffling reaction.

Damn it, Virginia, what the blazes haven't you told me? Nick thought, already in motion.

He heard indignant shouts and exclamations of alarm from behind him in the lobby as Truveau's Promethean henchmen (as best he could judge them) pushed travelers out of their way, racing after them.

Nick dashed out the door, past the gaudy lions and the pillars, looked to the left, then spotted the lad tearing off down the street to his right, past La Maison de Maxime.

"Get back here!" he bellowed.

Carr kept running.

Nick gave chase, sending a look of fury toward the balcony as he ran past. *I'm going to turn you over my knee in earnest for this one, girl.* Then he pounded on, his stare fixed on the fleeing young idiot.

$\mathcal{W}$ith a gasp of shock, Gin burst out onto the balcony, still clutching the folding telescope in her hand. The last thing she had expected to see was Nick chasing John Carr down the street.

Oh, no! That wasn't supposed to happen! He was only supposed to be there on surveillance, not to intervene! More to the point, her deception was unmasked. John Carr was clearly not a kidnap victim. What Nick must be thinking right now, she could not begin to guess.

Something must have gone seriously wrong in there.

Then she realized it was even worse than she had thought, as three black-clad men came racing out of the hotel after them.

A curse left her lips; crushing guilt filled her. How could she have sent Nick in there without knowing the full story?

This was her fault. She had to help him.

Whirling away from the railing, she rushed inside and grabbed her pistol, then ran out of the room, slamming the door shut behind her.

Her bootheels pounding on the wooden stairs, she raced down the steps and across the lobby. Monsieur de Vence looked up in astonishment from organizing something under his desk as she went dashing out the door.

Out on the curb, Georges was holding a horse's bridle for a dandyish guest who was just returning, perhaps from a morning gallop. The gentleman dismounted and tipped his hat to her as Gin brushed past him in the doorway.

At once, she ran over and commandeered the horse. "Sorry, Georges, I need to borrow him." Swinging up into the saddle, she did not waste a second thinking about scandal—or basic property rights.

"Madame!"

"I'll bring him right back."

"But he belongs to that gentleman!"

She gathered the reins and kicked the tall, leggy bay into motion. "I'll buy him if there's any trouble. Tell him to name his price!" She turned the horse around and urged him into a canter.

It was cold without her coat and hat, but she ignored the chill, racing to catch up to Nick.

Thankfully, she spotted him as soon as she turned the corner, and being on horseback gave her an obvious advantage. Within seconds, she rode past the three black-clad strangers, and was already gaining on Nick.

When he heard hoofbeats coming up behind him, Nick looked over his shoulder as he ran. He saw it was her and glared. "Are you mad? Get back to the hotel!" he yelled, as she pulled ahead of him. "Virginia, what are you doing?"

Getting back what's mine, she thought, her jaw set with determination.

John Carr was now in her sights, the little thief.

Coaxing the horse to a faster gait, she was able to get ahead of the fleeing man; she turned the horse, abruptly cutting in front of John, forcing him to halt.

His chest heaving, his cheeks scarlet from his sprint, he glared at her and tried to back away. She used the horse to herd him and hem him in.

Shifting the reins into her left hand, she held out her right. "Give it back, you ungrateful little viper."

"Go to hell, redheaded witch!"

"Give back what you stole from me," she repeated.

He sneered. "I told you you'd regret the way you brushed me off." Then he saw his chance.

Without warning, John dodged sideways into a narrow walkway between the brick buildings.

The horse was too broad across to fit into that cramped passage, but Nick caught up just then and took over from there. "Go back!" he ordered as he slipped into the dark, narrow walkway after John.

She fumed at the command. She had no intention of doing that, obviously. But with an angry glance, she saw that the three men were coming.

It terrified her to contemplate what they wanted. Could it be that John had already found an interested party who wanted to buy her father's journal before it even reached the auction?

Her throat constricted with dread, she clucked to the horse and headed for the intersection ahead. She'd have to ride around the blasted block to continue her chase.

But when she saw the three strangers fling around the corner, dodging into the shadowed passageway, she saw fit to yell out a warning to Nick.

"They're coming!"

I know, Nick thought crisply, irked. He pounded on, racing at top speed down the bricked passageway. *I'm going to wring her neck if I ever figure out what's actually going on.* He could not believe she had lied to him.

Then he scoffed at himself for being surprised.

So John Carr had stolen something from her: the object he had not wanted to hand over back at the hotel. Nick intended to find out what it was.

God knew he needed some shred of truth, as he was suddenly questioning everything she had ever said to him.

There wasn't much time for getting answers when he

finally inched forward enough to grab the young fop by his coat near the far end of the passageway.

Chest heaving, Nick hurled him into the wall.

"What did you take from her? Give it to me."

"Get off me!" Carr kept thrashing, but Nick clasped his lapel and shoved him back, then pinned him there with his forearm planted across the lad's throat.

"I don't want to hurt you. Whatever it is, hand it over. Now."

Carr stopped struggling abruptly and laughed at him, taken aback. "What, you don't even know what it is? You mean she didn't tell you? How typical! Oh, you should stay away from her, my friend. She'll only make your life a misery."

Nick scowled while John Carr laughed, ignoring the three men who'd be upon them in another moment.

"I take it you're her latest gentleman friend?" the lad bit out, his voice dripping with sarcasm. "Don't worry, she'll be done with you soon, too."

Nick punched him in the face with a glower. "No time to chat, sorry." Having sufficiently stunned his quarry, it was a simple matter to reach into Carr's coat and find the item hidden in his waistcoat.

His fingers clasped a small, leather-bound book.

As he pulled it out, and found it tied closed with a leather cord, Carr rallied to try to wrest it back out of his grasp.

"What is this?" Nick demanded. He could hear the pounding footfalls in the darkness, only seconds away from them now.

"It's mine, is what it is!"

As they fought over the book, Nick suddenly saw the white Maltese cross, insignia of the Order, engraved on the bottom center of the book's back cover.

It shocked him.

This time, he grasped Carr by the throat as he slammed him back against the wall, and his habitual motion was so quick that the knife appeared in Nick's hand almost by magic. "Why were you meeting with Truveau?" he asked, bringing the blade up to the corner of the lad's too-perfect face. "Are you a Promethean?"

"What? Me? No!" Understanding flooded his eyes at last. "You're with the Order?" he whispered.

"What do you think?" Nick snarled in reply.

Carr looked at him, wide-eyed and stock-still, as though he realized for the first time in that moment the colossal scale of his mistake.

That would explain why, when Nick turned to deal with their pursuers, Carr took his chance and fled, abandoning the book.

Nick knew he had only seconds to choose his ground.

He instantly shoved the book into his waistcoat and ran out the far end of the passageway, placing himself in position with his back to the wall beside the opening.

Muscles tensed, weapons ready, he waited for them to emerge.

$\mathcal{W}$hen the three black-clad men—whoever the hell they were—came barreling through the dark, narrow passageway in single file, the first one who burst out of the opening got a back-knuckle blow to the face that possibly broke his nose on impact, judging by the crunch.

A bloodcurdling scream came out of him as he dropped like a stone, apparently not realizing he was lucky he hadn't been met with a bullet instead.

Immediately, Nick pivoted into the alley, lifting his pistol to halt the others in their tracks, but the second man calculated his options just as quickly; then he did the only thing he *could* do to avoid being shot point-blank. He put his head down and charged straight at Nick with a war cry.

Brave, Nick thought begrudgingly, but he pulled the trigger anyway as the man tackled him out into the alley beyond the passageway. His shot flew high, ricocheting off the brick side of the building.

Pain blazed through his back as the man slammed him to the ground, diving on top of him with a *woof*.

The wind knocked out of him, Nick saw the third man run out of the passageway, but number three barely spared the rest of them a glance. All business, he immediately fixed his sights on the fleeing John Carr.

The blond sneak was bolting up the alley, trying to escape. At once, the third henchman took a stance to shoot Carr in the back.

Time always seemed to slow in these sorts of situations, and as he brawled on the ground against the second fellow, Nick's mind had already been collecting details about these unknown enemies.

From the automatic way they worked as a team to the excellent form the gunman looming nearby took as he aimed his pistol at John Carr—to say nothing of the impressive left hook that suddenly rammed Nick in the side of the head, courtesy of henchman number two—it was obvious they were very well trained, possibly men of his own profession.

Ow. Nick was seeing stars but somehow managed to lunge partially free of the milling match; he gained just enough distance to stretch out and kick the gunman's knee without warning, knocking him off-balance just as he pulled the trigger.

The shooter's aim went wide: What was meant as a headshot glanced off Carr's right shoulder.

Snapping out an elegant French curse word, while farther down the alley, Carr stumbled to his knees with a scream, the gunman turned his attention now to Nick.

Only to find that Nick suddenly had a knife pressed to the throat of his comrade, the one who had tackled him.

"Put the gun down, or I cut his throat," Nick informed him, chest heaving. "Go on. Throw it out of arm's reach."

"Let him go," another voice responded.

Nick glanced over warily and saw that the fellow whose nose he had bloodied had rejoined the party, and unlike the man who had just shot John Carr, he had not yet expended the bullet in his single-shot pistol.

His was now aimed right at Nick.

"Put it down," Nick advised.

"Do it," his prisoner clipped out, and the way the other two glanced at him and obeyed informed Nick that he had immobilized the leader.

"Get up," he ordered his captive. Not taking his eyes off him nor removing the threat of his blade against the man's jugular, Nick backed toward the wall.

Once he was in a position where nobody could come up behind him, he instantly felt somewhat better about all this. Likewise, with the leader under control, it was easier to hold the other two at bay.

He scanned the alley and saw John Carr facedown several yards away. He wasn't moving. "You better not have killed him."

"Pah. He's only fainted," the leader answered. "If he didn't want to get shot, he shouldn't have run."

Nick scowled at this reply and gave the man a rude shake, as if they could dislodge his arrogance. "You work for Truveau?" he demanded.

"Not anymore, actually," he replied in a guarded tone. "Cheeky of you to try to impersonate the count, though. What is your interest in our book?"

Nick shrugged, slipping easily into his role as one of the criminal class, merely in town to enroll in the Bacchus Bazaar. "I heard talk that that young amateur had something highly valuable for sale. I was curious. Wanted to see what it was, that's all. But then he bolted off when he saw you. I don't like it when people run away from me in the middle of a conversation."

"Does that happen often?" the leader drawled.

Nick smirked. "All the time. Why did you call it *your* book?"

"Well, you are full of questions." The leader looked askance at him. "Who are you, anyway?"

The question eased Nick's mind a bit. At least they did not seem to recognize him as someone from the Order.

"I'm here for the same reason you are, I suspect. For the Bacchus Bazaar."

"Really," he said skeptically. "And what are you bringing?"

"I'm a weapons dealer."

This answer seemed to mollify his captive. "You haven't registered yet," he remarked.

"No. How do you know that?"

"I have my ways."

"What about you?" Nick countered. "What are you lot bringing?"

They exchanged sly glances and low, unpleasant laughs.

"Oh, a number of items," the leader drawled.

"Whatever we can scavenge," another said under his breath.

Nick furrowed his brow and studied the leader. "I could swear I know you. What's your name?"

"What's yours?" his captive countered.

Nick glanced around cautiously at them. "If we're done trying to kill each other, I'll tell you."

"Agreed," the man replied.

Nick disarmed the leader, removing his dagger from its sheath on his hip and his shoulder pistol from its holster under his coat.

As he threw both weapons several yards away down the alley, he noticed that John Carr was no longer in sight.

Not dead, then. A blood trail on the ground led out of the alley and around the corner.

Nick slowly let go of his new friend, quite prepared to stab him in the heart if the man made one wrong move.

Hands up in a casual surrender to show he had no such intentions, the Frenchman stepped away from him and cautiously turned around. "Your name, then, monsieur?"

"Jonathan Black," Nick replied. One of his many aliases.

The leader narrowed his eyes. "I know that name. You work for Angelique."

"That's right, off and on. I help her out now and then when I'm needed. I've trained mercenaries for her. Managed some of her weapons shipments. That sort of thing."

"Right . . ." The Frenchman nodded slowly. "Well, Mr. Black, our former employers were on friendly terms— though they did not exactly move in the same circles."

Nick looked at him in question.

"I was a bodyguard for old Truveau. He's dead. They all are." He shrugged, not exactly grieved by this reality. "I've got my own enterprises now. But it's surprising how much weight his name still carries."

Nick nodded, feigning admiration. "We all have to land on our feet one way or the other, don't we?"

"Indeed. Name's Simon Limarque." He nodded at his henchmen. "This is Cagnard, that's Brou."

"Sorry about the nose," Nick said.

Brou just scowled at him.

Nick shrugged, but privately gave thanks that the men's loyalties were not still bound to the Prometheans if what the leader said was true. It seemed credible.

No bodyguard who took his job seriously would look so apathetic upon reporting that the people he'd protected were all dead, while he himself had survived.

Nick concluded in relief that at least Limarque and his men were obviously not committed Promethean believers.

It was so much easier dealing with someone who was simply out for himself.

Then, as he lowered his weapon, it suddenly dawned on Nick how Limarque must be running his scheme. "Oh, I see . . . You've got someone on the inside who lets you see the list as people register for the Bazaar. Then you pick and choose what you want to try and steal."

Limarque flashed a smile. "Something like that."

"Clever."

They were scavengers, thieves.

A bloody pack of jackals.

"So many treasures gathered in one city," Limarque reasoned with a smirk. "Well, you have to admit it's tempting. Where is the harm in robbing from criminals, after all?"

"I see your point. But, then again, not all of them are men you necessarily want to cross," Nick replied with a warning stare.

"No," the Frenchman conceded. "I'm not stupid. When I meet an equal, I keep my distance."

"Good." *An equal? I kicked your arse.* He decided not to dwell on that point, though. Another thought occurred to him, now that they seemed willing to talk. "I don't suppose you chaps happen to know who Rotgut is, do you?"

"Of course we do," Limarque said serenely. "We know everyone and everything. Why?"

"I need to get in touch with him. He's apparently found some cooperative Customs official at the port of Bristol who's willing to help men like us get our shipments out without overly close inspection. I'd be willing to pay handsomely for an introduction to whoever the devil it is I need to bribe."

"If we see him, we'll let him know you were asking for a meeting."

"I'd appreciate that. Well, then, I'll bid you gents good day." He took leave of them with a curt nod, but as he backed toward the opening of the alley, Cagnard blocked his way. Nick stared icily at him. "What do you want?"

Limarque smiled coldly. "Before we part ways, monsieur, I'd like my book back. With all due respect to you and Madame Angelique, that book belongs to me. We both know the boy gave it to you."

Nick glanced around to stall for time, weighing his options. He had no intention of handing it over, but they didn't know that.

Besides, he still needed information. He did not bother denying that he had it, since they already knew.

"You're putting it on the auction?" he inquired.

"Of course."

"What good is it? The boy said it's all in code."

"Someone out there will care enough to decipher it."

"Why? What makes it so important?"

"Let's just say it'll fetch a fine price at auction from those looking to settle old scores."

"Hmm," Nick replied noncommittally.

"Very well, then. Come now, Black." Limarque put out his hand. "Give it here, and we shall part as friends—or at least, not as enemies. Trust me, you don't want me for an enemy."

Nick smiled darkly.

And with that, the fight exploded.

*W*hen Gin came riding around the corner, at once she spotted John Carr staggering down the street a short distance ahead. Racing toward him, she saw his perfect face was ashen, his right shoulder covered in blood.

Good God, had Nick done that to him? she wondered with barely a modicum of sympathy.

She slowed the horse as she approached him. "Give me the book!" she ordered, holding out her hand once more.

"I don't have it, all right?" he wrenched out. "He took it from me!"

"The men in black?"

"No, the other one. They shot me!" he wailed.

"Which way?" she demanded.

Still clutching his wounded shoulder with his left hand, he turned and gestured weakly with his right. "Back there. In the alley. My lady, don't! It's too dangerous!" he protested, as she started riding away.

She scoffed under her breath, urging the horse on. The dandyish owner of her borrowed horse had left his shiny dress sword in its leather scabbard attached to the saddle.

She drew the weapon and charged.

Within a few strides, her horse's hooves clattering over the cobblestones, Gin turned the beast around the corner. Slowing the bay's gait just for a heartbeat, she scanned the scene before.

There in the back alley, she saw Nick hemmed in by all three attackers, doing their best to cut her lover to ribbons. They were not yet successful, but they seemed very determined.

Nick, for his part, despite being outnumbered, seemed to have the battle well in hand. Her heart swelled with pride at his ferocity. He was holding his own, smoothly whirling to deflect blows from all directions and doling out pain to each of them in unpredictable patterns.

Still, Gin thought to give him the sort of decisive advantage that could help to bring this deadly confrontation to a swifter close.

Plunging into the fray without hesitation, she drove the horse straight into the fight, using its big body to separate one of the men from Nick.

Her arrival seemed to astonish all of them.

"Oh, for God's sake," Nick muttered, while his enemies, with a chorus of *"mon dieu's,"* fell back to avoid being trampled under her angry horse's hooves.

"Get out of here," Nick said.

"You have the book? Give it to me," she answered, holding off the bloody-nosed man with the point of her borrowed rapier. "I'll get it to safety. You finish them off."

"I'm going to wring your neck," he informed her, but when the large, square-headed fellow took a swing at him, the threat was forgotten.

Nick proceeded to fight with him while the rather handsome one suddenly reached up and started trying to drag her off the horse. "Well, who is this, then?"

Tall and lean, he had olive skin and cold, dead eyes. "So happy you could join our little party, *ma chérie*. Why don't you get down from there and tell me why you're after my book, too."

"Take your hands off me!" Still seated firmly in the saddle, she kicked him in the chest and flung him back, but about that moment, her horse was inspired with a similar idea.

Bloody-Nose Man was obviously not having a good day. The horse jumped; and the unfortunate fellow suddenly went flying backwards with a yelp. Thanks to a well-aimed kick from her angry mount, he was flung against the brick wall of the alley, where he crumpled to the ground, out cold.

"Good boy!" Gin started to praise the gelding with a startled laugh, but unfortunately, the horse was angry at her, too, no doubt for stealing him and dragging him into this unpleasant business.

Nick let out a shout of fear as the horse bucked her off its back. Her borrowed sword clattered to the ground as she went flying, too—only to land more or less in the arms of the cold-eyed Frenchman.

She gasped with relief that she hadn't broken her skull, but as the horse bolted, leaving her to her fate, she felt the Frenchman's grasp tighten around her and suddenly found she had a gun to her head.

"I take it this belongs to you?" he said to Nick.

Nick stopped fighting immediately. "Limarque, don't hurt her."

"The book, please."

"Nick, no!" Gin cried.

"What's this? I thought his name was Jonathan," her captor said mildly. "Jonathan Black, *non?*"

Gin winced at her mistake. Nick or whatever he wanted to call himself today was glaring at her, his obvious message to her clear: *Shut up.*

She did. But as she pressed her lips together, her scowl likewise informed him: *I was only trying to help you!*

"The book," Limarque repeated more insistently. "Fancy a swap, Englishman? Whatever your real name is. She'd fetch a pretty penny at the auction."

Nick's chest heaved with exertion. "Not if you value your life."

"It's that book I value. You don't even know what you're fighting for. Or, do you?"

"It's worth a lot o' money," he growled.

"It's worth far more than that, but only to someone with the right connections. You don't have them, Black. It doesn't concern you, anyway. Now give it here, or we take your little hellcat home with us and take turns having our fun with her until she's out of tears. Then she dies."

"You're vile," Gin hissed at him.

"Shut up." He jerked her arm.

"You'll let her go?" Nick barked. "I have your word? One hair on her head, and this is war. Do you understand me, Limarque?"

"Give the book to Cagnard."

"No, don't listen to them! Nick!" she protested in dismay as he reached into his waistcoat and took out her father's journal, handing it over to the square-headed blond man with a black look.

Satisfied, the leader shoved her forward, releasing her, true to his word—much to her surprise.

Stumbling when he pushed her, Gin tripped on the hem of her blasted skirts. But just as she caught her balance, she looked up and gasped to spy the Bloody Nose man standing right behind Nick.

Apparently, he had recovered from the horse's kick while no one was looking. He raised his weapon.

"Nick, look out!" she yelled, too late.

The man clobbered him over the back of his head with a brick he had found in the alley.

"*Stop!*" Gin screamed as the man bashed him a second time, snarling vengefully.

Gin cried out as Nick crumpled, bleeding from his head.

"Make him stop!" she pleaded with the leader as the vicious brute hit Nick a third time to make sure he stayed down.

He was unconscious.

"*Nick!*"

"Cagnard, give me the book. Brou, finish him," the leader ordered, to Gin's horror.

"Gladly." Brou tossed the bloodied brick away and paused to reload his pistol.

Ashen-faced, Gin turned to the leader. "You can't kill him. Please! Trust me, you don't want to do that."

"Why not?" Limarque asked pleasantly, holding up a finger to stay the execution for a moment. "Tell me why I ought to spare him."

She swallowed hard. "Not for his sake but your own. Believe me, you don't want to tangle with his friends."

"His friends? Ah, I see. Well, my dear, the only way they'll be able to trace his death back to me is if we leave any witnesses alive. Easily remedied, *non*? Maybe I'll just kill you both right now—"

"You mustn't! Don't you see that would be foolish?" she insisted, heart pounding as she found herself begging for both their lives.

"Foolish?" Limarque a brow.

She nodded fervently, knowing this was a desperate ploy. But he was intrigued. Obviously, it was a waste of breath to try to inspire this cold-eyed man to mercy. She had to appeal to his self-interest.

"How's that?" he inquired.

"That book you've got—it's all in code. But I know what it says. Spare him, and I'll give you all its secrets."

Limarque eyed her warily. "You can decipher it?"

"I've been working on it for months."

"It was in John Carr's possession."

"We were supposed to share the money we'd get from bringing it to this auction. But that little thief double-crossed me and stole it. When I tracked him here, I met this Jonathan person. He told me his name was Nick— typical man, liar. But I persuaded him to go after Carr to get it back for me. He looked like he could do the job."

"Persuaded him how?" he drawled.

"How do you think?" she retorted. "That's the only reason he was there in that hotel, aside from the Bacchus Bazaar. Other than that, he's got nothing to do with any of this. The book is mine."

"I see. Well, fair lady, I'm sure you can be very persuasive." His downward glance skimmed her body. "I suppose if he wants you back, he can buy you at the auction—*after* you've decoded all the secrets in the journal for me." He leaned down to whisper a warning in her ear. "Try anything stupid, and you die. Slowly."

"I won't, I understand." She swallowed hard. "Just leave him out of this. I don't want his blood on my hands, and neither do you, if you're smart. He's very well connected."

He seemed amused by her attempt to come across as fierce. "Clever girl. I think I rather like you. Cagnard, get the carriage. Brou, drag that English bastard into the passageway where he won't be seen until we're gone. But leave him alive," he added crisply.

"Limarque! He can't be trusted!" Brou objected with

his nose swelling by the minute and beginning to look a little like an eggplant.

"Of course not," Limarque replied. "Nevertheless, the hellcat has a point. I don't need a war with Angelique's army of mercenaries. He's not worth it. *Allons.* Let's get out of here."

Mere moments later, Gin was pushed into a closed carriage that pulled up to the mouth of the alley. Limarque got in beside her, her father's journal tucked inside his waistcoat.

"Where are you taking me?" she demanded, but the tremble in her voice gave the lie to her defiant mask of bravery.

"That is none of your concern." Limarque tied a blindfold around her eyes, then set his hand possessively on her thigh, and ordered his henchman to drive.

Chapter

17

$\mathcal{N}$ick slowly opened his eyes and found himself looking up at the blurry oval of a face. Someone was anxiously peering down at him. "Doctor, he's awake!"

Barely.

Movement shuffled about in the room. It all seemed far away. He blinked a few times, struggling to shake off the confusion as a second pale, blurry oval appeared and hovered over him.

"Young man, can you hear me?" a kindly, aged voice asked with a thick French accent.

He nodded slightly, glad to find at least his neck still worked.

Where am I?

The smell of good food that permeated the building and the familiar softness of the bed where he lay hinted that somehow he was back in their room at La Maison de Maxime. He had no idea how he might have got there.

As his vision cleared, the two faces came into better focus. The first belonged to an old French surgeon with a white goatee, who was squinting at him in a scientific way.

"Can you tell me your name?" the doctor tested him, holding his chin up to look in each of his eyes.

Nick struggled with the question, but not for the reason the doctor probably thought. Countless names and identities he'd used over the years tumbled through his pounding head like a rockslide. *Who am I, again?*

It alarmed him that he could not remember under which alias he had registered at the hotel. But it wasn't Jonathan Black, obviously.

Black was wanted by the *gendarmes* as a known associate of the quasi criminal Angelique.

"Your name?" the surgeon repeated in a steady tone. But the other person nearest him was apparently so distressed by Nick's silence that could not help himself. "He is Baron Forrester of England, sir! He's my mother's friend."

With that, the familiar boyish voice penetrated the dark fog of his likely concussion, and Nick sat bolt upright—which in turn brought on the sensation that his head had just exploded.

"Thank God you're alive!" Phillip cried.

Skull throbbing, Nick glared at the boy in disbelief. "Of course I'm alive," he muttered. "What . . . are you doing here? Your mother's going to kill you," he grumbled, then his stomach clenched as the sickening memory returned of how everything had gone awry in the alley, and he nearly groaned aloud in panicked anguish as he remembered they had taken her.

He immediately started to get up, but the doctor pushed him back gently to the pillows propped against the headboard. "Not so fast, *monsieur*. Lie still. You need to rest—"

"I have to go," Nick informed him, heart pounding with horror at the thought of her held captive, while the room spun and black dots zigzagged across his field of vision. "I just need a moment . . ."

Phillip frowned, watching him.

"Nonsense," the doctor answered. "Look here. Follow my finger."

Nick scowled but obeyed, trailing the doctor's fingertip slowly back and forth. "How did I get here?"

Phillip nodded across the room. "Carr brought you in."

"Carr?" Nick followed his glance and was mystified to find John Carr sitting in the armchair with his shoulder bandaged. He was silent, watching everything unfold, his expression a mix of relief and sullenness.

"It's a good thing he did," the doctor informed him. "You were still unconscious when I arrived. Monsieur de Vence sent Georges to fetch me," he added.

"Ah," Nick answered, scanning the chamber.

Good God, the room was full of people. The hotelier stood a few feet away, looking personally stricken and aggrieved at the attack on one of his guests.

A woman Nick supposed was Maxime de Vence herself stood in the doorway, holding a cheesecake as if she had brought it to him for its medicinal properties, while her gangly son Georges peered, wide-eyed, over her shoulder.

Bloody hell.

Monsieur de Vence stepping forward, hands clasped in distress. "I am so sorry this has happened to you, *monsieur*. I must apologize for my city! *Mon dieu,* this is outrageous! That you, a visitor, should be attacked in broad daylight! Rest assured, we've called the *gendarme*. He should be here in a moment. Now that you're awake, you can make a report. Whoever has done this to you and the young *monsieur*, he must be punished!"

Nick tensed at the news that the Paris police were on their way—as if finding Gin missing and himself in this vulnerable state were not already horrible enough.

"Well," he managed, "it seems I owe you all my thanks." He gave Carr a guarded nod, which the blond lad returned.

"Did you know your friend was also wounded in the robbery?" the doctor remarked. "You must have got the club while he got the bullet. He's lucky, though. His is just a flesh wound. You're the one we were worried about. We'll have to keep an eye on you over the next twenty-four hours or so to make sure this mild concussion of yours does not bring on any latent effects."

I don't have twenty-four hours.

He wanted her back safe, now.

"Any double vision? Strange taste in your mouth?"

"Honestly, I'm fine."

"It took ten stitches to stop the bleeding."

Nick scowled. "Bloody hell." Raising his hand, he gingerly fingered the bandage tied around his head.

"Georges, run to the icehouse and fetch more ice for the gentleman."

"*Oui, Maman.*" The hotelier's son dodged off while his wife stepped forward.

"Poor *monsieur!*" Maxime exclaimed, bringing him the cheesecake, much to his bemusement. "Cheesecake always helps," she said fondly, following his bemused glance at her offering.

"Thanks, ma'am."

"*D'accord.*" She set it on the table. "How do you feel?"

"Like a lion has been gnawing on my skull," he admitted ruefully.

"I am not surprised. You bled all over our lobby."

"Sorry about that. We'll pay for any damages—"

"Nonsense," she declared.

"Ugh." Nick closed his eyes as a wave of pain hit.

"You see?" the doctor chided. "It isn't good. When the boy brings the ice in a cloth, keep it on your head. That will help to keep the swelling down. I'm afraid we cannot let you go back to sleep for several hours, though. That could be dangerous."

"I understand." He did not open his eyes. It was

hardly his first concussion, nor the first time he'd ever
been beaten senseless.

He didn't recommend it.

"Here. Drink this," the doctor ordered.

Nick dragged his eyes open and stared at the offered
glass skeptically. "What is it?"

The old man shook his head. "A headache powder dissolved in some nice English tea for you. What, do you
think I will poison you just because I am French, eh?"

Nick gave him a sardonic look and took the glass,
downing the stuff. "Thanks," he mumbled.

"That should help to dull the pain," the doctor said
with a satisfied nod.

As Nick swallowed the medicine, Phillip could no
longer contain himself and worriedly demanded,
"Where is my mother?"

Lowering the glass from his lips, Nick faltered. He
had no idea what to tell the boy, especially in a roomful
of people.

"Carr claims he hasn't seen her, but you never know
with him. Then Monsieur de Vence said she 'borrowed'
a horse from right out in front of the hotel and went
galloping off without explanation. That's odd behavior,
even for her!

"Don't worry, I paid for the horse, so the *gendarme*
won't arrest her when he gets here," Phillip added with
a dismissive wave. "I just want to know if she's safe!
Please tell me she wasn't with you during the robbery!"

Robbery. So that's what we're calling it. All right.

"No, no, of course not," Nick soothed. "She said she
was going out. She's probably shopping or something."

"Oh, thank God," said Madame de Vence, clutching her bosom in relief. "I'm so glad to hear your wife
wasn't there."

"She's not his wife," Carr spoke up.

His low, cynical drawl embarrassed everyone in the
room.

"Thanks for that, John," Nick muttered, flushing at the bald accusation after he had lied to these good people—and especially after the sort of brazen conjugal sport that had gone on in this very bed, around which all of his visitors had gathered with such tender concern for him.

He hung his head and mumbled, "Sorry."

"Ah, *monsieur,* this is Paris," Maxime replied with a discreet wink. "We understand such things."

"So, she wasn't with you when this happened?" Phillip asked beseechingly.

Nick strove to clear his head. With the *gendarme* on the way, he had to get his story straight now—and best to keep it simple.

The sooner he could get rid of the policeman, the faster he could get on with rescuing Virginia. He did not want the Paris *gendarmerie* poking their noses into this.

Even if he managed to keep them from finding out he was also Jonathan Black, they were unlikely to take his side.

Napoleon's ex-military police were famous for their corruption. And given Limarque's connection to the powerful Truveau clan, chances were high that Limarque's gang already had some sort of understanding with the local police force—bribes, to make sure the law left them alone.

"No," he assured the lad. "She wanted to go out and visit some of her favorite shops along the Champs-Élysées. Carr and I had no desire to go shopping with a lady, obviously."

Monsieur de Vence let out a sympathetic humph.

"So, where did *you* go?" Phillip persisted.

Nick hesitated, racking his addled brains and wishing this conversation would simply go away. "To a place where you don't bring a lady," he mumbled.

But apparently there was little point in trying to shield the lad by speaking in delicate terms.

Phillip scrunched up his nose in disgusted under-standing. "You two went to a brothel while my mother was out shopping?"

"Ahem!" Monsieur de Vence interjected. "Well, that would explain the attack. Bands of footpads have been known to wait outside such places to, er, rob the gentle-men as they're leaving."

"In the middle of the day?" Phillip shook his head at Nick in reproach. "I knew you weren't good enough for her!"

Nick gave him a pained look. And to make matters worse, at that moment, the *gendarme* arrived, smart and polished in his uniform. The soldier-policeman knocked curtly on the open door, then entered the bed-chamber with the strut they all had, all these French veterans who had ever stood within a ten-mile radius of Bonaparte.

"You wish to make a report, *monsieur*?"

Nick sent Carr a warning look to let him handle this.

With a wry, subtle shrug, Carr invited him to have at it. *He's all yours.*

"Yes, of course. Thank you for coming." As the *gendarme* ordered the hoteliers out of the room, Nick swung his legs off the side of the bed and sat up with a flinch. The doctor warned the *gendarme* not to overtax him, but thankfully, the headache powder was starting to take the effect.

The questioning commenced.

Damn it, I don't have time for this, he thought as he coolly made up a string of credible lies.

He had to be on his way to go and save Virginia.

Of course, he was not entirely sure he could stand up yet without falling down. He didn't care if he had to crawl on his hands and knees. He would rescue her from Limarque or die trying.

If he could just get rid of all these kind, meddling busybodies!

The *gendarme* was all business, meanwhile, scribbling notes in his little book as Nick answered his questions on various points. "And did you get a look at your attackers? Could you describe them?"

He shrugged and shook his head. "I really couldn't say. There were three of them, I think. We never saw them coming."

"Did they take anything of value?"

The question pained him exceedingly. They had torn away the *most* valuable thing.

Nick's voice failed him; he shook his head.

"That's enough for now, officer. He's white as a ghost from blood loss," the surgeon insisted.

"Is there anything else you remember?"

"No. It all happened so fast. There isn't much to tell. But thank you for coming."

"If you remember any more details."

"Of course." Nick nodded. "I will come down to the station."

The policeman did not look entirely convinced by his story, but since Nick and Carr were clearly the victims in whatever had happened, there was nothing else for him to do but withdraw.

At last, the old surgeon took leave of him, as well. He pooh-poohed Nick's thanks as he gathered his things into his black bag. "Just doing my job, lad. Keep the ice on that head. I've left the headache powder over there for you."

Nick touched his hand to his heart in sincere gratitude as the kindly old Frenchman stepped out and pulled the door closed behind him.

Finally, Nick was alone with Phillip and John Carr.

All three exchanged dark glances. Phillip started to speak, but Nick raised a finger to his lips until the last pair of footsteps had faded off down the stairs.

He gestured to the boy to go and make sure no one was listening outside the door. Phillip went; the hallway was clear. Phillip shut the door and locked it, then he turned around slowly and leaned his back against it, gazing grimly at Nick. "She's not really shopping, is she?"

"No." It was an excruciating moment, having to explain his failure to her son. He rose a bit unsteadily and crossed the room to the boy. "Phillip, I'm so sorry. Something bad has happened."

"I knew it," he said with a gulp. "Is she dead?"

"No! God, no. Of course not," Nick exclaimed, laying his hand on the boy's shoulder. "She's not dead. Don't even say that. It's going to be all right."

"Well?" he countered with a wide-eyed look.

Nick struggled for how to say it.

John Carr supplied the words in a blunt tone: "They took her."

"What? Who took her? What do you mean? Where is she?" The panicked boy looked again at Nick. "You promised you'd keep her safe!"

"I know," Nick forced out in a strangled whisper. "I tried, Phillip, I did. She kept secrets from me. Everything went to hell, then they took her. But don't worry, I'll get her back. I swear it to you on your grandfather's grave."

Phillip stared at him in bewildered dismay. "I guess even Order agents fail sometimes, don't they?"

Nick flinched and lowered his head.

It was all too true. Still, he'd had stab wounds that hurt less than the boy's artless words.

God, he had to make this right. Whatever it took.

Steadying himself, he glanced across the room. "Mr. Carr, I appreciate your getting me back to this hotel. But you need to tell me now what the hell is going on."

Carr frowned warily at him.

"Come, man, her life is in danger! I know you stole the book from her. And *you* must know by now that whatever sort of deal you thought you had with Limarque, his true intent was to take the book and kill you. So tell me everything," he commanded, "from the beginning."

"Tell him what you know!" her cub growled.

"Phillip, I'm not sure what we'll be discussing is suited for young ears—"

"Quit treating me like a child!"

"You are a child."

"I am nearly sixteen!" he thundered.

Nick gave up on that fight with a shake of his head. He turned his attention back to Carr and went to sit down again, feeling slightly woozy. "How did you know to come and find me in that alley? I thought you ran after you were shot."

"I started to, but then I crossed paths with Lady Burke around the corner. She was on horseback. I told her not to go after you, but she never listens. So I followed her back toward the alley. I was scared she'd be hurt. I didn't know what to do, so I just hid, but I was close enough to see the whole thing. You're pretty good in a fight," Carr conceded with a begrudging nod.

"Thanks. What happened after that blackguard knocked me out? What did they do with her?"

"Put her in a carriage."

"Did they hurt her?" Phillip asked anxiously.

"No." Carr glanced around at them with a somber look. "She told them she would decode the book for them if they'd spare your life."

Nick flinched.

"What book?" Phillip echoed.

"Never mind," Nick mumbled. At least, if Limarque had a use for her, she should be relatively safe for a little while. He would have to get out ahead of this somehow, anticipate Limarque's next move. "Were you able to follow the carriage?"

"No. They went tearing off too fast. Instead, I came back for you."

"I owe you for that."

Carr shook his head, staring dazedly at the floor. "It all went so wrong. I had no idea . . ."

"How far out of your depth you were? Well, I trust you know that now. You can escort the boy back to England."

"No!" Phillip cried. "She's my mother, I want to help!"

"You're just a pup!"

"I'm smart and resourceful! Look how well I did, getting here! I sneaked into Mr. Haynes's detective office back in London and found a clue to where in Paris you two were going. Then I followed, and look, I got myself here, all the way to Paris without a tutor or a footman or anyone! You have to admit that's pretty brave of me, coming all this way."

"You're supposed to be at Deepwood," Nick said in disapproval, though he was hard-pressed to hide his amusement.

"I wanted to show you I have what it takes to make a good spy when I grow up! But, blazes, I certainly didn't expect to get here and find things in such a state! It's a good thing I came, I can tell you. Now that I see how you've botched it, I'm not going anywhere." He folded his arms across his chest. "She's *my* mother, and I'm going to help you rescue her whether you like it or not! And John must help, too, because all of this is his fault. Well, it is!" he added, shooting her former assistant a glare.

"Phillip." Nick sighed. *Can't you see that if you stay, you're just another person for me to protect?* But he didn't have the heart to say it out loud after the boy's bold speech.

"You can't send me home, Forrester! What if it was your mother who was missing? Would you leave—even if you were my age? Of course not! Besides, you can't do this yourself. Look at you! You're half-dead."

"I'm fine."

"Order agents always work in teams of three. So here we are. You, me, John."

"Oh, Lord," Nick groaned, leaning forward, elbows on knees, to rest his pounding head in his hands.

If this was not him reaping what he had sowed in life, then nothing was. For years in the field, he always preferred to play the pain-in-the-arse skeptic and leave the rigors of leadership to Beauchamp.

How his former team leader would have laughed and laughed to find Nick in command of two distraught, immature boys. One itching to be a hero, while the other couldn't stop glancing into the mirror.

"Please?" Phillip begged him.

"All right, fine." One had to pick one's battles, after all. "But you have to do exactly as I say. All our lives could depend on it. You see John's shoulder? They were aiming for his head. I can't protect people if I'm not told the whole story. Are we clear on that?"

Both of his baby troops nodded.

"Good. Now, then. Carr, tell me everything, from the beginning. And make it quick."

Carr explained how he had stolen the mysterious book to sell at the Bacchus Bazaar when Virginia had refused his advances.

"I can't help it," he defended when Phillip gagged. "I've always preferred women a few years older than I. They're more . . . mature. I thought the attraction was mutual. But she just laughed at me. Brushed me off. I know I'm not the sort of rich, titled lord she usually likes—but I never expected to be treated as a joke!"

"She only hired you because she felt sorry for you, you idiot!" Phillip snapped. "Because you're a by-blow like she is! She wanted to give you a chance. And this is how you repay her? Lord Forrester, what is this book he stole from my mother?"

Nick shrugged, eyeing Carr skeptically. "Well? Answer the question."

"It came from her father. Not the Earl of Ashton," he pointed out, "her real father. He was some sort of shadowy government agent. She never really went into much detail about that."

"What do you know about its contents?"

"Well, of course, it's all written in code, as you saw, so I couldn't read it. But she was always consulting it and once showed it to me. She knew the code, of course. Her father had given her the key. She told me she had memorized it, then destroyed it. Though I should think she's got a copy of it hidden away somewhere . . ."

"A book from Grandpa Virgil? Did she tell you what sorts of things it said?" Phillip asked eagerly.

"It was a record of her father's exploits as a spy, in case any of his old enemies ever came after her. Names, dates, places."

Nick drew in his breath. *Oh, Virgil, what have you done?*

"All his secrets were in there. She told me that when he was a young man, he had loved a woman up in Scotland. His enemies kidnapped her to try to force him into turning traitor. He never betrayed his country, but he never saw the woman again, either. His enemies killed her."

The room fell silent.

"I guess, as an old man, her father didn't intend to let those he loved be used as a pawn like that again. That's why he trained her to fight and use a gun. The book was probably meant as her insurance policy. And yours," Carr said to Phillip. "That's why I knew it would infuriate her so much, my taking it. I knew she'd chase me. Maybe I wanted her to." He shook his head. "But I swear I never meant for it to come to this. I don't want to see her hurt. I still care for her."

"We all do," Nick said.

Phillip shook his head dazedly. "What are we going to do?"

"Give me a moment." Nick leaned forward and

rested his pounding head in his hands again, trying to think around the pain. *So that's how she always knew so much about me,* he thought, *but, God, Virgil, how could you do this?*

Hearing this, at last, explained so many things. Like why she had been so secretive and why she kept saying that everyone makes mistakes.

In hindsight, Nick realized that was why she had come to him in the first place. She must have known that, more than anyone, he would understand what it was like to muck up royally. She must have known he would help—not just to fix this—but to protect her father's reputation.

She would not have wanted the graybeards finding out that the great Virgil Banks had committed the ultimate indiscretion to protect his only living kin: Had put his secrets into writing and handed them off to an outsider.

Good God, that was worse than what Nick had done, trying to quit the Order.

It was shocking to find out after the man was dead that the great Virgil had had an Achilles' heel, after all.

His little girl, and of course, his grandson.

If word of this got out, it would certainly taint Virgil's reputation. But in an instant, he was equally committed to protecting the memory of his beloved handler. It was the least he could do for him after the way he had let everybody down. There was only one real question in his mind. *Why didn't she tell me?*

Especially after their night together.

It should have been the first thing on her lips the next morning, but she had said nothing. It stung to think she still didn't trust him—but then again, why should she, considering where she had first found him?

He shook his head, longing to wrap her safely in his arms. He swore that once he got her back, he was never letting her out of his sight again.

In the meantime, unfortunately, by holding on to her secrets, she had endangered everyone, not just herself.

In the wrong hands, that book could lead old enemies to hunt down the unsuspecting Order agents and pick them off one by one. All his happily married friends, thinking they could finally get some peace and settle down . . .

No. He had to make this right, no matter what it cost him. He'd protect his brother warriors, make it up to them all for his previous failures. Rescue the lady who had stolen his heart and save those kidnapped girls, as well.

God. He lowered his head. It was still throbbing with pain when her son approached him cautiously.

"Lord Forrester?"

"Yes, Phillip?" he asked wearily without looking up.

"Maybe you should take this back."

Nick slowly lifted his head and felt a startled pang to find his medal from the Regent sitting there in the boy's cupped hand.

"Mother asked me to keep it for you while you were away. But I think now's a good time for you to have it back." Phillip offered it to him. "Maybe it'll bring you luck."

Unexpected anguish closed his throat. Nick reached for the symbol of everything he had once prized more than his life.

His honor.

"Let's hope so," he said in a strangled voice, examining it. "We could use a little luck right now."

The boy laid his hand on his shoulder, bringing him back from his dark brooding. "So, how are we going to rescue her?"

Nick glanced up at him in wry affection. "I'll think of something." His hand closing around the white Maltese cross, he ignored the throbbing pain that filled his skull and stood to his full height, his eyes blazing with renewed fire. His mind churned.

"Should we try to find their hideaway?" Carr suggested.

Nick shook his head. "They'll be expecting that. It would take too long to find them, and even if we did, we're badly outnumbered."

"Why don't we go tell the *gendarmes* they took her? They could help us! The police must have some idea where these criminals like to hide—"

"Phillip, the *gendarmes* are probably corrupt. If we start asking questions, we're the ones who'll probably disappear. Limarque and his men are going to be leaving Paris soon, anyway."

"Then maybe we could lay a trap for them somewhere on the road, ambush them—"

"Would you shut up and let him think?" Carr interrupted the boy impatiently. "We don't even know where the auction will be held yet, let alone what route to take to get there!"

"It's all right, lad," Nick murmured to her frightened son. "There are other cards in play that have to be considered, not just your mother, but the missing girls she was investigating, as well. And your grandfather's book. We've got to get it back and make sure it is destroyed."

"How in the world are we going to do all that?"

Nick considered it. "If all else fails, I need to get enrolled in that auction. Secure my last line of defense."

He stalked over to the armoire, opened it, and reached up to feel around to the back of the upper shelf. When his searching hand found the velvet-wrapped lump of the emerald, he grasped it in relief.

Considering that the jewel might prove his last resort for buying Virginia's freedom on the auction if he could not save her sooner, he put it securely in his inside waistcoat pocket, where neither John Carr nor any Paris footpads could steal it.

He did likewise with the game piece from Hugh Lowell, aware that she had concealed it inside a hidden compartment of her reticule, which she had left behind.

Now all he had to do was set up his own entry into the Bacchus Bazaar. He would not be going, of course, as Lord Forrester, but as Jonathan Black of the criminal underworld. "Let's go, you lot."

"Where?" Phillip asked, watching him, wide-eyed.

Nick shrugged on a brace of pistols, then reached for his coat. "We need to go see a friend of mine outside the city."

"Who?" Carr asked as he rose and followed.

But Nick remained evasive as they headed for the door. "Someone who can help."

Asking a favor from Madame Angelique was making a deal with the devil, to be sure, but Nick was past caring.

Whatever he had to do.

In the meantime, Virgil's daughter was just going to have to use all her wits, wiles, and skills to stall and delay, confuse and confound Limarque until Nick—or Jonathan Black—could come to her rescue.

Chapter
18

$\mathcal{A}$t about the same time Nick had been brought back unconscious to La Maison de Maxime, Gin was sitting tensely, bound, gagged, and blindfolded, in Limarque's black carriage, speeding through the streets of Paris.

She had no idea where he was taking her, but every time the carriage jolted over uneven streets and broken cobblestones, she collided into Limarque, who was seated much too close beside her.

To her chagrin, he chose to take these accidental bumps as an invitation to touch her. He made free with her person in the most outrageous manner; the gag in her mouth muffled her curses.

Wrists tied before her, she tried to push him away, but he enjoyed that too much. Enjoyed her anger and her fear. He was simply making sport of her, having rendered her powerless.

Maybe he could tell somehow that this was the thing she hated most—being under another human being's complete control. Indeed, if she was honest, that was the very reason she had landed in this situation.

Her own stubborn secrecy.

Refusing to admit her mistake. Refusing to share power in the form of information. Determined to stay in control of the mission, she had opted not to tell Nick her father's secret days ago, when she should have.

And now she might have got him killed.

Guilt crashed through her, flaming down every nerve ending, overriding even her terror. *This is all my fault. How could I let him go into that hotel without his knowing the whole story?* It had been utterly immoral of her. She saw that now. *Please, God, let him live.*

It was bad enough she had driven her husband off to his death. The thought that she might have got Nick killed, too, was more torment than she could bear.

She despaired of ever knowing why she was so bloody proud, ornery, and difficult. Her mother used to say it was because of her red hair. She just never could see why she should have to do what anybody said, especially a man.

Unless perhaps he proved himself.

What arrogance! Judging everyone like that, as if she were the standard of all knowledge.

Truly, she had been too proud—but now came Simon Limarque, a devil sent to humble her and put her in her place. Never had any man dared to treat her so much like an object, demeaning her and savoring it.

He was laughing at her fury, taunting her, asking did she like this, did she like that as he touched her neck and face and chest in the most annoying fashion. When she succeeded in elbowing him forcefully in the stomach, he quit laughing and pinned her to the seat with a whispered threat of something worse.

Gin went motionless, feigning submission, even as she longed to cut his throat.

Satisfied with her rigid stillness, he finally got off her, sitting upright again.

Her heart pounded with rage.

But as disgusted as she was with him, even more so, she was in a panic over Nick. Vicious blows to the head like that could kill a person or send them into a death-like coma.

What if no one came along and found him in that alley?

How long would he lie there, bleeding and unconscious?

In this cold, damp chill of late November, he could catch his death quickly. She had to get back to him, help him.

Nothing mattered but that.

Unfortunately, as the carriage raced on, she was well aware that she could face some very unpleasant times ahead, herself. For she had no intention of telling Limarque any of the secrets in her father's book.

She intended to handle it by lying through her teeth, but if he caught on, she would probably face torture.

Of course, she had realized that fact even before she had volunteered to go with them. No matter. It was worth it to have stopped them from pulling the trigger and finishing Nick off when he was defenseless, lying there unconscious.

Unfortunately, there wasn't much time to ponder her own best strategy for not getting murdered. The carriage slowed to a halt. The next thing she knew, they were getting out.

Limarque tossed her over his shoulder, piratelike. As he carried her several steps across some pavement, she tried to see around the edges of her blindfold, identify some nearby landmark to help her figure out where she was. Then she could feel him climbing up a couple of steps, and she could tell they went inside because the gusty wind suddenly stopped blowing her hair around.

A door slammed, quite close behind her, while, below, she could hear Limarque's bootheels striking hardwood floors.

"Put me down!" she insisted, her words muffled by the gag. Her attempts to struggle against his hold only got her a clap on the rear end and another whispered threat of an intimate act of violence.

Then Limarque's gait changed. "We're on a staircase. Keep squirming like that, and I could drop you. Do you want to fall and break your neck? No? Then hold still."

Another door creaked ahead of them.

She heard a low-toned, clipped exchange between the leader and his underlings, then the door slammed.

"Shut the blinds," he ordered someone.

She heard the *snick* of wooden shutters clicking closed. Then Limarque bent down to spill her off his shoulder onto a hard wooden chair beside a desk.

A moment later, the blindfold slipped away from her eyes. Hands still bound before her, Gin blinked rapidly and looked around at the plain, sparse room.

Directly in front of her, Limarque loomed, studying her, arms folded across his chest.

He passed behind her and removed the gag from her mouth, then he walked away to confer with his men across the room.

Gin struggled to get her bearings. After a brief exchange of information, he nodded their dismissal.

The broken-nose man trudged out among the others, probably to see a doctor. Gin glowered at him in hatred as he left.

Limarque closed the door after his men and locked it, then returned. Opening a desk drawer, he pulled out a small notepad and pencil. "Now then. If you're ready to get started, madame." He pushed her chair in for her, bringing it snugly to the desk, then he pulled the candle toward her. "Time to get to work." Slipping her father's journal out of his waistcoat, he set it on the desk before her. "Go on. Impress me."

Gin stared down at it, heart pounding.

"Well? What are you waiting for? You said you know the code. So start deciphering." He grasped her chin and roughly lifted her face, forcing her to meet his gaze. "I don't allow women to make a fool of me. I spared your lover in exchange for these secrets, and I must warn you, I'm all out of mercy for today. So, no games. Start writing—and make it worth my while." He released her face.

Gin swallowed hard. "Would you untie my hands, please? How am I supposed to write like this?"

"You'll manage."

She scowled at him, gingerly picking up the pencil. It was awkward with her wrists bound, but not impossible. *Deceive, delay, confuse.* Revealing the true contents of her father's book was, of course, out of the question. *I'll just make something up. He has no way of verifying it, after all,* she thought. *I'll make him think I'm cooperating, win his trust, and keep my eyes open for any chance to escape.*

Fortunately, she knew enough about codes at least to keep him guessing for a while. "I'll need a Bible. It has to be the original King James—the Protestant Bible. In English," she added pointedly.

Her expectation that this would send her French Catholic captor off on a fool's errand was thwarted as he smiled.

Damn, why hadn't she asked for something more exotic. But this was the most believable source code for a book cipher, as it was so common. Easy for any British spy in the field to get his hands on, according to her father.

Limarque obviously knew his business. Maybe he wouldn't be quite so easy to fool. At once, he pulled a King James Bible off the bottom shelf of a cluttered bookcase against the wall and brought it to her.

When he dropped it on the desk with a thump, she managed a taut nod, mentally cursing. "Thank you."

"So, it's a book cipher, then."

"No, it merely starts that way." Better think of something fast. *Right*.

Pulling the pad of paper over to her, she began drawing crisscross lines as for a game of tic-tac-toe. Below it, she drew a large X, then she started filling in the letters.

Limarque glanced over her shoulder. "Book cipher mixed with the old Masonic code? Interesting."

"Just be glad I didn't require a Caesar wheel."

"I hate a cipher wheel, myself," he remarked. "It's not very practical in the field."

She arched a brow at him, full of questions that she opted not to ask.

Limarque began to pace back and forth across the room, waiting for her to produce results. "So, who are you, anyway?"

"No one of any consequence," she replied absently as she worked. "Could I have more light, please? It's too dark in here with the blinds closed."

"Of course." Instead of opening the shutters and letting her look out the window, which might tell her where they were, Limarque lit a match off the low fire in the hearth and brought it over to the nearby candle.

She nodded her thanks. "Now could I have a penknife? The pencil's point is dull."

He gave her a knowing smirk. "Do you take me for an idiot? If you are not going to uphold your end of our bargain, I've got no particular reason to leave you alive."

"You don't have to threaten me," she retorted. "This book is full complex code! It's going to take some time."

"You have an hour . . ." He turned over an hourglass on the mantel. "To produce three pieces of information from this book I can verify."

She hid her terror at this challenge. "Any specific area of interest?"

He shrugged. "Give me a secret about the Order's dealings with the Truveau family. I used to work for the count. That way I'll know if it's true."

"That's not fair! My life depends on whether or not the information in this book is true? That's ridiculous! I cannot even say for sure if this book is authentic! Just because I was going to sell it doesn't mean I can vouch for its accuracy. For all I know, it could be a hoax!"

"John Carr said it was absolutely real."

She snorted. "Carr would have said anything to get your money, *monsieur*. That blackguard stole it from me. I came to France to get it back."

"Lot of trouble to go to for something you claim is a fake," he drawled.

"It's the principle of it. It's mine. He took it. But I don't know for certain if it's real or not! I'm not prepared to stake my life on it."

"I'm afraid you already did, madame. What was that name he called you? Virginia?"

She nodded reluctantly, hating that he knew even that much about her. There weren't many Virginias running around in London. Her mother had named her after Virgil. It wouldn't be too difficult to track.

"How did you come by this thing, anyway?"

"I stole it," she mumbled. "I'm a thief. Carr and I work together."

"Who'd you steal it from?"

"Some eccentric old man in London, a recluse. We broke in when he was not at home and cleaned out his valuables. When I glimpsed this old journal on his nightstand and saw the insignia on the back of it, I had an inkling of its significance. The Order of St. Michael the Archangel had just been exposed in all the London papers. Shocking, really, to hear that something like that had existed since the Crusades. Anyway, I realized the senile eccentric was probably an old, broken-down Order agent. He's dead now, anyway. Natural causes. I kept the book and became obsessed, I suppose, with figuring it out. I've always had rather a passion for puzzles of the mind. Chess, mathematics."

"Bluestocking, eh?"

She shrugged.

Limarque sat down nearby and continued staring at her. "Well, best crack on, then, as you English say, my little thief. Time is wasting."

Gin saw in relief that he seemed to buy her story. But, heart pounding, she felt like she was damned either way. She did not want to give him real information from her father's journal, but she had no doubt this ruthless man would kill her if he decided she was lying.

"Very well," she forced out in a strangled tone. She decided to give him something true out of the journal in the interests of survival, but it would be dated information. Secrets that could no longer do any active harm. "As you wish. The Truveau family. I believe I've come across that name in here before . . ."

He waited impatiently while she flipped through the pages, which, when decoded, were arranged alphabetically by topic. One just had to know where to look.

Rather than putting the topic heading in the obvious place, in the top outer corners of the page, Virgil had listed it on the bottom line, all the way to the right, next to the binding.

On every page of the journal, the letters were carefully grouped into neat blocks of five, alternating with similar groupings of numbers. Her father had been very thorough. There was a whole section on the great Promethean families. Given that she knew the book well and had used it often, she had a fair idea of where to turn.

She scanned down to the bottom line and furtively got to work decoding the subject heading working off her greatest secret, the one they would have killed her for. The keyword: *Serpentine.*

Of course Virgil had chosen a keyword that had special meaning between the two of them. It had been there, one sunny day, at age thirteen, on the banks of the Serpentine lake in Hyde Park that her mother had first introduced her to the gruff, braw Scotsman who was her natural father.

They had become instant friends.

Her heart ached with missing him as she finally found the pages dealing with the Truveau clan. In this situation, her greatest hope was to make him proud.

"Well? What have you got? I'm done waiting," Limarque snapped after a quarter hour.

She cringed away from him slightly as he stomped toward her. "Um . . . there's a story in here about something that happened in 1802."

He looked disappointed by the age of the information, but he nodded nonetheless. "Go on. I worked for him then."

"In 1802, Count Frederic Truveau ordered his men to burn one of the villages near his castle to the ground."

He eyed her warily. "The fire would have been reported in the papers. That proves nothing about this book."

"You're right, it says here that the newspapers reported the blaze as an accident. But according to the book, the truth behind it is a great deal more sordid. It centers around the death of a young footman, Luc Minot, who supposedly committed suicide, hanging himself from a tree."

Limarque's lips curved in a sinister half smile, as though he remembered it well. "Go on. You have my full attention, *chérie.*"

She swallowed hard, unnerved by his snakelike stare. "Minot was new to the household, and apparently before his death, he was shocked to have stumbled across certain perversions going on among the family members of the Truveau clan. He must have confided in someone what he'd seen, for local rumors exploded.

"A few days later, Minot's body was discovered hanging from the tree, then came the blaze. According to this, the Count Truveau set the fires as a warning to the people to keep quiet about his family secrets." She glanced up at him with her heart in her throat. "I'm sure they didn't put that part in the papers." She swallowed hard. "So, is it correct?"

"Oh, yes. I was there," he said softly. "I helped light the fires. Give me another one."

Her heart sank at this command.

"Something about the Order this time," he urged her. "We know they keep a safe house in Calais. Where is it? Give me the address."

Gin dropped her gaze. "There's nothing about that in here."

"Fine. Then let's try another one. Which of the court ladies around the Empress Josephine was their informant?"

"It would take me some time to find that. I haven't got to that part yet."

"You're boring me. Let's try an easy one."

"Yes?" She lifted her gaze to his in dread.

He leaned down close, until their noses nearly touched. "Tell me who killed old Count Truveau. That mystery was never quite solved."

As he stared into her eyes, Gin felt like a hare trapped, mesmerized by the beady gaze of a snake.

Her heart raced with newfound panic.

The wild gleam in Limarque's eyes brought on a sickening realization. Just as lying about the book's contents would have guaranteed her death, telling the truth—showing she really *could* decipher it—would surely condemn her to untold years as his prisoner.

Not to mention what he might do with the information if and when he finally forced it out of her.

It would likely lead to the eventual destruction of every one of Virgil's boys, the valiant men her father had loved as his own sons.

She couldn't let that happen.

The only way she could think to turn the tables on him in that searing moment was to quit trying to feign cooperation and go on the attack.

Seize the element of surprise and find some way to escape.

"Well?" Limarque prompted. "Tell me who the book says killed the Count Truveau."

Holding his stare, she gathered her courage, and whispered coldly: "You did."

Now, there, my love, is a gamble, she mentally told Nick, wherever he was.

And as it turned out, she was right.

Stunned incredulity flashed across Limarque's face. He straightened up, staring at her, his mouth open, as if to ask, *How on earth could the Order know that?*

She pressed her attack, eager to keep him off-balance. "You killed your own employer and blamed the attack on some unknown Order agent. Why did you do it?" she persisted. "Did you ever confess it to your comrades—"

He suddenly grasped her by the throat. "Stop playing games with me!" he roared in her face. "Who are you? Who do you work for? There's no way they could know that!"

In answer, she seized the chunky pewter candlestick nearby and bashed him on the head with it.

He cursed, his hold around her throat dislodged. Leaping to her feet, she fled past him, but he was right behind her. She shrieked in terror when he grabbed her by the hair and threw her onto the nearby couch.

"Little bitch. You need to learn some manners before we proceed." He came toward her with blood trickling down the side of his face from the cut on his temple. With a smooth motion, he reached into his pocket, then snapped the spring on a folding knife as he stalked toward her.

The look in his eyes was terrifying. Gin righted herself on the couch and, heart pounding, glanced past him toward the locked door. The chances of making it past him seemed slim, let alone his henchmen in the other room and all throughout the building.

But this could not happen to her—of all women.

He stopped in front of her, cutting off her yelp of fear as he took hold of her throat again and pushed her onto her back.

His nasty little blade glinted in the candlelight as he held it up before her face. "I think . . . you never intended to help me in the first place. But you will, by the time I'm done with you. Like you, I can be very persuasive." His hand on her throat slid around to grip her nape; he kissed her neck, his lips on one side, his knife on the other.

Gin squeezed her eyes shut and strove to stay calm.

"I must confess, I'm going to enjoy this," he said in a husky tone as he squeezed her breast roughly with his free hand.

She considered kneeing him hard in the groin but feared she'd only be making it worse for herself.

"*You'd better hope he's dead.*" The words escaped against her will in a terrified whisper.

"What?" Trapped under him, she eyed Limarque in seething wrath as he pulled back to meet her gaze. "What did you say?"

"You heard me."

He scoffed. "Black?"

"You think that's his real name?" she countered, the truth her last resort. "Don't be a fool! He isn't a criminal. He's one of the Order's deadliest assassins—who personally saved the life of the Prince Regent not long ago.

"As for me, I'm no thief. I happen to be a baroness, related by blood to half of London's aristocracy, and that man in the alley, he's also a peer, and my lover. He's better connected than you have any idea and more dangerous than you can possibly imagine."

He hissed and jerked back a bit, but a spark of doubt sprang into his eyes.

"More than that," Gin charged on rather brazenly, "he happens to be in love with me. If he hears you forced yourself on me, the pit of Hell itself isn't deep enough to hide you from his wrath. Touch me again, and you can rest assured, Mr. Limarque, you and all your men are already dead."

Limarque recoiled from her, obviously rattled. "You're lying."

She stared into his eyes and shook her head. "Let me go, and maybe he'll let you live."

He climbed off of her abruptly, studying her as though weighing the truth of her words.

She could see that she had shocked him.

Excellent. She pressed her attack with the direst warning she could manufacture as she sat up on the couch, nodding. "You should have killed him while you had the chance. You're going to wish you had. Because he's going to come back with all of his fellow warriors from the Order. And they're going to burn your little kingdom to the ground, tear you all to pieces—"

"Even if what you say is true, you think the Order's going to authorize all that just for one man's harlot of a mistress?"

"Oh, *monsieur,* you don't understand. The man who wrote that book was my father. I'm like a sister to them all. All those mean, vicious lords who brought down the Prometheans. Let me go, or I promise you, you haven't even seen them angry yet." She shook her head with a chiding smile, while Limarque turned white.

"Abducting me was the biggest mistake you ever made. I'm the only chance you've got of getting out of this alive."

He gulped, backing away from her. "It was your idea!" he accused her. "You offered to come with me if I spared him!"

She was thrilled to see him looking so unnerved, but she merely gave a cool shrug. "You've only got your own greed to blame." Then she nodded toward the door. "Why don't you go tell your comrades how you've just painted the biggest possible target on your whole gang? One visible all the way from Dante House in London?"

His dark eyes flared with fear, then all of a sudden, he slammed out of the room.

Gin let out a trembling exhalation.

Limarque had looked so shaken, she was almost certain that when he came back after a brief consultation with his henchmen, it would be to let her go.

But as it turned out, she was wrong.

$\mathcal{N}$obody knew better than a spy that a straight line was not necessarily the shortest distance from point A to B.

Though it was torturous not to follow his raging protective instincts directly and start tearing Paris apart to find Virginia, Nick knew such action would only waste time and probably prove more dangerous to her.

Besides, there was brave, and there was idiotic.

Even if he knew where to find them, single-handedly attacking a whole gang of criminals in their hideout would have been stupid, indeed. Instead, a circuitous route would take him to her side much faster—and would avoid cornering Limarque.

Nick knew a coward when he saw one, and with his back to the wall, Limarque was more likely to do something drastic.

Like killing her to get rid of the evidence.

In the interests of racing ahead of this double crisis so he could stop it from reaching the next stage of disaster, he rushed off to the outskirts of Paris and arrived at last at Angelique's decadent establishment.

The day's gray gloom and the bleak, bare trees of the wooded grounds made the sprawling, towered chateau look all the more sinister. At this hour, the flambeaux that lined the straight formal drive up to the castle were not lit, and the ornate, wrought-iron gates stood open.

Nick drove right in.

It was odd to see the ancient house in such a state of stillness, but of course, the revelries here never really got started until midnight. Pulling the horses to a halt, he told the boys to wait in the carriage while he jumped down from the driver's box and stalked toward the heavy front doors.

Banging the huge metal knocker against the door, he hoped the "vampire queen," as he had once privately dubbed her, was not sleeping the day away. He had to talk to her.

A harried servant woman finally answered the door, some poor, haggard, old maid probably tasked with mopping up vomit from the previous night's guests, judging by the terrible smell of the place when he stepped inside.

The chateau was a different place by moonlight, magical, alluring, but in the harsh glare of day, Nick found it all deeply disturbing.

The old woman recognized him as the former top mercenary employed by her mistress. Wearily letting him in, she told him to do as he liked. He answered with a nod that he would show himself to Madame's apartment upstairs.

God knew, he knew the way.

Bracing himself for her reaction to his return and barely daring to wonder how many people he might find her in bed with this morning, he strode through the chateau, passing the wasteland of the card rooms and the little, velvet-curtained theatre where the most exotic acts were performed at night.

He passed a parlor where the whores without their makeup sat sipping their morning coffee, swathed in loose dressing gowns, dark circles under their eyes. Without the glamour of candlelight and wine, the ill, pallid cast of their complexions rather startled him, but not as much the apathetic dullness in their eyes, the hardness of their deadened souls.

Marching on, his bootheels ringing over the dirty marble floors, Nick passed the heavily guarded banker's chamber, where Angelique's current head of security, Luc, a man he had trained, was overseeing the counting of money from the previous night's haul.

Leaning on the accountant's desk, Luc shot to his feet in shock when Nick walked by. He rushed into the doorway.

"Black!" he called after him in astonishment.

Nick tensed, unsure of the welcome he'd get and resenting any delay. Nevertheless, he put on a smile and turned.

"It is you!" Luc strode toward him with a grin. "Sweet Hades, man, I thought you were in prison!"

Nick smiled wryly and shook his offered hand. "Ah, they let me out for good behavior."

"Right." Luc laughed and clapped him on the back. "*Ça fait longtemps!*"

"I know, six months. Believe me, I counted." Though smiling, Nick stayed on his guard, well aware that his friend would turn on him if Madame gave the order that he was not to leave.

Luc gave him a knowing look. "She'll be thrilled to know you're back."

"Can't stay," Nick replied in a breezy tone. "Just popped in for a visit."

"I'll bet. She is alone up there." He glanced meaningfully toward the ceiling.

Nick raised a brow. "What is the world coming to?" he drawled. "Must be pining for me."

"Actually, it's possible," Luc replied.

Nick frowned. "Bloody hell," he said under his breath.

Luc snorted. "Good luck, then."

As Nick started to walk away, his friend called after him, "Some cards with me and the boys this afternoon?"

"No, thanks, can't stay. I'm in a bit of a hurry."

As Nick jogged up the curved, marble staircase, he wondered how much poor Luc currently owed the house. For as beautiful as she was, Angelique was a shiny black spider who lured in her flies, then sucked the life out of them. In more ways than one.

He braced himself outside the door to her bedchamber.

If there was no other way, he supposed he could play the whore for her one more time. He had done it for the Order. She liked him, and she always had good information.

He just hoped it didn't come to that, or if it did, that at least she was no longer quite so enthralled with whips and chains. He supposed he would endure anything to save Virginia, but it was the middle of the day, he was on the brink of multiple disasters, and frankly didn't have time to get as drunk as he'd need to be to play her dirty games.

Of course, he understood that Angelique herself was not entirely to blame for what she was. Surviving the Red Terror could warp a person in any number of ways. Life had made her ruthless from the time she had been the sixteen-year-old mistress of a duke who had gone to the guillotine.

Nick did not believe she had let her guard down for one second ever since. But maybe, just maybe, for once she'd do something for somebody else out of the goodness of her heart. He steeled himself and knocked.

"*Qui est là?*" she barked from inside the chamber.

"Jonathan Black."

He heard a gasp and light, running footsteps, then the door whooshed open. And there she stood in all her dark beauty, wearing nothing but fluffy heeled shoes and an open silk dressing gown that swirled around her naked body.

Her dark eyes wide, she suddenly launched herself into his arms. "Oh, my darling! They let you out? I am so glad to see you!" She pulled him into her room, pushed him up against the wall, and kissed him, picking up right where they had last left off nearly a year ago.

Nick was rather taken aback.

But things had definitely changed. The last thing he felt like doing was kissing her, but he was wary enough of her vanity not to protest. Oddly enough, though he did not have a monogamous understanding with Virginia, he felt guilty anyway—and tainted by Angelique's passionate onslaught. He saw it for what it was, after all. Simply her way of claiming what she believed to be her property.

"Mmm." Ending the kiss, she stepped back just enough to cup his face between her hands, staring up into his eyes. "I knew you would come back to me. Oh, my darling. We shall have such times together! Come. Let me give you a proper welcome home." She took his hands and started drawing him toward her huge, feverishly carved canopy bed.

But Nick could not hide how he recoiled at the order, let alone that she should call this place his home.

God, no.

This was not where he belonged. It couldn't be. He was no longer one those dead-eyed people wandering around downstairs like lost souls.

Not anymore.

She tilted her head, scrutinizing him, her dark eyes shrewdly narrowed. "What is it?"

Nick abruptly remembered he was supposed to be a

well-trained spy, cool and calculating. "Business before pleasure, love," he murmured, capturing her chin with his thumb, caressing her cheek with a fond air. "I have a proposition for you."

"Ooooh, this day is off to a good start." She released him and flitted over to her sumptuous velvet chair, tucking her feet under her as she posed pertly. "Do tell."

Nick sauntered toward her. "I was wondering, Madame, if you would like me to take a shipment of weapons to the Bacchus Bazaar and sell them for you. I'll get you a good price."

She toyed with a lock of her long, dark hair, studying him. "Hmm. I wasn't *planning* on participating in the auction this year . . . but . . . Is this for the Order?"

He nodded.

"I thought you wanted to part ways with them for good," she said in surprise.

With a rueful sigh, he sat down idly on the arm of her chair. "Let's just say they helped me see the error of my ways during my incarceration," he answered dryly.

"Ah, that bit of nastiness. Poor Nicky." She laid her hand on his knee and caressed him. "So that's why you're here, then. Another mission. Why do you never come simply for *me?*" she asked with a petulant, little-girl pout.

"I have come for you many times," he reminded her with a dark smile.

She bit her lip as she dug her fingers into his thigh appreciatively. "And I for you."

"Next question. Do you know a man named Simon Limarque? He used to work for Truveau."

"Oh, Truveau's bodyguard, right. Hmm, he shows up to gamble here every now and then. Never had much of a conversation with the man. Not sober, anyway. But he's on my list of beddable guests."

"Who isn't?" he drawled.

She smacked him lightly and laughed.

"Do you know where he keeps his headquarters?"

"No idea. I could probably find out for you if you give me a few days."

"I don't have a few days."

"Why?"

"I need to track him down, and I haven't got much time," Nick said vaguely.

She leaned her head against the chair back and frowned at him. "I know that look. What, you're planning to kill him?"

He petted her silky head to distract her with a façade of affection. "Let's just say you may have missed your chance."

"Ah, must you? You're no fun. What's he done?"

"Abducted an English lady. A baroness."

She looked at him suspiciously. "The Order sent you to rescue her?"

"Yes," he said firmly, praying that he concealed all signs of his deeper bond to the baroness in question. "This is my chance to redeem myself in their eyes. I'm sure you know how important this is to me. If I don't get her back, Limarque is going to sell her at the auction."

Angelique winced.

"The Crown won't countenance the insult," he added. "Her husband is a good friend of the Regent."

"I heard you got shot for him, by the way!"

Nick shrugged. "You know me. Always getting shot. Hobby of mine."

She gave his thigh a hearty slap. "Luckily, you're very hard to kill."

"Yes," Nick replied rather wistfully.

"So, what can I do for you, darling?"

"Well, we both know the sort of bad, disreputable folk who attend the Bacchus Bazaar—"

"My kind of people!" she taunted with a grin. "So what do you mean to do, enter the auction and buy her back? Using my guns? You almost make me jealous."

"No, I plan to get her out of there before it comes to that. They want this woman back alive and preferably unharmed. What I need is a solid cover so I can get into the auction and find out where Limarque is keeping her." He lifted her hand and kissed her knuckles. "So will you help me? Jonathan Black could go to the Bacchus Bazaar as your representative."

"Hmm," she said again, scanning his face before she asked the usual question. "What's in it for me?"

Nick laughed. "Egads, they should put that on your headstone when you die."

"Who says I'm ever going to die?" she asked tartly.

"Of course, how silly of me. Everyone knows goddesses are immortal."

She rose and turned to him, crossing her arms, tilting her head, staring into his eyes. He arched a brow in question. "What are you up to? You're never this nice to me."

"Maybe I missed you." He reached out and grasped the edge of her robe, pulling her to him. When she was in arm's reach, he wrapped his hand around her nape and kissed her deeply, ignoring the stale taste of last night's liquor on her breath. "I'll tell you what," he whispered.

"I'm listening."

He knew he was being ruthless, but he also knew her character. Angelique would never help him unless she got exactly what she wanted. "Let me take the weapons, and when I come back, I'll arrange to stay here with you for a while. Would you like that? We can make up for lost time."

"You expect me to wait?"

"The Bazaar takes place in a few days, Ange. I have to go. I don't even know yet where I'm traveling to. Come on. I need your help."

"And you shall have it," she breathed, arching against him. "But first, I need *you*."

His heart sank, and a rush of vicious curses at this waste of time blazed wrathfully through his mind, but he was a consummate actor and didn't have time to argue.

He scooped her off her feet with a roguish laugh. "Oh, do you, now?"

She wrapped her arms around his neck in breathless delight and started kissing him as he carried her over to her bed.

He set her on her knees on the edge of the mattress, where she proceeded to help him pull off his coat and start taking off his clothes.

Once upon a time, it had been easy to perform for her with reasonable enthusiasm. But something had changed. The moment she slipped her hand into his trousers, Nick experienced an inexplicable malfunction.

For the first time in his life, his member simply refused to cooperate. He glanced down at himself, aghast: Angelique looked up from his peacefully slumbering cock to meet his stunned gaze. She arched a brow in mildly vexed amusement.

"What's wrong, darling?" she drawled.

"I-I don't know," he stammered, reaching up to touch the back of his head. "Maybe it's the concussion . . . Bloody hell!" *And I thought prison was humiliating.*

"Don't worry. I'm sure I can remedy this," she said, but she couldn't.

Good God, had Virgil's daughter ruined him for all other women? Angelique had mastered every sensual trick known to man, and did her best with mouth and hands, but it was clearly no use. Someone simply wasn't interested in her, and within minutes, to Nick's relief, she lost patience and backed off angrily. So much for his legendary status as a stud.

Still at a loss, he saw he now had a bigger problem: Angelique took it personally. "What's wrong with you?" she demanded. "Are you ill?"

"No! No, I—" He bit back the truth. *I just don't want to do this. With you. At all.* "I don't know. Worried about the mission, I guess, maybe. Tired."

She folded her arms across her chest. "Or maybe you just don't want me anymore."

"Don't be absurd. You're the most desirable woman on the Continent," he lied, as he quickly fastened his trousers again, there being no point in leaving them open.

"Hm, but that doesn't include England, does it, darling?" She pinned him with a cold stare full of suspicion. "Who is this English baroness you're out to rescue, exactly?"

"She's no one," he said flatly.

But the underworld queen stared into his eyes and slowly shook her head at her realization of the truth. "You bastard."

"What? Come on! It happens to every man at some point."

"Not to you. Your mind is obviously elsewhere—or should I say your heart. Hell must have frozen over, because Nick the bastard Forrester has finally fallen in love. And it clearly wasn't with me."

He opened his mouth to deny it, knowing from experience what her jealousy could cost him, but the words would not come out.

Angelique looked askance at him in cynical understanding, but for his part, Nick was baffled.

What the hell was wrong with him? He couldn't fuck another woman, and now he couldn't lie? He was a goddamned spy. What the hell had that redhead done to him? "Angelique, please. I can account for this. I got bashed in the head with a brick earlier today—"

"Poor boy," she said, bored, as she turned her back on him and finally saw fit to close and tie her robe.

"I still need your help," he forced out. "I'm begging you."

She laughed and lit herself a cheroot. "Usually I like it when you beg, but this is just pathetic. Get out of my chamber."

Nick shut his eyes and banged his head once softly against the bedpost with a low groan of self-disgust.

"She must be really something else," Angelique continued, as though she couldn't help herself.

Nick opened his eyes wearily and found her staring at him in withering scorn.

"I knew there was something different about you, but I assumed it was from everything you'd been through, prison and all. How dare you come in here and think that you can use me?"

"You do it to me all the time!" he barked back without warning, glowering at her as his true feelings burst through the façade.

She blinked.

He had never raised his voice to her before, but Nick was past caring. "Can't you just once in your life, do something decent for somebody else? I thought we were friends."

"And I thought we were much more than that," she said icily. "Apparently not." She threw his shirt at him. "Get out of my house and don't come back."

He floundered at the order, his heart pounding. He pulled his shirt on slowly, stalling for time. But, God, if he didn't have his body with which to barter with her, how was he supposed to get the cutthroat seductress to go along with his plan?

He had to get into the Bacchus Bazaar.

There had to be something he could offer in exchange. Something else. He bit his lip, racking his brains as he found his cravat and put it around his neck.

Give her the emerald?

Can't.

He might have to use it to buy Virginia's freedom.

He had no gold, no information to pass along, no

nothing, he thought with a furious curse under his breath.

But then, as Nick wearily picked up his coat, cringing at the thought of having to return empty-handed to the carriage where the boys waited, and having to admit to Phillip that he had failed, a diabolical inspiration suddenly flashed across his mind. He froze.

Maybe he had one item, after all, that might interest Angelique . . .

Oh, but I can't, he thought, shaken that he should even think of such a thing. *It's too evil. Even for me.*

"Would you leave, or do you want me to call for security?" she snapped.

What choice did he have?

"Angelique," he said tactfully, taking a wary step toward her. "Before I go, I actually do have a present for you."

"Oh, really?" she asked dubiously. "What is it?"

"A new toy. May I?"

She shrugged, skeptically willing to accept a parting gift.

"One moment," he said.

She watched him in suspicion as he stepped out into the hallway, where he called for a servant and sent him on his errand.

She slanted him an aloof, questioning look when he returned to the doorway of her chamber. "What are you up to?"

He shrugged. "There's someone I want you to meet."

"Who?" she demanded.

"You'll see," he said, leaning in the doorway to wait.

Mere minutes later, the servant he had sent out to the carriage returned with the sacrificial lamb.

Nick beckoned to him, and into the room stepped Virginia's beautiful boy, John Carr.

The young man gazed at Nick in question, but Nick steered him firmly into Madame's chamber.

The minute she saw him, Angelique stopped scowling.

Her stare homed in on him, scanning him from his princely golden locks to his dusty black boots. "Well, well. Is it Christmas?"

An intrigued smile curved the rouged lips of the vampire queen, her silk dressing gown mysteriously falling untied again as she glided toward the lad.

Carr stared, mesmerized by the way the garment skimmed her white, pearlescent body.

She was equally pleased with the offering.

"Wherever did you find him?" she murmured to Nick, but did not take her eyes off John Carr. "Look at you . . ."

He backed up a few steps in blushing confusion as she prowled toward him. But she laughed in delight. "Don't worry, I won't bite. Yet." Then her hands alighted on his chest. "Come in, you pretty thing. We must get acquainted."

Nick did the introductions.

"Angelique, allow me to present Mr. John Carr of England. John, this is Madame Angelique. She is very rich and powerful."

"And also very beautiful," he answered breathlessly.

"Oh, you're too kind! Isn't he adorable?" She was hanging on him, caressing him and licking her lips like she could already taste him. "How old are you, Monsieur Carr?"

He swallowed hard, bewildered by her attentions. "Twenty-three."

"*Là!*" she exclaimed, probably because the lad was half her age. "And do you have a wife?"

"Oh, no!" he answered, wide-eyed, already half her slave.

"That's good. Very good. Poor thing, you're hurt. What happened to your shoulder?"

"I got shot, ma'am."

"How awful." She cupped his boyishly smooth face and whispered, "You can call me Angelique."

"One of Limarque's men shot him," Nick informed her. "Just a flesh wound. It'll heal soon," he added like he was trying to sell her a horse. "Until then, you'll have to go easy on him."

"Young man, you're staring at me."

"Sorry." Carr swallowed hard. "It's just, your, um, your dressing gown isn't . . . quite . . . fastened."

"Really?" She slipped it off on shoulder, showing him even more, and Carr moaned softly, averting his fevered gaze to the wall.

Nick rolled his eyes.

Angelique laughed in delight. "Ah, look at him blush! You never did that. Very well, I accept. He's adorable."

"We have a deal?" Nick demanded.

Carr turned to him with a questioning frown.

"Maybe," she answered, sidling closer to her prospective new plaything. "Face of an angel," she murmured, returning her attention to the lad. "Oh, you beautiful thing, you could have anything you want out of life with a face like that. What do you want most of all? Tell mama."

Carr stared at her, finally sensing that his opportunity here was real.

"Well?" she whispered.

"To be rich," he confessed.

"Mmm, I can teach you that. Among other things. Would you like to stay here with me for a while as my very special guest?"

He nodded mutely, his chest heaving as she stroked him. Then Carr surprised even Nick, gamely made a move and kissed her.

Angelique dove in, running her hands all over him. Her sure, sensual explorations produced the effect that was to be expected from any healthy male in his early twenties being caressed by a beautiful, depraved seductress.

Well, as long as that man wasn't *he*, Nick thought wryly as he looked away, heaving a sigh of impatience.

Carr ended the kiss, letting out a small gasp when her fingers found the growing bulge in his trousers.

"Mmm," she purred, "now that's more like it."

"Sorry," he croaked.

"Don't be ashamed, darling. Honestly, I'm flattered." She cast Nick a pointed look of mocking reproach as she played with Carr's erection through his clothes. "Does that feel good?"

"For God's sake! Can we please finish our business first?"

She kissed Carr's neck in amusement, holding Nick's angry gaze. "Leave him here with me, and you can take your guns. Have Luc load twenty crates of rifles on a wagon."

"I want a few howitzers, as well."

"Fine. But my proceeds from the sale had best be sitting inside my bank by the end of the month, or you're dead."

"I understand."

"And Nick?"

"Yes?" he asked, pausing as he turned to go.

"I don't ever want to see your face again."

"You won't," he answered, then he pulled the door shut and left the couple to their pleasures.

Match made in heaven, he thought in annoyance, or more likely, the other place. An insatiable sophisticate with a taste for domination, and a spoiled prince who craved the pampered life of playing stud to a wealthy patroness.

Those two deserved each other.

Nevertheless, Nick felt a little guilty about bringing them together. The lad *had* arguably saved his life.

But it was not as though John Carr was going to be corrupted. He was already well on his way to that condition on his own before their paths had ever crossed.

Nick gave Luc the message about the twenty crates of

rifles and the half dozen howitzers that he'd be taking to the auction for Madame.

While Luc got some men on the task of loading up the wagon, Nick returned to the carriage to check on Phillip.

The boy was waiting anxiously, consumed with curiosity, craning his neck to take in the view and watching everything. "What's happening? Did it work?"

Nick nodded. "They're loading up the wagon for us now."

"What took so long? Hey! Where's John?"

"He'll be staying here," Nick answered vaguely.

"Why? Is everything all right?"

"He's going to be keeping a lady company here for a while."

"A lady! But don't we need him?" Phillip exclaimed.

Not as much as she does.

"We're better off without him. He might've saved my life dragging me out of that alley, but he's the one who stole your mother's book. He's proved he can't be trusted. Better to leave him here, out of trouble."

Phillip studied him. "All right. You're sure about this?"

"Trust me, he'll be very happy here. Can you drive a carriage?"

"Pfft!" Phillip answered with a scoff.

Nick laughed, startled by the boy's indignant response. "Good," he drawled. "Then get up on the driver's box and follow me. I'll take the wagon. We need to get back to Paris before dark."

There was no time to waste. With the game piece in his pocket and the shipment of weapons for the auction secured, all that remained was to rush back to L'Hôtel Grande Alexandre and register at last for the Bacchus Bazaar.

*M*eanwhile, back in the criminals' hideaway, Gin waited while Limarque conferred with his mates in the other room.

Unfortunately, her fierce satisfaction with having scared him off was short-lived.

After all, her threats of doom about how Nick and his brother warriors would descend on Limarque's gang to avenge her would quickly prove hollow if Nick had died in that alley, or even if he simply couldn't find her.

Since the thought of his dying was too agonizing to contemplate, she reminded herself of all the many scars on his body that proved how hard he was to kill. Then she focused her attention on listening to the low-toned exchange among the men in the adjoining room.

Maybe her dire warnings were enough to inspire them to release her, simply let her go.

Or . . . maybe she had frightened them into killing her as soon as possible to hide the evidence of their crimes.

Her hands still bound, she got up and crossed the room silently, listening at the door.

The fear clouding her mind made it more difficult to translate their quiet, rapid words from their French, but it seemed fairly clear that Limarque did not relish the thought of becoming the target of Nick's wrath. She closed her eyes and concentrated.

"The bitch claims to be a baroness."

"What do we do?"

"We need to get rid of her. Fast."

"But she can translate the book, no?"

"We don't need her. She revealed enough about the codes just now to give a leg up to whoever buys it from us. It's a book cipher crossed with old Masonic code."

"Ahh," they said, much to her satisfaction, considering she had been lying through her teeth.

The real code her father had used had been a Viginere cipher—a much more difficult affair. Still, they or their clients were sure to figure it out eventually.

"All right, if we don't need her, what do you propose? Kill the wench or let her go?"

"I don't dare let her go! She'll run straight to the *gendarmes* and make such a noise, with her title, that they won't be able to cover this up for us."

"So we kill her, then."

Limarque was silent. Gin listened in dread although without surprise.

"If we do, we mustn't leave a trace of her."

"Burn the body?"

"That, or dump it far out at sea," he replied. "If we do this, no one must be able to trace it back to us, or there will be hell to pay."

"Would it be simpler to keep her alive? We've got places we could stash her—"

"It's not that easy! She's a hellcat and tricky as a witch. She could escape. And be warned," Limarque told them, "somebody taught her to fight."

"I'll beat the fight out of her," one of his henchmen said, probably Brou.

"We're not animals!" Limarque rebuked him.

Oh, yes, you are. This claim of chivalry on his part was nothing but a cover for his cowardice.

"We need to back away from this," Limarque concluded. "She's got connections."

There was a silence as they pondered the problem: Gin listened keenly at the door to learn her fate.

"I have an idea," one of the men suddenly spoke up.

"What?" Limarque replied.

"Why don't we give her to Rotgut?"

Gin's eyes widened.

Limarque let out a sinister laugh. "Ah, Cagnard, I could kiss you! What an excellent idea! But not *give* her. That piece of shit would be suspicious. We'll sell her to him."

"Cheap," Brou replied.

"Problem solved." Limarque sounded wholly relieved to have finally found a way to wash his hands of her. "If Jonathan Black or whatever his name is wants to buy the wench back at the auction, that's up to him."

"You think he can really outbid the sheiks?"

They all laughed.

"Not my problem," said Limarque.

"And the book?"

"Oh, we're keeping that."

The hell you are. Gin locked the door from the inside to buy herself some time and crossed at once to the desk where she had left her father's journal.

"Set up a meeting with Rotgut right away," she heard Limarque order his men. His voice sounded louder; then the door handle jiggled.

He immediately cursed.

Gin grabbed her father's book and took it to the only window in the room. Slowed by her bound wrists, she fumbled with the window latch while Limarque pounded on the door, cursing at her and yelling for one of his men to bring a key.

Heart pounding, she swung the window open, then drew back and threw her father's book as far as she could out into the street.

Better it should be trampled, rolled over by carriages or land in a puddle where the writing would be smeared than remain with them, knowing what they meant to do with the information.

But it was a poor throw, a girlish throw, because of her bound wrists, and as she cursed in fury, the door banged open, and Simon Limarque saw what she had done.

He immediately barked at his men to run out into the

street and retrieve it. Then he came for her once again, a tenfold fury in his eyes.

But there was nowhere to run.

His fist flying at her was the last thing she saw for quite some time.

One blow to the face, and the world went black.

Chapter
20

As soon as he reached Paris that night, Nick returned the hired carriage, then got permission from Monsieur de Vence to leave his wagon full of crates in the shed behind the hotel, just for a few hours.

Though the stacked crates of rifles in the wagon's bed were hidden under a tarp, Nick didn't want anyone snooping around his cargo. But then came the problem of how he was supposed to be in two places at the same time.

Somebody had to stand guard over the weapons while Nick went to register for the Bacchus Bazaar. He had only one option at this point: the red-haired fifteen-year-old.

Phillip looked at him, wide-eyed, as Nick loaded one of the fine Baker rifles and explained his next assignment.

If entrusting the lad with driving the carriage weren't enough to give *him* a fit of apoplexy, (though in truth, Phillip had proved perfectly competent), Nick now had no choice but to leave the pup standing guard alone over their extremely valuable shipment of weapons.

Well, the kid wanted to be an agent, Nick mused grimly, and with Virgil for a grandfather, it was hardly the first time Phillip had ever held a weapon.

Besides, there was no one else on hand that Nick knew he could trust. Anyway, he did not intend to be gone for more than twenty minutes or so.

Praying no disaster would befall the plucky lad in his absence, Nick locked him in the shed. His last glimpse of Phillip was him sitting atop the wagon with the rifle resting across his lap and a confident gleam in his eyes.

You'd make your grandfather proud, he thought. "I'll be back in half an hour," Nick assured him, giving the boy a bolstering nod.

He glanced at his fob watch and went.

The Grande Alexandre across the way was arrayed in its elegant evening attire, crystal chandeliers aglow.

The tourists and visitors to Paris bustled about on their way to the opera or some fancy ball, gentlemen in formal black and white, ladies clad in satin gowns with stylish feathers on their heads.

Nick strode past them all across the shining marble floors. He had the game piece in his pocket, but on his way to the suite upstairs where Hugh Lowell had instructed them to go to register, he decided to take a brief detour.

Despite all the upheavals of this day, he had not forgotten where he had started out this morning: in the café down in the lobby. He could not help Virginia directly at this moment, but each of those abducted girls surely meant as much to someone out there as she did to him.

Though he was anxious to get back to Phillip as quickly as possible, he took a moment to investigate E. Dolan, the suspicious man he had noticed in the restaurant this morning and identified as a possibility for Rotgut.

Nick promptly found his way to Room Fourteen, as

noted on the mysterious E. Dolan's bill at the restaurant. He knocked on the door and waited.

No answer.

He glanced to the right and the left down the hallway, then picked the lock. Opening the door discreetly, he poked his head into the room—and instantly whispered a curse.

The room was empty. He stepped inside and looked around. Nothing. No clothes, no papers, no traveling trunks. Whether E. Dolan was Rotgut or just some random traveler, Nick was too late to learn.

Whoever he was, it was obvious he had already checked out of the hotel.

"*Y*ou caught me just in time," a gravelly voice was saying with a tinge of a Birmingham accent, but Gin could not see the speaker through her blindfold.

She had woken up from Limarque's clobbering blow to find herself once more bound and gagged, rough hands holding her by her elbows. No longer locked up in the criminals' hideaway, she could smell the Seine and hear the river's current pouring past.

The ground was shaky underfoot. It creaked, as well, but she couldn't say for sure if they were standing on a dock or had already boarded a boat.

If she was not mistaken, she was about to become a passenger aboard the infamous *Black Jest*.

The gag in her mouth stifled any screams of protest she could have made; instead, she could only listen in disbelief to Simon Limarque selling her to the very man whose underworld trade in women she had been investigating.

"You'll have to watch her," the Frenchman warned. "Redheaded hellcat, this one."

"Good! The gentl'men like a lass with spirit. More fun for 'em to break." She jerked away violently when unknown hands squeezed her breasts. "Ah, calm down. You're not to my taste. Just making sure these nice round globes o' yours is real. No, no cotton stuffing here."

She was still cringing when Rotgut let her go. God, that man stank. But she noticed that Limarque still hadn't seen fit to warn his vile colleague that she was a titled aristocrat with connections to the Order.

Well, ignorance wasn't going to save Rotgut when Nick caught up with him, she thought.

She heard the clink of coins changing hands and wondered how much she had gone for.

But before Limarque handed her over to Rotgut for good, he paused to give her his own cruel farewell. "Don't worry, *chérie,* if your lover really cares for you, he'll come to the auction and buy you back. If he's still alive. Just hope that he has pockets deep enough to outbid the Arabian sheiks. With that flame-colored hair and milky skin of yours, I'm sure they'd find you an exotic addition to any of their harems. Did you know they don't believe in allowing women to experience sexual pleasure, by the way? Seems an abomination to me as a Frenchman. But it's true. They'll give you a small surgery, just there." He thrust his fingers in between her legs, causing her to jump with revulsion. "Make a female eunuch of you. Pity, eh? Ah, well. You'll still have your memories. I hope he was worth it."

She was still reeling from his horrifying words when he pushed her into Rotgut's arms. She recognized the latter by the rank stench of body odor and stale whiskey.

The slaver clamped her in a pitiless hold and grunted a goodbye to Limarque and his friends leaving.

Then Rotgut slung her over his shoulder like the merchandise she was and carried her down into the bowels of his ship.

Her head still throbbed thanks to Limarque's various punches, leaving her with a black eye; Gin felt sick to her stomach from the stink of her brutish captor, the swaying motion of the moored vessel, and, most of all, from fear.

For a lady who had been so determined to remain the mistress of her own destiny, under no man's control, this turn of events was, in short, the ultimate nightmare.

She could not comprehend being bought and sold like an animal. But was that not why this case had got to her so badly in the first place? It was precisely *because* she hated the insult of such powerlessness so much that she had made it her business to help those girls.

And now she was one of them.

Rotgut halted. She heard a jangle of keys and a rusty lock's turning. A heavy door creaked open. The next thing she knew, she was being tumbled off his shoulder onto a hard floor.

He pulled the blindfold off her roughly. She winced at the jar to her black eye from where Limarque had punched her. Wherever Rotgut had brought her, probably a section of the cargo hold, it was dark.

"Lift your hands," he ordered.

She looked up at him in wide-eyed terror as he took out a large knife.

"Calm down. You don't need these bindings down here," he said impatiently, pausing to frown at her black eye. He shook his head in disgust, but only because such bruises were unflattering to any woman's beauty and might bring down the price that he could get for her.

Then he slit the chafing rope that bound her wrists. Putting his knife away, he straightened up, turned around, and headed back for the door.

He left her to pick apart the knot on her gag herself, so he wouldn't have to hear whatever she might want to say when she could talk again.

Not that pleas to let her go were anything new to him.

He had probably learned how to ignore them long ago.

The heavy door slammed shut, and the keys jangled again as he locked her in. By the dim glow of the lantern in the passageway, she got her first glimpse of Rotgut's stone block of a face when he peered through the little, barred window on the door. "The rest of you, look after her," he ordered before tromping off.

That was the first moment Gin realized there were others in the room with her.

She slowly looked around as her eyes adjusted and could just make them out. About a dozen figures huddled in the dark, cowering up against the walls around her.

Beaten and terrified.

*N*ick let himself out of the vacant Room Fourteen and pulled the door shut furtively behind him. He was too late to confront the mysterious Rotgut, but he fixed his sights on the next task: registering for the Bacchus Bazaar.

He strode back to the staircase of the Grande Alexandre and headed for the Imperial Suite on the top floor.

They had two large men on security duty at the door, but when Nick presented the game piece from Hugh Lowell, they let him in.

Inside the opulent sitting room behind the door, three bland, quiet, respectable men with the air of bankers waited to take down his information and ascertain that he was qualified to take part.

He gave his name as Jonathan Black, noted his cargo, and informed them where he was staying.

"Everything appears to be in order," one of the men said. "Very good, sir. The location will be sent to you by midnight."

"I wonder if I might leave a message with you here for

one of my colleagues. I understand he checks in on the registration list from time to time."

The comment made the bankers nervous. They glanced uncertainly at each other.

"I don't know about that, sir. But, of course, you are welcome to leave a message if you like."

"Thank you." Nick accepted a small piece of paper and leaned across the desk to dip the quill pen in the pot of ink. His message to Limarque was simple but ominous: three small words charged with dark promise.

I am coming.

$\mathcal{I}$t was amazing how much easier it was to ignore one's own terror when one had to be brave for others.

Down in the cold, damp cargo hold with the abducted girls she had set out to rescue, Gin had somehow managed to rally, and had gathered her fellow prisoners around.

Exchanging whispered introductions, she soon found that just getting them to talk helped everyone to fight back the atmosphere of choking fear in that dark, floating dungeon.

She did her best to encourage them not to lose heart. "People are looking for us. It's going to be all right," she told them with more conviction than she felt.

Sometimes hope was everything.

Still, she chose her words carefully, for the girls knew nothing about what their captors had in store for them.

"Please, ma'am, are they going to kill us?" a bedraggled young blonde choked out.

"No. As long as we are reasonably cooperative, we should be all right. Have they been feeding you?"

"Gruel," said another.

"Do you know where they're taking us, please?" the little one, Rose, asked.

She was no more than twelve, much to Gin's rage.

She put her arm around the child. "We'll find out when we get there, love."

All of sudden, the frigate groaned and began to slosh slightly from side to side.

"We're moving!"

They could hear a great rumbling of chains in the deep.

"What is that?" the sloe-eyed brunette asked anxiously.

Gin stared into the shadows, listening. "They're pulling up anchor," she murmured. Rotgut and his men must have received notice of the location for the Bacchus Bazaar.

Her heart sank. *Oh, no.*

Nick's window of opportunity to find her was fast closing, especially now that Limarque had transferred her to Rotgut. As frightened as she still was for *his* safety, the time had come to consider her own—and these girls'.

Presuming, God willing, that Nick had survived the treacherous attack in the alley, what if his injuries and any period of unconsciousness had caused him to miss the deadline to register for the auction?

Then he would not be privy to their destination. *As soon as we leave Paris, he's not going to have the slightest idea where to find me.*

God, she could not let herself think like that. Nevertheless, she realized that help might not be on the way. Any rescue of herself and these girls might truly come down to her, alone.

Then the ship lurched, leaving its moorings, and despite the dangers of a moonlight sail, the slavers' vessel entered the main channel of the current.

Soon, the *Black Jest* was gliding down the Seine, leaving Paris behind.

Destination unknown.

$\mathcal{P}$hillip's reaction to the announcement of their final destination was a puzzled, "Corfu? Where's that?"

"The Ionian Islands. Northern Greece," Nick told him. "Gorgeous place. Horrible reason to go."

Then came the mad dash in the wagon full of crates, barreling southeast from Paris to Dijon. There, he had the crates of weapons loaded onto a river barge and took the River Saône south through the lush countryside of Burgundy, all the way to its confluence with the Rhone at Lyons.

Nick was well aware that if they had attempted the overland route with their heavy cargo, they would have had to choose to contend either with the Alps to the east, the Midi-Pyrénées to the west, or the wild, rugged country of the Massif Central down the middle. To say nothing of the temperamental weather in that high country and the early snowfalls and the unreliability of finding fresh horses as needed. Instead, the rivers of France allowed them to float right past these mighty obstacles with all due haste.

Still, though it was the fastest route, Nick found it agonizingly slow and much too quiet, considering that Virginia's life was at stake. He sat restlessly on the barge hour after hour, watching the graceful landscape of France drift past like his life passing him by. Thirty-six years old, and what did he have to show for it but a lot of scars?

He tried to ignore the churning uncertainty about where his life was really going to go from here as the scenery slowly unfurled: quaint towns and tiny villages; picturesque bridges under which they glided; sleepy vineyards brown and spindle-branched, tucked in for the winter; glorious chateaux where the haughty local lords presided; ancient forts and castles in the distance; Roman ruins; spectacular mountain peaks that loomed against the skyline.

All the beauty merely pained him without her by his side.

Never in his life had any woman ever affected him this way. She had turned him inside out, and if Limarque hurt her while she was his captive, Nick also vowed the most savage sort of revenge on the man and his whole gang.

Bloodthirsty fantasies of doom and dismemberment seemed just a tad excessive as the Rhone finally carried them down to Avignon, past the palace of the popes. From there, it was an easy journey to Marseilles on the Côte d'Azure, where he hired a plain but fast vessel whose captain was willing to take his gold (well, Phillip's gold) without asking too many questions about what was in the crates.

As the French vessel pulled up anchor among the cloud of squawking seagulls, Phillip turned to him, the sea breeze running riot through his Virgil red hair. "Finally, we can head for Greece!"

"We go by way of Italy," Nick replied. "It'll be faster."

"Oh! I've never been to Italy before."

He clapped the boy on the back in wordless encouragement, then they stood at the rails and watched the fishing boats farther out working their nets.

Nick looked askance at Phillip, studying him with a watchful eye. He wondered how the boy was doing. They had become great chums on their journey, and Nick was doing his best to keep the lad's spirits high and his own dread to himself. He did not want to scare him any worse about his mother's safety.

Probably should have sent him back to England, he reflected, but figured he could keep a better eye on her son this way. There was no telling what the baby would-be Order agent might do if he were left unsupervised. No doubt, it would be something rash and foolhardy, more likely to get the little cork-head into some new scrape and only cause more headaches for *him*. Beyond that, well, truth be told, Nick was glad of the pup's company.

It kept him from obsessing any more than he already was about rescuing Virginia and ripping Simon Limarque limb from limb.

He was not proud of the fact, but he no longer really gave one damn about Virgil's missing book or those kidnapped girls. He could not even think about either of those disasters compared to the knowledge that the only woman who had ever really mattered to him was probably being tortured to reveal the book's codes.

He tamped down more fantasies of death and destruction at the thought and tried to join in Phillip's enthusiasm about the dolphins following their boat.

With a quick sail eastward along the Côte d'Azure, then, dipping south to swoop between Sardinia and Napoleon's home island of Corsica, it was not long before they reached the Italian port town of Livorno, where they disembarked.

Once more, the crates were loaded onto a hired wagon, and once more, he bribed the livery operator not to ask questions. They went thundering through

Tuscany into the Le Marche region, or, as he told the boy: "Right across the skinny part of the Boot."

It was nearly a straight shot through central Italy to Ancona on the Adriatic Coast. The weather here was not an impediment for travel as it had been in France. It was warmer and drier, and though the ground was hilly, the terrain had long been tamed by trusty, old, Roman roads.

Their hired horses, however, did not appreciate their insistence on haste. They lagged, refusing to budge at anything over a trot, as though personally insulted that any foreigner should come to Italy and not even care about the peerless beauty on all sides that had been the glory of this land from time immemorial. What sort of British barbarian could race past Venice with barely a glance?

"Get on, you nags!" He cracked the reins over their rumps. Then he joked to Phillip that they must be Italian horses, used to the strolling, *andante* pace of life.

Inwardly, it took all he had to keep a cheerful demeanor. He did it for the boy's sake, telling himself that once he had Virginia back safely—if, God willing, she wasn't too damaged from her ordeal and in need of many weeks of recovery—their trip back to England would be leisurely and beautiful.

The three of them, almost like a family.

But for the moment, haste was of the utmost.

It was now early December, and as they passed through Italy, they saw glimpses of Christmas preparations under way: Advent processions with candles, statues of the Virgin, and ancient hymns, children in white running from door to door making their traditional visits to elderly neighbors in a token of goodwill and bringing them little presents. Nativity scenes were under construction in every village square they passed.

As a rule, Nick hated Christmas. For a spy, it was

undoubtedly the most painful time of year. Even more so now.

Finally, arriving at the horseshoe-shaped port of Ancona, their eyes bombarded by the shocking cobalt blue of the Adriatic, they changed transport one last time. Nick hired a small ship, the brig *Santa Lucia*, two-masted, square-rigged, with six guns for protection.

The *Santa Lucia* was large enough to carry their cargo but small enough that it took only a dozen hands to sail—in this case, all the grown males of the colorful Fabriano family. They were a good-natured lot, continuously taunting and teasing each other: the captain, Antonio, and his crew of his seven grown sons and five assorted nephews.

Nick immediately liked them and felt they were men he could trust. He took the captain aside and told him this could take a while and that at some point, there could be trouble. The old, tough, weathered Italian had merely smiled in a manner that gave Nick to understand that, indeed, this was a very good crew to have on hand.

Phillip, for his part, was delighted when he discovered that the Fabrianos sang opera buffa instead of sea chanties when they worked the sails. They were also avid fishermen, constantly trailing their hooked lines off the sides of the ship, and they invited the young English lordling to try it. They told him they would try to net a swordfish.

At last, the Fabrianos were ready to go, promising all their wives that of course they would be back in time for Christmas. They got all the crates loaded in short order and finally pulled up anchor.

"*Now*," Nick told Phillip, "we sail for Greece."

Fortunately, the Ionian Islands were the northernmost island cluster of Greece in the Adriatic, so they reached the archipelago quickly.

Well north of the island of Ithaca, the legendary

home of Odysseus, Corfu had been a holiday spot since
Roman times. It had spent the past four hundred years
under Venetian rule before being taken over by the
French.

As of 1814, however, it had passed from French to
British control. To the best of Nick's knowledge, his
country's interest in the sultry, golden island was not in
the day-to-day management of local affairs but mainly
as a strategic base of operations for the Royal Navy.

The Navy was headquartered, however, well south,
on the eastern side of the island at the capital, Corfu
Town, facing the mainland.

Nick had been directed to the remote northern shore
of Corfu, to the town of Sidári.

He was to report to a quayside *taverna* called the
Seahorse Inn, where he would be given directions to
the Villa Loutrá, a luxurious hillside estate where the
private auction would be held.

As they sailed to Sidári, he wondered what the Navy
would make of all the foreign vessels arriving at this
sleepy coastal village, especially at this time of year.

It was hardly the usual season for an influx of holidaymakers. With winter rainfalls and temperatures in
the sixties, in December, Corfu was hardly the sum-
mery paradise that it became in spring.

Of course, given the crop-killing cold snaps and bizarre middle-of-summer frosts they had seen in most
of Europe this past year, due to the giant volcano erup-
tion on the other side of the world, a winter visit to the
Greek islands was a welcome change, indeed.

Perhaps if questioned, the organizers of the auction
planned to tell the Navy that the visitors were merely
Christmas guests of some local grandee.

More likely, Nick mused, they had already taken
care to pay off the right people and were not concerned
about the Navy's interference.

At any rate, when they finally dropped anchor off the

coast at Sidári, Nick left Phillip aboard with the merry Italians and rowed ashore alone to scout out the territory. He wanted, above all, to see if Simon Limarque had already arrived. Poor citizens of Sidári, he mused as he rowed through the placid waves, they had no idea what manner of visitors were about to descend on their village.

They were to be overrun by criminal merchants of all stripes, along with their henchmen. And that was the role Nick knew he must play, as well.

Thus, it was not Baron Forrester but the wicked Jonathan Black who stepped out of the rowboat into ankle-deep seawater. With the shallows sloshing around his black, waterproof boots, he dragged the dory up onto the golden sands, then paused to glance around, his eyes narrowed against the beaming sun.

He scanned the various ships moored nearby in acute suspicion, then spotted the Seahorse Inn among the several *tavernas* lining the docks. Heavily armed as usual in light of the dangers lurking at every hand, he took a stroll through the seaside village to get his bearings first and scout out the territory, looking for threats.

Without the presence of summer-season visitors, Sidári seemed nearly deserted. He wandered the cobbled streets, between rows of little stucco houses, either whitewashed or painted some pastel color, all with red-tiled roofs and flower boxes waiting for the spring.

From some of the houses, he smelled the food the women inside were cooking: fish and turtle stew simmering, lamb roasting, pork frying, pastries baking.

Hearty, welcoming smells of Greek food.

He passed a palm tree here and there, lemon trees shivering in the chill, and a few old olive trees with dramatically gnarled branches, their silvery green leaves slightly grayed with winter. Walking past the Orthodox church, he nodded to a long-robed monk who was sweeping the tiled floor at the church's entrance. The old bearded monk with his pillbox hat nodded back to him, but warily eyed the sword and pistols at his waist.

Not wanting to wear out his welcome, Nick returned to the quay and stepped into the Seahorse Inn. The little seaside pub was nearly empty but for a few old peasant men, rustic locals in traditional garb playing backgammon by the hearth.

He ordered a shot of ouzo from the curly-headed barmaid, then nodded politely to the villagers. Living on an island favored by holidaymakers, no doubt, the people of Corfu were used to being visited by strangers.

Still, Nick did not yet ask for directions to the Villa Loutrá, for that would only invite these folk to start asking questions of him, in turn.

He wanted to remain as anonymous as possible for now. There'd be time to start cultivating the locals— always a useful spy tactic—once he got accustomed to the place and ascertained who else among the criminal participants of the Bacchus Bazaar had already arrived.

Especially Limarque.

Unfortunately, as he downed his ouzo, he was beginning to suspect that in his push to make the best possible time, he had beaten most of the other participants here.

That meant, maddeningly, that he was going to have to wait and do nothing until they began arriving.

Bloody hell.

Finishing his drink, he paid for it with one of the Greek *drachmai* he had changed for Italian *lire* back at Ancona. They no doubt would have accepted British coins, but that would have announced him outright as an Englishman.

When he noticed the buxom barmaid with her rosy cheeks and raven curls watching him, he smiled at her. She might be a useful source of information later.

"*Efcharistó,*" he murmured softly as he set his empty glass on the counter.

"*Parakaló!*" she answered in surprise.

He made sure to tip her well and gave her a wink full of promise that they would meet again. Then he left the *taverna* and returned to his boat.

*M*eanwhile, down in the cargo hold of the *Black Jest,* the "cargo" had no idea where their captors were taking them. They only knew it was very cold, with great, wild tossings of the ship and howlings of the wind, and then it got warmer, the seas calmer.

Gin concluded that they must have rounded Gibraltar and sailed into the Mediterranean. It seemed the most likely explanation. The warmer temperature obviously spelled a southern latitude, but she doubted Rotgut was taking them to Africa.

Besides, she was certain that nowhere near enough time had passed for them to have reached some far-flung tropical destination like the West Indies.

And it wasn't *that* hot. It was enough of a boon simply not to be freezing every moment anymore.

Whatever their current location, she had done her best to keep the girls' chins up. They had played simple games, sung songs, told stories, explained to one another how they had been tricked or outright kidnapped by Rotgut and his men, and talked about their families.

Gin thought often of her father and missed her darling son even more than she missed Nick.

But she could not let herself dwell on them.

Having quickly emerged as the leader of the captives, she had to keep her wits about her. Especially since she had long since realized that any plan of escape she might hatch could be jeopardized by the traitor in their midst.

Susannah Perkins, the very girl she had first set out to find, was a risk to them all.

The headstrong lass had made it clear that she was chiefly out for herself. She meant to survive this, no matter what. She had taken to pleasuring a few of the sailors with the most clout in order to get out of the cell now and then and to procure a few simple comforts for herself. Better food, extra blankets.

When one of the other girls called her a whore, Miss Perkins slugged her in the face. Gin had had to break up the fight but she knew full well that any girl who would get down on her knees for such trifles could never be trusted.

Moreover, she had no doubt that Susannah would use any information about a mutiny brewing among the prisoners for her own gain, too.

Unfortunately, the only way to escape the traitor's hearing in their closed prison was to wait for her to fall asleep.

But it scarcely mattered. There was no point in making an escape plan if they were in the middle of the sea.

One day, however, Susannah returned from one of her visits with the crewmen to report brusquely to the others that they had just arrived in Greece.

Still no sign of Limarque.

Nick had been constantly on the watch for him, but the Promethean's ex-bodyguard and his gang had not yet joined the gathering horde of criminals descending on Sidári.

That day, Phillip was fishing off the side of their boat, determined to net an octopus. Captain Antonio, as patriarch of his clan, was also something of a chef. He had promised to prepare this great delicacy for the boy to sample if he succeeded. And so, the octopus hunt was on.

Nick, meanwhile, was hunting more dangerous prey. He peered through his telescope from the rails of the brig and spotted another person of interest tromping into the Seahorse Inn: E. Dolan from Room Fourteen of L'Hôtel Grande Alexandre. Rotgut, if his suspicions were correct.

At once, Nick ordered the dory lowered into the waves and duly told Phillip, "Of course not," when the lad asked if he could come along.

As soon as Nick had buckled on his brace of pistols, he was climbing down the ladder, stepping into the boat.

After all, he was going out of his mind waiting for the opportunity to rescue Virginia; but since Limarque had still not appeared, he might as well see about saving those kidnapped girls. It was what she would want, and at the moment, it was the only task that he could fix upon.

He seized the opportunity, his first goal to find out where the son of a bitch was keeping his human cargo.

Once again, he rowed ashore, past the pair of towering rock formations that rose from the shallows on both sides of him. He dragged the boat up onto the sand and strode back to the Seahorse Inn.

The pub was now crowded with all the visiting members of the cutthroat class—though most were respectably dressed. Pausing in the doorway, Nick's stare homed in on the tall, husky Mr. Dolan, sitting at a table, washing down shots of whiskey with tankards of ale. He wondered how long ago the man had reached Sidári. But one thing was certain.

The direct approach was out of the question.

Fortunately, Nick had a fair notion of how to reel in this Geordie bull shark. The man sold women, after all.

Thus, as Nick crossed the pub to order his usual ouzo, he decided on the spot that this was the perfect day to get very drunk (or seem so) and come on very strong to the curly-headed barmaid.

This he did, without so much as a glance at E. Dolan.

He got louder, laughing with her, complimenting the lass on her body; he pinched her cheek, downed another shot of the fiery stuff, and pulled her onto his lap with a hearty laugh.

The barmaid squealed and giggled; that was rather unexpected. Bloody hell, she was not supposed to react with naughty interest to his loud, obnoxious flirtation.

E. Dolan scowled at his rakish display, Nick observed from the corner of his eye. He had certainly got the man's attention now. Dolan was studying him, eyes narrowed with recognition.

Nick ignored him, capturing her hand. "Come, take a walk on the beach with me," he cajoled her. "You're the prettiest girl in this town."

"I can't!" she insisted, her English better than his Greek though her accent was strong. "My father does not let me walk out with the customers."

"But I can pay you," he whispered loudly.

"What do you take me for?" she scolded, blushing.

"Come, my little Aphrodite, don't be cruel. A man needs some company every now and again."

Pinned on his lap, she struggled against his hold around her waist, but when he laughingly kissed her on the cheek, she seemed inclined to let him do it.

Fortunately, her proud Greek papa came out from the back just then, saw Nick pawing his daughter, and flew into a rage, as expected.

Now that's more like it, Nick thought, as her father promptly threw him out of the pub.

Nick went peaceably enough, but pretended outrage. "What's wrong with you people?" he yelled in a slurred, drunken voice. "Don't you have any wenches around here? Good *God*!" He straightened his jacket and staggered away from the door.

But within a few seconds, he sensed someone behind him. "You, there! Don't I know you?"

He spun around with a mean, drunken glower. "Who the hell are you?"

Dolan took a wary step toward him across the wooden planks of the dock. "I recognize you from Paris."

Nick looked him up and down suspiciously. "So?"

"You here for the auction?" the Geordie demanded.

"Aye. You?"

Dolan nodded, studying him. "What's your name?"

"Jonathan Black. You?"

"They call me Rotgut," Dolan informed him with a cagey nod of greeting.

Nick raised his eyebrows. "I heard about you from my friend, Limarque! I've been meaning to talk to you!" he said.

"Why?"

"I've got a business proposition for you. Shall we?" He gestured toward the docks; Dolan sauntered along beside him with a wary look, one hand on his pistol. But the slaver heard him out as Nick explained how they were in parallel lines of business and perhaps could profit by sharing transportation costs on their various shipments in future. Coordinating their efforts could also be a boon to help them both evade the Water Guard.

Rotgut was intrigued. But he needed proof that Nick was really the gunrunner he claimed to be.

"Come aboard, I'll show you the stock Angelique sent me to sell. In fact," he said, giving the Geordie a hearty clap on the shoulder, "I'll give you a crate of Baker rifles as a token o' good faith."

Rotgut was still seemed suspicious, but he agreed to come aboard the *Santa Lucia* and take a look. After all, Nick had done nothing threatening. The hostility he had shown toward Rotgut before they had been properly introduced was to be expected among criminal colleagues.

So, Rotgut joined him in the dory, and Nick put out again for the *Santa Lucia*. Soon they had both climbed aboard. Phillip and the crew watched silently as Nick led the shifty-eyed stranger down to their hold, where the crates of guns were stacked. He cracked one open and showed him the ten shiny rifles inside.

"They're yours," he said with a generous flourish. "I'll even throw in some ammunition for you. Think about my offer."

Rotgut was pleased, but Nick kept their visit short, especially when he saw how interested Rotgut was in the light, nasty, always-useful howitzers. He lidded the crate again and nailed it shut with the store of black powder and bullets inside. Then he hefted it abovedeck and carried it over to the crane, where he strapped it in to be lowered to the dory.

"My pleasure, where do you want it?" he asked.

"Might as well take it to my boat. And . . . perhaps since you couldn't snare the barmaid, I can repay the favor in kind." He grinned. "Would you like to see *my* merchandise?"

Nick laughed. "More than you know."

As soon as they had the crate securely in the dory, Dolan pointed to his ship anchored farther out.

Ah, Nick thought, the infamous *Black Jest*. A merchant vessel, it was smaller than a frigate—about ninety feet long—but rigged like one, and three-masted.

Nick rowed toward it, biding his time. It was going to be difficult seeing those poor girls paraded before him like cattle for his choosing, but at least now, he knew which ship belonged to Rotgut.

"So what do you fancy?" the slaver asked as he pulled against the oars. "Blondes? Brunettes?"

He grinned. "Don't really care, long as she's got bottom. Spirited filly is more fun to tame, I always say. But . . . I suppose I am partial to redheads," he added wistfully without quite meaning to.

"Well, you might be in luck," Rotgut said with a snort. "You'd probably like the new one I got in. Redhead. Fighter! Got her through Limarque, actually."

Nick nearly dropped the oars in shock at this casual remark. He stopped rowing for a second, suddenly queasy with the waves.

"Somethin' the matter?"

"No, no." He slammed himself back to his criminal role. "Now you've piqued my interest."

"Well, if you want her, she's yours. More trouble than she's worth to me. Too much of a handful for me to be bothered with. Besides, my clients don't usually have much use for anything over thirty."

Nick nodded, but was so horrified by his near certainty that Limarque had handed Virginia over to Rotgut to be auctioned as a sex slave that he couldn't say a word.

If this was Limarque's way of apologizing for the misunderstanding, giving Nick a scare, but ultimately, making it relatively easy for him to get her back, that was *not* going to let the French bastard off the hook.

Limarque was now officially a dead man.

And if he had tortured her to reveal her father's codes, then his death was going to be very painful and very, very slow.

Despite Nick's years of hiding his emotions, it was difficult to mask his seething hatred, fury, and revulsion as they neared Rotgut's ship. Thankfully, a plume of seafoam splashed up and hit him in the face. It helped to clear his head and focus on the task at hand.

When they reached the *Black Jest*, he counted five gunports along the ship's flank. They'd be mirrored on the other side, so ten cannons, he thought, as well as two swivel guns bristling off both the bow and stern.

In short, they were quite efficiently armed.

Some of the slaver's men let down a ladder, while others rigged the davits and lowered a line tipped with a chunky hook. When it reached the dory, Rotgut grabbed it and secured the hook to the strap around the crate of rifles.

As the crew began hoisting the crate up onto the deck, Nick tied the bow line of his rowboat to the bottom of the ladder. Then he and his odious new friend climbed aboard.

He immediately counted up the armed men he saw, noting a rifleman posted in the crow's nest. About thirty crew on deck, but there were sure to be at least another dozen below. You couldn't sail a vessel of this size without at least forty or fifty men, he thought.

With an unfamiliar knot of pure, cold fear in the pit of his stomach, he reminded himself he was Jonathan Black and flashed a cocky smile as he opened the crate to show the men. While they admired the fine weapons, he loaded one so Rotgut could test-fire it into the air.

It took all of his considerable self-discipline to hand the loaded rifle over to their captain instead of aiming directly at the bastard's head and demanding that all the girls be set loose, including Virginia.

Of course, that would have been extremely foolish.

He had a knife in his boot and pair of single-shot pistols at his waist, but that would only take care of four of these devils. He doubted they'd give him time to reload.

He dared not take the risk with Virginia aboard, nor with Rotgut's cannons within firing range of the *Santa Lucia,* where Phillip waited.

All that mattered was getting her safely out of here, and if Rotgut was willing to simply hand her over, that should soon be accomplished.

Rotgut fired skyward and murdered a seagull for no particular reason. His audience applauded, and the slaver nodded in approval, well pleased with Nick's gift.

"Crate 'em up again and take 'em down to the arms locker," their captain ordered one of his men.

"Would you like some help?" Nick offered, stepping forward in the hopes of getting a look around to find out exactly where the girls were being kept.

"That's all right," Rotgut said, clapping him on the

back. "Your turn now." He turned and barked another order: "You two!" He gestured at a pair of seadogs standing by. "Fetch the redheaded wench from Limarque. Bring her here. And watch yourselves! She's mean. Of course, our friend here likes a lass with spirit." He laughed heartily, but Nick could only manage a taut smile, his stomach churning with dread at what sort of condition he might find her—the woman he loved.

A few minutes later, he could hear her coming even before they had brought her topside. "Take your hands off me, you disgusting brutes! I can walk by myself, thank you very much!"

Heart in his throat, Nick could have wept to hear the fire in her voice. Whatever they might have done to her, she hadn't lost her Scottish fighting spirit, and he nearly dropped to his knees to thank God for it.

"You hear that? A proper hellion, that one," Rotgut said with a smirk. "Hope you know what you're in for."

"Oh, I think we'll manage just fine," the mercenary Jonathan Black murmured, arms folded across his chest as he waited for his prize.

She burst up from the hatch still wearing the same gown in which he had last seen her weeks ago, in that Paris alley. She was pale and thin, the wind running riot through her auburn hair, which hung free, but her eyes had never blazed so wild, the cobalt blue of the Adriatic all around them.

Nick forgot to breathe from the minute that he saw her.

He had only a moment to steel his expression before she noticed him standing there in her angry scan of the decks.

She went motionless.

The two crewmen holding her arms laughed at how she had frozen at the sight of him, misunderstanding the reason for her shock. They took it for terror.

Nick held her stare in fierce warning, willing her not to give away the truth of the bond between them.

He glanced at Rotgut. "Well, well," he said. "Very nice, indeed. I'll take her."

The slaver gestured to the men to bring her closer. Virginia stopped fighting, staring at Nick in amazement, her complexion gone even paler, her eyes wide.

He could not bear to hold her gaze for long for fear that his relief and his love for her would be written all over his face. Or worse, that he would give in to the overwhelming need to take her in his arms and hold her as tightly as he could, forever.

"Aye, here's the hellcat I told you about, Black," Rotgut said, nodding as he, too, looked her over. "She's yours if ye want 'er."

Nick put out his hand to her. "Come here, woman."

The soft-toned order seemed to jar her out of her daze. "Why?" she forced out.

Nick figured she was just playing along with the charade. *Clever.* No doubt she wanted to run into his arms, but she kept her wits about her.

After all, a woman *ought* to be reluctant to be presented as a gift from one criminal to another.

"I'm taking you home with me," he replied, trying not to sound too strangled by the lump in his throat.

She stared at him soulfully, an anguished mix of joy and sorrow warring in her eyes, but she made no move to come to him though the sailors had released her.

"Come!" he ordered, waiting with his hand out to rescue her, every nerve ending thrumming with crazed protective instincts.

But either she was taking the charade of resistance too far, or, he thought with a sickening feeling, she was even more traumatized than he had anticipated. For, to his amazement, she shook her head slowly and once more, gave the answer: "*No.*"

Chapter

22

Gin could not take her eyes off him.

Everything in her longed to run to Nick and fling herself into his arms.

Fraught with emotion and fragile after all she had been through, she was shaking from head to toe with the shock of seeing him again, especially since she had been half-certain he was dead.

Boundless love flooded her at the sight of him.

But her refusal to go with him was genuine, and as she held his stare, she saw him gradually realize that.

The confusion in his dark, fiery eyes gave way to a flash of understanding. Disbelieving fury filled his face. "Come to me! Now," he repeated in a hard tone. God only knew what lengths he had gone to to save her.

But she shook her head again, her heart in her throat, for she knew what she had to do.

Perhaps he was catching on. He glowered at her like he would wring her neck, and it wasn't just for show. "I gave you an order, wench," he warned, while his midnight eyes pleaded with her, *Don't do this to me.*

She balled her fists at her side and held her ground, refusing to budge. The men snickered at her show of obstinacy, but Nick's eyes narrowed.

He cast a cold glance at Rotgùt. "Might I have a moment alone with the wench to apprise her of her situation?"

"Be my guest! But don't go rogering her in my stateroom," the captain drawled with a coarse laugh, gesturing toward the door on the quarterdeck.

While the crew laughed, Nick closed the distance between them with a few angry strides and grasped her by her arm. His touch was blissful, his nearness heavenly, even though she could tell he wanted to throttle her.

"Like to borrow a belt, Black? Give her a few snaps on the hind end, eh? That'll get her in line."

"Not necessary," he said through gritted teeth.

"Go on, ye little spitfire, go with him!" Rotgut taunted her, as Nick escorted her none too gently into the stateroom. "Willful witch, now you've met your match, haven't ye?"

The moment Nick had closed the door of the cramped, messy stateroom behind them, he turned to her in bewilderment. "What do you mean, no?" he whispered.

Gin couldn't hold back. She launched herself into his arms; he caught her up hard in his embrace, and she clung to him in trembling secrecy and silence.

She ran her hands almost frantically over his head and shoulders, glorying in the solidity of him. "You're a miracle," she breathed as she held him hard. "I can't believe you're really here. I thought I'd lost you," she whispered with a small sob.

"I'm here, sweeting," he soothed barely audibly. Then he cupped her face and pushed her back gently to examine her for signs of injury.

Thankfully, the black eye she had received from Limarque was long gone. She did not wish to stoke the wrath he already felt.

As they stared into each other's eyes, Nick touched her hair with a mix of adoration and fury on her behalf. He took her face between his hands and kissed her on the forehead with exquisite gentleness, then on the lips.

She closed her eyes. The man melted her entirely.

When he pulled her into his arms once more, she rested with all her soul against his chest. He stroked her head in soothing reassurance as he held her. "It's all right. You're safe now," he whispered.

"Oh, Nick. I've missed you so much."

"And I, you. More than you'll ever know." He kissed her head again, cradling her in his arms. "But there'll be time for kisses, sweeting. Right now, I've got to get you out of here. I've got a ship waiting just a stone's throw away. Rotgut and I have made an exchange of gifts, y'see, some of my guns for one of his women. Now, let's get the hell off this ship before he changes his mind."

She warded him off when he started to draw her toward the door. "Nick—I can't."

"Why? What are you talking about?" he whispered.

"I can't abandon these girls! They don't have a chance without me."

His jaw dropped. He stared at her incredulously, then blurted out, "I'll drag you!"

"Please don't. Can't you see? As one of Rotgut's prisoners, I'm in the best possible position to help the others escape. Nick, please. I can do this—with a little help. Show me you believe in me like my father never did."

"So that's it?" he whispered in outrage. "You always wanted to be an agent, and now you think this is your chance? Are you mad, or do you think this is a game?"

"Of course not!" she whispered back. "But I can't walk away from these girls just to save my own skin! We've got to do something!"

"*I'll* do something," he corrected with a glower. "You're a lady, for God's sake! And you've already been through enough. Let me take you to safety first, then I'll send for a contingent of Marines. There's a base on the other side of the island—"

"What island? Where are we?"

"Corfu. Adriatic. We'll come back here in force and stage a raid—"

"Absolutely not." She shook her head. "As soon as they see you coming, they'll kill the girls and burn the ship to hide the evidence. It won't work."

He scowled at her, amazed by her retort. "Well, what do you propose, then?"

"I don't know!" She searched his face in frustration. "What would an Order agent do? What would *you* do if you were in my place?"

"Well, that's easy. I'd take over the ship."

His answer startled her. "How?"

He shook his head. "Forget it. This is madness. There is no way I am leaving here without you."

"Darling, listen to me." She clasped his lapels, gazing up at him. "If Rotgut is allowing you to take someone off this ship, then you have to take the little girl, Rose."

His midnight eyes flared at this news. Then he let out a low groan of doomed exasperation and dropped his head back to glare at the ceiling.

"She's just a child, Nick. Please. You have to get her out of here, not me. I can fend for myself and help protect the others."

He could not seem to speak for a minute. Then he looked into her eyes, his own churning with frustration. "You're serious."

"Of course I am," she whispered. "I am Virgil's daughter, and I will not leave these girls behind to die."

He shook his head at her, at a loss.

"Nick, please. You've got trust me."

"After you lied to me about the whole reason for this mission?" he retorted in a whisper. He visibly checked his impatience with her and gave her a hard look. "I know about your father's journal. You should've told me."

She winced. "I know. I'm so sorry. I shouldn't have kept anything from you. I won't in future. Please forgive me."

His gaze softened and he ran his hand down her arm with a comforting touch. "Of course I forgive you. But, honestly, woman! Charging into that alley on that horse . . . You should have stayed out of it."

"They were going to shoot you! Was I to let them?"

"Never mind, we'll talk about it later." He captured her chin, lifting her head again to search her eyes. "Are you all right? You seem remarkably yourself after everything. More than I expected."

She nodded, pleased with his assessment. "I'm well enough. You?"

"I'm fine." He hesitated. "Has anyone . . . hurt you?"

She knew what he was really asking. If she had been raped. "Limarque tried. It didn't go well for him."

He seemed taken aback, then he melted at her dry reassurance.

With a soft laugh, Nick shook his head, pulled her close again, and held her tenderly. "That's my girl."

She smiled, dizzied by the bliss of his embrace.

He kissed her forehead as he sheltered her in his arms. "Sweeting?" he murmured after a moment. "About your father's book—I'm afraid I must ask. Did you give Limarque the codes?"

"No."

"Good," he murmured in relief.

"But he still has it," she warned.

"I'll take care of it from here. As for you—"

"I'll be fine," she promised. "Just help me figure out a plan to get everybody out of here. I'm not leaving just to save my own skin. I couldn't live with that."

He pulled back a little to give her a rather paternal

frown. "I still think this is daft. But, if you insist, and you swear to me by your stubborn head that you'll use the utmost caution—"

"I will, I promise!"

He nodded reluctantly, even as he eyed her with a speculative glance. "Very well, then. Where are they keeping you?"

"Cargo hold, behind a heavy, barred door that's always locked, except when they bring rations or carry out the slop."

"Can you pick a lock?"

"If I have a suitable instrument, yes."

"Here." He bent down and gave her the knife hidden in his boot, unbuckling the small strap that secured the sheath.

"Ah!" Her eyes lit up as she grasped it, sliding the nasty little blade out of the sheath and holding it up to the light. "This should come in handy!" she murmured with great relish.

It felt wonderful to have some means of self-defense in her hand again, at last. As Nick straightened up again, she noticed him staring at her. Did she seem too savage?

"What is it?" she asked.

"Your father would have been extremely proud of you."

She smiled ruefully as she put the knife away.

Then Nick leaned down and kissed her with mesmerizing softness. The silken caress of his lips on hers made her shiver with longing to make love with him again.

Perhaps his thoughts had wandered down the same wayward path, for he ended the kiss abruptly, as though unwilling to be distracted by desire when so much was at stake. Taking hold of her shoulders, he pushed her back sternly to arm's length and stared hard into her face.

"Right." From that moment, he was all business, all spy. "Here's what you need to do . . ."

He told her.

Gin listened avidly. She hung on every word until she had her full instructions, asking just a few brief questions.

"Have you got all that?"

She swallowed hard, nodding. "It doesn't sound too difficult," she said, though her heart was pounding.

"I'll see if I can't even the odds for you before you make your move. You'd better be safe," he added, pausing as he cupped her cheek. "Because it's beginning to look like I can't live without you."

She beamed at him. "Really? Does that mean you're not still planning to go to America?"

"Oh, I think life with you is plenty wild enough for me," he whispered. "Of course, when all this is over, I still fully intend to pay you back for scaring me like this. You've got it coming, just so you know."

She smiled, her lips inches from. "Mmm, that sounds fun. Nick?" she murmured in a dreamy tone after he had kissed her again. "I want you to know how much you mean to me." His eyes glowed warmly at her words as he pulled back just enough to meet her gaze. "I never thought I'd feel this way." She ran her hands slowly down his rock-hard arms. "Thoughts of you—and of Phillip—are all that's kept me going. At least, thank God, my son is still safe at home."

An odd look skimmed his face.

She paused, unsure what it meant. Maybe her love words had made him uneasy. "What is it, darling?"

"Nothing. Just promise me you'll use all possible caution when you do this thing. I can't lose you again."

"You won't. I promise. Well—I guess we'd better go back out there before our dear Captain Rotgut gets suspicious."

"Right. I'll tell him he was right, that you're too much damned trouble. Which is true."

She pinched his cheek for that, smiling adoringly at him.

"And then we'll see if there's any honor among thieves. If the rat will let me choose another female," he added in distaste.

"You'll know little Rose when you see her. Blond curls. Big blue eyes. Once you get her to safety, tell her it was all my idea. We've become quite close."

Nick took a deep breath, then let it out with a look of disgust. "I can't believe you're making me act the part of someone who would buy a child virgin. I kill those kinds of men. With great zeal."

"And I love you for it," she replied. "I know. I'm sorry, darling. But if there may be shooting, all the more reason to get the little one out of here before it starts." Gin shook her head. "God knows she's already been through enough, poor thing. She's scared to death. The only blessing is that she's too innocent to understand what these men intend."

"Good," he grumbled. "I'll see that she stays that way."

As he turned and grasped the door handle, pausing to gather himself for another round of playacting as one of the criminal cutthroats, Gin quickly hid the knife under her skirts, buckling the strap above her knee.

He glanced back at her. "Ready?"

"Not quite." She pulled him down for one last, passionate kiss. Heart pounding, she whispered a promise that they'd be together again soon.

"Now I'm ready," she breathed.

He wasn't, it seemed, hesitating for one moment more. "I love you, Virginia," he suddenly blurted out. "I just wanted you to know that."

She drew in her breath at his declaration—just as a shout from outside summoned them back to an unforgiving reality.

"You're not rogering her in there like I said, are you, Black?"

"I wish," Nick said under his breath. Then he opened the door. "Damn you!" he yelled at her, rubbing his cheek as if she had clawed him and cursing at her under his breath.

Gin followed him, trying not to laugh at his performance—though that was partly from nerves and partly from her sheer, giddy joy that the hero of her girlish dreams had just said he loved her.

"Hellcat! God, you were right, man! She's a vicious thing!" The men laughed heartily while Nick feigned sheepish indignation. "The little viper bit me! No thanks, you can keep the guns, I don't want her. Bloody hell!"

"Ah, poor fellow! Let's see if we can't find you another," Rotgut said with great humor, clapping him on the back. "You ruined it for yourself, lass. Try to get away with that when I sell your lily-white arse to some prince of Arabia."

Gin hissed at him in answer, but stole one last longing glance at Nick before they returned her to her dungeon.

Nick soon left the slavers' frigate with a screaming twelve-year-old slung over his shoulder as he climbed down the ladder.

He had played a lot of roles in his career as a spy, but this was by far the most distasteful.

His visit to Rotgut's ship had left him wanting to take a bath with lye soap at the first opportunity.

"Hold still!" he cried as his prisoner kicked him in the kidney in her frenzy of hysterical rage.

Good God! The brat might have a future career in the opera with those lungs.

"Calm down!" he ordered.

There was no comforting her. She'd raise the Adriatic with her rain of wild tears. Little Rose did not know she was being rescued, but was bereft and terrified at being separated from the older girls, and most of all, from

Virginia, to whom she had obviously developed some sort of mother-child attachment.

"*Let me go!*" she shrieked in earsplitting tones.

"*I am not going to hurt you!*" he roared back, not the most soothing reassurance, but it was all he could do be to be heard over the din of her heartrending screeches.

With all her flailing about, he nearly dropped her in the waves. Dear God! he thought when they reached the dory at last.

Obviously, he had never dealt with an angry twelve-year-old girl before.

She proceeded to scream and wail piteously and plead with him not to "*m-m-murder*" her, the whole way from the *Black Jest* to the *Santa Lucia*. Nick just rolled his eyes.

Even when he tried to inform her in the calmest of tones that he had no intention of murdering her, she didn't believe him. "Listen to me!" he insisted when they were halfway there, far enough not to have his words carried back to Rotgut on the wind.

She paused only long enough to take a few ragged breaths, pulling for air, while he attempted to explain that he was, in fact, rescuing her on Lady Burke's orders.

She shook her head, refusing to believe, found her voice again, and resumed her piteous wailing. "Take me back! Take me back to her!"

"Oh, for God's sake." Nick gave up and resolved to foist her off on Phillip the moment they arrived.

For his part, Nick hadn't finished his exchange yet with Rotgut. He still had to send over one of the howitzers to pay the vile bastard for this noisy, little, curly-headed fiend.

Turned out the going rate for a child virgin was a good deal higher than for a gorgeous grown redhead ripened to the perfection of her womanhood.

Well, who could comprehend the pervert mind, Nick thought in disgust while Phillip suddenly peered over the rails above them.

"*What* the deuce is all that caterwauling?" the boy exclaimed.

Eager to be relieved of her, Nick called back, "What's that, sorry? I'm afraid I've gone quite deaf."

"Who is that?" Phillip repeated.

"Oh, this is Rose. Rose, meet Phillip. He is Lady Burke's son. You see the resemblance? *Now* do you believe me?"

Rose looked up at Phillip and wasn't sure. She clung to the rowboat as it rocked back and forth on the waves, her round, reddened face a very theatre mask of sorrow.

Soundless sobs racked her little frame. Perhaps she had lost her voice, he thought dryly.

One could only hope.

"Quiz him once we go aboard, if you don't believe me," Nick told her. "Ask him any question about Lady Burke, and you'll see, he knows everything about her—as he should. That's his mother! All right? So you can hate me if you want, but at least you know you can trust him. Phillip's not going to let anything bad happen to you."

"What are you saying down there?" Phillip called above the noise of waves and wind.

"Nothing! Just help me get her aboard. Up! Up you go," Nick ordered, steadying the girl as she stood up cautiously in the dory and reached for the ladder.

"Take my hand!" Phillip reached down to help her as she climbed the ladder slowly, rung by rung, sparing a terrified glance or two down at the waves. "It's all right, almost there." At last, Phillip helped her onto the deck of the *Santa Lucia*. "Who are you, then?"

Rose cowered, looking around at the unfamiliar boat.

Phillip frowned, apparently grasping the gravity of the child's situation.

"Your mother sent her over," Nick informed him as he swung his leg over the bulwark and jumped down onto the deck.

Phillip's eyes widened. "You saw my mother? Where? How is she?"

"She's well enough. She's on that ship. No, no, don't wave. They don't need to know you have a connection to anyone over there. Besides, I don't want to take any chances of her seeing you."

Phillip turned to him indignantly. "You didn't tell her that I'm here?"

"I couldn't, lad." Nick gave the boy's shoulder an apologetic squeeze. "I'm sorry, but she'll never be able to focus on her escape if she knows you're this close to the danger. You know how protective she is."

"Right." Phillip's mouth tilted. "She's going to kill me for leaving England, anyway."

Nick nodded. "Probably so. Now, then. I've got to finish up some business. Look after the girl for me, will you?"

Phillip looked dubiously at Rose, then back at Nick. "Do I have to?"

He nodded. "Cheer her up. You're good at that sort of thing. As you can see, she's quite upset."

The well-bred young lordling looked again at their little damsel in distress and produced a handkerchief from his pocket for her tears.

Rose took it, wide-eyed, and blew her nose with great vigor.

Phillip frowned. "Who exactly is she?"

"She's Rose. That's all I know. She's had a terrible time, so we're all going to be very kind and gentlemanly toward her until we can return her safe and sound to her family. Agreed?" He glanced around at his jovial Italian crewmen. "No teasing."

Sensing the delicacy of the situation, they sent the curly-headed *bambina* compassionate looks.

"We make-a you something to eat?"

"Now, there's a fine idea," Nick replied. "Rose, I am making Phillip your official defender on this boat, do you understand? As I said, nobody's going to hurt you. Especially now, because nobody here wants to mess with him. You know why?"

"W-why?"

"Because Phillip's grandfather was a great Highland warrior who taught him how to be a knight, and knights protect ladies, you know. That's what they *do*. So you may rest assured from now on that you are completely safe aboard this ship. Sir Phillip himself is hereby assigned to look after you," he added pointedly.

Though blushing, Phillip did not look too enthused about having to play nursemaid to a wee girl.

Nick stared him into obedience.

"Fine," the boy muttered, then he glanced at their guest. "You can help me if you want."

"What are you doing?" Rose asked him shyly.

Phillip lifted his chin. "Catching an octopus. And when I get one, Captain Antonio's going to make us calamari."

"No, the calamari is a squid!" Captain Antonio protested. "How many times I gotta tell you?"

"Whatever," Phillip mumbled, then he flashed a grin at Rose. "You can have some, too—but only if you help me catch 'em."

She seemed intrigued by this project in spite of herself. She still clutched his handkerchief with a white-knuckled grip, but it looked like having another youngster around had already started to put her at ease. "Have you caught one yet?" Her voice sounded froggy from screaming.

"No," Phillip said with a sigh. "They're terribly clever. You wouldn't think it, would you? Give her a hat before she gets a sunburn." Phillip snatched Luigi's straw hat off his head and set it atop Rose's dirty golden curls. "Here, you want to help? Here's what you must do."

He thrust a clay pot tied with a rope into her hands, then fished a coin out of his pocket. "Drop this in the pot."

She did so, marveling at this strange advice.

"Octopi like shiny things. He'll climb in the pot and hunker down in there. Then we'll pull him up. Now we have to drop the pot over the side and lower it down to the bottom. Go ahead, you do it. I'll help."

Nick watched in amusement while the two undertook this operation. Satisfied that Rose was settling down, he left them to their octopus fishing and went to fetch the howitzer.

He sent a few of the Italians out in two of the ship's largest boats to deliver the weapon to Rotgut in pieces— one carrying the howitzer itself, the other transporting the disassembled gun-carriage. But he did not go himself. God knew, he could not face that foul beast again right now. The desire to shoot him in the head was much too strong.

Once they had departed to deliver the weapon to its new owner, Nick went below and retreated to his cabin, taking a moment to try to clear his head.

The fact was, he was more shaken by his meeting with Virginia than he had let on.

He couldn't believe he had agreed to leave her behind. Walking away from her had been the hardest thing he had ever done. Their strategy was solid, but he was scared to death about whether she could really pull it off.

He hoped she understood that he was, indeed, treating her like an equal.

Truly, he was placing as much trust in her to get the job done as he would've trusted any of his warrior brothers in the Order.

Well, he thought, taking a deep breath, this *was* what she had always wanted.

More importantly, they didn't have much choice. She was right. She did have the best chance of helping the girls from the inside.

Too restless to remain below for long, Nick left his cabin again and returned topside to see if the Italians were back yet.

At the rails, he looked through his telescope and saw the howitzer being slowly hoisted on a crane up onto the *Black Jest*.

He sent the frigate's odious captain a cordial wave, when all of a sudden, cheering erupted from the opposite side of the *Santa Lucia*.

"We got one! Look!" Phillip quickly pulled the clay pot up while Rose stood by, looking on. "Finally!"

Nick turned to watch, arching a brow.

"Oh, look at that!"

Captain Antonio was quick on the scene to help, cheering on the young fishermen. "*Molto bene!* Oh, he's a good one! A little small, but for your first one, is good!"

"Ew, he's ugly!" said Rose with a girly grimace.

Phillip grinned at her. "Looks tasty to me! What do we do now?" the boy asked with an eager glance at their captain-chef.

"Take him out of the pot."

"How?"

Antonio shrugged. "Just grab him."

It was easier said than done.

"Slippery fellow! Oh, drat."

Nick chuckled and Rose shrieked when the octopus thunked out of the pot onto the deck, along with all the water, which doused it.

Rose gasped as the whole of the bulbous, wriggly-armed creature was revealed. "You can't eat that!" she cried. "It's disgusting!"

"You want me to get him for you?" Antonio offered.

"No, no, I can do it myself!"

Phillip's answer to everything, Nick thought, folding his arms across his chest as he watched in amusement.

Rose bent down to watch more closely while Phillip crouched and tried to figure out the best way to pick up the animal.

The octopus stared at them, its arms waggling, its big, weirdly human-looking eyes blinking.

"How are you going to get him?" Rose asked.

"Not . . . quite . . . sure. He's all . . . squiggly."

Rose was silent for a moment. "I guess he's kind of cute."

"Too bad he's headed for the frying pan." Then Phillip gently picked him up, and Rose shrieked again when the octopus suddenly wrapped all its legs around Phillip's hand, as though it had just decided that its safest course was to hold on tight.

"Ho!" Phillip tried in vain to shake him off, his victory turning to panic. "Captain, get him off me!"

"He just a-wants to say-a *buongiorno.*"

Rose was now giggling uncontrollably. The rest of the Fabrianos roared with laughter.

"Do they bite?" Phillip cried.

"Only if you are a starfish."

Relieved by this news, Phillip offered his octopus-gloved hand to Rose. "You want to hold him?"

She shrieked and jumped back, laughing. "No!"

"Stop fooling around. You want me to cook him? You gotta kill him."

"Aw," Rose murmured in sympathy.

Phillip met her saddened gaze, then glanced over at the cook. "How do you want me to kill him?"

"Bite the head off. Quickly."

"*What?* Did you say . . . ?"

"Bite the head, yes. Is the traditional way."

"Oh, that's horrible!" Phillip exclaimed. "I'm not biting his head off! You didn't tell me that before!"

"Give him to me, I will bite it."

"No, Phillip, no! Set him free!" Rose shouted.

"Give him!" Antonio repeated, holding out his hand. Nick didn't dream of interfering.

"I say!" Phillip protested. "There's got to be a better way than decapitating the poor thing with your teeth!"

"Ah, come, little *signore.*"

"No!"

"Run, Phillip, run!" Rose shouted, as Phillip climbed over the rails to escape the cook, still trying to shake the octopus off his hand.

Nick merely shook his head, watching in bemusement as a wave suddenly splashed up and caused Phillip to lose his footing.

Phillip plunged into the sea with a shout.

Rose raced to see if he—or more importantly, the octopus—was all right. When it hit the water, the creature realized it was home and unwound itself from Phillip's forearm.

It swam away and disappeared in seconds while Phillip popped up from the waves, treading water with a grin. "Oh, well, he got away."

Rose cheered from the rails.

"After all that! *Mama mia,*" said Antonio, waving them off and returning to his galley with a shake of his head.

The eldest Fabriano brother threw down a rope ladder to the brave young swimmer, then he and Rose helped him up.

For his part, Nick scanned the area again through his telescope. The howitzer was now safely on the deck of the *Black Jest,* and his Italian crewmen were on their way, rowing back to the *Santa Lucia.*

It was not until later that evening that Nick turned his telescope toward the shore once again and suddenly froze, spotting Limarque entering the Seahorse Inn.

Excellent.

Vengeance filled him. If Limarque was finally here, then so was Virgil's book—and that meant he could set the plans he'd made with Virginia into motion immediately.

There was no further need to delay.

It was time to hoist the signal flag to let her know they'd work their plan this very night.

*M*eanwhile, down in the cargo hold of the *Black Jest*, the girls were crying, weeping bitterly that that shameless pervert had taken poor, little, baby Rose.

"Bad enough being paraded before that ruffian, but to have him choose the child!"

"Such debauchery!" the blonde from Herefordshire wailed.

"Why didn't he take me?"

"Or me? I wouldn't have minded! He didn't seem half-bad," another sobbed.

"Anyone but the wee girl! What sort of monster—"

"Oh, enough!" Gin bit out at last, unable to take any more.

They all stopped and looked at her, startled by her outburst. Gin glared at them in the darkness. "Rose is going to be just fine, I promise you."

"H-how can you know that?"

As she swept the bedraggled company with a guarded glance, she decided the time had come to entrust them with the plan she'd hatched with Nick.

Even Susannah Perkins.

Indeed, now that it had come to it, it seemed a little daft to expect such heroics from these pathetic, cowering creatures. On the other hand, most of them were farm girls from the shires, and God willing, had a basic understanding of how to fire a gun.

"Ladies, that man who came here today was not . . . what he appeared. Rose is in no danger. I myself asked him to choose her to get her off this boat and take her to safety."

"What?" they breathed.

"He is my dearest friend and lover, and he left us the means to escape."

"Your lover?" a few of them whispered. "Can this be true?"

"You mean you could have left with him today? But you stayed?"

She threw up her hands. "Did you expect me to abandon you all to your fates? Oh, botheration!" she huffed, coloring a bit at their shocked, admiring stares. "Now this is how it's going to go . . ."

Ignoring their wonder, she gathered them around and finally told them her role in all this, how she was a lady detective, and how Susannah Perkins's mother was the one who had first told her about her daughter's disappearance, which had led to the whole investigation and her finding them.

"Gor!" was the common response.

With the background information stated, she then began filling them in quietly on the plan, praying none of them started to cry at the mere thought of carrying out a mutiny. It was not for the faint of heart, to be sure, but after all they had been through, they were rather desperate, willing to do what they must to grab for any chance at escape, just as she had hoped.

She spoke with such conviction about their mission that her confidence and righteous anger must have been contagious. For rather than fainting, the girls caught her eagerness at the chance to put their captors in their place.

The only obstacle remaining was Susannah Perkins herself.

They all turned to her, unsure if she would betray them to Rotgut's crew for some sort of personal gain.

"Well?"

She gave no answer.

Gin took the hard-eyed, "fast girl" aside to confront her privately.

"What say you, Miss Perkins? Are you with me? You should be, considering you're the reason I ended up here in the first place. The time has come for you to choose a side."

She folded her arms across her chest and eyed the others in sullen wariness. "You're going to get everyone killed, that's what I think."

"No, I'm not. We'll choose our moment wisely and take them by surprise." Gin lost patience. "Are you with us or not? Do you want a chance to escape? Are you brave enough to try? Or would you rather be a slave to whatever man might buy you? Because I'm sorry to say, the success of our plan depends on you. Think of it. *You* have the power to rescue all these girls through the bond you've established with his men."

"What do you want me to do?" she asked uneasily, glancing over her shoulder, as if Rotgut's men might hear.

"The next time the sailors come to let you out for, er, a visit, I need you to find out where the arms locker is aboard this ship."

"The arms locker?" she echoed.

Gin nodded. "You also have to get up on deck and look for a red flag flying on a two-masted ship nearby. Whatever you have to do, I need both of those pieces of information if we are to make good our escape. You must *not* under any circumstances tell them what we are planning. Do I make myself clear?" she asked softly, lifting her knife for emphasis.

Susannah Perkins drew in her breath, staring at the blade. "Where did you get that?"

"From my lover. You see, my dear, he is a spy for the Crown. He'll be providing us with a little extra help when the time comes."

This revelation, at last, seemed to raise her confidence, at least enough to pry her away from her single-minded goal of selfish survival. Her tough bravado faltered. "He's really going to help us?"

Gin nodded. "Your job is to look for the red signal flag and also find the arms locker. That's all. Sounds easy enough, yes?"

"Maybe," she said uncertainly.

"Now, Miss Perkins, I know you are a clever girl. So let me make this clear. All these girls deserve to go home to their families, and all our fates now rest in your hands. All you have to do for this to turn out well is to get me the location of the arms locker. But, fair warning, if you should decide to betray us to save your own skin, I will cut your throat while you're sleeping," Gin said softly.

Her eyes widened; her face paled in the darkness. She swallowed hard. "I understand," she forced out.

"Good. I knew you'd make the right decision."

As Susannah Perkins walked nervously to the door of the cargo hold to call for her sailors, Gin eyed her, satisfied that she had secured the girl's cooperation.

Then she walked back to the others and sat down on the floor, looking on serenely while the sailors came to flirt with Susannah Perkins. She watched the crewmen unlock the door and let her little spy out of their cell for their usual lewd activities.

There was nothing more to do for now but wait.

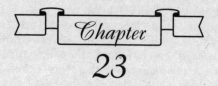

Chapter

23

"Whatever happens, don't tell your mother about this, or she might literally kill me," Nick muttered.

"Don't worry, I can do this!" Phillip assured him.

"Yes. I know you can. If I had any doubt, I would not allow it." Half a mile away from the warehouse, Nick pulled his hired wagon to a halt.

The night had come. Their plot was under way. Unfortunately, he had realized that he could not do it entirely alone. Even the Order's best assassin could not be in two places at the same time. Ergo, his recruitment of the boy. He looked at Phillip again, searching his face. "You're sure you won't freeze up?"

"No! My part's easy. And fun," he added with a grin.

Nick shook his head ruefully. "You're too much like your grandfather."

"I'll take that as a compliment!"

"So it is." He set the brake so they did not roll backwards down the steep hill with their heavy cargo. "All right then, into the box with you. Come on."

They jumped down and walked back to the wagon's

bed, stacked with long wooden crates full of rifles. Nick opened the lid of one for the lad. Phillip nodded to him firmly and stepped in. It was a good thing the wiry lad wasn't any taller. He had to bend his knees at an awkward angle just to fit, as it was.

"Got your fob watch?"

Phillip showed it to him, finally starting to look at least a little nervous.

"Good." Nick repeated his instructions: "Two hours, then you break out of that thing. Move carefully. Try not to make any noise. Find the book and get to an exit. I'll be waiting outside to take care of any guards. Any questions?"

"No, it's simple! Let's get on with it already! Before I lose my nerve."

Nick smiled wryly at him. "Proud of you, lad."

"Ha!" Phillip answered.

Then Nick covered the stowaway under a board to which a rack of rifles was secured.

"Can you see me?" came his muffled question.

"Not at all. Don't forget—start counting the two hours on your watch only once you hear the warehouse doors slam shut behind you."

"Righty-ho."

Nick placed the lid on the crate of rifles and banged it firmly into place, then checked on the single howitzer he had brought for display.

"Lord Forrester?"

Nick could barely hear him in the crate. "Yes?"

"If . . . anything should go wrong tonight and something happens to me, will you take care of my mother for me?"

"Of course," he answered gently. "You have my word. But don't worry, I'll make sure you come out of this safe and sound. Anything else?"

A pause.

Nick waited for Phillip's answer.

"You love her, don't you?"

He smiled wryly. "It shows?"

"A lot," Phillip declared.

"You got me," Nick replied. "She's the finest woman I've ever met, and the bravest. Now hunker down and keep quiet. We're heading for the warehouse." With his stowaway secured, Nick jumped down off the wagon's bed and returned to the driver's seat.

A moment later, the heavy cart rolled into motion. Another half mile up the road, Jonathan Black delivered the shipment of weapons to the warehouse for the main event of the Bacchus Bazaar, set to take place tomorrow night.

The guards saw that his papers were in order, all duly registered for the auction, signed and stamped by the bankers in Paris. Following protocol, one of the guards opened a couple of crates to make sure the contents were what they claimed to be.

Nick's heart slammed in his chest when the fellow cracked open the lid of the crate containing Phillip.

But the man gave it only a glance before he nodded to the warehouse. Two other guards pulled the wide double doors open.

"You need a hand unloading them?"

He nodded. "Thanks, that would be helpful."

Nick counted eight guards in all. *Shouldn't be a problem*. Their captain sent two large fellows to assist him.

Nick drove the wagon slowly into the huge warehouse, which looked like an old, disused barn. He scanned the rows of illicit goods waiting for the auction to see if he could spy Virgil's book.

He didn't see it, but he was trying not to be too obvious about his gawking. He just hoped the boy could find it in the dark. He also glanced around for exits and winced privately to note that the old barn was sealed up well.

Most of the old stall windows had been boarded over, but the fading light of sunset still shone in from the hay door off the loft above.

Phillip could certainly get out that way, but he was going to have to do some climbing to get down from there. Could prove tricky.

Maybe, with more time to explore the interior for himself once the warehouse was all locked down for the night, Phillip would discover an easier way out, closer to the ground. In any case, Nick would be right outside to help him when the time came.

The guards showed him to an empty space where he could unload his cargo. The hired soldiers helped him take the crates of rifles off the wagon and stack them on the ground.

"Careful with that! I'll do it myself if you're going to throw them around! Let me get that." He stalked over and personally picked up the crate containing Phillip.

While the guards smirked at his scolding, Nick set the precious cargo down on the ground and set his foot atop it, making a show of searching his pocket for a paper, as if he had just thought of something he needed to jot down.

"Can somebody get me a pencil? I need to mark the numbers of these crates."

This request annoyed the guards even more, but Nick accomplished his goal: simply ensuring that the box with the boy in it did not end up at the bottom of the pile. For if that happened, Phillip would be trapped under all that weight.

Thankfully, Nick succeeded in making sure that Phillip's crate was on the top of a pile that was only shoulder high. The lad should have no trouble getting out or down from there.

"All right then. Looks good." He gave Phillip's crate a reassuring knock to let him know he was leaving.

Satisfied that his cargo was secure, Jonathan Black threw a canvas tarp over his crates to deter the curious from poking around. Then he tossed each of the soldiers a coin for helping him and strode back to his wagon.

With night falling over the island, he had two hours to take care of his next little task and get back here. He hated leaving Phillip unchaperoned for any length of time, but his next errand absolutely required the cover of darkness. Besides, he'd only draw suspicion to himself if he were seen continuing to lurk around the warehouse after dropping off his crates.

Driving back to the town as fast as he dared on the rough and dusty Greek roads, he finally arrived at the fountain in the quiet center of the village, where he stopped to let the horses drink.

Leaving his wagon there, Nick picked up the hammer he'd used to bang the crates shut and prowled back toward the Seahorse Inn on the quay.

From a wary distance, he made sure that Rotgut's crew had accepted his invitation. He had sent over a message to the *Black Jest* telling his new "friends" he'd be hosting a night of revelry at the *taverna*—drinks on him.

They were there, all right. Loud and drunk and guzzling the free liquor as only sailors could. This cut the odds considerably for Virginia's work tonight aboard the *Black Jest*.

Unfortunately, it looked like only half the crew had been allowed to come ashore, and he did not see the despicable captain himself among them.

Damn. His eyes narrowed with displeasure, but he wasted no time in getting on with the task of sabotaging their boats.

He crept along the beach silently, unseen, taking out his knife. He used the hammer to drive the blade into the wood, widening each one with the hook on the end of their small anchors. He hoped the drunken sailors kept making noise until he was finished smashing holes in all five of their rowboats.

Virginia would still have the other half of the crew to contend with, but once she got her attack under way, at least these men would not be able to return to the *Black Jest* to assist their mates.

Dusting off his hands, Nick sneaked off the beach and hurried back to get his wagon. It was a little early yet, but staying around here would not be wise.

Besides, he was eager to get back up the hill to make sure Phillip was still relatively safe.

*A*t that same moment aboard the *Black Jest*, Gin glanced around at the silent, waiting girls in the cargo hold.

She lifted her finger to her lips, signaling them to remain quiet, while she crept to the door with the knife in her hand.

Though they could not see the outside world from their dungeon, they had known when their repulsive supper was brought down to them that that meant it was evening.

Then they had heard the boats being lowered as a goodly number of the crew went on shore leave.

This was part of Nick's plan, luring as many men as possible away, and indeed, when Susannah had returned earlier, she reported seeing the red flag flying.

Gin was startled that it was all happening so fast, but it was just as well, for now there was no time to lose her nerve. Her heart was pounding, but she'd get no second chance.

The time to start her mutiny had come.

Listening at the door for a moment, she couldn't hear anyone in the passage. So she slid the tip of the blade into the lock and wriggled it until it turned.

As soon as it sprang free, she opened the door without a sound. Beckoning to the others to follow, she slipped out of the cargo hold, Nick's knife clasped firmly in her hand.

She gestured to Susannah Perkins to come up alongside her. Gin didn't know and didn't want to know what Miss Perkins had had to do to learn the location of the arms locker. All that mattered was that the guns and ammunition Nick had given to Rotgut awaited them there: the means to their freedom.

Silently, the girls followed her down the passage, then climbed one by one up the ladder. As Gin shepherded them along through the darkness, she couldn't help but think of her father.

This sort of dangerous adventure had been his ordinary life. She hoped her courage held, to prove her worthy of the old spymaster.

What helped most to steel her heart against whatever this night held was thinking of all she had to fight for. All she had to do was get through this night, then a life with Nick and Phillip awaited. They could be a family.

She couldn't wait to see her son again . . .

*P*hillip could barely believe he was on a real mission with a bona fide Order agent.

Though waiting in a box smashed under a rack of guns was relatively boring, this was still the most exciting night of his fifteen years by far.

Danger was close, but safe inside the box, it was easy to remain optimistic about his chances of success.

This was actually fun!—considering he was fully confident that Nick was right outside to protect him and handle any unpleasantness if something should go wrong.

Moreover, he was further inspired by the chance to be a hero, now that he'd had a hand in chastely helping rescue a damsel in distress.

Poor little Rose. She was waiting safely for them back on the *Santa Lucia*. He knew old Captain Antonio was watching over the wee pip as if she were his own granddaughter. The Fabrianos would keep her safe.

Well, then, he thought, squinting at his fob watch in the darkness for the hundredth time. The tiny brass hands caught what little light there was and told him all he needed to know. *It's time.* Two hours exactly. *Off we go!*

He tilted the rack of rifles off him with a grimace and reached up to plant his hand against the lid of the crate. It didn't lift easily; the guard who'd glanced into the box had shut it well.

He had to kick the lid a bit to get it loose again, and doing that quietly wasn't easy.

But, at last, he lifted it aside and popped up out of the crate. The tarp confused him momentarily, but then he tented it over his head and carefully climbed out.

His heart pounded with wild excitement as he stepped down from the crate and ducked out from underneath the tarp. At once, he glanced around.

Good. The place was deserted. As soon as he got his bearings, he started searching for his grandfather's book. He strode up and down the darkened aisles between the goods that all the miscreants had brought to sell at the Bacchus Bazaar. *Not there, not there . . .*

He looked high, he looked low—then all of a sudden, he froze, hearing low male voices coming from outside.

Who's that?

It was hard to be certain, but it sounded like they were speaking French.

Suddenly, there was a bang from the front of the barn; one of the doors jumped on its hinges.

Egads, they're trying to break in. With a gulp, Phillip shrugged off a wave of dread. Whoever they were, Nick could take them, he assured himself. *Now, hurry.*

He redoubled his efforts to find Grandpa Virgil's secret book.

*N*ick was slightly delayed because he had had to abandon his wagon at the nearest village to avoid detection. He had gone the rest of the way to the warehouse on foot, striding through the moonlit countryside.

Watching his footing over the rocky ground, he passed through an olive grove, moving with added stealth as he approached the building.

As he got into position to check the location of the guards before moving in, he heard voices on the wind.

They were coming from around the corner of the warehouse. Without warning, a commotion broke out.

Yells, curses. The sounds of a fight.

Shots fired.

For half a second, his heart gave a jolt of sheer horror, fearing Phillip had been discovered.

But, no. As a couple of men came barreling around the corner, one chasing the other, he realized in astonishment what was going on.

It seemed he wasn't the only one who had had the idea to raid the place.

The jackals were back.

Bloody Simon Limarque and his men.

Well, it was certainly convenient that the Frenchmen were obligingly dispatching the guards for him.

But that left Nick to finish off Limarque.

Gladly. With a whisper of metal in the darkness, he took out his knife, an icy gleam in his eyes.

Time to even a score. Then he slipped out of his hiding place and stalked toward his prey.

"*Yes!*" Phillip breathed, seizing his grandfather's journal off the shelf where he had just found it.

He quickly leafed through it to see if any of the pages had been separated and were lying loose to be auctioned separately, but it seemed to be intact.

He tucked it into his waistcoat and glanced around for his exit. Hearing gunshots outside, he was in no hurry to go out there.

He told himself that Nick surely had the situation under control, then he focused on his own task of finding a way out.

Heart pounding, he jogged around the inside perimeter of the barn, warding off panic to find every exit boarded up, except for the main doors, where he could hear the fight raging.

That was the way the Frenchmen had been trying to break in, and he had no desire to come face-to-face with them.

His only other option was to climb up the ladder to the loft. Here, he was relieved to find the open hay door, but, of course, it was a long way down.

Got to be some rope lying around here somewhere. He hurried about until he found some. He grasped it with a mental cheer, then ran back to the loft and tied a series of strong knots around the nearest post.

Hope it's long enough to reach the ground! When he glanced down from the hay door, however, he stopped, riveted by what he saw below.

Nick came striding out of the darkness unloading a brace of pistols on his enemies, guns flaring as the powder flashed two, three, four times in a row. Men shouted and fell, staggering back with foreign curses.

When one fired back, Nick used his nearest victim for a shield, then dropped him. Out of bullets with no time to reload, he felled the next one with a knife hurled from an expert distance. Phillip gulped as the unfortunate Frenchman screamed and crashed backwards with the hilt sticking out of his chest.

Nick pivoted and warded off his next attacker with a bone-jarring kick in the chest. Another man closed in from his right, but he traded blows with both of them with smooth, swift savagery.

Good God, thought Phillip, staring in amazement at the spy-warrior in action.

Nick slammed the other fellow's skull ruthlessly onto his knee and dropped him in the dirt, out cold. The next screamed as Nick twisted him about-face and dislocated his shoulder. He gave it an additional wrench, and the man passed out from pain.

"Behind you!" Phillip suddenly yelled out.

Nick whirled around, ready to attack, just as a tall, lean, sinewy man threw a knife at him. He whipped out of the way just in time, but picked the blade up where it had fallen and hurled it back at the man.

It plunged into his side as he tried to twist away. The man screamed and fell to his knees.

With a look of cool determination, Nick strode toward him, reloading his pistol as he went. "I told you I'd kill you, Limarque."

"Please!" he choked out, holding up one hand in a token surrender.

"You should never have touched her."

Bang!

With a single shot at point-blank range, Nick took the Frenchman's life. Phillip stared in disbelief, well aware of who the "she" was Nick had been referring to.

The body twitched a little, then went still.

One last enemy had run toward the sound of the gunshot, but as he came tearing around the corner, the man took one look at Nick, then spun around and fled.

The area below Phillip's perch on the hayloft was strewn with unmoving bodies, some dead, others unconscious.

"See any more from up there?" Nick called to him, as they both scanned the landscape.

"No!" Phillip answered after a moment. He felt a little queasy at the ferocious display of prowess—and the utter lack of mercy—he had just witnessed.

Good Lord, did he *really* want to be a spy when he grew up if that was what it was like?

"Come on down," Nick ordered.

Phillip thrust his fears aside but was still a bit nervous about the descent. Of course, he did not even think about disobeying after what he had just seen. He wasn't stupid.

While he climbed awkwardly down the rope, his hands burning with his task, Nick took a moment to catch his breath. When Phillip reached the ground, dropping to his feet, he headed over to Nick at once to give him the book. As he approached, he found himself suddenly more than a little intimidated by his fierce Order friend.

"Did you get it?"

He nodded. "Here."

"Good lad," he said, but he must have noticed the wary look in Phillip's eyes, for he paused. "What's the matter?"

"Nothing," he blurted out, trying to sound natural.

The predatory glint in Nick's dark eyes dimmed as he realized Phillip had seen everything. "Oh, shit. Are you all right? Of course you're not all right," he muttered at himself before Phillip could reply. "Look, lad, it was us or them."

"Are they the ones that took my mother?"

"Aye."

Phillip swallowed hard. "Then they got what they deserved."

Nick's stare searched his eyes. "Are you ready to go?"

Phillip nodded.

"All right, then. Let's ride." He ordered Phillip to

follow him with a curt nod, then they stole the dead men's horses.

All in a night's work.

*H*aving broken into the ship's arms locker, Gin was loading rifles, one after another, and handing them off to her followers.

In the quiet of the night, fear and desperation haunted the girls' eyes as each accepted her weapon; but after their long kidnapping ordeal, Gin's firm air of command seemed to shore up their resolve. For herself, it was time to prove herself her father's daughter.

Having armed each girl with a weapon, she instructed them in soft whispers on the simple firing technique.

"Everyone got that?"

As farm girls, most of them had at least fired a fowling piece before. A few of them even knew how to load their guns themselves, thanks to the tutelage of farmer fathers or soldier brothers.

Only a few of the girls were complete novices without skills of any kind. "You're with me," she ordered these.

Just then, Susannah Perkins returned from her one-woman mission of locking the sleeping crewmen into the mess hall, which served as their communal bedchamber at night. As on most ships of this size, the sailors slept in rows of hammocks hung from the bulkhead, above the long, crude dining tables. "It's done," she whispered.

Gin nodded in approval. "Excellent work. That only leaves us the dozen men or so who are on duty now. It's almost dawn; their watch is nearly ending. They should be half-asleep on their feet at this hour. Now, listen," she instructed her wide-eyed troops.

"When we go up on deck, each of you pick one man to focus on. Don't try to cover all of them, just worry about your one target. With half the crew gone ashore and most of the others locked in their quarters, there'll be more of us up there than there are of them.

"Hold the men at gunpoint, but try not to fire, even by accident, unless you have no choice. The first shot will only wake the rest of the crew, so we must do this as quietly as possible.

"Besides, if we fire first, it'll make them fight back that much harder against us, do you understand? They're not going to want to hurt us if they can avoid it—we're the merchandise."

Gin did not say it aloud, but she considered herself the one exception to that last point.

When Rotgut realized she was the ringleader here, she did not doubt he would gladly kill her if he got the chance, especially after she had embarrassed him in front of his fellow criminal, Jonathan Black.

"Leave the captain to me," she added. "I'll see to that monster personally."

Then she divided the twenty girls into four groups of five. She designated three to be the other groups' leaders and gave them their instructions.

Two groups would head forward on the ship, two toward the stern. These, in turn, would split up, one going to the starboard, the other group to the port side of the ship.

From all four quarters at once, then, they would launch their attack, taking over the ship as quietly as possible. "Hide behind the hatches until you see me on deck. Then follow, and do as I've told you. Emotions will be running high, so decide now to keep your cool, and no matter how they laugh at us or try to goad us, don't fire unless you feel your life to be in danger.

"We don't need to kill these men—as much as we might want to. We just need to put them in the brig until Lord Forrester arrives. He'll be in contact with the Royal Navy at Corfu Town to come and arrest them, and then we're going to get off this cursed ship at last.

"Now, go, girls. And if your courage falters, think of Joan of Arc, or Good Queen Bess in her armor facing down the Spanish! We are women, but we can fight," she whispered fiercely. "Stand firm, and we'll be free within the hour."

Her words visibly rallied them. Steeling themselves, her fair mutineers padded off to get into position for their battle.

Gin couldn't help but feel that even her father would have been impressed.

*N*ick and Phillip raced back down the hill and through the sleeping town of Sidári. They returned to the beach at a safe distance from the Seahorse Inn, where half of Rotgut's sailors were three sheets to the wind, thanks to gallons of free ouzo Nick (technically, Phillip) had paid for in advance.

Perhaps the sailors thought it strange that the host of the party at the *taverna* had not yet appeared, but by now, they were probably too drunk to care. Yes, Nick mused, as they dismounted and strode across the sand, this half of the crew would not be a problem.

It was the other half that worried him.

He had to get out there onto the water to be ready to assist Virginia in her mutiny. Any minute now, he expected to start hearing shots coming from the direction of the slavers' frigate.

He and Phillip abandoned Limarque's horses in favor of the dory, running it out into the shallows, and splashing into their seats before picking up the oars.

Nick rowed as fast as he could back out to the *Santa Lucia*, where the Italians waited. When he called to them from the waves to get ready to make sail, they rushed into motion.

He tied the dory to the ladder to be dragged through the water. There wasn't time to lift it back up onto the ship with the davits.

Phillip climbed up the ladder ahead of him and was surprised to find Rose waiting for their safe return. She was supposed to be in bed.

As soon as Nick was also aboard, he took the captain aside. "Do you remember when I hired you, I said there might come a time when bad business afoot might require some action? Well, that time has come. Get me as close to that frigate as you safely can."

The tough, weathered Italian followed Nick's pointing finger with his gaze. He eyed the frigate darkly, then nodded. "That's the one that took the little girl?"

Nick nodded. "And he's got more girls on board. Tonight, the bastard gets what he's had coming."

The captain gave him a hard-eyed nod, then turned and clipped out a series of sharp orders to his sons. All their usual merriment vanished.

Satisfied that they'd be in range shortly, Nick called Phillip and Rose down through the hatch to the ship's galley. He beckoned them over to the stove, pulling Virgil's book out of his waistcoat. "I have a job for you two."

They looked at him eagerly.

He handed the journal to Phillip. "Start a fire in the stove and burn this thing. Every page. I want nothing left but ashes."

"Mother will be distraught," the boy warned. "It is her last remaining token of her father."

"I know, and I'm sorry. But Virgil never should have shared this information." Nick laid a hand on his shoulder, looking soberly into the lad's eyes. "Look at what it's led to. It must be destroyed. Can I count on you? And you, Rose?"

The girl nodded, but Phillip shrugged uneasily. "I'll do it, but I'm telling you, she's going to be furious."

"I'll explain it to your mother," Nick hastily assured

him. He was going to have a lot of explaining to do to her, actually. "After all that's happened," he added, "I think she'll understand. But if she does get angry, I'll tell her it was my fault. Now, I'm trusting you to take care of this for me. We can't risk anyone's getting his hands on it ever again. All right?"

Phillip nodded reluctantly. "Come on, Rose. Help me build a fire in this stove."

As the two youngsters got started on their task, Nick wasted no further time, rushing back up onto the deck.

*W*hen Gin set foot on the deck of the *Black Jest*, taking her first cautious step out from behind the cover of the hatch, the sudden face full of wind lifting her hair and the rocking of the ship made her slightly dizzy in her wound-up state. Heart hammering, she quickly shook off the sensation. Still, the war of fear and courage in her veins had heightened her awareness to a sharp edge.

She was acutely attuned to the rhythm of the waves and the creaking of the vessel. The intoxicating freshness of the free, open air. The smell of the salt-weathered wood and the tar they used as sealant, and the quiet chuffing of the furled canvas sails. She had never felt more alive.

The stars and planets seemed to sing out from the dark sky. The orange glow of sunrise gathered behind the eastward mountains of the Albanian mainland, where Ali Pasha, the Terrible Turk, reigned.

As she fixed her sights on the sleepy sailor leaning against the foremast ahead, his back to her, she was aware of her followers at her back. The other women glanced around, choosing their targets as instructed.

All around the sprawling deck, silently, her little army of mutineers were emerging in the predawn twilight, closing in on their hated captors.

Gin felt a welling rush of destiny. The moment of truth was at hand. Could she have done it? Could she have really entered her father's world of danger and intrigue and held her own?

But when the sailors suddenly started noticing that they were under attack, she brushed aside her musings and took command of the deck.

From stem to stern, the former victims seized control of the vessel, turning the tables on their captors. For their part, the men of the night watch were so taken off guard by this mutiny that they barely put up a fight.

One man started to give a shout, but stopped when a bayonet appeared inches from his eyeball. He shut his mouth abruptly. The sailors seemed to be in shock more than anything. Clearly, they had never believed such brazen action possible from a bunch of terrorized females.

It had all happened with startling speed and ease, smooth as clockwork. Gin's heart soared at the quiet, steady courage she witnessed in her mutineers.

They marched the sailors down to the brig and locked them in, stoically ignoring their taunts and curses.

Once these prisoners were secure, Gin ordered three of the women to go and make sure the sailors locked in the mess hall were still unable to get out.

Word quickly came back that the door was barred and the men inside still seemed to be asleep. They hadn't heard a thing. At that point, the only task left was to neutralize the captain.

Gin was looking forward to this. She nodded to a few of the girls to come along in case she needed reinforcements. Their eyes gleamed, fierce and bright, with victory. They, too, were eager to see Rotgut get his comeuppance. Rifle in her grasp, Gin strode toward the captain's stateroom at the stern.

"Everyone ready?" she breathed, glancing around at her followers.

They nodded, including Susannah Perkins. Indeed, rather than being the helpless victim Gin had expected, the kidnapped girl she had been hired to find continued to display an impressive knack for survival. She had proved to have a cool head so far dealing with danger.

Bracing herself, Gin lifted her hand and rapped soundly on the captain's door. She waited in anticipation for him to answer.

Wasn't old Rotgut going to be surprised?

"What do you want?" he yelled gruffly from behind the door.

Gin signaled silence to her troops.

No one answered him.

"Who's there?" he repeated.

She merely knocked again in answer, three times, slowly.

They heard the creaking of his berth as he arose, then his heavy footsteps tromping across the planks.

"Steady, girls," she whispered, as the footsteps came closer.

"This had better be good, or I'll string you up for botherin' me at this hour!" the captain growled, throwing open the door.

He froze abruptly to find himself looking down the barrel of Gin's rifle.

"Good morning, Captain," she said. "Would you kindly come with us?"

"What's going on? What is the meaning of this?" he shouted.

"Don't move another muscle!" she warned when he took a backward step, reaching toward the wall, where she figured he probably kept a weapon. "Touch it, and I will blow a hole in your guts."

He froze, perhaps seeing in her eyes that she was perfectly prepared to pull the trigger on this monster.

"Now, come out of there with your hands up," she ordered.

He considered this, his hatred of her and all the other females stamped across his ugly face.

She shook her head in warning. "Just give me one excuse, you piece of filth."

Rotgut must have decided that prudence was the better part of valor. "Where are my men?" he demanded, though he warily obeyed, lifting his hands and stepping out his stateroom into the passageway.

The girls smirked at the sight of the big, ill-kempt drunkard in his nightgown and cap.

"What *is* this?" he cried in bafflement.

"What does it look like? A mutiny, dear Rotgut. Now, move."

"Where are you taking me?"

"To the brig, with your men."

"At least let me put on me trousers!"

"Very well. Anna, bring the lantern. Step into his stateroom first and throw any weapons you find off the stern balcony. Susannah, help her."

Gin used her rifle to back Rotgut out of the way, so the two girls could pass.

"God, it stinks of old man in here!" Susannah coughed.

"Old drunkard is more like it," Anna agreed.

The girls quickly found a pair of pistols, a sword, and a knife, and carried all of them to the captain's balcony off the stern, casting them into the waves.

This done, Gin gestured to Rotgut with her rifle, allowing him to step back into his chamber. He quickly found some trousers and pulled them on.

Feeling generous with victory, Gin even allowed him to shove his fat feet down into his stinking old boots.

"You're a very evil man," she informed him.

"Ach, everybody's got to make a living," he grunted.

She could not help sneering in disgust, but a proper Order agent probably would have bashed him in the head with the butt of the rifle for that disgusting excuse.

"All right, you're dressed now. To the brig with you. Get up, it's time to go!"

"Wait!" Susannah interrupted. "Did you see what he just did?"

"What?" Gin halted. Still holding him at gunpoint, she sent her accomplice an uncertain glance from the corner of her eye.

"He swiped his keys off the dresser, there," she replied. "I'll bet he's got a key to the brig. We lock him up, he's just goin' to unlock the door and get right back out with the rest of his men. Hand 'em over, you pig!"

"I don't know what she's talking about. I don't have any keys."

"What you don't have is any credibility, Captain. Put the keys on the dresser."

"I don't know what the bitch is talking about!"

"I know what I saw," Susannah ground out. "Don't trust him, m'lady."

"I don't," Gin replied. "Put the keys down, Rotgut."

Rage came into his eyes. "You can go to hell, you little whore."

"Shoot him!" Anna cried.

Gin was holding herself back.

"Aye, do it. You don't have the balls." The gruff captain gave a coarse laugh. "But you wouldn't, would ye? Stupid wench."

Everything in her wanted to pull the trigger to punish this heartless ruffian for all the suffering he had caused.

But she gave him one last chance. "Give me back the keys, then we're going to the brig."

"You can go to hell, you redheaded witch. This is my ship."

Gin tensed, considering her options. "Very well," she said with a cold smile spreading over her face. "Then, you can walk the plank, instead."

*A*pproaching in the *Santa Lucia*, Nick stood at the rails, pistols loaded, weapons at the ready, his telescope pressed to his eye.

His stomach was in knots as he scanned the frigate with thwarted protective instinct, every fiber of his being full of anxiety over Virginia's plans for mutiny this night.

He hoped he had not made the biggest mistake of his life in agreeing to this, leaving her behind. *God, please let her be safe.* It was too damned quiet over there.

The sun was slowly peeking over the horizon, but the shadows made it difficult to see, along with the rocking of the waves.

The Italians sailed on, taking him ever closer to the frigate. Nick's heart pounded with a distress far keener than he ever could have felt about any brother agent's safety on a mission—let alone his own. She had to be all right.

And then, suddenly, he saw her.

A knot of women came into view on deck. She was at the head of them, a Baker rifle in her hands. Heart pounding, he scanned her in a trice and saw that she looked to be unscathed.

Then his jaw dropped as he realized she had taken Rotgut prisoner.

The hefty ship's captain was walking a few steps ahead of her, his hands up, fingers linked behind his head.

What is she doing? Holding his breath, Nick peered through the telescope. For a moment, he watched in avid fascination.

Then he suddenly laughed aloud.

"I don't believe it. She's a lunatic."

"What is it?" Antonio shouted.

"Look!" Nick pointed at the *Black Jest* as she made the vile captain walk the plank.

As Rotgut plunged into the cold, night-dark waves, the women on board cheered, the Italians saw what happened and hooted with hilarity, and Nick, if there was any doubt left, fell utterly in love.

"Oh, my God," he said softly, shaking his head in disbelief at her sheer, brazen pluck. *She did it.*

Here he was, beside himself with the need to save her. Ah, but she was Virgil's daughter, and she'd jolly well rescue herself, thank you very much.

"Get me over there!" he yelled to the Italians.

"*Sì, sì!*" All the Fabrianos were cheering, applauding, whistling. They set off a cannon in salute.

This got the girls' attention. They ran to the rails and started waving excitedly.

"Hey, Englishman!" Eldest brother Vincenzo cracked his knuckles as Nick climbed the mast. "You want us to go take care of de captain?"

"Be my guest!" he called back in amusement. "No hurry, though. Certainly would be a shame if the bleeder had to tread water for a few hours, don't you think?"

"Lots of sharks around this time of year," the second brother chimed in.

His cousin punched him in agreement. "Ha, ha! *Molto bene! Sì, sì!*"

When the *Santa Lucia* had drifted a little closer to the other ship, Nick grabbed a rope dangling off the yardarm and leaped off the mast, swinging over the rails and onto the other deck.

Dropping down onto the planks, he caught his balance, his heart soaring, his stare locked on Virginia.

As she turned, the rising sun kissed her cheeks and caught the way her blue eyes lit up at the sight of him, and her beauty nearly stole his breath.

She picked up her skirts and ran to him. Nick caught her up in his arms, twirling her around in a circle, but he did not, could not put her down. He had swept her off her feet, and the feel of her slender body in his embrace was heavenly. "You did it," he whispered. "You brilliant, mad pirate-lady."

She laughed and captured his lips. He gave her a lusty kiss, even as he smiled with jubilation. She was safe . . . and he was never letting her out of his sight again.

At last, he let her feet touch down on the planks and just hugged her, hard, for a long time. She held him tightly, burying her face against his neck.

He felt her tremble a little. "I'm so glad that's over," she whispered.

"Are we sure it is? Are all the men accounted for? Was anybody hurt?"

"Yes, and no. The crew is locked up in both the mess and the brig, and everyone came out of it unscathed."

"Excellent news. Well done, darling." He marveled at her. "Your father would be *so* damned proud of you. I know I am."

She smiled. "I couldn't have done it without you, Nick."

"Ah, that's nonsense," he murmured.

"It's true, I wouldn't have known what to do. I was blind down there in the dark and nearly too scared to think, but seeing you . . . gave me courage."

"Well." He smiled modestly, then shook his head, still wondering how a black-hearted scoundrel like him had ever ended up with this goddess. Here they were in the land of Greek myths, and he could not decide if she was love's irresistible Aphrodite, wisdom's warrior woman, Athena, or nurturing Juno, mother of the gods.

Maybe a little of each.

As she caressed his face and ran her fingers through his hair, Nick was as good as deaf and blind to everybody else there. She was everything, and his heart so full of devastated longing that he could not even speak.

He just gazed at her, mute and awkward; she kissed him again. He must have looked like he needed it.

When she ended the kiss softly, bit by bit, he opened his mouth to speak—to try to tell her how completely he adored her—but not a sound came out.

She smiled, caressing him. "I know, darling. Me, too."

"No," he informed her in a vehement tone. "You don't. You can't begin to imagine how much I love you. You can't. Sorry."

"Later, then," she said with a tender smile, "if you can't tell me, maybe you can show me."

"Count on it," he forced out.

She held his gaze in adoration. "Oh, Nick."

She started to hug him again, slipping her arms around his waist, but he halted her, capturing her chin between his fingers and his thumb; he leaned a little closer, staring sternly into her eyes. "As for you, madam, don't you *ever* scare me like that again."

She gave him a cheeky little salute in answer. "Aye-aye, captain."

He pinched her cheek in playful chiding.

"Come." She took his hand and started off across the deck, leading him behind her. "I've got to go check on my captives."

"Are you sure there's no one left that I can kill for you? Please? Can't I at least beat someone up?"

"There's always Simon Limarque."

"Done. The blackguard's already dead, along with that horrid broken nose chap."

She glanced over her shoulder at him in surprise. "Nicely done, sir."

"We got your father's book, as well. I'm sorry, but we've already destroyed it. It's safer that away for everyone."

Regret flashed across her face at this news. "Yes. I suppose you're right . . ." Then she furrowed her brow. "Did you say 'we'? Who? Did John Carr help you?"

"Er . . ." Nick lifted his eyebrows and froze. *Damn.* "Um, not exactly . . ."

In the next moment, however, she learned the truth.

"Mother! Mother, down here!"

She jolted like she might fall over, her eyes widening.

"Mother, halloo! I'm down here! It's me!"

"Is . . . is that *my son?*" She whirled out of Nick's arms and raced to the rails, staring down at the *Santa Lucia* in disbelief. "*Phillip?*"

Nick followed her, only to find the boy waving up at them in crazed excitement. Little Rose was right beside him, likewise waving to the females who had been so distraught when Nick had carried her off the frigate.

"Rose!" the girls yelled, waving back to her joyfully, no doubt relieved to see their little friend unharmed.

"Hullo, Mother! So glad you're safe!" Phillip exclaimed. "What a relief! I want to come up there and see you!"

"Phillip, be careful!" She gasped when the lad climbed up onto the rails of the *Santa Lucia* and leaped off nimbly onto the ladder on the frigate's hull.

Virginia whirled to stare at Nick in disbelief. "Did you see that? Did you see what he just did?"

"Don't look at me, he's your son. It's not my fault the apple doesn't fall far from the tree. For what it's worth, the pup has got the makings of a damned fine agent."

She pursed her lips and smacked him in the arm for that opinion. Nick laughed.

But when Phillip vaulted aboard, she pulled the beaming youth close and hugged him for all she was worth.

Tears sprang into her eyes. Nick watched, unsure what to do. Give the close-knit pair some time alone? It was a moment for mother and son.

But just as he started to back away out of respect, she reached out and grasped Nick's arm, pulling him over firmly to share in their little family's embrace.

"You should've seen Nick, Mum, he was brilliant—"

"You both are," she interrupted in a choked voice. "That's all I need to know."

Then she did a most un-Virginia-like thing and started bawling, overcome by her emotions.

"Oh, stop that, old girl," her son teased. "I never took you for a watering pot!"

"I can't help it!" She sobbed. "I just love you both so dearly." She kissed Phillip's head and Nick's cheek and got her tears on both of them.

"And we love you. Both of us, Mum. Don't we, Nick?"

"We do," Nick whispered. "Loads." Then he put his arms around them both, stunned at how naturally the whole new purpose for his life slipped into place in that one shining moment.

As if it had been waiting here for him all along. Just waiting for the sunrise . . .

And now the sky glowed.

Chapter 24

A few days later, they sat shoulder to shoulder on the beach, savoring each other's company and relaxing at last after all the unpleasant business had been sorted out.

They were both dressed in light-colored clothing and barefoot, toes in the sand, neither in any hurry to rush back to England. They had decided to stay until after Christmas.

Nick put his arm around her. "So," he murmured with an intimate smile in his voice, "how does it feel to have accomplished by yourself something that even the Order failed to do?"

Gin sent him a warm smile. "You mean disband the Bacchus Bazaar forever?"

He nodded.

"It feels good. Really good. But I can't take all the credit," she said, leaning her head on his shoulder. Still, she could not hide the satisfaction in her eyes.

His point was well-taken.

During her father's tenure as spymaster, the Order

had allowed the criminal gathering to remain in opera-tion as a useful source of intelligence. But with the Pro-metheans defeated, there was no longer any reason to allow such wickedness to flourish. She was glad to see it brought to an end.

To be sure, it had been an interesting couple of days.

After her mutiny on the *Black Jest,* Nick had sent down to the Navy base in Corfu Town, summoning re-inforcements.

When the Navy patrol boat had arrived, Nick and she had met with the captain to explain the situation. He had never heard of any such thing as the Bacchus Bazaar and looked at them as if he suspected they were either lunatics or pranksters, making such wild claims.

But then Nick had presented his credentials: namely, the Order medal the Regent had pinned on him at West-minster Abbey.

It was lucky that Phillip had brought it.

The Navy captain realized they were telling the truth about the assembly of criminals happening right under the British government's nose, considering that Corfu was now a protectorate of England.

That was all the captain needed to hear. He had quickly summoned a raiding party of dozens of Royal Marines, who stormed the Villa Loutrá just when all the rats were gathered for the illicit auction to begin.

Some of the criminals had indeed managed to scatter, but the Navy had men hunting down those who had escaped.

For the most part, the guilty had been apprehended. There had been many embarrassing arrests of high-level emissaries from all over the place. The Bazaar was done for, hopefully forever—though, admittedly, these sorts of things had a way of popping up again like so many poisonous mushrooms.

In any case, the girls were now safely in the care of the commanding officer and his wife down in Corfu

Town. Gin had bade them all a fond farewell, especially little Rose, whom she could barely stand to let go. She had come to think of the child as the daughter she'd never had.

Rose cried at having to say good-bye to her, as well, but to Gin's surprise, the little curly-head looked even more upset to have to say good-bye to Phillip.

Gin was further surprised when Susannah Perkins lowered her bravado enough to hug her abruptly in thanks. The brazen hoyden had wiped away a tear and said she couldn't wait to return to her mother and inform her what her stepfather had done to her—selling her to the likes of Rotgut simply to be rid of her for causing the family embarrassment.

After this experience, the girl looked ready to reconsider her wild behavior for a tamer mode of life. Gin thanked her for all she had done to help bring about their escape. It couldn't have been pleasant for her.

Having said their good-byes, all the girls were presently recuperating from their ordeal under the watchful eyes of the commander and his wife, but a ship would soon be dispatched to take them home to England.

As for Rotgut, or Ed Dolan—who had eventually been fished out of the water by the Italians—he, too, would be returned to England to stand trial for his many crimes.

It would have been just as well for him if some passing shark had bitten him in half, for he only had the gallows to look forward to at this point.

Still, he had already provided the authorities with useful information about his kidnapping ring. More arrests would be made back in England.

The last order of business was selling Gin's emerald so they could pay the Fabrianos for their services, among their other expenses. Together, they had sent the warm-hearted captain and crew back to their wives at Ancona well rewarded, home in time for their *Buon Natale*, as promised.

Now that all the excitement had died down, this left the two of them at last to make up for lost time.

Phillip understood they wanted to be alone, but Gin had even found a way to keep her son out of trouble for a while (though this was always slightly doubtful).

She had hired a local professor of antiquities to take Phillip around to see some of the ancient structures left over from classical times, both on Corfu and the surrounding islands.

"If he's missing school," she had said, "he might as well get something educational out of this trip."

Nick had snorted. "Oh, I think he has."

She had smacked him again for this bit of cheek, which he seemed to enjoy.

"Why are you always beating me?" he exclaimed.

She loved seeing the scoundrel laugh.

He was so different now from the brooding, angry mercenary she had so cautiously freed from the Order's dungeon. But then, Gin supposed, she was different, too. Not as hell-bent on keeping control of every situation. It was exhausting to live like that, anyway.

Life was much more peaceful and easy to enjoy when one was able to let go . . .

"So, here we are," Nick said at length.

Just the two of them, alone in a Greek-island paradise, wildly in love.

Life was good.

"Yes?"

"Finally, my dear Virginia, all is revealed, and I even figured out why you first came to me down in that Order dungeon—"

"Um, Nick," she interrupted. "Actually—my friends call me Ginny. Or Gin."

He turned to her in astonishment. "They do?"

She laughed. "I daresay we ought to be on less formal terms by now, don't you think?"

"Ginny!" he echoed in surprise. "Huh. I like that."

Then he shrugged and muttered, "My friends call me a black-hearted bastard. Actually, I'm not even sure I have any friends."

"Oh, don't make me smack you again!" she chided, giving his shoulder a kiss. "You know full well all of Virgil's boys are still your brothers. Now what were you going to say, my darling—before I so rudely interrupted?"

He smiled. "The reason you came to me, of all people, down in that dungeon . . . It was more than just the fact that I could get you in to see Hugh Lowell, wasn't it?

"You needed someone who would not only help you get the book back but wouldn't tell the greybeards about your father's breach of protocol, writing all those secrets down in the first place. That's why you kept telling me everybody makes mistakes."

"Including my own, trusting John Carr more than I should have. But you're right, I needed a rule-breaker," she said ruefully, playing with his strong, long fingers as she held his hand. "Someone who doesn't think like everybody else. Who knows that sometimes, you have no choice but to stray outside the lines—and who wouldn't condemn my father for doing the same. He only did it to keep us safe, you know, Phillip and me," she added. "If any of his old enemies ever came after us, the information in that journal would have helped protect us."

"Well, you've got me to do that now," Nick answered softly. "And you might as well know I have decided this is my life's whole duty from this day forward."

She beamed at him. "Really?"

He nodded. "Actually, it started a while ago—and this goes for both you and Phillip. Of course, you seem rather a dab hand at protecting yourself, I admit. But a man's got to have something useful to do. And as for you, my girl, Lud! You can be so dashed impetuous. Somebody's got to keep you out of trouble."

"Look who's talking!" she exclaimed. "But Nick?"

"Hmm?"

"What about America?"

"Oh, my love. All the freedom in the world would be a prison without you," he whispered, then he kissed her.

Gin wrapped her arms around him and lay back invitingly on the sand. He deepened the kiss, stroking her tongue with his own, while his hands caressed her arms and her waist. He moved atop her, braced on his elbows and knees as he kissed his way down her neck. She thrilled to the weight and heat of his hard body pressed against her.

At length, he paused in kissing her and gazed down into her eyes, the sun dancing through his tousled black hair, his dark eyes full of glowing softness.

Gin ached with love for him. She could barely find her voice as she cupped his cheek longingly. "You weren't the only one in a prison, darling," she whispered, "and I'm not talking about Rotgut's cargo hold. I was in a cell of my own making . . . for so long. Keeping my heart locked away so nobody would steal it. But I give it to you freely now. It's yours, whether you want it or not."

"I do." He paused, as though hearing his own words. "I do," he said more slowly, savoring the two simple syllables spoken at every wedding. "I do?" he suggested a third time, arching a brow at her in question. Though the quirk of his lips was sardonic, his midnight eyes were earnest.

"Are you asking me . . . ?"

He nodded. "What do you think, Lady Burke? Would you like to become Lady Forrester?"

"Oh, Nick! Yes! I would. I love you so much!" She arched up to capture him in her embrace.

He enfolded her in his arms and, after a moment, rolled onto his back, bringing her atop him.

She sat astride his lean waist, her hair blowing, loose and long, around her. Nick searched her face with his heart in his eyes. "I love you, my Ginny. How could I not? You are the cleverest, most beautiful, the bravest, most amazing woman on earth. And look at all you've done for me."

"What have I done?"

"Turned me back into a human being," he drawled. "You didn't have to help me. You didn't have to be kind to me or treat me with the respect that I no longer deserved. But you mended me, whether you know it or not. You've given me a whole new life. A second chance."

"I knew you'd do brilliant things with it. And you have."

"Well, I owe it all to you. Thank you . . . for everything. Believing in me. Even after I had lost all faith in myself. You gave that back to me. My pride." He sat up, holding her on his lap, his arms around her.

Gin stroked his hair, staring into his eyes. "You've done great things for me as well," she informed him softly. "You gave me the courage to surrender to love. Because I trust you, Nick. Not just with my life—and my son's—but with my very heart. I know you'll never let me down."

"I never will," he vowed. "I swear it to you, on . . . well, let me not say on my honor, since that's been known to fail me in the past. On something better. Stronger. On something eternal, like my love for you." He glanced around at the beach. "I swear it on the sea and the sky above us, and these rocks!" he declared with heart-tugging earnestness.

She gazed at him in melting, doting amusement. "Even on the rocks?"

He suddenly furrowed his brow. "Are you making fun of me?"

"Never! I adore you, you sweet man. And I've realized something profound about you, darling," she added in a whisper, hugging him close.

"What's that?" he asked with a teasing little harrumph.

"You are frightfully romantic."

"The hell I am." He pulled back and gave her a warning glower. "If you tell the fellows that, I will stringently deny it."

She laughed. "Don't worry, your secret's safe with me."

"Good. They'd never believe it anyway."

"I love you, Nicholas." She kissed him thoughtfully, suddenly wondering about something. "When do I get to meet them, anyway?"

"Who?"

"The rest of Virgil's boys. Your fellow agents."

"Hmm, I suppose I could arrange a meeting . . . in exchange for a certain favor."

"Oh, really? What sort of favor?"

"I want you to do something with me."

"Oh, dear. I hope this doesn't involve tricks you learned from your old friend, Angelique."

He scoffed. "If you'd behave yourself, I'd like to tell you the real reason I brought you to this particular spot."

She glanced around at the sun-kissed beach and the turquoise waves. "Because it's gorgeous?"

"No, though it is. You see those rocks?"

"The ones on which you swore your eternal devotion to me?" she asked, smiling in hopeless adoration of the man. "Couldn't miss them."

Two giant sandstone boulders thrust up from the shallows several yards apart.

"What about them, you adorable man?"

"I am not adorable. I am a trained assassin."

"Yes, you're very, very scary," she assured him. "Even so."

"Ahem." He ignored her playful teasing. "I was told by an old Greek man at the Seahorse Inn that the passage between those rocks is called the Canal d'Amour."

"Is it really?" she exclaimed.

"Legend has it that any couple who swims through it together will have eternal love. So, let's go."

"But darling, it's December."

"Who cares?"

"It's cold! It's in the sixties."

"Gin, we're Order agents. What the hell do we care? You're an honorary one," he informed her before she could protest. "Besides, I'll warm you up after. Believe me." With that, he tumbled her off his lap and climbed to his bare feet. He held out his hand to help her up, looming over her like a dark god limned in sunshine.

She bit her lip and gazed up at him, dazzled. He was her beloved, and he was much too hard to resist. "I suppose we *are* talking about a guarantee of eternal love here."

"I do think it's worth it," he agreed in a pointed tone, nodding wryly.

"In that case, I'll race you!" She grasped his hand, jumped up from the beach, and dashed headlong into the breath-stealing water.

She shrieked at the cold, but kept running, splashing through the shallows. Nick laughed, chasing her. He was right behind her. Running out into waist-deep water, they started getting used to the chill as the waves flowed past them. Then they were swimming side by side, gliding in breathless exultation toward the twin towers of the timeless sandstone rocks ahead.

"Ready?" Nick asked, treading water when they had neared the rocks.

She nodded, too joyful to care that her teeth were chattering with the cold.

Then they swam together past the famous love-spell rocks of Corfu, making the watery journey that lovers had been taking together since the days of Odysseus and his faithful Penelope.

Nick stopped between the giant boulders and drew her into his arms, sporting in the waves. Exchanging salty kisses, they lingered there to let the magic wash over them completely. Just to make extra sure they had sealed their pact according to ancient specifications, they then swam well past the huge rocks, out into the deep open water, where they turned back to see how far they had come.

"Well, it's d-d-done," Gin declared.

Nick's black hair was slicked back against his head. Water droplets starred his inky lashes, and his white shirt clung to his skin in the most seductive fashion.

He gazed back through the Canal d'Amour. Then he cast her a roguish, sideways glance. "No turning back now."

"Who'd want to?"

He flashed a roguish grin and reached for her, pulling her close to kiss the saltwater off her frozen lips. "Come on, my little icicle. I'll carry you." Drawing her by her wrist, he turned around and put her on his back.

She held on to his broad shoulders. Then he swam through the bright aquamarine waves, but instead of returning to the beach, he bore her over to one of the great rocks. They climbed up onto it, dripping and shivering, but exuberant.

At the pinnacle, they lay on a flat, narrow bed of sun-warmed stone, and there, her true love kept his promise: With the fire of his passion, the magnificent rogue soon made her very warm, indeed.

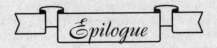

Epilogue

"*Virgil had a daughter?*"

They all kept saying that.

Gin felt a trifle self-conscious as six pairs of eyes trained to scrutinize people studied her in amazement.

True to his word, Nick had made sure as soon as they reached England to assemble his fellow agents to meet her. In fact, he had gone one better and arranged for the introduction to take place inside the Order's London headquarters of Dante House. The ancient Tudor palace by the Thames had been Virgil's domain. She got to meet the illustrious Mr. Gray, butler to the spies, as well as the fierce German guard dogs.

Mostly, she was relieved to see Nick welcomed by his brother agents, fully forgiven and restored to their friendship—even Lord Trevor Montgomery's.

Then, one by one, her father's protégés greeted her: Max, the sly Marquess of Rotherstone. Rohan, the Duke of Warrington, the mighty Beast. Jordan, the Earl of Falconridge, the calm, cool diplomat.

Even Drake, the heroic Earl of Westwood, had ventured into Town with his wife, Emily, to meet her. As Gin shook his hand, she could see he wasn't mad, only a little touched and perhaps still slightly damaged by all he had experienced, which had included torture at enemy hands. But Emily, Lady Westwood, was obviously devoted to him; Gin was moved to see how, from the moment they walked in the door, the two remained inseparable.

The dazzlingly handsome Viscount Beauchamp, Nick's team leader, gave her a hug and welcomed her to the family.

Trevor, Nick's former human shield, just kept staring at her and shaking his head in disbelief—not so much because she was Virgil's daughter, like the others were, but because of the changes she had brought about in the Order's lone wolf. "I've never seen anyone get through to him like this," he kept saying. "It's a miracle."

"Oh, he's a lamb," Gin teased.

But if they were astonished to meet her, their handler's daughter, one could have heard a pin drop when she called in Virgil's grandson.

At that, six unshockable spies who had been everywhere and seen it all stood around gaping in amazement over one fifteen-year-old boy.

"What?" Phillip mumbled, shrinking back slightly from the ring of tall, intimidating warriors around him, all staring at him like he was the eighth wonder of the world.

Gin couldn't help laughing.

At length, Rohan gave her son a friendly slap on the back that nearly sent the boy flying around the room. Cheerfully, the big duke boomed: "So, are you going to join the Order, lad?"

"Uh, I think I'm going to go back to my regular school, a-at least for now," Phillip responded.

"Smart boy," Jordan murmured.

Having seen what Phillip was capable of in Greece,

and acknowledging that being a part of the Order *was* his rightful heritage, Gin had cautiously agreed to let him try a year at the school up in Scotland if he so desired.

But to her surprise, Phillip had reconsidered after witnessing Nick unleash hell's wrath on Simon Limarque and his men. It was a lot for a boy his age to take in.

No doubt meeting these men also gave him fair warning of what he could expect in the spy life, besides just adventure and excitement. Their valiant service had cost each one of them, some visibly, like Rohan, with a scar on his face, or Drake, deaf in one ear and in need of tranquil surroundings, or in invisible ways, like Max, who could never quite trust anyone outside their inner circle, or Beau, whose sunny smile still concealed shadows he'd carry with him for the rest of his life.

All of these men had paid a price in one way or another—just like her sire. But they were heroes all the same, and each deeply loved by a good woman who had dedicated her life to helping him heal. Gin was set to meet the rest of the wives later that evening.

Thankfully, each of her father's handpicked agents— even Nick—had reached his own kind of peace now that the war was done. If only Virgil could have been there to see it, she mused as her gaze wandered up to the mantel, where the old Scot's portrait looked down on them.

Nick noticed her staring at the painting and came over to put his arm around her. "Are you all right?" he murmured in her ear, giving her shoulders an affectionate squeeze.

She nodded and kissed him on the cheek. "Never better."

"Gentlemen," Max spoke up all of a sudden. "And ladies," he added, with a nod to Gin and Emily. As the senior agent present, he called them all to attention. "I propose a toast."

"Gray! Bring us drinks, man," Beau called.

Gray was already on his way, passing around short glasses and a very fine, old bottle of Scotch whiskey.

When all had their share (except for Phillip), Max lifted his glass. "To Virgil and the victory he made possible."

"Hear, hear," Nick assented in a hearty murmur.

Then they all raised their glasses and drank.

Gin smiled, savoring the moment as she suddenly found herself a part of their world, as she had longed to be since she was a girl. *You did well, Father,* she thought, mentally toasting to him, too.

Then she tossed back her drink in a brash style that made them laugh and exclaim she was indeed one of them.

"And so Virgil's spirit lives on," Max declared as he threw his arm around Phillip's shoulders and rumpled his red hair.

The boy beamed, the future dancing in his eyes.

Author's Note

Dear Reader,

Thank you for coming along on the journey with Nick and Gin and me through this, the closing episode of the Inferno Club series. We've come a long way! Looking back, we started at the tail end of the Napoleonic Wars with top agent Max, Lord Rotherstone, (*My Wicked Marquess*) on the hunt for a bride beyond reproach and a marriage capable of restoring his family's tainted reputation.

Next, it was on to Cornwall with Rohan, the Duke of Warrington, (*My Dangerous Duke*) as smugglers who had crossed "the Beast" tried to soothe his wrath by giving him the gift of a girl. A girl who changed his world. After that, Jordan, Lord Falconridge, got a second chance with his first love, Mara, in *My Irresistible Earl*. Fourth was Drake, Lord Westwood (*My Ruthless Prince*) bringing the Order a major victory, but at great cost—a price he couldn't have paid without his quietly fierce Emily by his side.

From there, we moved on to Beauchamp's three-man team. Seductive charmer Beau (*My Scandalous Viscount*) faced the amusing dilemma of being a secret-keeping spy who falls in love with a ton gossip—oh, forgive me—"lady of information." Next came the noble Lord Trevor Montgomery, in a great sulk after his marriage plans fell through, but it was a blessing in disguise because only then did he meet Grace, the vicar's daughter, in *My Notorious Gentleman*. Last but not least, as you've just seen, bad boy Nick finally got his comeuppance—and a much-needed shot at redemption—with Virgil's daughter.

I hope you have enjoyed reading their stories as much as I've enjoyed writing them, and I thank you from the bottom of my heart for letting me entertain you for a while. Visit me anytime on the web at www.Gaelen Foley.com for fun story extras, articles, videos, and more. If you sign up for my e-newsletter, you'll be automatically entered into my monthly sweepstakes to win prizes like autographed copies of my books. You can also find me on Facebook. I look forward to hearing from you! And thank you once again.

Best always,
Gaelen

At Avon Books, we know your passion for romance—once you finish one of our novels, you find yourself wanting more.

May we tempt you with . . .

- **Excerpts** from our upcoming releases.

- Entertaining **extras**, including authors' personal photo albums and book lists.

- Behind-the-scenes **scoop** on your favorite characters and series.

- **Sweepstakes** for the chance to win free books, romantic getaways, and other fun prizes.

- Writing **tips** from our authors and editors.

- **Blog** with our authors and find out why they love to write romance.

- **Exclusive content** that's not contained within the pages of our novels.

Join us at
www.avonbooks.com

AVON

An Imprint of HarperCollins*Publishers*
www.avonromance.com

Available wherever books are sold or please call 1-800-331-3761 to order.

FTH 1013